Mack Daly is the product of a time and place that is no more and can only be embraced through knowing the heart and soul of this unforgettable gentleman. A big-hearted, beautiful Manhattanite who holds a high office within the Bureau of Prohibition and leads a necessarily Very Secret Life, he is branded with a glimpse of a Paradise All Too Brief, whose memories wink through their laughter and tears on the following pages.

Mack's syncopated coterie, led by his pretend-wife, Ynez, become wrapped up with him in fatal, forbidden passions, shocking scandals and ghoulish murders, eventually leading to the tragic eclipse of their moment in the sun.

HEYDAY

MICHAEL VIKTOR BUTLER

HEYDAY

Published by Arbor Books

Author's note: "Some of the events described in this book happened as related; others were expanded and changed. Some of the individuals portrayed are composites of more than one person and some names and identifying characteristics have been changed as well."

DEDICATION: For Louey.

For further information, please contact:

ARBOR BOOKS, INC.
19 Spear Road, Ste 301
Ramsey, NJ 07446
www.arborbooks.com
info@arborbooks.com

Printed in the United States

HEYDAY
Michael Viktor Butler

1. Title 2. Author 3. Historical Gay Fiction

Library of Congress Control Number: 2006923348

ISBN 10: 0-9777764-3-3
ISBN 13: 978-0-9777764-3-6

“Have you ever been happier before
than you are right now?”

—advertising slogan, circa 1928.

FOREWORD

HERE'S LOOKING AT YOU!

In 1919, the Volstead Act, as the 18th Amendment to the United States Constitution, made the consumption of alcohol illegal in all and any forms—except when sanctioned by the government.

While the initial concept of national temperance was noble, its subsequent implementation served as a mid-wife which forever stamped the entire course of American culture. Fatally alluring to those both within the system as well as outside of it, was the descent into corruption which almost immediately gave birth to the first invisible empire of all that seemed shocking and modern. It rapidly became that single vacation spot where almost everyone wanted to go as often as they could. At first known as being "smart," it later was labeled "cool."

Under both federal and state control, a vast internal bureaucracy known as Alcohol Bonding was born. Responsible for strictly limiting the uses of alcohol and withholding it from the general public, it was here that the most pure booze found anywhere in America was both manufactured and warehoused. These vast high-security citadels—thick-walled, trimmed in barbed wire and replete with guardhouses—were pipelines through which trickled censored libations for a thirsty nation. Their government seemed to be thrusting upon these first, modern Americansa very bad joke which merited flippant defiance.

Under this system, the only alcohol permitted for public consumption was released through these compounds to churches, synagogues, hospitals, pharmacies, or so-called "cordial shoppes" where syrups used in parfaits and phosphates were said to contain such a low alcoholic content it was assumed they could not inebriate. However, additives such a radiator fluid, turpentine and even formaldehyde found their way into every other kind of bootlegged product, providing a deadly "kick" to the otherwise pure stuff.

Not a drop could leave these confines without the petitioner first being subjected to a complicated system of red tape. However, at both ends of the game, everyone, it seemed, was in on the take. Rapidly, scandals erupted—the cleverest violations of the law being conceived from within the Bureau of Prohibition itself, at the top of the booze chain. The most highly respected politicians and lowest of social pariahs invented secret handshakes still with us today, yielding under-the-table profits amounting to millions and millions of dollars.

A new and syncopated version of Atlantis was thus born, afloat on an ocean of hooch, doomed from the start, but darkly, magically powerful. It still can be seen—there—at the bottom of your glass, gazing upward—the Mother of Us All.

WHO'S WHO

MACK DALY (aka Benjamin Leventhal, MacDailey, Mackie, Mackus): Man-about-town, owner and supervisor of largest government bonded alcohol plant in the entire Northeast.

YNEZ DALY: Mack's ornamental wife.

JOSEPH IMPERIO: Mack Daly's gangster beau.

DEUCIE DE VOL: Mack's friend, who served with him in the War.

BABY DE VOL: Deucie's devoted wife; former war-time nurse.

ELLIOT ARMSTRONG: Famous crooner who also served with Mack.

WINOLA ARMSTRONG: (Nolie): Elliot's "other half." Novelty singer.

PRINCESS JOHNNIE PARKER (Jonquil): Nolie's maid and "friend."

BRUNO IMPERIO: Head of crime syndicate; Joe's older brother.

WIGGILY JACK WRIGLEY: Elliot's college-boy beau.

BRIAN O'COURAN: Commissioner of Prohibition, New York City.

MARGARET O'COURAN (Peg): Brian's long-suffering wife.

ANNABELLE HARRISON (Belle): Dethroned millionairess and sculptress.

CAESAR PARKER (Keys): Belle's beau, brother to Princess Johnnie.

ALEXANDER PARKER: Keys' younger brother, devoted man-of-all-work to the Dalys.

COLONEL CALVIN CONNAUGHT: Commanding Officer of the Old Regiment.

THE COUNTESS XACHA (pronounced "Tzay-kuh"): a clairvoyant.

HUCK: The Colonel's beau.

VIOLET CONNAUGHT: Estranged daughter of the Colonel.

Blanche "Squirrely" King: Underworld secretary to the Imperio gang.

BOOTSIE CARSTAIRS: Interior decorator, owner of The Tumble On Inn.

ORCHID: Bootsie's beau.

Table of Contents

CHAPTER I

HIS LIFE BEGINS AT LAST

In the Spring of 1928, there came into the full glory of his gorgeous manhood a Jewish gent named Benny Leventhal. On a certain and most glorious of April afternoons, Manhattan Island was able to compliment herself because it was apparent to All and Any that here was a spot like none other in the whole wide world. She gazed back at what she had so suddenly become, seeing reflected in the new shining towers a metropolis which winked at other places and other times the rest of the world over, never imagining a single cloud in the sky.

We find our hero, about whom this often funny—and always tragic—tale is spun, just now walking East from Broadway, swinging his stick, whistling away and coming to the sudden realization that he had never felt quite so good before in his entire life. A gradual kind of awe possessed Benny Leventhal in that most singular moment in time. And it reached deep into his very heart, whispering something about a rapture just forthcoming. If ever there was anyone in both the right and wrong place at exactly both the right and wrong time—it was this gentleman.

"*Hell, but I AM a lucky son-of-a-bitch,*" he told himself, swaggering along now, pierced by this inspiration, just then experiencing this stirring sense of glory, never imagining the terrible sorrow which would soon accompany it.

A tall man of thirty-three, powerfully built, with dark blond hair stubbornly, thickly waving, lazily curling—in spite of daily applications of brilliantine. Eyebrows of the same shade, capable of a diagonal thrust when witnessing irony and folly. His eyes, made of topaze, rimmed in dark lashes, revealing an almost fatal kindness-of-heart. Eyes which betrayed, also, to anyone who might look long at him, a love and lust for other men.

Eyes which had—deep behind them—an awful, unspeakable pain of which you will hear much soon. A man made of burnished gold was our Benny.

The moment he would smile, everyone always fell in love with him. Not like any smile you've ever seen because in this angular grin there was sadness...and sex. So, they called him "That Splendid Animal" behind his back, and he laughed when he heard it, liking it.

They called him their Best Friend because if there was anybody whom you wanted for one, it would've been him. He was the kind of guy you prayed for; the kind of fellow you secretly loved without ever being able to admit it.

"You know, pal, I just love you!" you might find yourself blurting out. And he would never be embarassed, replying with just a trace of a continental accent mingled with New York-ese, "Thanks for that. You're very kind…" in that deep, sensual voice of his.

Benny Leventhal really loved men. He did not love women, although he had an ornamental wife, as many men of that persuasion did during this wonderous time. Pure façade—a sheilding of secrets that nobody would've believed anyway.

Except for the fact that his wife was insanely in love with him. And that didn't make it any easier on either one of them. Simply by the way his wife looked at him and spoke of him in such an adoring and unceasing manner, Benny Leventhal knew he could trust her with his Secret. There were others, naturally, who worshipped him. But she was his self-elected High Priestess and, within this office, there was no room for anyone else.

During the War, he had acquired the handle of "MacDailey"—so named because he resembled his company's Scottish chaplain freshly slaughtered just as Benny was entering the ranks. The moniker had stuck and soon enough he was known ever afterward as Mack Daly, and he wasn't a Jew anymore. He didn't look like one or act like one. For that matter, he didn't look or act like a fairy, either. After all, he was a very much married and sucessful government official. But he was also Jewish and also very much a homosexual.

On that day in April of 1928, anybody encountering this dapper, mannish, all-American guy would've shaken their head in wonderment had you told them he was a lover of men—and men only. This instant admirer would never have accepted or believed it. Not for a minute. And even if you told them he was a Jew, they would've said something like, "Never woulda guessed it! No siree! Not him. Not that guy."

You might imagine that he was lonely—this nonpareil gentleman, out of an Arrow Collar advertisement; this matinee idol; this dream come true. Was he haunted every moment of that charmed life of his by a desperate, aching emptiness? A Jew—and a swish to boot? You bet he was.

During the War, he had been picked from the ranks, landing in a regiment filled with with fellows who had that same gnawing desire to love other men. Who, in the throes of desperate sex with one another, while covered with their own blood, squirming naked on top of each other in the filth of the trenches, came alive for the first time in their sad experience. Strange to have found this forbidden ecstasy there—clinging to one another as, one by one, each was torn to shreds.

Nonetheless, it was sex as he and his buddies would never know it again. Still, nearly a decade afterward, this kind of sex haunted him. Right there, alongside his nightmares, seeing the lads being blinded, blown to bits, cut into pieces—were those all too vivid scenes of sweating, muscled bodies entwined. Kisses hot with tears, breathless panting and ghastly cries of joy so close in their throb to the screams of the dying boys whom he so loved.

Mack Daly might wonder if his wife Ynez, sleeping, of course, in the next room, could hear him sobbing when he would akwaken from such dreams. Naked, he would rise and go to the full-length mirror—there, to the left of the French windows—and run his big hands over his body, unable to ever fathom what in Hell had made him want to just curl up and die from being so alone. And what was wrong that he *was* so alone? And, after all,why did it have to be this way? Why?

"Mack? Are you o.k.?" (From her bedroom, this wife of his—faintly, but filled with terror.)

"Oh, just another one of those War dreams," he would call back, reaching for a white, silk, monogrammed handkerchief with which to wipe away the stain upon himself, shuddering.

Always, in these dreams, a horrible battle raging around him; ear-shattering bombs going off, showering the trench with dirt. The cries of his buddies, dying. And in the midst of it all, he was making such fierce, shameful love to some man. Who was it? Some man…who appeared to be near death and who claimed Mack Daly with his arms, with his whole, dying, bleeding body. Because he so required love and had never gotten it. As this man was holding onto life, Mack opened his heart to him, emptying out his own hunger. He wrenched from inside himself all the love he had, sheltering the wounded soldier, engulfing him as he quite suddenly shuddered, then…ceased to live.

He would hear his wife's hollow sigh, hear her turning over, imagine her face buried in her pillows, weeping as a woman might, who had married a fairy with full knowledge of what she was getting herself into. And also wondering: Why did it have to be this way?

How this wife wanted to run to him on those nights when the War would come back so vividly—throwing open his door, cradling him in her arms. But she couldn't do a thing like that. They had never touched. Never kissed, or even patted one another fondly. Ynez Daly—Mrs. Mack Daly—certainly was proud of the Somebody she had become by marrying him. Knowing what her husband was doing in his own sealed-off confines, and how his heart and soul ached in perfect rhythm with his body. She sought a weapon with which to kill this haunting emptiness.

Yet, she also wanted him miserable in this sham marriage of theirs, devoid of sex, of real love. Why shouldn't her husband feel such anguish? Ynez Daly felt it, because of her obsession with him. Why shouldn't it be a shared…misery?

And what would happen if he were to ever meet someone like himself? A mannish, grand-looking guy who would share with him that strange and terrible love? What would ever become of Mrs. Mack Daly?

Mr. Mack Daly, however, could imagine no such encounter. He would just go on covering everything up, working cleanly and efficiently in his government position; a war hero, a modern hero, meeting that gleaming standard which he found so vital in those long lost days. He would go on winking while telling the latest joke out of the Follies, giving nickels to little kids, acting the part of a Man's Man. And almost nightly finding himself, utterly alone in that room of his, choking back his tears. It was the War. That's what they always said if some poor guy acted off his nut.

But not in my case, Mack Daly—alias Benny Leventhal—would tell himself over and over. *Even so* (he would go on thinking), *what if I were to one day…just get lucky and meet up with some grand fella who could see right through me? Someone like myself.*

He was thinking about it just then, in fact, on that very day, prompted by this certain euphoric sense that something was going to happen which would, at almost any moment, transform this emptiness in him.

A billboard loomed overhead. It advertised a particular brand of breakfast cereal and posed this question:

HAVE YOU EVER BEEN
HAPPIER BEFORE
THAN YOU ARE
RIGHT NOW?

To which he answered right out loud, "No, I guess I haven't…and I don't know quite why!"

It was so all-encompassing it beggared even pondering. Taking it all in (whatever *it* was) this marvelous vision of a fellow went on his way—women ogling him, men tipping their hats. Nobody with even so much as an inkling.

"I guess it must be Fate," he decided, swinging his stick. Yes. Fate. Fully preparing Mack Daly to go about this business of falling in love. And why not? Discreetly, of course. "That particular type of guy whom no one could ever guess might be…well, just like myself, in fact!" Well, where was this happy accident of Fate?

That Fate, already on its way, was just then driving a truck in from Brooklyn to a strictly appointed spot, just a few hundred feet off. Here was the perfect antidote to Mack Daly's every misery if ever there was one.

Having turned onto 46th Street from Broadway, the very truck, holding this Answered Prayer, went rumbling by. And the young man, there, at the wheel, stuck in traffic, swearing in both Sicilian and English, was, in fact, driving one of Mack's own vehicles.

Both were proceeding in the same direction; one, in a sweaty undershirt, gaudy gold crucifix around his dark, thick neck, a cigarette hanging from his full lips; the other with a song in his heart, neat as a pin, gallant and as noble as a knight.

But Mack didn't see the truck or who was in it. Perhaps what caused him to look just ahead…there, and to his left—where, by now, the vehicle and its magnificent charioteer had passed—was the shadow which lay in his path across the pavement. A cripple—also a veteran of the Late Conflict; a wretched, legless casuality slumped upon a crude, wooden sledge was waiting there for him.

This poor beggar had once screamed in agony at a field hospital where his limbs were separated from him. Now from those partched, twitching lips of his came no sound—yet, still around him, there was whistling. It was an eerie melody, this whistling, echoing up into the concrete canyons. And it grew louder as Mack approached.

They'd met a while ago, on the streets along the Great White Way, aknowledging one another with a mutual salute, both always wearing their veterans' pins on their respective lapels. Mack had not known Blackie the Whistler during the War, but got to know him, and the spurious kind of fame which surrounded him—and had come to need him. This was the famous beggar known to all *au fait* New Yorkers as the one person in town who got wind of certain secret things before anybody else. He was literally one in a million and valued by everyone whose lives were lived in shadows, from the Underworld to Park Avenue. Mack had made it a habit of visiting with this creature every week or so, rain or shine, as he was parked on any mid-town street corner—tin cup, toothless grin—a ruined, pathetic monster. Over the years, they had become friends.

From as much as twenty feet away, you could hear the old vet wheezing like a pump organ. Caught in the middle of a gang shooting in '21, Blackie the Whistler took a bullet in his left lung. Yanking it out himself, he left the hole wide open. This was a mixed blessing because it brought him his bread and butter; he found that he could whistle out of that hole in his lung. He could let go of jazzy numbers, sad ones, novelties with either pep or poignance, songs both old and new.

As his fame spread, so too did his contacts, high and low, great and small. In this way, he found out things. And of all the pals Blackie the Whistler made over the years, Mack Daly had become his favorite. Oddly enough, both men possessed a similar smile and had that same look in their eyes. They had a lot in common. And they also had an agreement. Mack had come to be very, very careful for years now—because of the government position he occupied in the Bureau of Prohibition—and Blackie the Whistler made it his job to look out for him.

Stopping before Blackie, bending toward him with a wink shielding a concerned look, Mack asked him, "Is my old buddy doing all right today?"

And, oh, you would've thought it was Jesus Christ himself who asked him that question. The poor thing lit up, exposing a toothless chasm, lifting a gnarled, filthy hand, to tip his old cap and offer a salute, joyously answering with a snappy: "Yessirree, *Mon Capitane*—just copasetic!"

Mack tossed a silver dollar into his cup and Blackie gestured for him to bend even closer. "Listen! Listen! They're raidin' The On Time tunnight, sir! The heat's on since this new commissioner is comin' in, yuh know."

"The On Time" was what those who had never studied French called The Club Intime, a speakeasy up on 54th Street, presumably heavily protected by pay-offs.

With a great gulp for air, the Whistler continued, "With you and yer pals op'nin' yer new jernt, I thought I'd pass it onto yuh! Oh, God, yes and there's more, too!" (Mack nodded for him to continue.) "Whatever you do sir, you find a way to get yourself covered and you steer clear of this new commissioner. Oh, God, you could get in real dutch wid' yer associations such as they are!"

"We're opening tonight no matter what, Blackie. We've no choice. It's been set for weeks now," Mack continued, as Blackie shook his head, shutting his eyes tightly, "Listen, if you hear that they're sending the paddies down this way, will you come by as quick as you can? You know where we are—right up there near Fifth Avenue…" He indicated the building itself by a very subtle nod of his head.

"I do. I do. I do, Sir…My God, I'll sprout wings if I have to. This is no joke, an' I don' mean maybe neither!"

Mack slipped him a twenty dollar bill and pulled Blackie's old hat affectionately over his eyes. Requesting his favorite song, "My Album of Dreams," Mack, standing over him while Blackie delivered himself of that tune, went into a brief reverie.

"Well, if that wasn't the sweetest damned rendition I've ever heard, Lieutenant," Mack said when Blackie finished, all out-of-breath.

The Whistler managed a valiant smile of sorts and Mack, giving him that knowing look which he always accomplished so beautifully, turned away. He never said good-bye to Blackie the Whistler, because he always thought it would be his last.

And so, heading just a short distance East for the new *boite* he had bankrolled (come Hell-Or-High Water to open that very evening), he also whistled. Just because they raided that speak, there was no reason to believe they would visit the Club deVol tonight, was there? And as for the new commissioner—well, he hadn't been sworn in yet. So what was there to worry over?

Mack had invested considerably in this new nite spot—not just money alone, but his whole reputation as well. And not for his own sake, but for two of his dearest friends. Better not tell them in any event, he quickly decided. They'd had enough of the rough-and-tumble world.

Blackie was left behind, worried and scared for Mack Daly. Never had he seen his pal so all aglow, and he couldn't quite figure it out. Probably simple enthusiasm over this new club of his. *The swankiest and swellest speak in town. Anything Mack Daly touches is pure Klass. And that's as true as the telephone book*, Blackie the Whistler thought.

As Mack contined East, Blackie rolled in the opposite direction, back toward his hovel in Hell's Kitchen. The night before, while Mack was having one of his unsettling dreams, Blackie had also tossed about on his horsehair mattress in the fastness of his Tenth Avenue cellar. He was fretting something terrible about Mr. Daly and the plans he and his pals had about that club, and how he'd be certain to see him strolling up toward the jernt on the morrow. He'd tell him all right. Blackie knew Mr. Daly would lose everything if even the least little leak got out. It wasn't just that, either. It was something terrible. So very peculiar and godless...yes, that was the word...it was godless.

He didn't want to alarm his old buddy, and, anyway, it was awfully hard to put it all into words. But Blackie still had a keen mind, and over time he'd mapped it all out! Oh God! It was terrible, filthy, rotten stuff. The worst thing mortal man could ever contrive aginst his own species. Miracles! What were miracles!? Somehow, it was all tangled up with Mr. Daly and his government position...and his secrets.

Blackie didn't want to think about it; still, he couldn't help himself. So, taking a deep gulp of April air, he decided to be on his way, propelling himself slowly back toward Broadway, rolling along back into the caverns of steel and concrete.

Mack approached the building he had leased for the new spot, which stood unobtrusively on the South side of the street. Across from it, he'd rented a small, second-floor flat atop a cobbler shoppe. Here, another trusted veteran whom he knew well would watch for the police, with a telephone hook-up going directly into the office of the club itself. The Club deVol—that was what they called it. A genuine private club, and not a speakeasy at all. But it still sold illegal liquour to the public, so it was still a speakeasy—any way you cut it, if you thought about it like that. But Mack never thought of it as anything other than a dream come true. Not for himself but for his two friends who were running it—Deucie and Baby deVol.

For many years now, Mack had hoisted them out of any variety of fly-by-night schemes; this pair, like all of Mack Daly's closest friends, sharing one another's joys, heartaches and dark secrets since their days in France. Deucie and Baby were always safely tucked under Mack's wing. He had most certainly adopted them. But that was all right because, well, whenever he thought of how much they both meant to him, he got a big lump in his throat.

Mack and the deVols had all met in France in 1917. After the War ended, it was Baby who—regretting it ever afterward—had introduced Mack to Ynez, his wife.

A little older and a lot tougher than Deucie, Baby had made it her life's work to protect Mack from whatever Cat Might Get Out of the Bag. Baby was that kind of dame, always somewhere between laughing out loud and sobbing into a hanky, chain-smoking, swearing like a fish-wife, and adoring every pansy she came in contact with.

The deVols would get themselves into the damnedest messes, and Mack would get them out. They adored Mack Daly with a fervor that was formidable, and God help anybody who thought differently. Theirs was a unique outlook on life, embracing a place for all God's creatures, in loving acceptance of one another, no matter how screwy your proclivities might be.

Deucie required a wooden leg and had a blubberly constant grin beneath a bald head that was decorated with three or four threads of hair plastered down in the middle. He reminded everybody of a cartoon character right out of the funnies. Grumbling quietly now and then about Mack's heart of gold, he humbly accepted his patron's hand-outs, which were often and generous. Always ready to repair whatever might be broken, or invent something that soon would be, Deucie was irreplaceable. All his War buddies (all of whom were queers, but what the hell?) believed him to be a genius. Baby took care of him with an ardor that was far beyond mere devotion.

Both of these characters were dead sure that this new nite club project would finally make their friend, Mack Daly, happy. Baby had never forgiven herself for introducing Mackie to his wife, and in the two years since they'd been "married," she had observed (loudly) that it was Missus Daly who was making Mister Daly so secretly blue by clinging to him and driving him nutso. But Mack knew that Deucie and Baby were also pretty blue, and he'd put the whole idea of a club together for their sake, to finally make them happy. So that they could have a real home (right up on the third floor, over the club) and a steady source of income. He'd dumped over twenty thousand clams into the 46th Street place and didn't mind it, or even feel it a bit.

A sturdy four-story affair, built of granite at the beginning of the century and imbued with a dignity—a quiet charm—so essential to that kind of...*speakeasy* where nothing on the outside of a building of that sort could betray itself. The whole idea was strictly hi-tone, appealing to the Sophisticated Moderns who were making lots of money and loads of whoopee.

Mack didn't like to put himself in any category at all, but if there was one into which he (and Ynez) might fit perfectly, it was that one. More than anything else in this world did Mack Daly want to be really and truly American and up-to-the-minute in every possible way.

Now he stood there in the front of the building. So proud, smiling to himself, rubbing a bit of dust from the small square window just above the center of the door. No bigger than a playing card, with the name of the place, done in wrought iron with letters hardly bigger than a couple of inches, was placed there a grille. Deucie had put it in backwards, so that the shadow of these letters would be cast on the sidewalk as light passed through them. CLUB DEVOL—that was all it said. No sign. No jazzy, attention-getting gimmicks. No, siree. To Mack's mind, that was enough.

It was a risk all right—opening a nite club like this, serving the best liquor in town, a drawing card as the very best band in town, and, most probably, the swellest patrons in attendance. But what the hell? A dream come true couldn't be classified as a joint, could it? Illegal or not?

Mack breathed a sigh, let himself in with his key, and stepped into the circular Egyptian style foyer. This, like everything inside the club, had been the creation of Bootsie Carstairs—a venerable old queen who insisted on absolute control of the decor, in spite of Mrs. Mack Daly's attempt at horning in. As he parted the entrance doors, he could hear Elliot Armstrong—his best friend—rehearsing that now-famous orchestra, bearing not only his name, but that of the old regiment as well: Elliot Armstrong's Army of Charm.

How amazingly marvelous Elliot's sound was, thought Mack. You talk about modern and sophisticated! Nobody in all of radioland ever quite got it right. But Elliot did! And, how miraculous that everything was coming together so beautifully—so perfectly. Tonight was going to be some stew all right!

Ahead was a dark, cavernous rotunda with chairs sitting upside down on tables. Dimly, a hat check area elevated to the left, a reservation desk to the right, and far at the end of the dance floor, a stage upon which Elliot and his band were now rehearsing. Having just come in from out of the sun, Mack could barely make it all out. Except for the rehearsal lights, there ahead, nothing of the splendor of the place yet revealed itself. Nothing of the planning, the days and nights of work, the dreams being made reality, and money—oh, the money!—spent so lavishly.

Still, it was pretty damned thrilling. *"It reminds me of Paris during the zeppelin raids!"* Mack thought just then. In those days, all the restaurants and casinos of Toot Paree were wrapped up in black cloth, yet went on providing the hysteria so necessary in times like those.

Striding into the darkness and waving with hat in hand, he hailed Elliot, who called for a break. Turning, shielding his eyes with his white enameled fiddle, Elliot beamed, "Mackus! You're here! He's here, everybody! Our boy is here. Rejoice o' tribe of Benjamin!"

It was pure rapture, but it was very funny, too. Elliot could be very funny, very nasty, very beautiful and very, very much a star. His Army of Charm Orchestra gave Mack a fanfare in jazz, as its leader jumped off the bandstand, his blond, curly hair fairly leaping out of place. Grabbing Mack by the arm, he pulled him toward the bar, and there, in almost total darkness, planted a big smacker on his lips. Everyone in the band broke into laughter. They put up with this stuff all the time, and were well-paid to keep shut up.

"Hey, stop that! You're supposed to be crooner, not a pansy, Elliot Armstrong!" Mack whispered.

"Oh, nerts. For a minute there I must've sssssssslipped!" Elliot snapped his fingers. Then, with a tone that implied Mack wasn't holding up his end of this whole opening night stuff: "Looks like every little thing is all set for tonight, old pal o' mine, old pal o' mine—everything except for the bar here!" Motioning over Mack's shoulder, it was plain to see—a completely empty set of shelves.

Mack's eyes now adjusted to the lack of light. He grabbed Elliot by the neck. "Well, I thought I'd leave the spirits for the last minute so you wouldn't empty every godammed bottle before we even opened the door!"

His drinking was a problem to say the least. Elliot did, however, swear up and down that he'd go on the wagon starting that very night, if the club were a success.

"Aw, you cut me to the quick! Is that really true, Mack?" he responded, a little hurt.

"No, of course not! You know how careful we have to be. The plan was to bring it in with the fresh-baked goods—and that's what's happening. No slip-ups. Better that it should be done in broad daylight with the bakery trucks, than at night..."

Elliot hung on every word. A bit shorter than Mack, and easily the sweetest-looking band leader around, he was blessed with the combined appearance of the proverbial lad with his hand caught in the cookie jar and a fallen angel with a distinctly dirty mind.

As Elliot looked up at him like a kid might, Mack looked down at him like a big brother might. "I smell gin over your shaving soap, kid."

"Oh, no, you don't! Ask Nolie, Mackus! I'm as dry as a Methodist minister, I swear I am." He held his right hand up before Mack. "You just got a whiff of my violin rozin, that's all."

"You told me you used jizz for that, Elliot. Don't fool me."

"Well—" Elliot burst into laughter, then searched for an excuse. "Since I have to sing tonight, I just started gargling, that's all. Anyway, it was *your* gin—the very best made."

Mack sighed. Hopeless. "I wish you could get back together with that innocent college kid who kept you away from the watering hole, Elliot."

"Listen, I'm going to be as sober as a judge tonight. I promised I would, and I never break a promise." (Mack gave him a narrow look.) "Besides, Nolie said she'd scalp me if I drank after four o'clock today." (Nolie was Elliot's ball-and-chain.)

"Ah-hah! Just as I thought, you goddammed husband, you! Well, just make sure you swim in it until 3:59 arrives, won't you?" Mack pulled at his bow-tie, leaving it hanging in two shreds. "Nolie is a saint to put up with the likes of you, kiddo. Now go and rehearse." He whacked him on his ass.

Jumping up on the stage with the band, already tuning up and ready go, Elliot turned back to Mack micheviously. "Yeah, but when exactly is the booze shipment coming in, Daddy?"

Mack waved him off with a grumble. "Four-oh-one! God! Half-cocked already…" he muttered to himself, then headed toward the far end of the bar where velvet drapes concealed a corridor running the length of the building. Here, Bootsie Carstairs had chiseled out space for dressing rooms, and, at one end, a staircase leading to the second floor office. Just to the left of the curtain and burrowed deep within the walls was a utility closet, presumably placed there for holding mops and brooms. Behind all of this subterfuge of cleaning devices was the cellar where all the hooch was stored—perhaps a hundred thousand smackers worth of the real thing, Deucie had figured, and all supplied by Mack Daly himself.

Against the opposite, back wall of the building, a sliding iron door had been installed opening to the alley, heavy with Deucie's own system of locks. Arriving to find it wide open at first surprised Mack. Then he saw, in the back driveway, a spotless, cream-colored truck identified, in cozy, curly letters, as belonging to LEVENTHAL BAKERIES—which was Mack's family business and the name of the company.

"At last," Mack sighed, nervous as Hell.

Coming toward him, carrying three wooden crates bearing that same name, face unseen, sun-baked arms straining under the weight of what was obviously not fresh-baked bread at all, apparently there came a very attractive delivery man.

And because it wasn't a good idea to leave the iron sliding doors open like that, Mack called out, from a distance of fifteen feet, "Is that you, Abie?"

To which a voice answered from behind the crates, "No, Abie I ain't." He slowly lowered the crates, and because the sun shone so brightly behind him, Mack could only tell that this guy was certainly not Abie at all.

Outlined, he saw a wonderfully built individual, his undershirt dampened by perspiration, his cap askew, his black hair in shining arrows over one eye, a cigarette hanging from his mouth."So just who are you?" Mack asked him suspiciously.

Now, the person who was not Abie, came closer, out of the sun and under the door frame itself. Abie, Mack thought, never looked like this. Someone you wouldn't want to meet in a dark alley, that was for sure. But probably the best thing Mack had ever set his eyes on because, from head to toe, this particular delivery man was too good to be true, as Mack found himself murmuring, followed by a low exclamation of, "Oh, my God…"

"I'm duh new guy what's replacin' dee old guy. Dat name you jus' said," answered this new delivery man.

"I didn't hire you…did I?" Mack asked him, feeling beads of sweat forming on his brow, and thinking, *Cause if I did, I sure as hell would've remembered this one—*

The voice, profoundly husky, blue-collar, dangerous: "You musta given Mr. Goldenberg the o.k. 'cause they put me on dis mornin'…sir."

"Do you know who I am?" Mack asked carefully, his eyes taking in the arms, the chest, the everything of whoever this man was.

"Youse is duh boss. Youse is Mr. Daly," the other fellow replied, without inflection, enthusiasm or, apparently, brains.

Mack now strode closer, as if inspecting some glorified species from out of an Edgar Rice Burroughs book, startled into something between anger and an awkward, white hot sense of being horribly, instantly, aroused. He was in every way the most astonishing human being Mack Daly had ever seen. Whoever this man might be, he took Mack's breath fully away. Not just because of his appearance—he was, in fact, a kind of masterpiece—but the absolute feeling he gave off. A sensation like no other ever experienced was overtaking Mack Daly from his trousers to his homburg. Where on earth did this speciman come from!

"Are you—are you…trying to tell me that Shem Goldenberg entrusted you to this particular job?" Mack finally exclaimed, a bit archly.

"I guess he musta, 'cause here I am…sir." The man's eyes, like two black olives, watched Mack Daly's brows furl, giving him the once over.

"Let's just get these doors closed behind us and bring that stuff inside," Mack motioned, staring at the other's get-up. A normal delivery man would've worn the uniform of the Leventhal bakeries. This fellow looked as if he'd just climbed out of a muscular development magazine. His broadly striped pants, rolled up over work boots encasing a large and, thought Mack, charmingly clumsy foot, were soiled and far, far, too tight—so terribly tight—and that undershirt had shrunk in the laundry—blessedly so, thought Mack, for it hugged his chest, outlining rather large, erect nipples, a garish gold cross about his neck and a tattoo on his left bicep which told the world he loved his "MOM."

Mack's eyes at last took in his face, and courageously stared long enough at it to make this big lug look quizzically at him.

"Somet'in' wrong?" he grunted. (Mack shook his head as if in a kind of daze.) Removing his cigarette, flicking it a good distance, then inserting chewing gum between his brilliantly white teeth, he asked, "Wan' some gum?" In his not too clean hands, there was a spare stick of Beeman's Pepsin.

"Wha—what?? Oh—no. No, thanks," Mack replied, his mouth dry, thinking, *Whoever this fella is, he certainly takes the cake!*

There was a pause during which time both stared at one another; Mack frozen, the other slowly taking the gum wrapper off, wadding this piece up and putting it obscenely into his mouth. It then occurred to Mack Daly that this guy was not a delivery man at all, and so he said, "Maybe you'd just better leave those crates just where they are."

"Well dere awful heavy." (Mack was hearing a strong Lower East Side accent.) "Don't yuz want me to put 'em where dey belong?"

Mack thought a bit. After all, that bakery truck was full of booze. Nobody was supposed to be in on this except Abie. And where was Abie? How did this guy get the job? Who was he anyway?

And so Mack asked: "Say, who are you anyway?"

"Joey Imperio," came the reply, looking straight into Mack Daly's eyes now, waiting…waiting…as if for a challenge. A real mug.

Through Mack's mind raced the fact that he never, ever hired Italians—nobody at the plant would accept them! Goldenburg himself would never have even considered such a thing. He ought to tell him to just leave, right then and there. Leave the truck, hand him the keys and get lost! That's what he should do. Still.

Mack felt he had to compose himself. Attempting a thoroughly business-like tone, aloof and detached, he asked, after clearing his throat, "Are you one of those day laborers who get hired when a regular employee can't fill in?"

Joey Imperio's eyes went heavenward and his mouth to one side. He stopped, for a second, chewing his gum. Then he said, "Oh, yeah. Dat's it. Exacklee."

Mack didn't buy it.

Joe looked at him, resuming chewing his gum, only now with great caution. "So? You want me to unload dis stuff and bring it inside now?"

"Actually, I really don't," Mack heard himself answer.

"Well, den, you want me to go back instead? Am I done?" the Italian asked in the same tone—almost expressionless except for a hint of apology and another hint of…something else.

(Do I want him to go back! Mack asked himself.) "No…no, you might as well…just take a break…you, um, you must be tired after loading 'em up and driving all that distance."

Joey Imperio looked at Mack as if he were nuts. "Well…I might jus' take a glass ah water." And then, out of nowhere, he started to smile—a broad grin crossing his face, making dimples at either side of his mouth.

Mack was thinking, *We who are about to die, salute you*—for, smiling right at him was the reincarnation of a Roman gladiator, only then, in that Spring of 1928, he had come back as a street tough. Wasn't that what they called types like him? One of somebody's gang. A criminal, in fact, to put it plainly. *Come to shake me down.*

Mack felt himself smiling back—but not because he wanted to. Because he thought this guy named Joe Imperio was extraordinarily, miraculously, perfect and—he almost dared not think it—perfect for him. Something was happening for which there was no sane explanation—a voice inside his head, over the beating of his heart, was saying, "*This is it, kid. You have met your destiny.*"

But the question now was—how could he go get him a glass of water, leaving him there with all that booze and the keys to the truck? How could he let him go inside and have him, at once, case the jernt, as they said in those gangster novels? How could he leave the booze out there unattended?

"Come on, I'll help you. Let's get that stuff inside, and then we'll both have some…um…soft drink."

"O.k. by me," Joe replied, the smile fading, as he watched Mack strip off his jacket, place it over the railing, and pick up the crates himself. "I'll get some more of 'em outa duh truck—" this person named Joey Imperio said.

Watching him from behind, Mack tried to find the right words for how he felt. "Dazzled. Impressed!" he found himself saying almost out loud, shaking his head in disbelief.

Mack commented, "Quite a haul, isn't it?" not knowing quite what to say when Joey returned bearing his own load.

"I seen woyse—" came the retort from behind the crates. "—must be awful stale bread, 'cause it sure is heavy!" And then, poking his head around the crates, Joey Imperio gave Mack a wink.

"Um—just follow me…" Of course, this guy knew very well what was happening. Bread! Bread indeed! Cute. Awfully damned cute, too. Gorgeous. Gorgeous as hell. A simple soul—an animal and a comic. Sweet as hell. Tough as hell, too. "Right this way, Mr. Imperio—"

"I'm right behind yuz—MISTER Daly!"

They had reached the phony broom closet. A decision had to be made. Elliot was too much of a star to lug the booze down to the cellar, and Deucie, because of his war injury, was out of the question. And just beyond the drapery, over and over, Elliot was making the band repeat the same five bars, the same difficult part of that week's hit tune.

Mack stopped and put the crates down. "Listen, we have a bit of a problem here...we're pressed for time. This place is a...a...um...supper club and the opening is tonight. I'm used to having men on my end of this...business...whom I can trust implicitly."

"Well, I can see what yuh mean. Me bein' a dago."

"No! No! That's not it all."(*Not much it wasn't.*) "...but, you see, well—"

Joe nodded a little. "I guess you'd have tuh hire me. I mean full-time. See if yuz could get to trust me dat way."

Mack, at that point, had to sit on the crates and take a deep breath. "But I don't even know you! I don't know anything about you. This is very, very—important to me—and my friends as well. If anything ever went wrong, well—you just couldn't imagine."

The Italian suddenly let out with a kind of grunt, and then began pacing back and forth, rapidly, right there in front of the broom closet, hitting the palm of his hand with his fist, and repeating, "Jeez! Jeez!" over and over.

All of this caused Mack to say; "Say! Calm down! This is my problem, not yours!"

Joey Imperio stopped dead in his tracks, muttering something that sounded like, "I didn't t'ink you wuz gonna be so great, damn it."

"What did you just say?" Mack asked.

"I didn't t'ink you wuz gonna be so great, damn it."

Mack rose up as if hit by lightning. "Wait a minute. Wait a minute. I think you'd better explain yourself, before we carry this whole matter any further."

It was now Joey's turn to have a seat on those crates. His head hanging low, he said in an angry whisper, "I never shoulda said I'd do dis. Jeez, I feel terry-bull." Off came his cap, which he murderously slapped againist his hand.

Mack was getting nervous. The clock was ticking. He still had to go home to Great Neck, change into his tails, pick up Ynez, and get back there by nine o'clock. All of that booze—some two dozen crates of every variety of hooch—had to be put downstairs, then categorized—the champagne put on ice, the bar stocked, and so on and so on. All of this was supposed be up to Abie. And where was Abie?

Mack bent over, trying to look at Joe. "This just isn't going to work, I'm afraid. I'm going to have to call my office and have them hunt up my regular man!"

Joe's head jerked upward. "Oh, don't do dat! Please!"

"Listen. I know this is some kind of set-up. What'd you do with Abie?"

"Nuttin'. I swear tuh Christ. He got some dough for not comin' in, dat's all."

"Abie Goodman accepted a bribe?"

"Well, lemmee tell yuh," Joe laughed mirthlessly. "It was some bribe. Jeez. I never knew it was gonna get like dis."

"Like what!" Mack almost shouted.

"Oh...oh...you know."

"I do?" Mack paused.

Both look blankly at each other, Mack sensing Joe's rigid, muscular shape so close to his, the smell of his sweat mixed with his cheap Italian perfume. The kind gangsters always wore. It was unmistakable. But they looked and looked, and kept looking at each other.

Could it be (Mack was incredulous) that this big ape was...queer? And—*attracted to him*?

Mack said, "Listen, Mr. Imperio, I don't know quite what to do. Abie is out of the question, I suppose. Now there's the boys in my friend Elliot's band, but I can't take them away from their rehearsal, see. I could do this all myself, but I just don't have the time right now, and I can't leave all this stuff in the corridor because we've got a floor show here and everybody'll fall all over the place. And I can't leave the truck out there because of what's in it, and I think you know what's in it. And there's something else—"

They were almost touching now. Mack could feel Joe Imperio's breath, catching the pleasant scent of Beeman's Pepsin Gum.

Joey whispered, "So I'll *help* yuz. And we'll take it from dere."

"Meaning—*what*?"

Then, from the top of the stairs, Mack heard his name being called. It was Deucie.

"I'm right here, Deuce. Just unloading the stuff! No need to come down."

"How's it all comin'? Baby can help if..." (As if either one of them could help! And if either one of them knew what was going on with a dago yegg right inside the club!)

"No! No!" Mack fairly sang back in a booming voice. "Everything's just jake!"

Both were breathing very heavily, Joe patting Mack's arm, as if to calm him down. "And by the way..." Mack continued his whispering. "Did you mean what I—um—what I think you meant just now...about taking it from there?"

"I'm awful sorry," Joey whispered back. "Did I rile yuz?" Joe's lips were touching Mack's ear. Mack, with great caution, lifted his hand to the Italian's shoulder, then let it rest there briefly.

Mack replied, with an unfortunate gulp, "Yes. You riled me. But, listen, we've got to talk about this…" (almost cooing now).

"Sure. After I help yuz down with duh stuff. Whatever yuh say."

The last few words barely audible, as their bodies neatly met, the textures of their vastly different clothing, sliding along, shielding the growing firmness of each muscle. It was only a brief second or two. Mack pulled away, not being able to take his eyes from the Italian's.

Quckly, in silence, they went back outside together, first unloading the two dozen crates of liquor and placing them in stacks before the broom closet. Finally, Mack, now perspiring himself, shoved the mops, pails and brooms aside, lifted the false back off, and revealed the locked door to the cellar. He stood directly before it as he rapidly spun the locks—knowing the combinations by heart, making certain Joey Imperio could not see what he was doing. But Joe was a gentleman about it all, and with a surprising degree of finesse, turned and lit yet another a cigarette.

Then, quickly, they carried the booze below, never saying a word. Once only, when they met on the stairs, did they both smile at each other. Mack kept thinking perhaps it's not going to happen. There was still so much to do. The spark—the magic might be lost!

Standing together in the cellar, surrounded by crates and crates of booze, one bare light bulb overhead, with every single crate put in its proper place, Joe wiped his brow, sighing, "Gotta rest. Long day."

He sat down on a chair—the only one down there, placed beside a small desk upon which was a ledger used for keeping track of the stock. Pulling off his undershirt, he wiped his arms, his chest, and his face with it, then, carefully, draped it over the back of that chair. "Whew," was his only comment.

"Whew," was also Mack's, responding to the Italian's smile, lips curving slowly, dimples emerging. Standing over him, Mack allowed Joe to slip off his tie, slide off his suspenders,unbutton his shirt, help with his cuff-links, pull off his undershirt, and unbutton his trousers. With so much to accomplish in so little time, both of them silently realized how well they were working together.

Now they were in each other's arms, puddles of clothing about their shoes. Mack felt for the first time in ten years as if he were once again really and truly alive.

It didn't matter to him if this guy was as crooked as Hell—and he was sure Joey Imperio was just that—an engulfing, strange kind of desire was being fufilled. This big, bulging, crude, goofy son of a bitch, the golden skin slick with sweat, the face as beautiful as—*more* beautiful than—any man's he had ever seen. He kissed him everywhere because every part of him gave, at last, satisfaction to the hunger he had felt for so very long. He held onto him with a grip like a fighter's, and Joey's body responded.

"Not…too…rough…Mr. Imperio?"

"Come on…come on…we got time, Mr. Daly." Joey would not let him free. Mack was in a vice made of the Italian's whole physique. Holding him in turn just as closely, Mack bit into his chest, just above his nipple, hearing him groan—then laugh. "Don't stop dere!" Joey Imperio whispered. And Mack Daly didn't.

When both in unison yelled out at the perfect moment, they hid their mouths and their shouts of incredible joy on one another's skins. They slid together, down, down on the floor, panting like two animals. First they both laughed. Then Mack felt tears come to his eyes. He knew he wanted to cry and he didn't know how to stop himself. And so, he buried his head in Joe's arms.

Incredibly he heard Joe say softly and tenderly to him, "I know. I know what it's like…I'm sorry. I'd never rat on you, Mr. Daly. Please, please don't let me go. Hold me just a little while longer. See, I bin through Hell. I didn't wanna do dis tudday—but I had to—I never t'ought you wuz gonna be so han'some and so goddamed hot. Christ, you're the hottest, grandest guy I ever saw. I never…I never t'ought—"

Mack held Joe's head up in his hands. "Hey! Imperio! Dry up!"

He couldn't believe this man, naked, big and bronzed and dumb and wonderful, was crying like a baby in his arms. Mack laughed and socked him lightly in the jaw.

They both stood together, facing each other. "Oh boy," Joe said. "We're bot' of us big messes. How we gonna 'xplain dis one?" Slowly, they pulled on their clothes.

Mack thought aloud, "Well, I have a right hand man…Alexander's his name—and…let's see…if I left now and got home early, I could bring him back and he could stock the bar, but my wife would never be ready."

"Your wife? You got a wife!"

"Yeah. Didn't they tell you that?"

Joe made a funny noise. "Fffffhhht! Jeez." Almost dressed, he now helped Mack with his tie. "I don't know nothin' about you excep'…um…excep' I sure do like you a helluva lot and I didn't never bargain for dis."

Mack nodded, deep in thought, stopping to stroke the back of Joe's neck. "Here's what we'll do. You'll take the truck back to the plant—I'll follow you. Then, you'll come with me in the roadster. Then we'll get cleaned up at home. Then I'll put you in one of my monkey suits, we'll come back here, and Ynez can follow in the limousine with Alexander driving."

"You lost me, pal!"

"Joey Imperio, that's one thing I hope never happens. Because now, kid, you're working for me."

"Holy shit." Joe slowly put his cap on. "How am I gonna 'xplain dis to Bruno?"

"Come on, we've got to hurry," Mack said, grabbing his arm and pushed him up the stairs, giving him a crack on his ass as they went.

In the alleyway, Mack heard Deucie once again calling out to him. He was hanging out of the second floor window.

"Hey, ain't you comin' up, Mackus?" he shouted.

With Joe getting into driver's seat and Mack going around the front, Deucie needed a fast explanation. "Not this minute, Deuce. Gotta get the truck back to the plant—but we'll be back early."

In a stage whisper, Deucie asked, "Who's the wop? Where's Abie?"

And Mack replied in the same way, "I'll tell you everything later," giving him a wink and a series of very confusing gestures.

Mack pointed Joey Imperio down past Broadway, where he had discreetly parked his roadster to avoid attention due to the fact that he was involved in a nite club scheme. Meanwhile, Deucie deVol, now sitting on the windowsill of the upstairs office, was telling his wife what he had just seen.

"This guy who was with our Mack was nobody from Leventhal's, that's for sure. He was kinda swarthy lookin'…had a kinda sexed-up look, makin' googly eyes at Mack."

Baby deVol, intently perusing the guest list for that evening's opening, looked up. "Well, it's about time somebody made googly eyes at our Mack!" Adjusting her glasses, she absently added, "I wish you'd quit worrying, honey—but wishing it never did me any good anyway!"

Deucie had already risen and was hobbling in the direction of the stairs. With a sigh, she went back to her work, pulling kid curlers from her hennaed hair now and then to make certain she wouldn't look like a Hotentot later on.

Lighting her hundredth cigarette for that day, she gazed wistfully across her nice, new desk (Mack had furnished the place just swell) at two framed photos she had placed there with a vase of fresh posies next to them. One was of Mack in his uniform, taken in 1918. So darling and so brave! The other was of an infant, beneath whose rather pitiful coutenance was a tiny brass plaque reading simply "Junior." Their kid who died at three weeks old.

"My two angels," she said to herself, crushing the cigarette in the naked lady ash tray to her right. Whoever Mack had with him downstairs was going to be Just All Right with Baby deVol. Maybe Mackie took some time off to find a fella! As if Mack Daly ever took time off to do anything that was even the least bit selfish! As almost always happened whenever matters of the heart and Mack Daly were concerned, a tear formed on the rim of her right eye. "Crazy galloot," she sighed, getting back down to work.

How far she had come from those strange days and nights at *La Maison*! And now here she was preparing a reservation list for some of the swellest folks on the Main Stem! Doesn't Ynez Daly wish that she had this privilege?

Well, whatever might happen down the pike between that ginnie Deucie just espied out the window and her Mackus would certainly be interesting—in light of the fact that Ynez Daly had her Mackus by the balls!

Not that she trusted ginnies. She trusted them about as much as trusted Ynez Daly—which was not at all. But never mind. Mackie would see to it that the guy was made to walk the straight and narrow, she concluded, whoever the Hell he was—wondering, even as she was making that conclusion, what in Hell the whole thing was about anyway.

Deucie was making his way laboriously back up the stairs toward the office. Even before he entered, he loudly announced, "Well, guess what! The bar ain't even stocked yet and I went down to the cellar and found a pair of polky-dot BVDs somebody used to wipe up goo-goo with!"

Baby didn't bat an eye. "Looks like he found himself some outside help, hmm?"

Deucie lowered himself into the club chair in front of her desk. "I'll say he did! My own worry is how they both took off like that tuggether, leavin' things undone. Say now, you know, honey, that ain't at all like Mackie."

Baby put out her cigarette. "No. But he did say he'd be back soon. You've gotta leave things up to him like the liquor, Deuce. It's his business!" She stopped, looking at his gristled face, his plump form all in a heap. She had been his nurse when they had to saw his leg off during the War. From that time on, she was still his nurse.

Deucie thought the world and everything of his Babe. This woman possessed a soul as white and pure and starched as the uniform she'd worn for most of her young years—which still hung neatly in her closet, along with a bag of mothballs. There are certain types of females whom all men come to love in one way or another. They might be a mother one minute and a whore the next. They can scold, they can even turn away and say they'd never talk to you ever again—they were just that mad—or they could be just horribly, horribly hurt. But then they'd always come back, and always call you Their Very Own, their Sweetheart, their Lover Boy—or their Cross to Bear.

As Baby always said, a woman who's been around is the easiest to get around. But it didn't matter what type of pain they took on—these gals were True Blue Lou's right down to their dyed orange roots. Turn them inside out and you'd find a Mary Mother of Jesus, or Joan of Arc, or a red Hot Mama who could drink any fella right under the table.

All the boys in Mack's regiment felt that way about their Baby. They would kill for her. And she would do the same for them. Because all of these boys (those, at least, who were still alive and hadn't died from latent injuries, lousy booze or going crazy) were all still buddies, and Baby was their mascot.

Baby deVol would also tell you that she'd been around the block so many times—she actually had to have it re-paved. She would tell you that she was such a sucker they had slug minted wth her profile on it. But if anyone in God's whole world knew what her Mackie needed, it was none other than herself.

Sure she and the Deuce were worried about what Mack was doing—being that he worked for the government within the Prohibition Bureau!—but, the fact remained, he desperately wanted to open the club for them…and that was all there was to it. It made him happy, and that's all that mattered.

Stretching her arm loaded with cheap bangles across the desk and patting Deucie on his one real leg, Baby consoled him, "Just work around it, honey. There's plenty to do without worryin' about the bar."

"Yes, but that's the real reason why folks are comin' here! It won't take any time before word gets out that we've got the very best stuff on the entire East Coast. All it takes is one toot!" Deucie shook his head. "Gawd help us all if any Prohibtion agents sneak in tunnight. We'll be cooked."

Baby deVol rose and went to the window, automatically dousing her hanky with cologne and wiping her temples, neck and wrists with it—something she did a dozen times in one day. Looking out at the back alley, she listed in her mind how particularly careful Mack had been. It was so like her Mackie to justify what he was doing in a way that only Mack could. Oh, my God Above, was she proud of him!

Landing that big government job, feeling the brunt of all that predjudice…having his own family, those goddammed Leventhals, turn on him.

("You shouldn't worry about bein' a Jew, Mack! Keep your name as it is! Why, just look at the show business! Everybody's a Jew and nobody changes their name!")

But Mack reasoned that he hadn't been known as Benny Leventhal for years following the War. He was right. Nobody really knew where he'd come from…he was just there: married, rich, charming…getting to know All the Right People because of his associations with government—and with liquor.

Deucie, meanwhile, had to calm down. Getting up and pouring himself a drink from the bottle he kept hidden in the toilet tank, he couldn't help but notice what the label said:

MEDICINAL LIQUOR
INSURED UNDER AUTHORITY OF THE NATIONAL PROHIBITION ACT
BONDED BY THE FEDERAL GOVERNMENT
AVAILABLE ONLY THORUGH PRESCRIPTION
DO NOT REFILL OR TRANSFER UNDER PENALTY.

Mack always let the deVols have his stuff in its original bottles, because Baby's nursing background could explain her reason for keeping it about. After all, Deucie had been seriously shell-shocked.

Pouring himself a shot in the toothbrush glass, he called out to Baby if she'd like a quick refresher. Baby rarely drank anyway, and wasn't in the least concerned about this dago or the bar not yet being filled. But she was worried. (Mack couldn't ever get over how they both were always nervous wrecks about something.) She had told herself, however—over and over—that he was in no danger of being caught.

Deucie yelled at her from the bathroom, "Do you remember how surprised Mack was when he got that offer from Uncle Sam? Jesus, weren't we proud of him, though!" How he loved to reminisce about almost anything, laughing and coughing all at the same time as he took his toot. "He'd done so grand in the Fightin', and his family was in so good with Pres-dent Wilson!"

Baby sat back down, now carefully writing out the reservation cards for each table, her tongue sticking out between her teeth. "Uh-huh, " she replied, deep in sudden concentration.

"Why you coulda knocked him over with a feather! Say, if it wasn't for the Volstead Act, our Mackus would prob'lee be bakin' cookies at the Leventhal plant. And we'd be out on the street! Funny how things work out—now he's got himself a good four acres of warehouses out there in Brooklyn devoted only to hooch! And it's all legal!"

He let go a deep burp then barrelled on. "Here he is manufacturing bonded alcohol for the government—from his family's grain, right next door at the Leventhal bakeries. It's s'posed to go to our hospitals, or wash away the stain of sin in church—but, Hell, most of it goes right down the very politicans' gullets who act so godammed high and mighty about never having taken a drink!"

"Yes and most of 'em will be here tonight! Doesn't it make you just want to laugh!" Baby replied. "Mackie's gotten one over on 'em all right!" (Baby had to keep convincing herself of this.) "The poor darling went into our so-called Noble Experiment with great hopes, Deucie. Mack was a progressive if I ever saw one. Say, that's our Mackie! Never touched a single drop of alcohol in his life! You listenin' Deucie? The way I see it, one reason he's openin' this club is just to thumb his nose at those bastards up in Albany and down in Washington."

"I don't see how they could miss a couple ah thousands gallons, the way they got it rigged now—might as well go to us as to anyone!" Deucie added, having cleaned out the soap dish with his pen knife throughout this entire conversation.

In the mirror over the sink he saw the reflection of his wife, going over all the RSVPs. Gee, things had certainly turned around. He pondered how Mack had made it all happen by way of a what Baby had always termed "A Mixed Blessing." Talk about a silk purse out of sow's ear! He began to recall how, just after the War, none of his bunch really had very much at all.

Then came Prohibition.

• • •

The year was 1920 and the Volstead Act was in full national enforcement. Those so suddenly put in charge had already suggested that Mack siphon off a certain amount each month from his quotas, fake his overage reports to Washington, then bottle it up and deliver it secretly to those haunts where the rich, powerful and politically ambitious frolicked. He was shocked.

But the big boys in government assured him that if he would only "help them out" in this way, they would make him rich. Well, he certainly got rich—with no direct help from them!

"Supplying" all of the Best Families in the country from Palm Beach to Cape Cod in a most discreet manner...that was what they needed. He was perfect for the job, too, and truly–how could he refuse? After all, these First Families of our Great Land could not possibly deal with bootleggers! It would hardly be dignified if any one of them went blind or choked to death on his own blood!

They also required him to cache all pre-War booze that could be had under their names, because it belonged to them. They'd bought it. After all, when the great distilleries had to close down, what was to be done with all that inventory? It was still there—in the warehouses out in Brooklyn—he never dared touch that stuff. Mack was under their thumbs all right. He'd always said they'd given him the government contract because he was a Jew and they knew they could treat him any way they wanted. But he was also a polished gentleman, cultured, urbane...and somehow inordinately private.

But the fact that the Wilson administration had so favored his family during the War didn't hurt either. Mack found himself doling the legalized liquor out left and right, providing phony bottles and labels, and comandeering the bakery trucks to deliver it right to their homes out on Long Island.

"And for this," he would joke, like a Yiddish comic, "I don't get paid?"

That was how he'd gotten his first taste of American Capitalism. With only the help of Abie and his Negro Right-Hand, Alexander, Mack had to deliver all the shipments himself. During the height of the Season, from the Summer of 1920 until only three years ago, he'd traveled up and down the Eastern seaboard with lists of local and state police (as long as your arm) who were in the pay to the politicians. From county to county, state to state, Mack had made it without a single arrest. Abie joked with him, calling him the Wandering Jew. He called his little gang the Three Musketels.

As a son of Zion and a of son of the Leventhals, Mack Daly was not prepared for the display of wealth he saw first-hand at those parties, fund-raisers and conventions. Nor was he prepared for the fact that he had to work with these people behind closed doors to clinch the deals—being invited right inside—while Abie, a kike, and Alexander, a nigger, waited out by the garages. And was he prepared for the fact that they didn't even cover his fuel expenses, or offer to feed his friends? He certainly was not.

"How come you don't look like the rest of your family?" one old souse asked him—who was just celebrating his new seat in congress. Mack tried to tell him that everybody on God's earth was different, as they were supposed to be. But the congressman just laughed ruefully. He ended by offering Mack a cigar and advising him he could get places if he didn't let anybody know that he really was a mockie.

Another time, there was a troupe of lawn dancers—then the rage—at a swell house party on the Gold Coast. Mack tried to strike up a conversation with the young man of the company, who was responsible for hoisting the girls above his head and twirling them around. His muscles attracted Mack, and he was a gentleman, too. But Mack couldn't get to first base with him.

The dancer, clad only in a silk loin cloth, took him aside, behind the gazebo, warning him: "Listen. You'd better not talk to me. They'll think you're a fairy and give you a beating."

"I'd like to see them try it," Mack answered.

"Sure. I get you. A fellow like you would use his fists. But they've got billy clubs around here, and kick you where it hurts most."

"You look to me as if you nicely avoided any of that!" Mack smiled.

"Well, it's a living, I'll say that much. Just last week they put a tenor in the hospital—all of them so drunk—got him around the neck with ice tongs." Then he added, "But you've got a nice, deep voice and you're very manly."

All of this did Mack Daly store within his heart.

Then, in 1924, he started charging these big shot clients of his. Oh, his prices were fair enough and he added on travel time, too. He decided not to charge more simply because the stuff was pristine. After all, the cream of High Society would have it no other way. Nor would Uncle Sam. His friends had a lot of laughs over that one.

"Listen, they're hooked. That crowd loves their booze," he'd tell those few war buddies whom he could trust. "You think they're not going to pay for it? You think they're going to risk calling up a bootlegger for bathtub gin made with radiator cleaner instead of coming to me?"

Those big shots were breaking the very laws they were put into office to enforce, and now they were paying the guy they'd hired to supply them, and looking the other way! Well, if that didn't take the cake. Mack could easily have told the few honorable and respectable politicians he'd gotten to know that he'd been railroaded into this racket. After all, he was finding himself in meeting rooms where there were free-and-easy girls present; he often overheard these men plotting their secret agreements which would emerge, days later, in all the papers as whitewashed highway projects or allotments for phony charities.

They couldn't say no to him; they wanted it, needed it and feared what would happen to them if they couldn't get it. Pink elephants and a case of the shakes when delivering their speeches.

That damned yiddle has such a fine appointment in our government—a booze baron for Uncle Sam no less! Better pay him. Besides, nobody would ever suspect what he was up to. And he looks so–so–well...American!

Besides, there's something so honorable about him...pure, you might even say. Striking—almost too good-looking, really! Not married, you say? How old? And a vet? Hmmm. I just wonder...

He was hardly out of ear-shot when they began talking about him. Of course they resented paying. They resented the fact that this fellow was not only heroic-looking, but a real hero as well—going over with the AEF took a lot of courage. They resented the fact that he was a kike, and even if he hadn't been queer, they might've said he was anyway. But mostly they resented "shucking out their sheckels" (as Mack put it) for the stuff they felt entitled to imbibe because of Who They Were.

Mack had felt it all, and it had made him seethe. It had also created in this newly invented man—formerly known as Benny Leventhal—an arrogance which even surprised himself. And so he started on this new path, stopping at nothing. He would get himself a wife—clearly and carefully explaining everything that was expected of her, treating her like a goddess, putting her on a pedastal. Requiring only that she would allow him to go his way, and she would go hers.

He would show them. All of them. He would buy himself a smart house and socialize with smart people—as long as they were good-hearted and accepting of the world as it had emerged after the War. And, after all, with Prohibition turning everyone into neurotics—what choice did they have?

All of this was done in a remarkably short period of time. The opening of the Club deVol, he had thought, was going to be the crowning achievement. Deucie and Baby deVol, muddling endlessly over the real reason why their best friend in the whole world was risking everything to start this enterprise, finally chalked it up to just thumbing his nose at everyone. That had to be it.

• • •

Deucie blinked several times and, right there in that new little bathroom, came to the relaization that he'd had a realization about the whole thing. Just why Mackie put the whole deal together as he did. Turning, he ambled out and into the parlor.

"Well, now I guess I've got to worry…" Deucie said under his breath, hoping that Baby would not throw the paperweight at him, "…that he don't go and pick up with that dago!"

"He's got everything but what he really needs, Deucie. What he always did need. A *man*. And if that guy you saw with him just now can be that man for him—well, all the better sez I, and God bless 'em both for it, too!"

"Guilty as charged," replied Deucie, grinning down at her.

• • • • •

CHAPTER II

DOUBLE STANDARD

Mack was at the wheel of his purple Marmon convertible, Joseph sitting—or, rather, slouching—beside him, on top of the lap rug keeping the upholstery from getting dirty. The idea was Joey's, not Mack's. Legs were open to the breeze, arms up behind his head. Happy as Hell. He looked *good*.

"Hey, can I start callin' you by your foyst name one ah dese days?" Joe asked, looking Mack's way with a sudden smile.

"What's that supposed to mean?" Mack looked sidelong at him.

"Well, if yuh must know, I feel awful uncomfor'bull. I sorta feel like youse is stuck wid me and—after what we jus' done. And I guess you picked me out for duh kind of low-life I yam. And dere's dat udder problem as well—"

"—what other problem?" Incredulous.

"No…see—I jus' mean…well…you know—me bein' funny and all—a sissy."

"Listen, right now that stuff takes a back seat to you being a gangster, Joe. And yes, you can call me Mack. And I'm hoping you won't shoot me if I call you Joe."

"Well dat makes it all a lot better, don't it! Yessiree-bub!" He picked up his left arm and hung it over the back of Mack's seat. Then Mack heard him laugh, and loved what he heard.

"Hey, did I give you permission to do that?" Mack asked.

"No! No, you did not! But somet'in' made me do it!" He paused. "I'm awful glad I'm here wid youse, Mr. Dal—I mean *Mack*. You coulda made an awful asshole outa me, yuh know."

"Well we've got a lot to discuss, Joe. Not for one minute do I intend to let you think that you're going to move in on me and what I've got going."

"Listen, I'm just a shill, see. If I had my way, I'd move in *wid* you not *on* you! Facks is, I gotta just do what I'm told. So I do. I hope you don't t'ink it's easy bein' someone like me! Hey, can I have one of dem Egyptian gold tips yuh smoke, huh?"

"There's several packs in the glove case. Take one." Joe was getting nervous. Mack decided on letting him talk—fascinated, captivated.

They now were in the middle of a traffic jam in Queens.

"It was planned dat I show up and meet youse. But—shit! You sent me to Heaven on sight!" Joe performed a gyration which appealingly placed his body in yet another position of sensual repose. On his side now, he looked over at Mack.

"Don't let me wreck this car, will you, Joe, with those eyes of yours."

Mack honked the horn. "Listen, how old are you?"

"Last time I checked I was twennie-eight, but when I got tested up duh river, dey said my mental age was 18. I guess you could say I ain't too bright."

Mack started to say something, thought a bit (*He is adorable!)* looked sidelong—looked again, (they had come to a stop light) then, smiling in spite of himself said, "You really are one piece of work, Joey Imperio."

The big beefy Italian grinned up at him, "Ain't I just dat, dough?" Then, noticing a shiny look to Mack's classically chiseled profile, took his index finger and gently slid it down his nose. "Gee, if you don't quit sweatin' I'll have to slip dis lap rug under youse! Say, I'm duh one who's noyvous here! You ain't noyvous about me bein' wid yuz like dis are yuz?"

"I think we're both a little 'noyvous,' Joey, as you put it."

"Aw, shit, jus' make like we're out on a date! I never get dis lucky! You draggin' me along tunnight to yer dump! Hot dog!"

Mack laughed, at first trying not to—but Joey joined in. Then Joe suddenly became serious, cleared his throat and, looking off at the approaching intersection which would point them toward Great Neck, said, "But we gotta talk 'bout what's goin' on here. I wouldn't want yuz tuh t'ink I don't trooly like yuz nor nuttin'. The fact is, dat's the problem. I do like yuz. Lots, too."

This caused Mack to get a lump in his throat; grasping for words, and not finding them, he pulled the younger, not-too-bright street tough closer as they roared off with the late afternoon sun behind them, painting with amber benevolence the last remnants of Queens—little bungalow backyards hung with wet sheets, clouds of gray smoke emerging from chimney pots; the sound of a victrola playing the latest Paul Whiteman record; a kid yelling for a dog named Sparky.

Mack didn't want any explanations at all. If it wasn't going to be the Underworld, then it would be the cops. After all, he'd gone into this project having weighed all the consequences. And if what was sitting right beside him was a consequence of his actions—then to Hell with it.

This tableau of a contented world now whizzed past as Mack and Joe felt a magic descend on them both. As husbands came home from factories to suppers spread on clean white tablecloths, and flappers chattered away over telephones, life was sensible—fitting itself sweetly into everyone's heart. The world had become a romantic backdrop for these two big fellows who were both as queer as three-dollar bills.

"Say," Joe reverantly observed, "do you believe us two meetin' like dis or what?" He looked at Mack, who kept on smiling, holding Joe close with his strong right arm, driving fast now, one hand on the wheel, feeling masterful.

"Do I?" Mack wanted suddenly to define for himself his exact feelings at that very moment and drew from the bard: *"'Now I will believe, That there are unicorns, that in Arabia, There is one tree, the phoenix's throne, One phoenix at this hour reigning there…'"* he sighed.

"Wha-at? Say, dat's a little deep for me! Dat's po'tree, ain't it?"

"Sure is, Joey. Shakespeare, from *The Tempest*, and the phoenix is the bird that rises triumphantly out of the ashes. See, for a long, long time, I never had anyone in my life. I really just gave up. Now, here you are. It's pretty goddammed strange. I realize now my strange and wonderful feeling today was just a harbinger of all of this!"

"—whatever *dat* means!"

Mack paused and took the cigarette Joey had lit for him. "We had fun back there, didn't we?"

"If you aksts me, it's destiny. Now dere is a woyd I know! Dat's what duh judge sez to me when I go up duh river. 'Son,' he sez, 'it's yer destiny!'" His tone changed. "Oh jeez, I guess you don't wanna talk about nothing serious now, though, do yuz?"

But Mack didn't mind. "You mean about what's *really* going on here? What you did with Abie? How you found out my game?"

"Listen—if I tol' everyt'ing, would it make any difference?"

"Any difference in what? We seem to be getting along just fine so far…"

"Oh…*you* know."

"All I know is that you seem to have been informed about a few things that aren't generally supposed to be known, and I didn't know what to do with you because of that. So here we are." He glanced over at Joe. "You smile at the oddest times. Can I ask you why you do that, Joe?"

"Listen, I don't always smile, see? And when I do, it's cuz I got somethin' to smile about." It was as if he had completely changed. "Finally—I hope!"

"Well, may God forgive me, Joseph, I didn't mean to get you going there! We'll just have to see where this all leads, right?"

Both said nothing for quite a while as they drove along. By now, it was nearly sunset.

"O.k. Here it is," Joseph took a deep breath. "When I met youse today, I sez to myself, holy Christ, what a real gennul'man he is and how am I gonna do dis to him!"

Mack now also took a deep breath. "—and what is it precisely you intended to do to me? You've got to forget about shaking me down—not you, but whoever it is you're working for. Why, they'd have to be crazy, Joey!"

"Pull over, will yuh?"

Mack did so, assuming Joe had to pee, but the big, brawny Italian went for Mack Daly, not to hurt him, but to cover Mack's mouth with a passionate and deep kiss, wrapping his arms around him firecely—powerfully shifting his body toward him, pressing himself against Mack, and feverishly attempting to get his pants down at the same time.

"Hold on! Let's get off the road a little more!" Panting.

"Yeah, hurry up, though, or I'm gonna blow my load!"

It was looking that way, because Joe had already lowered his trousers and revealed it all—throbbing and hefty. "Oh jeez! I musta left my skivvies back at yer club," he realized.

"Don't worry, Joey, it's less to think about." Mack whirled under a grove of trees, shut off the engine and began the laborious procedure of once again denuding himself, as cars sped past at a distance of not more than thirty feet off.

As soon as they were both entirely naked (this time, off went the shoes and socks), Joe, breathlessly on top of him, noted a mutual discomfort, "This ain't too successful..."

"Open the door there and let's slide down into the grass—quick!"

Both tumbled out, laughing, and attacking one another like two marvelous beasts.

• • •

Mrs. Mack Daly had earlier lunched at the Ritz with her chum Annabelle Harrison, who was, for all practical purposes, the only real chum Ynez Daly had. And, at almost exactly the same moment that Mr. Mack Daly was entering the inner confines of his Italian young man on the road to Great Neck, his wife was entering a Domestics Agency not far from that most chic of chic restaurants.

Annabelle, poor thing, who was not "poor" at all in that sense of the word, who was, in fact, one of the richest women in America, loped alongside Ynez's clipped mince, and filled her in on the particulars of the establishment.

"It IS a Domestics Agency and yet—it *isn't,*" she was saying in a half-whisper, somewhat breathlessly, half-smirking, her tone vaguely scandalous. "Darling, if you can't get it there—you don't need it. DO you get my drift, my dear?"

"Well, whatever it is or isn't, you're looking at a gal who needs it, Belle, sweetie, desperately! So lead on!"

With a fluttery hand banded by a deep red fox cuff, Ynez Daly, her head held high, high, high, followed the kind-hearted, brilliant and equine millionairess, onward and upward to the second floor of an office building with a lobby somewhat frayed at the edges. The elevator girl, giving them both the eye, hadn't even asked what floor they wanted. She knew. And as they departed her cage, she was heard delivering herself of a snide chuckle. Ynez shot her a withering look, and the girl stuck her tongue out.

"The very cheek of her!" Annabelle Harrison whispered. "She's seen me here before...and probably in those damned society pages as well. I should be more careful, I guess. This is the place."

They stood before a door upon which was stenciled "Richards Dial-a-Domestic."

Hardly had she so gingerly knocked when a heavily powdered woman with pince-nez and cheap lace trim pinned artlessly to a shiny, crepe, navy blue frock, hissed that they should enter and be seated. Ynez Daly looked about, blasé.

It was a sort of waiting room where stale cigarette smoke hung in the air, a half-dead sansivera rose and fell like a withered green hand on top of a sputtering radiator. Two Maxfield Parrish prints hung on the walls, crookedly. And there, in the middle of an office that could have been for any kind of business—or no business at all—this sleazily clad person, standing before them, fairly ogling them both with eyes evidently enlarged by hop, gurgled a greeting in bad French.

"*Bone joor maze damns. Essay yey vooz see vouze plate.*"

Lowering themselves down on the greasy varnished oaken bench, Ynez murmured, "*Really*, Belle—" successfully. Once again, Ynez thought to herself, how well she had put across that such common surroundings were loathe and strange to her most exquisite self. Little did Annabelle Harrison know how close her new friend was to that class.

"We offer only the finest gentlemen only here," the woman was saying, not ever blinking, "for those who desire the most discreet kind of service. We pride ourselves on...on...on..."

Apparently the dope had gotten to her.

"Never mind," Annabelle offered helpfully, in a ultra-cultivated voice hardly above a whisper, "we know why we're here, and so do you. I've used your agency before with satisfying results, and so today I've brought my friend. We telephoned ahead—*if* you recall. You *did* get our message, didn't you?"

The woman's eyes fairly rolled to the back of her head as she croaked a shaky, *"Ah! Oui!"* then managed with, "You wanted—I believe—a chauffeur, is that not right?"

"That's right," Annabelle nodded. "My friend must be very, very satisfied. She desires someone who can drive her around—as well as—be a mechanic. *You* know what I mean! If we might meet someone who would…fill the bill, as it were?"

The woman then so loudly cleared her throat that both ladies jumped. Suddenly, as if on cue, from the only door in the room, there emerged a man of about 27 years possessed of a singularly visceral and sordid countenance. He knew it, too, and had evidently studied long and hard the films of many such Latin Threats, for he smoldered from the tip of his glossed black head to the toe of his patent leather shoe.

Slender and tense like a cord of knotted amber beads, he was the kind of man who, even though dressed in an off-the-peg suit, looked somehow shamelessly, indecently, hardly dressed at all. There was not a pore in his body, thought Annabelle Harrison, which did not exude perfectly nasty thoughts. He was like some gorgeous cobra, she decided. He would do, for Ynez, nicely.

The manageress gestured his way. "Permit me to introduce to you Signor Reynaldo di Rose. He comes from a fine aristocratic family of old Spain. He is our finest."

"Finest *what*?" Ynez tittered to Annabelle.

After clicking his heels, he crossed the tiny room and lifted Ynez's gloved hand to his lips, turned it over, palm up, and placed a kiss therein, closing it gently, as if forever sacredly sealing it. (Later on, Ynez told Annabelle: *"I saw that movie, and thought, oh, my Gawd, I'll just have to laugh. But then when he looked at me, let me tell you—I was sold.")*

"I hahb references, of course, " he purred.

The woman produced a wrinkled envelope from behind the dying plant somewhere. Ynez quickly dismissed it, knowing the game inside and out, but nodding as the Empress of China might.

"You do possess a driver's license, don't you?" Ynez felt business-like all of a sudden.

"Shooah," he replied and winked at her. (Ynez was hit with just a tiny thrill by that wink, and managed to crack just the tiniest of smiles.) "Would joo like to see some photy-graphs?" he then asked, flashing his slitty eyes.

"Of you driving?" Ynez asked.

"Hardly!" he replied with something between a sneer and a smarmy grin.

Annabelle turned to Ynez's cloched right ear and quickly explained that these were the pictures she must see; each prospective client was entitled to do so, although no one else ever got a peek. The woman placed before her five, eight-by-ten-inch photographs of the snakey-looking man standing in the nude, executing (or trying to, at least) various art poses.

"Pliss note, Madame: *pennus erectus*," he pointed.

("Who could help but note that!" Ynez later confided to Annabelle. *"He was hung like a horse!")*

And indeed it was so; wearing nothing more than coat of salad oil, the studies showed Reynaldo di Rose in all his glory.

"Joo see! I neffair deesapoin'!" His thick lips parted to reveal a set of enormous choppers, the diadem of which was a gold tooth. The effect was vulgar, for, in every possible way, he epitomized a slithery gigolo. But Ynez felt a chill of long forgotten joy and was sold. Then, just as he was admiring himself, the photographs tumbled from his hands. Ynez and the odd-looking woman both stooped to retrieve them. There was a chorus of lackluster apologies and don't-mention-it's. And then came the calm after the storm.

"We always, *naturallement*, require a cash retainer," the woman said in her sepulchral voice, standing up again.

As Ynez was putting the hundred bucks in her unusually hairy hand, rattling off explicit instructions on how to get to her Great Neck house, all being taken down by means of a chewed pencil stub onto a small, much-thumbed pad, Annabelle breathed sigh of relief. Now, at last, her poor dear friend would be relieved of her sexual torment!

Anxious and racing to closure, the manageress nodded as if almost in Nirvana. Ramon, shuffling his erotica and phony references again into a neat pile, bowed and vanished back from whence he had come, slipping through that single door, wraith-like. The date was set: tomorrow evening for his trial run. If she liked him—well! he could perhaps even be put on steady.

Ynez experienced a moment of very understandable panic. "There must be no questions asked and he must, of course, be utterly, *utterly* trustworthy!"

"That, Madame, goes without without saying—*a demain*!"

Out the door with them! BANG.

Before both ladies knew it, it had been slammed, almost in their faces. Hungry for clean air, they found a certain relief to be once more in the hallway.

Hoofing it back to Annabelle's limousine, parked a block away—just as Mack Daly's car was—so that her own (real) chauffeur would not know of this assignation, she assured Ynez further, "I've had two or three of them from that agency, with no trouble at all, darling. Now don't you worry about a thing."

"I don't quite know *what* to think—or how to *feel*. You understand my plight, Belle, dear," Ynez confided, eyeing the passing throng, certain they were hanging on to her every word. "Two years into a marriage with a man whom I simply *idol*ize and yet I even scratch my own back! I need LOVE! I need someone to—*make love* to me. But you didn't let them *make love* to you, as I recall, did you?"

"I didn't need to find fufillment that way. Call me abnormal, I don't care!" she laughed dryly, slipping her arm through Ynez's. Annabelle Harrison had decided her calling in life was that of a sculptress, thus estranging herself from her family. "Fact is, they were ready, willing and able—but I wasn't interested in anything more than using them as models. So, I did do a few nude studies of the boys sent out to me instead. And that was that, as they say!"

Now only a few feet from the car which would take them both back to Long Island, Belle became grateful. "Honestly, 'Nez, I didn't know what was *wrong* with me for the longest time—until *you* figured it out for me!"

But there was no time for that now, it seemed; for Ynez, who only liked talking about herself anyway, loftily diverted. "Well, I know *exactement* what's wrong with *me*. *Nothing's* wrong with me! My libido is in eclipse, that's all. Whose wouldn't be, with the deal I got myself into?"

At the opened door of the car, Annabelle, getting in first, said. "Of course it is, poor muffin, and this is what you need to rekindle the fire of your soul. You must have no doubts!"

But Ynez was not herself, smoking endless perfumed cigarettes on the way home, rolling her gloves into a ball, then putting them on all over again. Annabelle was one of the few "outsiders"—that is, those not within Mack and Ynez's secret circle of chums—who really knew how things stood in this marriage of theirs. A free soul was Annabelle, constantly playing devil's advocate to Ynez, because she, herself, was also without a single girl-chum in the whole world.

Annabelle Harrison was simply too eccentric for the females of her set. She had taken to Ynez at once. Here was a stunning, exotic newcomer, of whom she did a wonderful statue! And after those sessions together, giggling and gossipping, molding clay and drinking a lot of gin, the two were best of friends.

Mysterious was this Mrs. Daly (an understatement) and self-admittedly in need of schooling in the trecherous art of Getting In and Staying In. Her advice to Ynez, culled from nothing more than a stultifying upbringing of rigidly imposed innocence, consisted of one cliché after another about the *Haute Monde* which Ynez naturally swallowed whole.

But Ynez considered Annabelle a real sage because she thought all Old Money People were wise and could never do or say anything wrong. This lonely Junoesque artiste, the unfortunate female product of a Patrician American family, was a real catch for Mrs.Mack Daly, steering her unwittingly toward what she was certain would avail her (Ynez, that is) of every possible advantage the other woman could offer. Namely, melting in, seamlessly, with all of the Best People.

Through Annabelle, Ynez was now continually rubbing elbows with that crowd whom she idolized. And, even though Annabelle had ostracized herself from the whole Harrison brood by becoming a sculptress, she was still cleaved, naturally, to all the rest of the Old Guard. Yachting parties, riding to hounds, charity teas—Ynez wormed her way into all and any via Annabelle Harrison, who never seemed to want to know where on earth Ynez Daly had come from, or what had spawned her.

So streamlined and eloquently stylish—such an example of that modern type of beauty—rather hard, oddly superior, and imbued—for no reason in the world—with a poetic and lovely painfulness, Ynez Daly was simply taken for being one of Annabelle's models from somewhere else—wherever that might be!

Whenever she could get her story straight, Ynez babbled about how her father, who was a French count, met her mother, a White Russian grand duchess.

However, during the 1927 season, since they were seen together constantly, everyone started to wonder…"Who IS that woman poor Annabelle Harrison always has hanging about Her?" Mrs. Somebody Something, hissed at one such affair when first this duet was seen out and about.

"—her husband just bought that Broadway producer Tuthill's place out in Great Neck. Nobody knows very much about them. He's rather *Mittleuropa*, you know."

The other Blueblood laughed. "Too bad *she's* not! Those *ges*tures! And that posturing! One wonders if she didn't get left behind by some second-rate vaudeville company."

"Well, I for one wish they'd come back and get her! Did you ever hear such a phony accent in all your life?"

Through it all, and in spite of it, Ynez did manage to help Annabelle with her awkwardness when it came to making intimate choices. And so, today's adventure had transpired out of Belle Harrison returning a favor which had utterly changed that woman's life for the better.

In a vaguely audible voice—even though the tonneau glass was up—Annabelle admitted at last, to Ynez, as well as to herself, "I had no idea *that* was what ailed me. I feel, now, so—so—so *unbound* within my very heart! It's all so shocking, 'Nez, that I can't quite take it all in just now…but I DO owe it all to you, my dear friend…and yet—who—who—would've thought it?"

"I'm the most broad-minded person you might ever come across, Belle, and I'm not saying that it ever did, really, occur to me either—I mean that you liked *Negro* men. But I *knew* it had to be something like that. To each his own, say I."

Ynez had done such a simple thing. She had introduced Annabelle to the brother of their own trusted servant, Alexander Parker. She'd just had a hunch that Annabelle and Keys (whose real name was Caesar, which ended up being pronounced Keezer) would hit it off. And did they ever.

Belle leaned forward, opening the exquisite little back-seat bar, mixing drinks for them both and letting go a sigh of relief.

"Keys is such a perfect love,too. A truly noble soul. And such fun! He's so bright and such a guiding light for me! Darling, I just adore him and I owe it all to you." She wrapped her capable artist's hands, about to give the cocktail shaker a good jostle.

"Just bruise it, darling!" Ynez reminded her.

"Yes, I know—you're just like all those Irish Catholics out on the Island," Annabelle laughed. "Bruise the gin, boil the potato and burn the beef!"

It was then that something puzzling and vaguely disquieting crossed her mind. *Something* she had intended to tell Ynez. But, now—oh, well—it was gone.

Pouring, then sipping along with Ynez, "Mack is *such* a love to supply me with these spirits. Ah! To each his own, indeed, my 'Nez! I have found my true calling in the magnificent black man's majestic beauty and soul! And you have found yours in the tortured and untouchable idolization of the *homosexual!*"

"Well, I hope you get further with Keys than I have with my Mackus." Ynez sat forward now, her drink swishing in its glass. "I really don't *want* to cheat on him, Belle! I really don't! But you know how it's been since we got married—really, it's a wonder I haven't cracked up."

"The wisest thing you ever did was to stop crawling in bed with that divine *Unter der Linden* hubby of yours," sipping away, Belle proclaimed.

"It was simply eating me *alive*. Seeing him so perfect and so vital, day in, day out—and loving him so! *Truly* loving him so! God, I do hope everything goes smoothly with this Reynaldo di Rose person—if it doesn't, I'll just go mad, that's all."

"Do you intend to tell Mack what it's all about? This fufillment of your sex urge at long last, I mean?" Annabelle asked, pouring herself another drink.

"It will come as an awful shock to him. But I'm not going to *skulk* around hiding this, this, this—" (she almost said "trick") "—this *person* from him. If we put him on full-time, he can work during the days, and have his nights off working for me! After all, Belle, I've been such a good wife these past two years—acting the part. Well—*you* know."

"Oh, I know, I know." Sip. Sip.

"Of course, he'd never *expect* it of me. But, after all, Belle, dear, I *do* have my needs, too!"

"And so do we all, 'Nez darling."

And so do we all. Encased within the plush confines of Belle Harrison's huge Daimler, as twilight lowered its great train of blue and saffron across the North Shore, Mrs. Mack Daly, who never thought to look out the car's window, sped onward to her home, to be dropped there by her kind and ridiculously wealthy pal.

However, had she looked out from her window, she would've seen, right along that very road, her husband's purple Marmon of which she was so very fond, sheltered by budded trees. She also might've wondered—what in hell was her husband's car doing there, by the roadside?

But it was a blessing, at least in this instance, that Ynez was not at all observant.

Mack, however was always observant. Hiding behind that very vehicle, lifting himself up, divested of every stitch of clothing, he murmured to Joe—now, also, perfectly and gloriously nude—"There goes Belle Harrison and Ynez! Can you beat that?" He quickly tabulated in his mind how long it would take her to make it home and then begin getting ready for that night's blow-out.

But everything was just jake. There was time enough. With Alexander and Ynez fussing over her gown, jewels, coiffure and manquillage, why, they had time to spare. And so he lowered himself back down upon the golden body of the Italian god, who, greeting him with a smile and open arms, was ready to "go at it" yet again.

Mack had moved the car farther still off the road, tossed the lap rug down behind it. A mad, fevered abandon swept over them, there, in the late afternoon light. Tumbling around the now much-soiled lap rug, finally rolling off into the field, they lost all and every inhibition they might've had.

Mack had never known anything in his whole life to be this good, amazed at how Joe was his perfect equal and seemingly unstoppable. Now and then tender, at other times like a wrestler; but never letting go, or letting up. It was incredible how nothing mattered to Joe. No limitations at all.

"You like it goddammed good an' rough don't yuh, Mack?" Joe snarled lovingly.

Gone was the "Mister Daly"; gone too was even the thought of Joey as a gangster or a messenger of threats or danger. Now it was just Mack and Joe, as it would be for that twilight, and all twilights to come.

Stopping breathlessly, briefly, they would look at one another and both be captured by this terrible love; both being aware of it, wanting to shout, laugh, cry together.

They could not let go of each other; sweat made them glossy from the heat of their electrifying love as each was re-ignited to ravenously devour the other. Sometimes Joe would roll on top of Mack, and, lifting up on his haunches, stare down at him, tracing fiercely, with his big hands, those fine proportions of his instantaneous lover's slim and perfect form, pouncing on him, then engulfing him with this dark, rough kind of sex that Mack had only dreamed of for years—ashamed, starved for it and, at last, dying for it now.

Mack would then overpower Joe, who plummeted him against his body, harder, harder, never letting him go. Joe had always wanted a man like Mack—a tall, masterful, civilized, hood ornament of a man, with honest eyes and a swagger to his very spirit; heroic and strong like a champion swimmer; kind to him, most of all. Kind and yet fully understanding of this sex he craved so desperately.

This young gangster might've requested in his simple nightly prayers a man who would never let him go—dominating him, enslaving his heart so that he would never venture out again into the awful streets alone and terrified, to be beaten unconscious, day after day, night after night. Bleeding away, crying silently on the way home. Telling no one. A dozen black eyes, scores of knife fights—leaving more than a few scars which spread over his muscles, as embers of a living Hell.

Mack looked beyond the expression in Joe's eyes, and seeing past the animal, child-like desire to please, sensed, as if by some mystical divination, that his very soul was scarred as well. Those scars which stayed—there, at his left cheek, or the faint skimming of a bullet hole by his right shoulder, the knife wound on his left thigh, were kissed by Mack—each one.

The invisible ones which had cut deep into his heart were seen reflected back into Mack's own eyes, when, stopping in their love-making, both having become breathless, they looked in wonder at each other. Fate would cast them now as one. And whatever that meant to either of them, there was in their every touch a pact. No turning back.

Joe could not imagine what Mack had been through. Joe was 28. Mack was 33; old enough, then, to have fought in the War and to have come Home so changed…so numbed. He had gone into the trenches thinking that he did, after all, love men, and only men—needing them fully. He had returned weeping for them; knowing what he was and what they—who were like him—also were. And that another kind of love existed which enfolded, in the most secret of places, terrible strength and terrible gentleness all at once.

Joe knew this about Mack, and yet had no idea how he knew it. He loved Mack Daly at once. All of him and instantaneously. He also knew and felt—all at once—everything that Mack Daly required…to go on living at all…to be made whole. And he knew he had been chosen to heal him, because Joe thought only with his heart. He was brave and fearless because of this. Here was his beloved. He had met him. Finally.

It was true—all that Mack had said. Joe had been sent to shake him down by the Imperio mob. Bruno, Joe's older brother, had just heard a few unsavory rumors about this most discreet of New Yorkers. Bruno also knew that Joseph, his very own brother, was not normal. He decided to put them both together, to see what would happen.

It was Bruno Imperio who was, then, their match-maker. An intelligent, ruthless and well-educated man whose handling of the family's rackets had, since the advent of Prohibition, turned them into a regular post-War capitalistic enterprise. Joe's brother Bruno was no dago—he was a crooked businessman. Having heard from his new assistant, a bloodless mob girl named Blanche King, that Mack Daly possessed interesting proclivities, he, himself had come up with scant information hardly useful at all in influencing Daly toward a merger with the Imperio family. Even so, thought Bruno Imperio, if the Jew could be made to merge, the results would be just incredible. From what Bruno did gather, Mack and his kid brother Joe might just get along. Get the Yiddle where it would hurt most, that was it. Then take him down. Just a hunch, but worth a try.

• • •

Joe was driving now.

"Say, if dis ain't a t'rill, I wish someone would tell me what is! I'll tell duh woyld!"

"Yes, but you oughta slow down a little, Joe—there's a sharp turn coming—here it is!"

Shrieking around the bend, the great machine proceeded up a narrow road all but enveloped by tall elm trees. "Now take it easy from here on in or we'll both end up in the greenhouse."

Just ahead, the lamps from the Marmon revealed a sprawling Spanish villa with a circular drive before it, in the middle of which was a marble naked lady sprouting water. An alabaster glow from tall windows shed mysterious shadows on kempt lawns.

Maneuvering the purple beast to the front portico, Joe looked before him, giving off a low whistle.

"Quite a pile, huh, Joe? Used to belong to the Broadway producer King Tuthill," Mack commented, never ceasing to be awed by his own home.

Quietly, they went toward the front door.

"It's duh nuts," Joe whispered back, now imitating him on tip-toe as they entered. "Jeez. I feel like I'm at a funeral parlor."

That made Mack laugh. "Elliot calls it 'The Villa Hotsy Totsy.' Wait'll you see the inside!"

He then stopped, explaining to Joe that his wife's whereabouts had to first be determined before they went much farther. Introducing them was going to be a delicate matter.

There, in the foyer, as Joe gaped upward at the stairway curving to a long balcony over which was tossed a droopy Spanish shawl, tango music was heard drifting from some nether region. To the left, where the great drawing room yawned out from giant potted palms flanking an archway, a few lamps, with their fringes pulsating in the breeze, had been lit.

"JEEZ," Joe exclaimed again, loud this time.

"Sshhh—let's see. Well, she's had her first cocktail. That's a good sign." Mack, entering the room itself, spied one glass and a shaker on the sofa table. He was about to say something else when, from above:

"Alexander! Draw my bath like a good baby, will you, toots?" came over the music, special emphasis being placed on the pronunciation of the word "bath" like "BOHTH."

"Sure will, Miss Ynez!" was the echoing answer from a distant set of lilting, masculine pipes.

Mack grabbed Joe and hauled him into the darkened confines of the drawing room. Then both peered around the arch, looking up to see Mack's most trusted (and only) full-time servant trotting from one wing of the house toward the other.

"Pssssst! Alexander! Come down here quick!" Mack called up.

A lanky young black man, with an expression so sweet he appeared to be illuminated from within, glided down and toward Mack, who stepped from the shadows, waving Joey to stay well behind.

"Mr. D.! What happened to you!" he asked Mack, looking him up and down. "Were you in some kinda fight or somethin'?"

"Listen, Alexander, I've…I've brought a big surprise home, and we've just had an awful lot of fun, that's all. Is the wife in any kind of mood?"

Alexander looked behind Mack to see Joe. Insistent and alarmed, his voice rose several octaves. "Where you both been all rumpled up like that! What happened to you? Who's he?"

"He's my new friend, Joseph Imperio. I've just decided to hire him as our—oh—our…bodyguard."

Alexander stood, taking it all in for a moment, his long, curly lashes batting away. "MMMMMMMMM—huhhhh! *Body*guard is right," he beamed. "This does seem to be the day for new employees."

"Oh? Did she get us a new chauffeur?"

"Seems as if she did. MMMmm-huhhh! She's not talked 'bout nothin' else since she got back. Miss Harrison dropped her off just an hour ago, and they was both goin' on about—oh, all kinds of stuff!" Then he stopped, giving Joe a once-over from head to toe. "Looks as if both of you needs a good pressin' and hosin' down. Whatchu both been up to—as if I even need to ask!"

"Listen, Alexander, take Joe upstairs to my bedroom and let him get a nice bath. Then get out a monkey suit for him. He'll be getting ready for tonight along with all of us, and while he does, I'll explain all of this to Ynez. Please?"

Aleaxnder, laughing and overjoyed, replied, "When you gonna explain it all to me? I'll just bet it's good and hot, hey, boss? Follow me, handsome!" He motioned to Joe, leading him up the stairs.

Mack, winking at Joe, whispered, "O.k. with you, pal?"

"O.k.? You kiddin'! Say, you got bubble bat'?" Joe replied ascending, dazzled by all he saw.

Alexander let go peals of laughter. "We got three or four varieties—you can pick out a combination if you want!"

As they vanished out of sight, Mack heard Joe asking him if he shot craps and, again, Alexander's reply was absolute hysteria. Mack heaved a sigh of relief, shaking his head, then retrieved his mail on the round table before him. How on earth would he tell Ynez that things were going to be different all of a sudden? And would remain so from now on? And what would she say?

Mack always had to prepare himself for the worst whenever reality entered into Ynez's life. Absently glancing over that day's post, he began rehearsing how he would broach this subject.

Meanwhile, Ynez was in her sunken salmon-colored tub where, behind a haze of exotic aromas, she was stroking her ivory body with her long, expressive fingers ending in varnished blood-red nails in her favorite shade called "Was My Face Red?" Raising her eyes slowly upward, her lips pursed, her head and marvelous long, blue-black hair (dyed, but never bobbed) imprisoned in a white turban, she rehearsed what she would say to her husband. It would be a blunt and to-the-point notification: she had found herself a "chauffeur." Mack would know *exactement* what that meant!

Mrs. Mack Daly's face took on an expression like those she had seen thrown upon the silver screen—a mixture of exultation and pity. Pity for him, pity for her. Pity theirs was such a rotten marriage. Pity he had never once responded to her sexually, as any husband should even though that was not their agreement—ever. Pity she loved him so; sacrificing everything, everything, everything, for him and that he had made her whole life such a tortuous mess. Pity she was so beautiful, supple, born to be immolated by his manhood. Pity, too, that he was so divinely handsome and successful and rich—getting richer it seemed by the day! Pity most of all that he liked *men* and not women. But! that was their agreement. Pity.

Well, that was all behind her now. He was downstairs and soon enough he would be asking her about the day she had. Well, she would tell him all right.

Just below, Mack also felt a wave of emotion for her. Poor Ynez. He did really feel sorry for her. She hadn't realized all she was getting into—that was all.

Just a little over two years ago, right after *La Maison* got closed down and she lost her gig there, she really had no place to go. She'd said oh-so-blithely, "What the Hell," after he'd so carefully and almost clinically explained what kind of man he was and what he liked (men) and what her role would be as they both got closer and closer to the kind of life which she'd always dreamed of. Ynez thought her aching heart might become an ongoing, chronic pain—forgotten after a while. Just something one had to live with. Like a boil on your ass or something.

Well, it wasn't like that at all. And the pain just got worse; it didn't go away. Mack sighed, flipping through his mail quickly. So many invitations for things—so many bills. Ynez tore through Paris fashions like a deadly hurricane. And there was another letter from the Colonel! His old C.O. had been having a tough time since the War. Mack carefully opened the envelope.

This time, more vague, disturbing, disconnected thoughts. Calvin Connaught would not, after all, be attending the opening of the club, just as Mack had figured. But he was so looking forward to the birthday reunion of all his men this year. So sure it would make him feel better about the current mess he was in.

Whatever that meant. So damned meloncholy once again. Mack didn't bother to read on.

He went at once into the library, placing it in the ivory box the Colonel had given them as a wedding gift, with all the rest of the great man's missives. Mack could never bring himself to throw away a single letter from Colonel Connaught since first they began corresponding, just after the Armistice—filled as they were with aimless yearnings.

Going back out into the foyer, he looked up to the second floor. Slowly, slowly mounting the heavily carpeted steps, he prayed that everything would pan out now that he'd met this marvelous guy, as this sudden new chapter of his life unfolded.Was it going to entirely drive poor Ynez crazy?

He'd only wanted a wife who was nothing more than a dress shoppe dummy, after all. She came up with that one. Why, oh, why couldn't it be just a little bit more than THAT? Oh, she never, ever let up!

But Mack couldn't bear even being touched by her, making an effort to circle around her—to not even brush her skirts, or pat her on the shoulder in passing—for fear of their bodies meeting.

There, on the way up the stairs, he recalled her pleading, "But can't you just consider such a thing even for a moment, my darling?" always walking about quite nude, which did nothing at all for him.

"No, Ynez," he would patiently explain, "and I'm so sorry I can't—for your sake. I just never have and never wanted to. And I don't. And never shall."

Mack was always filled with self-recrimination after these encounters. He hadn't been cross with her—ever. Always patient, that was Mackie. Yet, almost throughout their whole first year together, Ynez had kept up her advances...until, well, she guessed, it just further alienated him! Then she had grown so cold toward him.

Well, he sighed, now at the landing, and why not?

Lately, he had felt Ynez staring right through him—Mack himself had gotten so surly...gone at night sometimes, coming home—very blue. Talking about the War again. She knew he was out trying to find a lover boy—and never could. She hoped he never would, for it made her seethe with almost ghoulish joy at the thought that he soon might join her in this misery which was their life together.

"Poor Mackie," was her litany, slightly touching his wavy hair as she stood over him, slumped there, at the edge of his bed. The scene repeated itself over and over. Coming back to that modernistic mausoleum, looking so forlorn and desolate, but never ever sharing with her what kind of living Hell it was for him—this gorgeous man—to be a swish! What a waste, she would say, shaking her head at him. What a terrible waste of manhood.

He insisted on never wanting to know where she went or what she did. He'd urged her to live her own life. She knew what he meant, too. But in all those two long years, she'd never slipped from her pedestal! He always haunted her and, as Mack so well knew, this spectre scorched the arrangment which was their marriage, causing a ring of fire to surround her, isolating her from normal men.

"High and mighty Mackie!" she would chide Mack, gently pushing her from his bed. "It kills me to see you so frustrated...so—*unfufilled!*"

Noticing that the white roses in the vase at the second floor landing were as fresh as when he left that morning, Mack withdrew one perfect blossom, thinking he might offer it to her because he now had a lover. And she had no one. But then...he thought again, and put it back with the rest.

• • •

Ynez's bathroom, like the entire rest of the house, there on the outskirts of Great Neck, had been totally re-done to suit her whims with the aid of the decorator Bootsie Carstairs—teeth-gnashing and swallowing headache powders by the gallon throughout. Somewhere half-way through his efforts, Mrs. Daly had seen a Nita Naldi movie in which a Chinese bathroom appeared. Thus inspired, Ynez's private powder room became Nita Naldi's, to the constant despair of Bootsie who threw fits over it, then simply gave in.

Dawned the day when every single room in the so-called "Villa Hotsy Totsy" was straight out of Cecil B. deMille. Mack just shook his head at Carstairs, then both shrugged.

Entering this chamber, he came upon Ynez, eyes closed, head thrown back, submerged in her sunken tub. Feeling as if he had entered some sort of strange shrine dedicated to Sin and self-enchantment, he approached his spouse gingerly, sitting quietly on the seat of the toilet (which was disguised as a throne chair).

He whispered carefully, "Hey, Ynez? Are you with us?" (He snapped his fingers.)

To which, immobile still, she replied, "Am I? *I'll say* I am, baby!" Her eyes began to open, slowly, like two trap-doors through which green orbs gazed out at her husband. He instantly saw within them a somehow changed woman.

"Today, Mackie, I went and got that chauffeur we'd talked about."

"Well good. I'm so glad. With Paul's wife having her baby so soon."

"Paul schmaul, Mackie! I not only got a chauffeur to do our driving, but I got someone who can also do *me* as well! They let me keep a picture of him. Look—right there, near Buddha." She gestured with a limpid hand.

"Well, I hope," Mack said, looking at the photograph, "he wears a bit more than this when you're driving around!" He propped it up against a powder box. "What's he do—moonlight as an artists' model?"

"Heheh. Wouldn't you like to know?" Then, not giving Mack a chance to reply, "Well, *I* found him, and he's all *mine*, and that's all there is to it, Mackie-whacky!"

Mack started to laugh.

"Do you think it's *fun*ny?" she lifted herself from the tub, dripping, staring wildly at him now. "Do you think it's *fun*ny that I have to go and hire a gigolo masquerading as our chauf*feur* in order to satisfy my mildewed *libido*?"

"No, no, no. Not at all, Ynez. I applaud the move, in fact. This really might set things right from here on in." His smile widened from ear to ear.

She stared at him for what seemed a long time, slowly—at the same time—reaching for a big, fluffy Chinese green towel embroidered with a parrot sitting on the initial "D." During this awful silence, from just past the next room (off Mack's own bedroom), the sound of another bathtub conversation could be faintly heard.

Alexander was saying to someone, whilst water was running, "You shure got a nice shape for a white man!"

The answer came, "Used to be a boxer. Hey, will yuh put more ah dat bubbley bath in, please?"

Alexander: "Shure thing! Oops! We's all out! Hol' on, big boy, while I go and steal some from Miss Ynez!"

Big splash and a deep voice singing at the top of its lungs:

"*Crazy woyds, Crazy toon, He'll be drivin' me crazy soon, Vo do dee oh vo do do dee oh do…*"

"Who's that in there?" hissed Ynez, fiercely wrapping the towel around her and nearly going ass-over-teacups as she climbed from her tub.

"Well, Ynez, today you hired a chauffeur and I hired a bodyguard."

Alexander threw open her bathroom door. "Jus' me!—Say, Mr. D., who-ever he is, you shure found yourself a he-man. From head to toe, that honkie is one speciman! Uh-huh! I'll say!"

"Don't you *knock* before you come into a lady's *salle de bain*?" Ynez snapped.

Looking about for someone who might be lady, Alexander rapped on a teakwood table, holding a roll of toilet paper disguised within a ginger jar. "I'm in! Evenin' folks!" and reached for her bath salts.

"*Who's over there and in this house!*"

Mack cleared his throat. "I just told you. My new bodyguard."

Alexander must've thought the answer sufficent, for he started to leave.

"I don't want my things taken from me and used *over there*—" she yanked out a thumb.

"Oh, come on, Ynez," said Mack, crossing his legs and lighting up a cigarette. "It won't hurt to share with him. He's full-time. And, listen, the guy's a peach."

Alexander cast Mack a look which verified that. Now, Joe was splashing wildly, singing at the top of his lungs.

"*Share with him?* Share what—or *whom*, shall I say? I'm going in there right now and meet this fellow. Give me my salts!" She grabbed the bottle from Alexander's hands, and slammed them down beside the t.p.

Out she bustled, with Mack and Alexander on her heels…the door to Mack's bathroom was wide open and Joe, packed into the tub, all soaped up—a wad of it in his eyes something terrible.

"Oh, *shit*! Oh, Cripes! Oh, God!" He stood up and blindly motioned for a towel. Mack handed him one and Joe's left eye looked out over it: "Oh Jeez—a *woman*."

"This is Mrs. Daly. Ynez, meet Joseph Imperio, my new best friend."

Ynez had not turned crimson, the way most women might under such circumstances. Naked people (herself included) were nothing new to her.

Alexander did note a little quiver of her turbaned head, however, and that was all. At length, her nostrils flaring, she demanded, "What's *that* supposed to mean?"

"Well," answered Mack. "Just what I said. You know. Use your imagination! We just met this afternoon and we're certainly getting along simply swell." (Joe lowered himself back into the masses of bubbles, sensing a scene.)

"*Well*…I see!" was all she said in reply. Then, turning regally, she began to make her exit.

"Hey, what about the bubbley bat', Mrs. Daly?" Joe called after her, smiling politely, but still completely in the dark.

They then heard the toilet flushing.

"*There's* your goddammed bubbly bath! Right down the crapper—where it belongs!" she screamed from across the hall. It was clear that Joe felt awful.

"Oh, let her go, Joe. I'll buy you a whole ocean of bubbley bath, don't you worry," Mack assured him.

"Should I go an' aplogize?"

Both Mack and Alexander put up their hands and shook their heads simultaneously.

From across the hall: "ALEXANDER! Get in here and wash my goddammed back!" Ynez commanded, in a voice filled with rage and, as if shot from a cannon, he fled.

Joe let go a sudden laugh, imitating her. "Mack! Get in here and wash my goddammed back!"

Mack, closing his bathroom door once more, tore off his three-piece suit, dropped his suspenders, trousers, shirt, tie, and eventually whatever else remained, then climbed in the tub with Joe.

"Dat wasn't *really* your wife, was it?" Joe asked, blowing bubbles at Mack.

"Sure it was. Who'd you think it was?"

Joe shrugged. "I couldn't tell…some relation or other, I guess. You got the same color hair."

"No. Ynez has black hair, Joe—it's dyed. But how could you tell—she had it all wrapped up in a turban…?"

"Oh, I get it. On her bush it's blonde, but on her head it's black. She wasn't too careful wid dat towel, yuh know."

• • • • •

CHAPTER III

BIG NIGHT

Almost as soon as Ynez and Annabelle Harrison had beat their retreat from that peculiar office—that denizen of lounge lizards and dope fiends—the creature called Ramon di Rose realized something.

"Dat dame musta pinched one of my peectures! How do you like dat?"

"I knew she wasn't born to the purple like the other one," said his partner in crime, now doffing the wig, the *pince-nez*, the phony accent and wiping off the *poudre de riz* with a soiled shirt-tail. "Let's split up the dough so I can go and get calmed down."

Digging into his pocket, the oily gigolo gave this person, who now proved to be a cadaverous young man and not a woman at all (yet, still a hop-head), half of his retainer. "Joo know, Trevor, eet takes a purty chipp article to pool the wool over MY eyes!"

The human spectacle, speedily stripping and jumping into waiting suit and tie, was almost out the door when he affirmed the observation, "—see what you can find out about her and maybe we can peddle it to You Know Who and get in good with him!"

He was gone.

Left alone to ponder how such a chic lady could pull off such a sleight of hand, Ramon di Rose, as he was then known, read again the address and time of his appointment. There just could be something about this Ynez Daly which might be worth looking into…once he had the goods on her. It just might be his big break.

• • •

The launching of the Club deVol that evening was the maiden voyage of a pleasure barge of dreams, set sail for paradise. A definite mystery had surrounded it for months now; word had gotten round that it was Broadway's latest Alladin's cave—the best band anywhere, and the best booze; the best food, the best floor show with the hottest mamas wearing the least amount of clothing anywhere on the Main Stem. What would be awaiting the throng once inside?

From champagne to gin to scotch to whiskey, the libations were said to be emerging from a pipe line whose origins were in Olympus. The decor, by the new rage of the Hotcha Set, the extravagant and wildly eccentric Bootsie Carstairs, would shock and amuse everyone. The crowd which would gravitate to the place, rumoured (by those on the outside) to be as modern as a minute—probably a little decadent, all of them troubled by sex complexes, rich, spoiled, carefree, jaded, and almost too beautiful—would most certainly set the tone for what to wear, what slang to use, and how to really live! live! live!

Outside the single door on West 46th Street clustered the Cream of the Crop. Looking down from Fifth Avenue, one might've taken the crowd for a first-night Follies audience. Gentlemen in white tie, tails and opera cloaks; ladies in glittering wraps trimmed in Spring furs, loaded down with jewels and massive corsages; limousines dropping off baby-faced show-girls clinging to rotund Wall Street Papas; shamelessly painted dowagers, bewigged and befuddled as young catamites held up their velvet trains, heaving them from the perfumed confines of their ink-black autos into the alabaster glow of the streets.

A crowd of college kids—boys in pork-pie hats, racoon coats, girls in far-too-short skirts and cloche hats, all but hiding their lovely mascara'd eyes—waited a little off to the side, hoping to get in. The girls wanted to see Elliot Armstrong in person and hear him croon; the boys yearned for Nolie Armstrong, having her pictures plastered all over their dorm rooms. Elliot Armstrong's Army of Charm was fast becoming the only music America's Flaming Youth could endure. Everywhere they went, this music followed.

Elliot and Nolie were the new-found saints of the Fast Set. Ironically, though some bluenoses disapproved, they were adored by everybody—young and old alike. Radio had helped. This pair were the personifaction of the positive, fresh way of thinking which truly inspired everybody who listened to them and saw how wholesome and happy they were!

Whether it was planned or not, Elliot himself marched right outside, past the priviliged, and straight over to his most ardent fans. His appearance caused an immediate stir. Togged out in his white tuxedo, all smiles and waves, he was mobbed by them.

"Now if you kids promise to be good widdle girls and boys and not dwink anything excepting Orange Crush, we'll let you in after these swells are all seated!"

Oh, he had won their hearts.

"I've got free passes to our next radio broadcast right in my hot little hand. Here. Let's see—how many of you are there?"

At the door, big burnished Keys Parker, Miss Annabelle Harrison's personal "model," outfitted in a sweeping white Russian uniform—making him look like an ebony soldier in the Czar's White Army—made certain each invitation was lifted up to the iron grilled peep-hole before he so grandly swung open the door.

It all seemed so perfect, so easy, so elegant…so almost legal. But, across the street in the cover flat, Mack's Hired Owl watched nervously for the dry agents. If so much as even the glimmer of a red light atop a cop car was seen, his nervous damp hands would spring for the telephone, while his toe pressed the floor buzzer. Mack had told him: it had to be like clock-work. Tonight was Deucie and Baby's night.

Once inside, those lucky dogs who RSVP'd in the affirmative were treated to what surely must've been one of the finest and most hi-toned evenings Little Old New York was ever to have seen.

"My Gawd, Ethel," some wealthy Midwestern zillionaire drawled, "ain't this something to tell 'em back home."

"I'll say it is! But how could you ever descibe it, Paw?"

Calculated to elicit breathless oohs and ahhs upon entering, Bootsie had hung the walls with backdrops from snappy Broadway shows which Mack himself had purchased once they'd flopped. These depicted maps of mid-town Manhattan done in cubistic fashion, street scenes of New York from the Bowery to Grant's Tomb, a symbolic tableau of America, Making the World Safe for Democracy and an allegorical one of Wall Street with ticker tape machines dancing in a chorus line.

Importantly, the tables, chairs, sconces, cocktail lamps, and even all the stemware and china were designed by Bootsie Carstairs himself, producing a syncopated look throughout. So exhausted was the poor thing on that night that he collapsed in a heap while putting on his corset and had to send regrets. Everyone thought it was such an uncharacteristic thing to do—especically in light of the fact that he had been taking monkey gland serum to restore his youth and vigor!

The bar, which was entirely made of mirror and glass, ran like a sleek locomotive along the left side of the room. Patent leather tablecloths shimmered on the tables, reflecting the silver and orange color scheme of the club. In the center, the dance floor, painted to look like the streets running East and West from Times Square, made the guests stop and point with their toes to their favorite restaurants or shows then running.

But, best of all was the moving platform upon which Elliot Armstrong's band played. Deucie's genius for invention was behind it all; the stage supported a dais which rolled forward, right out into the dance floor. Holding the whole band, and even Mae, the 250-pound pianist, and her white piano jazzing like mad, the Army of Charm emerged from a complete black-out like a platinum dirigible floating into everyone's hearts.

The lights dimmed. Preceded only by the screech of the clarinet, followed by the roar of the whole ochestra, the club was transformed by this invasion of sound and swank. The platform, on huge rollers, glided out and into the center of the club. A standing ovation met the band.

Nolie Armstrong, wearing little tom-toms on each hip and not much else, sprang out from a smoking cauldron. Compared to cotton candy with a whiskey chaser, her beauty was that of a cloud-perched cherub. There were wild cheers, whoops of joy. The chorus line advanced into the room, tom-toms on their hips, holding drumsticks in their hands, inviting the guests to pound out the madly jazzy rhythms with the nite club hammers placed at every table. The Club deVol was pulsating, everybody gathered there in unison and hilarious, ecstatic joy.

Elliot sang to her and then, the moment the college kids so wanted to see—Nolie burst into her fantastic black bottom. Off came the tom-tom's and the little skirt that held them. Now, in lace panties sewn with pink and green brilliantes, she climbed up on the premier table right before the band itself and thereupon, set the town on fire.

Seated at that very table was a young Walter Winchell, who wondered how he could keep his ten fingers from typing away a paean to that moment of moments on his typewriter. Tom-tom, peck peck.

How did all of this suddenly come about? What was behind it all…this painting of the town in shades so very pink? This wasn't just any old speakeasy. A private affair—with money and class and a helluva lot of chutzpah behind it—that was what was really going on here, wasn't it? Most of those gathered were still standing, or dancing helplessly, madly around their tables. Jesus, young Mr. Winchell thought, looking around him, *it's just like a great big firecracker went off on the Main Stem!*

Every Broadway Brite-Lite and more than a few of The 400 were therein gathered, all in the throes of losing their iron-clad inhibitions, all unanimous in this caterwauling which hailed the club, and who in Hell ever thought it all up, as Hot and Heavenly.

*Somebody's worked magic here tonight, and I've got to know who it is…*he was thinking. *Somebody with very big balls, too.*

Nothing had been left to chance. It was all so deliberate. So—well, so exquisite—for want of a better word. He would remember that word and use it, too. Now, Winchell noted, when the crowd imbibed their libations, a kind of collective passing glance drifted over everybody in the place.

"Smooth and neat stuff!"

"—Ex*cep*tional booze!"

"From whence comes this chalice?"

"Oh, boy! Haven't had hooch like this since before the War!"

But back in Great Neck, things were not so perfect. Mack did not like being late, and he certainly was going to be if Ynez didn't stop making things difficult. Having sent Alexander ahead in the limousine in order to stock the bar, it was left to Ynez, Joe and Mack to climb into the Marmon, which was a coupe.

In addition to Ynez's ensemble getting impossibly wrinkled, both she and Joe wanted to sit next to Mack. Finally, Joe thought it would be a good idea if he just stayed behind in Great Neck, but that hadn't really made sense. So Ynez simply snuggled on Joe's lap, making him very nervous throughout the trip.

"Hope you don't mind if we share your gorilla here, Mackie. This is the closest I've been to a *real* man in two long years!" With her arm around Joe, she proceeded to laugh. "Say, big boy, you aren't really going to tell me you're an authentic 100 percent pansy, are you now?"

"Oh, jeez—" Joe kept repeating over and over, his face crimson.

"I'd ask you for a loan-out Mack, but as I was trying to tell you earlier, I went and did the unthinkable this afternoon," caressing Joe's cheek with her hands.

"Let's just hurry up and get there, Ynez. We'll have to park a little way down the street, because I will not alight in front of the club like this!"

"Are you gonna make him walk three steps behind us?" she asked coyly.

However, they arrived three abreast, each gleaming with elegance. Mack introduced Joe to Keys as his bodyguard. And if Keys Parker raised an eyebrow, it wasn't seen because of his big Russian hat.

Inside: "Well there you are!" Baby threw her arms around Mack, planting a tattoo of carmine lip rouge on his cheek, then cordially nodding to Ynez.

"You do look stunning, 'Nezzie," she granted. "And this must be the fella who volunteered his help today!" Mack introduced him. "Well, listen, honey, any friend of Mackie's is a friend of mine!" (Eyeballing Ynez.)

As they were escorted to their table—the farthest one at the back of the club which Baby called the Royal Box, she made all kinds of faces at Mack, conveying to him that the dago was just the darlingest thing on two legs.

"Why do we have to hide out way back *here*?" Ynez whined. Mack told her once more that his presence had to be virtually unknown.

"Anyway," he said, "I'm sure you'll table-hop all night."

She whispered back to him, "You just wanna get *rid* of me so you can play footsies with that big ape!"

Off went Ynez at once, aswirl in nude lace and a vast ostrich feather fan. But Mack, A little nervous, a little pale, declining to dance, sat drumming the table with his Cartier pinky ring, smoking a cigarette now and then, sipping his Orange Crush, and rubbing Joe's leg under the table.

"If this ain't duh nuts, I don't know what is," Joe commented, glowing, edging his chair closer to Mack. "Is dis racket all yers?"

"Sure is, Joe. But the question is—are you all mine, sweetie-pie? I mean, you're not the type to be attracted to my wife, are you?"

"Say! I don't go for no tomatohs." (Mack breathed a sigh of relief.) "Not dat I haven't tried it. Besides, I don't like duh way she treats yuh, if yuh don't mind my sayin' so."

"Well, you just have to have patience with her, Joe. She's really not a bad egg. People tend to be mean to her—but I know you'd never be."

Mrs. Daly now approached the table far off to to their right, where Annabelle Harrison, handsome in her severe Callot, headed a contingent of Old Guardsters. Like everyone there gathered, they seemed to be whooping it up in spite of themselves.

"Halloo! Halloo there Belle!" Ynez waved, levitating toward them all. Belle stood up, cooing; "Oh I'm so happy for you both, Ynez! And for the deVols, too! This really has everyone floating on air! It's such a triumph! Who's that with Mack?" Ynez told her. "Bodyguard? We're not in any danger here, are we?"

Ynez whispered in her ear over the band. "No, not here...but my home! It IS in danger—about to be wrecked, it appears. Annabelle, that's Mack's new buzz-saw."

A pause. "Well at least you seem to be about to lead parallell lives, muffin!" she replied with a giggle. It was so awkward. People were staring. As galvanizingly beautiful as Ynez was, she looked all out of sorts this evening.

"Oh! Oh, here's that lovely new waltz!" Annabelle trilled. "Come on, everyone, let's all dance!" Then, calling out, "Mack! Mack Daly! Get up and dance with your wife this very minute!"

Ynez stood before all that Old Money, smiling tragically as Mack, caught up in howling laughter with Joe, was not even noticing Miss Harrison's plea. She actually had to go back over to their table and tug at his sleeve.

"Mack, let's *dance,* for Gawd sakes," Ynez snapped. "Do it for Deucie and Baby, will you! They want to know you're having a good time!" (All he'd done so far was laugh at that guinea goofball's awful cornball jokes!)

"Hey, can I dance, too?" Joe asked Mack, looking up at him with that same half-witted grin.

What, Ynez was made to wonder, were they doing to each other beneath that damned tablecloth? It was clear that they were certainly doing *some*thing!

Mack laughed and nodded in the direction of Annabelle who apparently needed to be asked. "Say, Belle, meet my amanuensis—Joseph Imperio!" he called out as he and Ynez danced past.

Standing, Joe approached her with simply, "Wanna dance, babes?" Caught all unawares, Annabelle nodded and off they twirled.

Whenever Mack and Ynez did anything in public, they cleared the way. People were awed by their grace, their beauty. What a perfect, perfect couple they made. On the dance floor, delivering a sublime Hesitation Waltz, they soon had the whole club as their audience. Deucie threw a pink spot on them, and a reverant air of romance spread over the place. Some Broadway-ites knew them slightly and proudly said so, too. Some people who were dancing even stopped to admire them. Ynez, her flesh-colored lace almost transparent, moved like a lovely vision, clinging to her husband, who might've been carved in bronze.

"They're truly gorgeous, aren't they!"

"I'll say! She's right outta the rotogravure! What's he do?"

"Dunno—stands around and looks good, I guess."

"Naw, he's a gov'ment official. A big wig in city polly-ticks, yuh know."

Ynez was in her glory: all eyes were on them.

She murmured upward toward his majestic chin, her head resting on his starched shirt-front, "Somehow, Mackie, moments like these make all the heartache and the bullshit I've had to put up with almost bearable."

Mack groaned, dancing on perfectly, never missing a step, his eyes always on Joe, whom he noticed was not leading.

"Why, oh, why'd you have to bring that meatball along?" Ynez whispered.

"Listen. You know exactly why, Ynez. Don't play dumb with me! (Now she whimpered, hurt at his retort.) "Well, anyway, there's more to it than you think. He's part of some kind of Syndicate who want to ruin me—you know, shake me down, as they say."

"What?!" Incredulous. "Well, how can you sex it up with with him when he's after you like that!"

"Because I'm in love, Ynez. For the first time in my whole goddammed life." That shut her up.

Joe was now dancing right next to them, sawing away with Annabelle, shooting Mack a look that made him laugh right out loud, throwing his head back. Ynez, making believe this was the result of her saying something amusing, looked about at those guests whom her friend had invited, shrugging her shoulders with a "can't help it if I'm cute" look.

Annabelle was thinking that having Joe wrapped around her was almost like having Keys wrapped around her—both were so well-defined. Why, she could feel every single muscle right through his clothes and identify each one by name, too!

"Would you like to pose for me sometime perhaps?" she whispered in Joe's left, slightly cauliflowered ear.

He must've not known quite how to reply, for he was looking at her oddly, so she added, "I do statues! I'm a sculptress, you see!"

"A—what?" he almost shouted.

Poor man. Just a beautiful primordial type. Utterly himself! "I'd love for you to *model* for me!"

"Yeah? Bare naked?"

"Naturally!"

"Hot dog!"

The song ended amid applause. Annabelle, catching Ynez on the way back to their tables, motioned for them to go to the powder room. As soon as they were inside, Annabelle turned to her.

"Ynez! Is it really true?"

Ynez, putting on her lip rouge with a shakey pinky finger, unable to make her bows match, answered hoaresly, "Not only that—I was just informed of the fact that Mack's new trick is not only a pansy, but a *gangster* as well!"

Annabelle was so entirely shocked, she stood looking at her friend's reflection in the mirror, speechless.

Ynez went on, "—but it doesn't matter. Not really. By tommorrow night I'll be a fully sexed woman again!"

Absently, she picked up an atomizer of perfume, shooting clouds all around her. "Pretty soon I'll be surrounded by a spray of gun fire instead of this stuff!"

"But, darling, it's all rather *sad*, isn't it? You do love Mack so *very much*!" Annabelle said softly, touching Ynez upon her lovely, pale shoulders.

Fighting back tears, she looked up at her friend—angry, stripped of her artifice.

"Well, I won't change my life for any dago missing link, that's for sure. He's not gonna wreck *my* marriage, gangster or not."

She could not ever admit to anyone how deep her love for Mack was.

When they returned, Mack and Joe were nowhere to be seen. "And just how do you like *that*! A widow already!" Ynez pouted.

The two had threaded their way through the crush to see Elliot and Nolie Armstrong, in reply to a note sent to their table reading:

"GET BACK HERE NOW.

WHO IS THAT GLORIOUS PIECE OF MEAT!!!????"

The Armstrongs had only a few moments between their next set, but it was enough time to inaugurate a private party all their own. Mack poked his head around the half-opened door to their dressing room, with Joe bringing up the rear. He'd heard all about Elliot and Nolie Armstrong and was familiar with their hit tunes.

Emblazoned thereupon in a star, was the legend: MR. AND MISSUS U NO WHO. Opening the door was almost impossible. The tiny dressing room was packed like a sardine can with Negroes. Through a haze of blue smoke, ear-splitting, shrieking laughter, the tinkling of cracked ice in glasses, Joe, looking over Mack's shoulder, could only spot two white folks—Mr. and Mrs. Armstrong themselves. Perched on the make-up table, they were serving champagne and fried chicken to a sea of high-stepping imports from Harlem.

Nolie waved, shouting, "Oh, Mackus, you absolute sweetheart! Get in here and see where the real party is!"

Elliot, struggling through the crush toward him, beamed, "Where did you disappear to this afternoon, Mr. Mackus Dallyus!"

Then he saw Joey. "*Jesus H. Christ*! I noticed you from the stage, but you're even better-looking up close!"

"So aren't you," Joe observed shyly.

"Say! Thanks!" and with that, he slammed Joe's face between his palms and planted a big kiss on his lips.

"I should've prepared you for Elliot," Mack said in a fast aside, then made casual, rapid-fire introductions at the top of his lungs ("Nolie and Elliot, meet Joey Imperio! He's my new buddy!"), leaving Joe wondering further what strange arrangement Mr. and Mrs. Armstrong had, and why the room was filled exclusively with Black folk.

Nolie, putting forth a sincere effort to make Joe comfortable after they were introduced, led him into the room, poked him in the ribs, and shouted in his ear not to mind Elliot's ways. "It would take me too long to really explain what's wrong with him, but you'll come to accept his per-wersities. You've *got* to! He's Mackie's best friend!"

Even Joe, who had seen mostly everything, was not prepared for how Elliot Armstrong was acting...panting and barking like a dog at him, then pulling out wads of dough pantomiming a voracious desire to have him at any cost.

"Down, boy! Down, boy!" a perfectly lovely colored girl with her arm around Nolie scolded.

Mack shouted out gallantly, "Oh, yes, this is Jonquil Parker, known to all as Princess Johnnie, Joey." Bowing and kissing her hand, "Johnnie, meet my Suppressed Desire, Joe Imperio."

Princess Johnnie did a silly curtsey.

"Say, I don't see Alexander here," Mack added, looking about.

The princess answered with a slight lisp, "He got word from Deucie that the bar was runnin' low, and so he's gone down cellar—" and offered Joe a drink.

"I hope he finds my shorts!" Joe added, refusing it.

"Don't you drink, sugarpie?" she asked. Joe shook his head.

Elliot slipped his hands beneath Joe's jacket, giving him a thorough feel. "Fellas like this one here are physical culture nuts! They don't imbibe—do you Joey, huh, huh, huh? Ooooh, he's just made of iron, that's all."

"Elliot, you behave!" Princess Johnnie waved her finger at him, then back to Joey, "Where you from, sugarpie?" Joe told her. "Hmm. I thought you were Italian. You and I are gonna get along. Precisely! Just stick with me, honey. These upper East Side honkies all need to have their heads examined."

Joe had never seen a colored girl like this one. There was something unusual about her, made-up the way she was, sort of the queen of the whole little party, acting so familiar with Elliot Armstrong, with one arm around him, the other around Mack. She couldn't have been over 23 or so, but looked like she possessed a wisdom far beyond her years. Johnnie's laughing eyes, green and just then full of mischief, flirted Joe's way.

Mack seemed to be leaving her in charge. "Listen, your Highness, you entertain Joe here, while I go locate your errant brother."

Joe was looking more and more like a mongrel mutt who'd lost his master. "You ain't leavin' me, are yuz?!"

"Just for a minute, Joe—don't take it so hard! I'll be right back. Gotta check our inventory."

And as Mack was squeezing his way out the door, Joe overheard Elliot Armstrong whispering, "Mackus, I'm so jealous of you I could just scream! In fact, I think I will." He did, at the top of his lungs, and everybody cheered. It was all very confusing.

Left engulfed in this Black Sea of whoopee, awkwardly blushing before Mr. and Mrs. Armstrong, yet sheltered by this sleek version of 125th Street royalty, Joe felt pretty goofy.

Valiantly, in an effort to make some sort of conversation, he asked the Princess, "Is that guy, Alexander, that woyks for Mack, yer brudder?"

"Yep! Flesh and blood! And my other brother, Keys, is Mrs. Harrison's muse. The one at the door tonight. It's all very incestuous!"

"Cripes, you people sure use big woyds—"

"Well, all I mean is we're all somehow in this together. Here, have an Orange Crush—you'll soon get the drift of what goes on here—if you plan on stickin'." (Joe blushed crimson.) "I'm assumin' you and Mack are *simpatico, mais oui*?" (Joe shrugged, nodded, made a face.) "I hope you don't think I'm pryin', Joey. But Elliot said you both ran off together this afternoon and did funny things with each other. So's, we all put two and two together—"

Suddenly, Joey felt himself getting goosed. Looking down, he came face to face with Elliot Armstrong, who had taken a seat on the floor and was drinking champagne from a dancing slipper.

"Hey! Hey! That tickles!" Joe giggled, embarrassed.

"Yes! The bubbles just go right up my nose!" Elliot winked.

"No, I mean where you got your *hand,* buddy!"

"But you said you needed a proctologist!"

Joe was feeling abandoned by Mack. "I might wanna just step outside," he muttered. He just didn't get any of this.

Mrs. Armstrong, meanwhile, had climbed up on the lap of Princess Johnnie, demanding her slipper back. "Oh, please don't wander off, Mr. Imperio!" she fairly hollered over the throng.

"Say! Watch it dere!" yelled Joe.

Elliot, getting to his feet, had gone a trifle too far.

"Elliot, lay off him, will you!" Nolie shouted and Princess Johnnie, right behind her, "Give the guy some air, you big whore!"

As Joey quickly closed the dressing room door, gasping for fresh air, he noted to himself that, even though he couldn't spell C-A-T, he sure as Hell knew something pretty funny was up among all these people he was just meeting. Never before had he heard a moolie talk to a honkie in that manner.

As Mack was heading toward the cellar stairs, he was rightly thinking, "Maybe I shouldn't have left him in there. Maybe it's too much too soon. Still, he'd never figure it all out without my explaining to him. Who could?"

Oh, but what the Hell, he still had to find out everything Joe was really up to—being sent to shake him down! So, sooner or later they'd both get around to spilling it all. Mack had to check himself, then and there.

Was he afraid? Could this new fallen angel really cause all that much trouble? "When he finds out how complicated my whole life has gotten to be, he'll just forget about everything. Except me—I hope to God!"

Below, Alexander stood in a shallow puddle of booze, an inventory sheet and pencil in hand, counting emptied bottles all around him, each turned upside down in their dozen or more crates, the sides of which read in profusion LEVENTHAL BREADS AND CAKES.

"I'm bringin' 'em down myself and accountin' for every one, Mr. D.! So far, nobody's made off with a single bottle." Alexander then straightened up to his lanky, imposing height.

Always to the point, he paused to look squarely at Mack. "You ain't thinkin' of replacin' me with your new friend there, are you?"

"Why, Alexander, it never even occurred to me! Nobody could ever replace you! My friend—as you call him, is going to be part of our family…watching my back, as they say."

"You think you can trust him?" Alexander asked.

Mack drew a breath. He began, "Listen. I'm not really sure at this point. I only know this: I'm keeping him around." Then, lowering his eyes, "And the great thing is, Alexander, he does seem to want to stay around!"

Alexander let go a deep sigh, then smiled a little. "You always know best,

Mr. D.—but I sure hope you allow yourself *beaucoup* time to get to know him—and that's all I'm sayin' 'bout it."

Alexander would very nearly die for me, I believe—Mack was thinking, now looking up again, seeing him smiling his sad smile, his eyes so full of innocence and devotion and something else—a kind of instinct. *But, it didn't matter. Joe was perfect. Right time. Right place. He was Sent. And that was all there was to it.*

"Well, so far nobody's hipped one single bottle." Mack forced a laugh. "And as far as I can tell, everybody's enjoying themselves—so, *they're* sticking around, I guess, and doing all their drinking right here on the inside!"

Quickly, they both refilled the crates without speaking, Alexander humming along with the melody being played upstairs. Then a shadow crossed the light hanging from the staircase.

"Who's there?" Mack yelled at once.

"Just me…Joey! You guys need some musckle down dere?"

Mack, suddenly thrilled, "Hold on, Joe—um—guard the door up there, will you please? We're bringing more stuff up."

Mack arrived at the top of the stairs carrying three full cases of which Joe at once relieved him, beaming.

"Evenin', Alexander!" he greeted Mack's right-hand man, who was following right behind. "You need me tuh go down and get yuz more?" Joe walked along, following Mack toward the back entrance to the club.

Mack looked over the top crate at him. "Sure. Put those down right here. Have to be careful when the bar needs re-stocking. We'll let Alexander do it."

Following Mack back to the cellar steps, Joe admitted, "I guess I'm a little shy, bein' around all these foe-sisstiketts. I don't see my undies aroun' here no place. Hey, how come you got all these empty bottles down here?"

Mack, in the ice-box, yelled out to him, "Because of the manufacturer's mark on the bottom. They're all made just for me. I don't want get traced."

Coming back with two cases of champagne, he found Joe scratching his head, trying to figure out what Mack had just explained.

"You mean everyt'ing in here comes directly t'rough your racket? Even that champagne?" Joe asked.

"Yes. If that's the way you want to put."

Joe let go a long, low whistle. "Jeez. You must got some set ah brains, dat's all I can say."

Baby's voice was now heard hollering down from above. "Hey, Mackus! We're about to serve the midnight supper!" The evening was flying by.

"Oh, swell! I'm coming up right now!" Then to Joe, "I bet you're ravenous, Joe—you know, 'starved.'"

"Huh? Oh, me? Yeah. But I'm more hungry for you, Mack." Joe looked puzzled, starting to say something, then stopping himself.

Mack held him in his arms. And after they kissed, he said, "You'd better level with me right here and now, Joe. Everything. What this is all about...other than you and me."

"Well, see...it's like dis. Are you int'rested in a partnership?"

"You mean—if it's going to be you and me all the way, I have to be first inducted into the Underworld, then go in with your mob, right? That's it, isn't it?"

At this Joe laughed and laughed until he doubled over. "Oh, God! I'm gonna pee my pants! Oh, God! Oh, boy! Ain't that a hot one! I never heard nobody put it like dat!" He threw his arms around Mack, still laughing helplessly.

But Mack was frowning. "Well, put it in your own words! Make me understand it!" But Joe could not stop laughing, tears in his eyes, his face red. Mack loved him more for it, and had to laugh, too. "Listen, listen, Joey, can you please come back to my house with me—overnight?"

"Oh, Mack, I wanna like anyt'ing...I wanna but—but I don't t'ink it's a good idea." Joe suddenly stopped laughing. "If you knew what my life was really like, Mack...I mean really, really, really like—you wouldn't believe it." He rested his head on Mack's shoulder like a kid.

"So just tell me—come on—we've got to get upstairs." Both hefting the crates, they proceeded again upward.

Joe nodded vigorously behind his crates of booze. "I'll try and, aw, Mack, I ain't gonna lie about it. I don't know if my brudder found out for sure you wuz queer but...he'll honest-to-God kill me if I don't get some mileage outa you."

Mack placed his crates at the top of stairs, looking up at Joe, still hidden behind his. "Mileage? Joe, hold on—put those down a minute. I don't know how he could have found out...and this is very serious. I'm relieved you've come clean."

"I'm wid yuz all the way, pal!" Joe said.

Alexander came around from the front then, ready to continue his restocking, eyeing them both, sensing that they were involved in something serious.

"I've got to talk to Joe in private for just a minute, Alexander. Would tell Deucie and Baby that we'll be right along?" Alexander gave a fast nod and disappeared as Mack led Joe to the second floor. "Let's go up to the office and hash this out—"

There, by the single glow of the desk lamp, Mack sat himself on the couch with Joe standing before him.

Joe began, hang-dog, "You don' hafta trust me. Nobody ever did. Just cuz of what I come from." Here was a new side of Joey Imperio, one Mack had not yet seen. "I don't got nothin' to do with dis 'cept dat my brudder, Bruno, knows I'm queer and sends me out to try an' vamp yuz, an' den, Jesus Christ! Next t'in I knows, I'm fallin' in love!"

Mack couldn't believe the change in him. He looked about to crack. "Well, don't take it so hard, Joey. You're afraid of him—this brother of yours. You say he'll kill you if you don't comply—do what he tells you. But here's the problem: I work for the state and federal governments. By simply knowing what you've just told me, I could make one telephone call and that would be the end of your brother Bruno."

"Well, so couldn't I. And dat would be the end ah you." Joe slumped down beside Mack on the couch. "Aw, shit."

"O.k. Here's what we'll do. Let's telephone him—Bruno! I'd like to talk to this brother of yours in the meantime."

Joe shook his head. "You gotta be kiddin'. You don' know what yer playin' wid here, Mack. If you t'ink you can talk any sense into him, well, all I sez—good luck!"

"Where is he? Call him—there's the phone."

Joe put in a call to his family's restaurant.

"Where's Bruno?" he asked someone. Mack leaned in, overhearing.

A short wait produced a surprisingly smooth, civilized voice, inquiring in a strictly business-like fashion if Joe had done his job thus far.

Over the wire, Joe said, "I tol' him. Sure I was 'pacific. Yeah—he's right here. He ack-shullee wants to speak to yuz. Talk to him." Joe handed Mack the receiver and the telephone.

Mack heard the voice belonging to Bruno Imperio. "Now why wasn't I invited to that clam-bake over there at your new nite club, Mr. Daly?" Not at all what Mack had expected.

He genially, answered, "What a terrible mistake! I do apologize. But you're well-represented by your brother here."

"Hmmmm. So, have you two hit it off yet?" Bruno asked.

Mack replied, "Oh, sure we have."

"I guess he's spoken with you about our plans, then?" he said, sounding nothing like his younger brother, except for a faint trace of the accent.

"Yes, he mentioned it. But not in any detail."

Bruno drew a breath. "My brother sometimes doesn't absorb things like he should. I want fifty-fifty. Did he tell you that?"

Joey was at once on edge, holding tightly onto Mack's arm.

"Fifty-fifty—and what do I get in return for a deal like that?" Mack answered, smooth and as cool as can be.

"You get him—anytime you want him. *If* you want him."

(Joey whispered, "Oh shit.")

"It was nice of you to send him over. But I'm sure if we'd met under more auspicious circumstances, we would've hit it off anyway." No reply from Bruno. Mack continued, "But as far as my business goes, I'm assuming you know what's at stake here..."

"I do," Bruno replied, then paused, breathing harder now. "But I don't think you know what's at stake *here*, Mr. Daly."

Mack let that go, changing the subject. "I'd like to keep Joe with me. Have him work for me—if you could spare him."

"Joey's my brother, Mr. Daly. He's a part of our family."

"I know what you mean. I have a family as well."

"I know you do. Leventhals, I believe. Dirty rich kikes you don't get along with."

Mack was taken aback just for a moment. "You're right about that. You must've found out enough to know why. It's a sort of double life, just like your line of work. Both of us keeping certain things undercover because we have to. Funny how we seem to have that in common. And now we have Joe in common, too, I guess."

"Yeah, but we're going to have a lot more in common, Mr. Daly. That is, if you want to hire Joey—make him a part of your life, maybe." Bruno Imperio chuckled darkly. "I never thought this whole set-up was going to take such a turn. So it looks like you owe me one," Bruno concluded, his tone changing now to that of a killer's.

Mack hesitated; his eyes met Joe's. "Yes. I guess I really do."

Looking away, he shrugged, handing the receiver to Joe.

"I wanna stay on overnight wid Mr. Daly, Bruno—" And whatever came back as the reply made him as white as his shirt-front. Numbly, he returned the ear-piece to the hook.

"Well," Joe murmured. "I guess dat's it for me. No soap. I'm headin' for downtown. But fast."

At the side alley, outside the club, Mack and Joe said good-bye.

Joe wanted to walk down Sixth and take the El., but Mack insisted on putting him in a taxi. It was two a.m.

Both spoke little, and it was Joe who said, "I'll get back to yuz tomorrow. I'll try to show up over in Brooklyn."

"O.k. But listen—" Mack, feeling as if he were losing him forever, not knowing at all what to say, was leaning into the cab with Joe looking up at him.

"I'll be there. You know I will. Oh, Joey...you call there, at Leventhal's, if anything's wrong, see..."

"Oh, it will be!"

"Joe, don't say that."

"Naw. I guess I'll be o.k."

The cabbie was getting impatient. Mack had his hand over Joe's, clinging to the door of the taxi. He whispered hoarsely, "So...you'll just tell him—tell him—I'll meet with him and we'll talk. We'll meet and talk. Only please, please, Joe—you watch it."

Mack bent and kissed Joe on the back of his hand. As the cab sped off, Joe leaned out, waving, with haunted, yearning eyes.

Off he went and, distantly, the howl of sirens and the clanging bell of the paddy wagon could be heard down around the Main Stem. They had raided The Club *Intime,* the place everyone called the Ontime—the speak that Blackie the Whistler said they would raid.

So, once again the Whistler was right.

It began to rain. Mack stood watching the cab go. And when it turned down Broadway, he leaned back so that the rain mingled with his tears, so that when he went back in, nobody would ever guess that he was crying out there—crying like Hell.

And from far, far away, he swore he heard old Blackie whistling.

• • • • •

CHAPTER IV

CAME THE DAWN

Someone had covered the star on the Armstrongs' dressing room with a bit of pasteboard. On it was scrawled:

FOR COLOREDS ONLY

Elliot and Nolie didn't even see it when they left to go and do their set, but Johnnie did. She pulled it off and hid it underneath her maid's apron. No reason to spoil anybody's fun tonight.

That sort of thing was bound to happen, anyway—but it was starting to worry Johnnie and Nolie. Elliot was oblivious to everything except the increasing glare of the spotlight in which he basked, becoming more and more aware that he, and Nolie, too, were quite suddenly famous.

That fame surrounding them was due to their talent, and thank God for that—yet, with it had come a thirst for imitation and idolatry. All the kids seemed to want to be like them, and to know every single thing they did, every minute of their lives. And that wasn't what they'd bargained for at all.

Elliot didn't want anybody imitating him. He knew what he was, and he lived with it. But it drove him nuts. Nolie was sane. Lovable. Elliot wasn't sane. Not at all. He frightened himself; he was frightened *of* himself. So was Johnnie. Frightened for them both.

The way they lived! It wasn't just Nolie's colored friends, but the type of boy Elliot sought out, too. Nolie had Johnnie...Elliot—well, Elliot had that truly self-destructive thirst for wild Rough-Trade Boys. At least, thought Johnnie, returning to the dressing room and politely beginning to throw everyone out, he liked only white fellas.

After her kin and their ilk left, Princess Johnnie Parker tossed off her patent leather shoes and sat a spell. Picking up one of Nolie's gardenia scented cigarettes, she began to ponder what a funny life she was living; lighting up, she deeply inhaled and lovingly toyed with one of Nolie's garters.

She put it back where it belonged—giving it a kiss first—then turned to the make-up mirror, ablaze with lights. There she was, a young colored gal who'd come Downtown to pretend she was the personal maid to a Lezzie named Winola Armstrong who loved her like anything; and about whom Johnnie felt precisely the same way. Nolie Armstrong—who was the Jazz Baby that every college girl envied and emulated. Brilliant, but nobody knew it, a martyr to Elliot's drinking and whoring—but nobody cared. A Dedicated Daughter of Sappho who found herself adoring black women and only black women (*"Adoring, in fact, only me…and thank you, Jesus, for it, too!"* Nolie prayed.) Johnnie wondered why it was exactly that Nolie loved her so. Oh, but why question happiness!

In the reflection, she saw a girl whom her sweetheart described as a little panther, sleek and sacred, like an African idol. Johnnie could see all of that, but she also saw her stiff, white maid's cap and her ruffled collar and cuffs. Someday they wouldn't have to play this game. But, for now, as long as she and Noles were together, it was all right, she guessed.

Whatever would her family—all of the Parkers—have done if Mack Daly hadn't come along and hired that silly, string bean of a brother of hers, Alexander? Lord, how everything changed after that!

Johnnie always laughed when she saw, like some circus parade in her mind, everything that had transpired through Alexander's hitching up with Mr. D.!

First, there was that crazy-ass wife of his who treated her brother like a lap dog—but who needed him and loved him like he was her son. Once, Alexander told Johnnie that Mrs. D. had said to him, "You're the son Mack and I will never have!"

What a thing to say! But all those people whom she, Alexander, Keys and Mama had met through Mr. D. were exceptional white folk. Crazy as hell, but exceptional like nobody—black, brown, white, yellow or red. Truly, like nobody she'd ever, ever encountered!

It was, after all, Mrs. D. herself who was seeing to Alexander's education, putting him through Night School at some Advanced Social Institution. My Lord! What a woman she was. Half the time you didn't know whether to love her or hate her. Too bad she couldn't get over being so in love with Mr. D. Now that was some way to live! But then, just look at how they all were living. Ye gods!

Johnnie recalled how, when she and Keys were little, they'd put a blanket over two chairs which had their backs to each other, hide under them, and truly think nobody would ever find 'em. That was how all of these white folk lived! Precisely. Covered up by big a crocheted blanket which was intricately woven, then tossed over their lives.

"I never knew white folks were so goddammed nuts," she would tell herself over and over. First one thing, then another. Still, she loved each and every one one of 'em. Even that Miss Annabelle Harrison—now there was a study for you.

Nolie would never forget that day!...when Mrs. D. told Alexander to bring Keys over to Great Neck to meet this wealthy social lady who was an artist, because she needed a figure model to pose for her statues. Miss Harrison was suitably impressed enough to send her chauffeur up to Harlem to retrieve Keys—not once, but on numerous occasions. Numerous and more numerous! Pretty soon, to everyone's genuine shock, he started staying out there with her.

In a little while, Keys came back with a big diamond pinky ring; then, a little while later, a platinum wrist watch, then some fine silk shirts and suits enough to fill a whole closet. Then, pretty soon, a wave to his konk and if he wasn't a new man with some strut!

Mrs. D. told Alexander that she always knew Miss Harrison needed a Big Black Beautiful man and Keys precisely filled the bill, because he looked just like what she always drew and sculpted and must've dreamed about. And suddenly, due to Mrs. D. becoming a match-maker, there was that dream come true in all his big, black, beautiful glory.

So Miss Harrison was no longer an old maid and Keys said he really loved her; and since he never lied, everyone knew he precisely did.

When Johnnie asked him—with everyone around the dinner table at Mother's, "Is it because she's so rich, is that all?" her brother laughed like Hell.

"Not directly," he answered at length. "Mostly I guess it's because she's almost as big as me, white or not!"

Johnnie had to admit, Keys and Miss Harrison were two of the broadest shouldered, tallest people she'd ever seen. She imagined how significant they'd be when side by side...certainly if they walked down Broadway together (and that would be some occasion!) passersby would have to hop off the curb right into traffic!

Outside the dressing room, she could hear Nolie singing up onstage. She closed her eyes and hummed along, marveling at how different her sweetheart was in real life! Just now, Nolie was putting over a torch song and sending that crowd out there to Heaven. She'd said to Johnnie, "I want to add some of the blues into this sad stuff—just see if you like it." Then she'd do it that way, and give Johnnie all the credit. Johnnie would ask her why, and Nolie would tell her that she could feel everything Johnnie felt from the time she was little, and that it almost hurt her as much as it did Johnnie.

Everything was almost precisely copasetic since she and Elliot rented out the penthouse apartment on 55th Street, because Johnnie could now live with her sweetie. Even though, coming and going, Johnnie still had to use the maid's entrance and traipse around in that silly uniform. Nolie had seen to it that they were pretty happy, and Johnnie was the happiest she knew she was ever going to be for all her life through.

Except for Elliot's drinking, his crazy kind of tortured love for those terrible boys he'd drag home…and except for how Elliot and Nolie had to act married…everything was going very well.

Except for how they had to act married! What if any reporter—or ANYbody for that matter—asked to see their marriage license? What then?

Johnnie sat up and emptied the cocktail shaker into her mouth. Only a few drops left anyway. It really was just that one little thing—and only that—which gave Princess Johnnie Parker pause. She looked about the little dressing room. Everything in there told of a couple who were the brightest young pair around; talented as Hell, contented as could be.

Strewn about were articles from newspapers and magazines which Nolie herself had clipped out for gluing into their scrap-book. Each detailed Mr. and Mrs. Armstrong's marital dreamlike existence. Nolie cooking eggs at their new gas stove, helping Elliot shave; Elliot cutely scolding Nolie for eating one too many bon-bons. Why, every White Young Couple in America was buying this gag without question! They were, in fact, modeling themselves after Mr. and Mrs. Elliot Armstrong. Nolie said she didn't mind any of it at all except the kissing part, and that kind of made her sick.

Johnnie could see how, as Nolie had told her many times, it had all begun innocently enough. Even before the War, Elliot and Nolie had sung and played together. Both were what Nolie called child prodigies, both encouraged to develop their musical gifts, writing songs, dancing, playing almost every instrument you could name.

Then, when the War did come, Elliot went and enlisted in the AEF—at only sixteen, lying about his age—and not to make the world safe for Democracy, either. But just to get away from his Mother. It seemed like a bad reason to go through the Hell he had to endure, but that was it. And, anyway, that's how he met up with all his friends who were pansies just like he was and who went to all kinds of trouble to hide it…just like he did.

Nolie, staying at home, took care of the Father. He was—what was the word? *Neurasthenic*. He was also a pacifist, and the War made him more neurasthenic. The problem had always been precisely Nolie's taking care of everyone and nobody ever taking care of Nolie! Well, Johnnie had fixed that.

Yet, when Elliot came back from Across, he needed a lot of care, and, of course, there was Nolie. He was a real wreck. But she knew what to do. It was his music that saved him.

What had begun as a crisis splitting Father and Son apart—because, not only was Mr. Armstrong, Sr. a neurasthenic and a pacifist, he also loathed syncopation. And this was shared with even greater ire by his wife, who was a concert pianist of worldwide renown.

"But both of 'em were as neurotic as Hell," Nolie told Johnnie of the Senior Armstrongs. "You know, coming out of the Mauve Decade and being so artsy-fartsy as they were!" Just completely wrapped up in themselves! Moping around in velvet frock coats and droopy tea gowns, taking laudanum, mumbling Swinburne! That's where Elliot got his self-indulgence!

All this from Nolie in a sad kind of reverie. And sometimes even though Johnnie didn't quite know what in Hell she was talking about, it was just so fascinating anyhow.

"To them, the stuff we hungered for was simply treacle, John! Why, we wanted to be just like Irene and Vernon Castle—and that's what started it all."

During the War, the craze for Jazz in all its evolutions had swept America. It made Elliot happy to get a band together, calling it The Army of Charm after his own regiment—and putting Nolie up in front of them, shaking her stuff and tearing a song to pieces as only she could.

It was this combination of everything, Johnnie imagined, that made their rise to fame so certain. Lord, were they good and were they hot! Elliot and his boys were very handsome and, at first, had worn their uniforms up on the bandstand. Nolie and Elliot sang and danced together; they also did comic routines that were just side-splitters. Nolie had the idea of painting everything white. Elliot's white fiddle and megaphone; their music stands, and soon their suits got ordered all in white. Elliot wanted to add more instruments—both of them reared on classical music—then a glee club; Nolie wanted a trio of girls backing her up. Well, it all helped, but mostly it was just the music itself. The way Elliot did those arrangements and the way they both sang 'em!

It was just about seven years ago, as Nolie had tabulated it, when they started appearing more frequently on the stage together, either for preludes or vaudeville shows, that the public—nobody else—started calling them Mr. and Mrs. Armstrong.

And then, well, it just got to be too much to explain. People seemed to want to identify them as the Premiere Purveyors of Pep...so young, so positive, so much in love...so...married.

Well, it did help their fame a good deal, that was for sure. Nolie herself said, "We didn't try and stop them. Hell, here we are in '28 with everybody believing we're hitched! Next thing you know..." she would add, grimly, with a mirthless smile, "...they'll want a little snook-ums to come along!"

Johnnie and Nolie would just stare at each whenever the question of the Stork loomed. And it did. And there it was—in those articles, right before Nolie's eyes. Enough to give you the willies...or the vapors.

When are you two going to bring a little kiddy into the world? Isn't it time? Or—*past* the time by now? People could just be so damned mean.

But the thing of it was, Johnnie decided, holding up an autographed photo of Nolie and Elliot, heads touching, looking all goo-gooey, they didn't look anything alike...not at all.

Nobody would ever guess they were...brother and sister!

After all, she and Keys looked nothing alike and THEY were brother and sister. And she was a lezzie herself, and he was being kept by a rich white lady! But...Elliot and Nolie were FAMOUS. And things were expected of them.

Lord. How much longer could they keep it up?

A knock at the door shook Princess Johnnie out of her trance-like wonderments.

"Honey, it's Baby...come on out and have some eats..."

As she opened the door, seeing Baby smiling there with a cigarette dangling from her mouth, she spied Mack just behind her, coming in from the alley.

"There's Mr. D....lookin' kinda glum..." Johnnie said. "Hey you!" they both called out. He did seem inordinately distracted. And on such a night as this, too.

Baby suggested, touching his sleeve, "Come on into the back and sup with us, darling—food's almost gone by now...Raining out, huh?" She knew exactly what was going on in Mack's heart. She never missed a beat.

"Yeah."

"Are you o.k., Mr. D.?" Johnnie asked as they went back into the dressing room.

"No—I'm not really. But I will be in a sec." Easing his way between them, not looking them in the eye, sitting down hard on the studio couch, he gave a deep sigh. "You two go on ahead. I'll be right there."

But both women, glancing at each other with looks that said he needed attention, decided otherwise. Baby gently closed the door; both looked down at their Mack.

"He'll be back," Baby said with poetic simplicity.

"He went on home, then?" Johnnie provided.

"Oh, yes. Sure. Had to. No other way."

There was a sort of silence—thick with knowing. Baby sat down next to him, patting his knee. "You're quite taken by this goombah. And he seems to feel pretty strong about you, I'd say."

"You know, I'm not dreaming. I'd never come right out and say it...but he's not kidding and he's not putting one over on me. I really do think he's just as strong for me as I am for him...you know that, too, don't you both?" Then he fell into a kind of heap, there on the couch. "But...you know, he is a gangster. A real, true-to-life gangster."

The two women looked at each other. "And he's after your business," Baby added.

"No, not him...but his family...you know, Italian gang stuff. Somehow they found out...found out...about me...that's why they sent him."

Johnnie bristled, "They can't touch you, Mr. D., 'cause you'll report 'em to the government and have their asses put right in jail!"

"I wouldn't do that to him. I tell you, girls, he's what I've always wanted and needed. He's—he's like a...a...miracle of love, that's what he is! You might not think so, but you've got to believe me."

Baby suggested, "At the risk of offering a bromide, opposites do attract, Mackus." She gently smoothed his hair back in place.

More silence. Then, Mack, as if thinking out loud, talking to no one in particular, said, "I'm going to have a talk with his brother as soon as possible...have to try and talk him out of it—or—or something. See, he runs the whole thing, not Joey."

"Talk him out of what?" asked Johnnie.

Mack gestured fatuously. "Oh—you know—if Joe doesn't get me on his side. I guess his brother will kill him."

Baby asked, "Or kill you first, more likely! Does Deucie know any this yet?"

"Well, it probably took him about five minutes to figure it out. But, see—if I didn't think Joey really cared for me!"

"You don't mean," Baby softly suggested, "you're trying to convince yourself, do you? Trying not to believe he's just selling you a bill of goods?"

Johnnie added, "You're some catch, Mr. D. Even if you weren't everything you are, you still would be an answered prayer to any queer fella, gangster or not!"

"Well, aren't you a sweetheart?" Mack managed a smile. "But you see, we might be in a fine mess if—Oh, just listen to me!" Shrugging it off, having a keen distaste for self-pity. "Aw! Hell's bells! I'm not going to let this spoil our fun! He does care about me heaps and nothing's going to come between us! Ever! I just know it. So let's go and tie on the feed-bag."

He took them both by the arm. "Hell! I've found my heart's dream, at long last, haven't I? Isn't that enough?"

"Oh, Jesus!" Daubing her eyes, Baby rushed to the mirror. "You're makin' me start again! I only hope to God that he feels the same away about you."

"Oh—he does—of course he does!" Mack quickly put in. Too quickly, perhaps.

"Let me finish!" Baby turned from the mirror. "—enough to choose you over his relations? You don't know dagos like I do, Mack!" Straightening his tie.

Johnnie, taking it all in, decided against saying anything just then, and made her way toward the door. Looking at Mack's reflection, she could only think of one thing: this new fella Mack was loving like all Hell had already taken something bigger and more priceless than his business. He had taken his very soul and wasn't intending on ever giving it back.

• • •

As dawn broke over Manhattan, the rain ceased. The City now shone a dark and sinful gold in the light of that morning. The inidigo lacquered evening was being slowly replaced by a promise of struggling, valiant sunshine, shameless in its certainty, causing everything below to glisten, sparring with yet undaunted clouds.

Pavements strewn with crushed orchids, jade green dance cards, lost telephone numbers scrawled on torn menus—all mirrored back the great drape of night which now rose from her stage, immensely pleased with the party she had thrown, wrapped in a self-embrace.

Silver slippers dodged puddles; trailing silver cloaks lifted to reveal legs which had danced the whole night through, shod in ravaged silk hose. Aromatic with gin, lips still sought lips, sleepily. Weary laughter—a ghost of that evening just ended—was faintly heard, hollowed by the empty steets. The joke was over—for now.

Men with pleasantly stubbled cheeks tattooed by kisses the color of blood went away with their battle scars still burning in this glaring light, fevered with aching memories of chorus girls.

Taxis and limousines rolled away—down the yawning canyons of the Main Stem, holding within magnificent causalities of an alabaster life illuminated, so briefly, so gaudily, by Nature herself. For had she not orchestrated the sun, the clouds, the black glass pavements, all for them in this year of Our Lord, 1928? They were her children—errant angels, tumbled from Heaven, bent on raising Hell. But for now, under this tented fallen star which was their City, they basked but briefly in the strange and lovely light before shutting up their dream-lives to slumber...and dream again.

One such child of both Darkness and Light caught up in the throes of this grandeur, at 6:10 a.m. on that Friday morning, was Mack Daly. He did not return with Ynez to Great Neck, but instead went in his roadster to the Leventhal plants in Brooklyn. Alexander and Ynez, driving back in the Pierce-Arrow, possessed of both exhaustion and exhilaration still lingering, vaguely heard him mention that he had work to do there, but would be home early to take a much-needed nap.

Vaguely, too, in Ynez's mind, something about her libido had begun to register...something about that gigolo coming to see her that night. But, as is often the case with libidos and morning-afters, the whole thing fizzled.

Mackie really oughta stay away from home for tonight. Go someplace else! Gotta 'phone him later. Tell him. Must be alone—with whas-hizz-name.

Mack did have work to do. He always had work. He never took a day off or a vacation, except when he went up to see Colonel Connaught. But on that morning, he was really only going there to wait for Joe. If Joe would, in fact, appear—and Joe would certainly appear. Wouldn't he?

Mack was self-describing that morning. He was thinking, "I'm a wreck about all of this. That's what I am. A wreck. If he doesn't show—what'll I do? Tell the police? No. Go find him? Maybe. Yes. That's it. I'll just go and find him, by God!"

And Joe, who had fought like Hell with Bruno until that same sun pierced the smoke-clogged, clothesline-thick tenements of his neighborhood in Little Italy, stood staring out his window, staring Uptown, concentrating on Mack and all he had so instantly become to him. With such child-like intensity, you would've sworn he was seeing, through that narrow alley, the Second Coming of Jesus Christ Himself.

Like the very statue which Annabelle Harrison envisioned Joe posing for, he stood naked there, bathed in light, stunned by a kind of love which meant to him immediate and absolute salvation. In his hand, he held a rag dripping with water and blood, soothing the bruise Bruno's fist had made on his left cheek. It didn't matter. Nothing mattered.

Joe never believed he was supposed to be happy. Yet, there it was. For the first time ever. *Still, I can't see him no more,* he was thinking. *It could get real bad if we kept on this way. There's no way he could ever sell out to us. We'd all end up in the hoosegow—or get the chair.*

Jesus! That whack he'd gotten hurt so bad! Plunging his fingers into the tea-cup size holy water font his Mother kept nailed by the door to his small bedroom, Joe miraculized his wound, then flopped back on his bed.

Christ, I love that guy. Oh, God, do I. What the fuck am I s'posed tuh do? He then proceeded, thinking of Mack and the fun they'd had, to once again blow his load.

• • •

As the morning-after turned into the afternoon, Baby and Deucie were still just so damned wound-up that neither one of them could even hope for any shut-eye. Sitting up on the third floor over the Club deVol, having cup after cup of coffee out in their kitchenette, each told the other one story after another about their whopping success.

Now, with the club a phenomonal success and their little nest right up above it, they had a real life and a place to call home. After so long a struggle with any variety of failed career efforts (finally ending in a humiliating brush with the Vice Squad back at *La Maison*) their troubles at last were over.

Sitting there, they reminisced once again about all they'd been through. Married in France, when both were on leave in Paris, Baby in her nurse's uniform, and Deucie still possessed of both his legs; then, but a day later, the brand new groom was back at the front. His stag party, made up of the original Army of Charm, was broken up by a sudden call to go over the top.

Then, the very worst happened. While saving Mack's life, Deucie's legs were crushed by the collapse of their trench under fire. He was rushed to the field hospital and found himself staring up at his newly wedded wife while she helped saw off one of his legs.

Baby succeeded (almost without assistance) in saving the other. Some honeymoon present that was. Baby said the goddammed Medico would've taken both his pins if she hadn't been there herself.

When finally all The Boys went Home, Deucie and Baby were separated; Baby on her own hospital ship, sick to her stomach night and day, hardly able to hold a bed-pan in front of any of her wounded boys because she was so busy holding it in front of herself.

"I don't get it, Dottie," she told her friend, "I never do this sort of thing. What ails me?"

"Dearie," Dottie answered in her best nurse-voice, "you're pregnant."

The infant died almost as soon as it emerged from her womb. This was the little boy whom they called Junior. Neither one of them ever really got over it. Just one more thing they never really got over.

Baby had been exposed to gas during the War and everybody agreed that must've been the cause. But that couldn't have been it. Must have been that the kid wan't intended for the Life Plane at that moment, that's all. Baby was an ardent Spiritualist, and had gotten Deucie hooked as well.

Never one for self-pity, she found a dump in the Bronx for herself and the Deuce, and went about seeking work. And there was her brand new husband with the thought of a dead baby boy to haunt him, his new wooden leg and no hope of a job because he was a gimp, and a veteran as well. Since every hospital to which she applied noted her exposure to the poisoned gas (in her medical records), she came to the realization that her career in nursing was forever finished.

She acted just as full of pep as ever but, with no hope of work and a man at home who sometimes talked of just blowing his brains out, she could get, now and then, terrifically blue. Naturally. *("But the blues do happen to us all every now and then,"* she would say.)

Sometimes, she'd get on a coughing jag without ceasing, frightening the wits out of all her pals—then get her breath and joke about her voice, saying it sounded like a train whistle with asthma. She still thought a lot about her kid—but talked to him over there on the Other Side and, say, listen, if he didn't talk right back to her.

Deucie, like so many of the boys who had returned, also could not really adjust to civilian life—or else civilian life wouldn't adjust to *him* and the way the War had left him. Eventually reduced to selling matches on the street, Deucie, with his ever-ready grin, his cornball sense of humor, his heart of gold and his phony leg, became one of the thousands of men who had Made the World Safe for Democracy and still were paying the price. It was in this way that he met Blackie the Whistler and told Mack about him.

"Do you realize how blest we are Deuce—to have a regular saint like our Mackus pull us through the way he has?" Baby reached across the table and patted her hubby's arm.

"Yes, and do you realize," he replied "how he seldom, if ever, speaks about all he's been through!"

She knew. Oh, she knew. But very few did. Baby and Deucie had heard all about it. That was why they loved him so.

Sure, those first years had been brutal for Mack as well. He had received word of his Mother's death upon returning to the States. Immediately, there followed a court battle over the Leventhal empire, and his claim as rightful heir.

Mack was the only son of a Polish Russian-Austrian union which joined two powerful families of the same backgrounds in matrimony. Theirs was an empire of grain, stretching like oceans as far as the eye could see. His Father's family had immigrated to America in the last century building a baking industry which made them proud, aloof—and rich in their own right.

In Europe, the same kind of business had prospered, until the fall of the Czarist regime. And then, the War—and the death of Mack's Father.

He died suddenly, in 1914, a broken man of 41, opposed by everyone around him, there in his native land. President Wilson had asked him to stop exporting grain to Germany, in order to starve the enemy. The Leventhal empire was already losing millions due to the troubles in Russia, and more millions would be lost if he were to comply.

But, the Leventhals had prospered in America and so they liked it there. Working to feed the Americans, to give them bread, to show themselves as patriotic, new citizens, they flourished. But what was Mack's Father to receive for helping the United States? Was there to be any reward at all?

President Wilson made him a promise: the United States government would allow those many tons of grain not shipped to Germany to go instead to America. The American embargo on European imports would be lifted for Mack's Father. Wilson had further promised that the Leventhals would even be partially subsidized by the United States for diverting their shipments in this manner. His own family urged the senior Leventhal to do this, sending endless wires from New York. His wife's family, originally Austrian Jews from Vienna, were horrified.

Her only child, called Benjamin, had always been closer to his mother and her family than to his father. He was taught all there was to know about his legacy, but his interests increasingly turned toward Vienna and away from the great farms they'd jointly owned.

Mack's mother, whom he called Muzzie, had always yearned for the culture which had given the Austrian empire its heady aroma of romance and meloncholy, and it was into this world that both now, innocently and so briefly, drifted—a very young widow of not yet 34 years and her beautiful young son of 19.

But the War had ruined the kind of life she'd remembered, and so, with her own millions now in the hands of the Leventhals, they had no choice but to go America. Ostracized by these pious Jews and by a country she could neither appreciate nor forgive, Muzzie sought to isolate herself and Mack—her Ben. They lived as if sealed away from their new World, and soon enough she became very, very ill. He would not leave her while she lived; she had always clung to him—and both were always so alone.

She died just because, Mack had always said, she wanted to—and so her son joined up with the American Expeditionary Force. He would tell you that it was his quickest way of getting back to Europe.

But Mack Daly had found America. And especially New York, which he loved with an ardor he had never known before. He could become something there, proving that he was his father's son to his family—and perhaps, finally, to his dead father as well. It was his refuge: he could forget who he had been. He could, and did, create a new being entirely. A thing he called a man.

At the end of the War, he returned to find that the Leventhals had placed themselves in charge of both his father's and mother's combined fortunes. Being gone for so long had not helped his case in reclaiming what was rightfully his, but being a veteran did.

And so he went to the United States government and asked that the entire contract originating with Wilson's agreement to ship the Leventhal grain from Europe to the United States, be his—with all its advantages.

He won his case, obtaining limited use of the Brooklyn plants, and unlimited potential to make a forune all his own; but then found himself frustrated. The Leventhals made baked goods for thousands of people. He could not compete with that! And the enmity was more unbearable than ever! All that grain. All those subsidies.

Then came the 18th Amendment, and Mack was put to use working for Uncle Sam once again. He would own and operate a bonded alcohol manufacturing plant for the Prohibition Board, under strict government control. It was a genuine reward. Those tons of grain which were free for him to use would be made into alcohol—to be sold strictly under state and federal supervision.

It didn't take him long to learn this untried business, or the racketeering, pay-offs and hypocrisy which quickly grew up around it. He didn't care. It was almost pure profit—a fast, covert business with an opaque veneer of respectabilty. It made him feel—American! And as Mack himself so often said, the rest is history.

He sent Baby and Deucie monthly checks; all the while he was doing better, the deVols struggled along. Baby mopped the floors of the Women's Reformatory, and Deucie did repair jobs—everything from clocks to carburetors. There was even talk of opening up a nudist colony on some land Mack had acquired up North, but Decie wisely noted the abundance of bugs and poison ivy in those parts. Mack had spoken of going into something which would put their dreams on the map—open a club for Elliot and Nolie to call their home; have them run it! And there it was. It had all happened.

Baby, lighting another cigarette, indicated the sideboard. "Deucie, just lookee over there—we took in just over five thousand smackers last night and that was without the *couvert.*"

Indeed, the till was overflowing with cash and more than a few hundred dollar gold pieces. "We've paid off our staff and even put in a bonus for each of 'em. We can take out the salary for ourselves which Mackie insists on us doing, and we'll still have a bundle left for a rainy day. And meanwhile, we're not payin' the cops off nor the dry agents neither."

Mack had told them to make a trap for the cash and let it just pile up. He wouldn't take a plum nickel…not that he would need it!

Deucie declared, "That rainy day money will pay somebody off—sometime in the not too distant future."

As Baby got up to get more coffee, she asked, "Where you gonna hide it, Deuce?"

Deucie grumbled. "Well, I'll have to ponder a spell. With Mack lettin' that blue jaw in on all our secrets—Chaaarrist! He was down into the cellar everytime I turned around."

"You mark my words, darlin'…if anybody comes calling to shake our boy down, it won't be long before he gets some of his friends in high places to take care of 'em. That Eye-talian is just a poor sap who's got no place to go. Watch Mack take him in. He always provides for stray mutts—just like us!"

"No more java for this old fart," Deucie smiled, wearily getting out of his chair, leaning heavily on his cane. He ached all over and stumped his way to the back of the flat. "Draw them shades, will yuh, sweetie…WHEW, yers trooly is tomacose."

So doing, Baby then pulled his wooden leg off and placed it at the foot of the bed. There it stood, covered with countless autographs, drawings and obscenities—also a member of their family. Removing her wrapper, she nestled down beside him.

"I imagine Mack'll handle it. He always does," she sighed, pulling her rosary out from under her pillow. "Just one decade is all you're gonna get, Blessed Mother! I'm just plain pooped!"

Turning toward her on his side, Deucie said, "My God Above, this mattress feels grand. Just lookit all we've got!" Baby's eyes were closed, but her lips were moving in silent prayer. "Say one for that dago, will yuh, sweetie? He might need some assistance." He saw her nod, and kissed her on her forehead. "And another thing…" But his wife had already begun to snore.

• • • • •

CHAPTER V

CORRUPTION COCKTAIL

Mack's own private office was at the back of his distillery over the garages, and it was here that he went to nap briefly on his leather sofa, and just wait for Joe. Outside, the gentle lapping of the Gowanus Canal helped soothe him to sleep. He had an hour or so to doze before the trucks started in with their engines and his employees began entering through the guarded gates—and hopefully, before one named Joey Imperio was among them.

And so, locking his office door, and shedding his clothes right down to his BVDs, he curled up, using his wadded up tail-coat as a pillow. Used to sleeping in the trenches, Mack Daly could sleep anywhere.

What awakened him was none of the above. Dimly, through his exhaustion, he thought that someone else was in the office with him. Opening one eye, he saw, stretched out in the Morris chair a few feet away from his desk, a pair of legs in repose. The edge of his desk hid everything else. Mack sat bolt upright.

It was Joe. Out like a light. So he came to work after all! God, thought Mack, was this guy beautiful—even moreso when asleep! His hat on the floor, a lock set beside it, his tie undone, adorned in a thoroughly horrible checkered suit, Joe's bronzed hands rested peacefully on his bulge. Standing up, Mack wondered to himself if Joe was ever, ever soft.

"Ahem! Did you pick my lock, Joe?"

In his sleep, Joe muttered, "Pick any lock. Just point me to—" and was out again.

Mack laughed to himself. It was 7:32 by his desk clock. In no time at all, things would start popping. First, there was the matter of Mr. Goldenburg taking Joe on as a hire. Next, there was the matter of Abie—the guy who was bribed by Joe (or his brother). But most important of all, there was the decision that Mack had made to put Joe in his life all the time. Not just as his own employee, but just as his own—his own—what? How would explain this all? Maybe they could hash it out together.

"Hey! Wake up, handsome!"

Joe was on his feet with a holler. "Holy shit!" But still not fully awake and apparently not aware of exactly where he was, or who was standing before him. Weaving a little, his eyes slowly opened, then his whole face lit up with a big grin. "Made it to woyk, didn't I?"

"I'll say! Now what's that clip on your jaw?"

They stood apart, each a bit uncertain of how to greet the other. Joe looked down at his two-tones. "Aw, never mind dat. My brudder and me, we always fight. It ain't nuttin' but a scratch." Then he stopped, as if frozen, his eyes lifting to Mack's. "We got into it over me not doin' my job for him. Jesus. I—I tol' him it was too complee-kated a operation, an' den he swings. He t'inks I'm jus' no good for nuttin'."

"Well, come in here and we'll take care of it." Mack led him into his private bathroom—all shining with tile and nickel fittings. Gingerly, he cleaned the dried blood away. "I'll put some stuff on it. But it might sting a bit."

"Aw, I can take it!" Mack zeroed in with a swab. "OHHHHH! SHIT!" Joe hollered, jumping around the little room. "Wow-dee-dow!" Finally sitting on the toilet, he sighed, "What a mornin'," then looked around. "Hey, you got a shower in here!"

"Yes. Often, I work late or come in very early, like today. Feel better?"

"Want me to wash your back?" Joe beamed.

"Well…I must shower, of course. O.k.! And look right here, Joe—I've got lots of suits, too." Mack pushed another door open which revealed a dressing room and a rack of beautifully tailored clothes'.

"You don't like what I'm wearin', do yuz?" Joe realized, downcast instantly.

"I didn't say that!—Sure I like it, but I'd like to see you in something less radiant."

"Maybe I better just take it off then?" Standing, his face giving birth to that grin-out-of-nowhere, Joe began to peel.

"Well, then, I just will, too!" Mack said also, dropping his underwear. "I'm glad you're here, Joe. At last."

"Are yuz really? Really now? You wouldn't shit me, would yuz?"

"Don't I look glad to see you, huh?" Mack looked down at himself.

Joe laughed. "Just about as glad as I look, Mack Daly!" and went for him.

"*—oof*!" Mack caught him in a bear hug, laughing. "Forget the formalities, right, kid?" His lips touched Joe's as he adjusted the shower then pulled him in.

"I hope you fixed my door so it would lock back up!" Mack said, realizing suddenly by catching a glimpse of them both in the mirror. "What would happen if—"

"Don't worry, pal! Now don't that feel good…" Joe began lathering Mack with soapy suds from his chest downward. From their vertical position, they evolved into the horizontal, out of the shower, locked together, on the tiled floor.

"Jeez! I never knew nobody who could take turns before—I'm just gettin' crazy!" Joe breathed. He was enslaved by him one minute, commanding him the next.

"Hold on to it, Joe. We've got all morning."

Afterward, as Joe was letting Mack pick out a suit for him, he related more on what Bruno had done.

"Fack is, I could squeeze him to deat' wit' my bare hands. He's not big like us, but well set-up anyways. He has an awful, awful temper t'ough, see, so I don't like to get him riled. I'd always rather catch a beatin' than get Bruno riled. I seen him stop at nuttin'. Nuttin'."

"But he ought to be more imaginative when it comes to this idea of his, trying to shake me down. Not that tie, Joe—this one."

"He can't figger out how you do what you do. And I couldn't tell him if I wanted to, 'cause I can't neither. Say, I like dem pokey dots."

"So he must've gotten wind of my sideline business from somebody? Somebody in local government, you suppose?"

Joe looked splendid in a pale beige silk suit with a double-breasted vest that he said "spoke to" him right off. He regarded himself, standing spiffily beside Mack, adjusting his own tie. "Is dat duh sideline business what I delivered yesterday dat got sold at duh club las' night?" he asked.

"Let's just say, it's stuff left over. Overage, it's called. Unclaimed. It doesn't really belong to anyone, so I use it—rather than throw it into the canal."

Mack also noted them both standing so close, reflected in the full length mirror attached to the dressing room door. How similarly they had been made, except for coloring and the boldness of strokes with which Joe was drawn! Like book ends really, thought Mack to himself.

Joe said, "Somebody who we used ta supply got rid of us in favor of youse, Mack."

"Somebody who suddenly made it big, huh, Joe? I wonder who! Oh, Hell, come on, let's go out here. We'll order breakfast up." Mack went ahead and opened the door to his office. "Anytime now, my secretary is going to breeze in—so sit there—on the other side of the desk—as if we're holding a meeting."

It was now 8:58 a.m. Mack, patting Joe on his unbruised cheek, added: "Whatever you say henceforward, dreamboat—cast a veil over it."

"Wha-at?"

"Oh, never mind. What I mean is, just be careful. Listen, do you know who these people were who dropped you as their suppliers?"

"Only dat dey wuz in wid duh Micks. Irish political bums."

"Oh, I don't deal with them. Ever. That West Side bunch is very suspicious." Then Mack handed Joe a menu, pensively.

"Don't you know what you want? Ham an' eggs mebee?"

"Oh, sure, Joe. I was just thinking about that ilk. Did any one of them suggest it was myself they'd taken on in your family's stead?"

"Say, you gotta talk plain English! If you mean did dem Micks tell us anyt'ing after dey'd 86'd us—naw. Dey don't even speak to our kind. We don't rate like you do!" He now intently gazed at the menu, his perfect brows furled. "Say, I'm gonna have duh steak and eggs if yuz don't mind. I woyked up quite an appy-tite in dere."

The door to the outer office opened and closed. "Good morning, Mr.Leventhal," a prim voice said from just beyond.

"Good morning, Mrs. Rozen."

In poked the cloched-hatted head of a bespectacled woman with a sweet smile and an unobtrusive face. "Oh, I am sorry! You're in conference!"

"That's all right. I want you to know Joseph Imperio. Mr. Imperio is going to be with us now."

Joe suddenly flushed, a great wave of nervousness passing over him. Standing, he nodded mechanically.

Mack instructed Mrs. Rozen to order them breakfast and just please close the door if she would. Her heels clattered down the hall to the powder room. Every morning it was a much unchanged ritual, as was Mack's Spartan breakfast.

"Dat all you eatin'? Orange juice with milk in it and a egg white!"

"Are you familiar the system of Physical Culture?"

"I ain't familiar wid no kinda culture! You never drink no alky-hol?"

"Never. Never ever. Anyway, I'm a great fan of Bernarr MacFadden's. Wait'll you see my gymnasium at home!" Joe was thrilled, hanging on his every word. "I noticed you don't drink either, Joe."

Joe made a face. "Uhk. It don't appeal tuh me. I'm too stuck on myself I guess."

Mack laughed. "Yes. Me, too! But it's more than that, Joe—it's the idea some Americans have about being your best! My mother didn't love this country, but she did admire that notion. And so do I..." He inidcated a photograph of Muzzie on his desk.

"Wow! She looks like royalty!"

"Well, in a way, she was, Joey. Things were much different in Europe then."

"—she passed?"

"Deceased? Oh, yes. Both my parents. How about yours?" Talking like this, seeing Joe sitting across from him, his big hands calmly resting on his knees, filled Mack with a sense that things were as they should be. Both of them…talking. Content. A real pair.

"My ma runs the restr'ant now. Since Pop's bin sick for sometime. Off his nut, yuh know. Bruno, he don't treat her right and it gets to me somethin' awful."

Joe was now in a kind of reverie. He just rattled on. "I'm closer to my ma dan anybody else, I guess 'cause I was always in the kitchen as a kid…helpin' out."

"Really! But I thought you were from a gangster family!"

At that, Joey began laughing helplessly again, slapping his knees, throwing his head back, then stopping, clamping his hand over his mouth. "Oops. Sorry—see—you just slay me when you talk like dat. We got a business goin'! Dat's all it is! Have for years! Right down across from Saint Anthony's choych on Houston. You gotta come over and eat sometime. My ma would just love yuz!"

"Well, I'm sure I'd love her, too. But your whole family is really involved in crime, aren't they?" Joey made a series of gestures which made Mack want to laugh instead.

"Listen to me, Mack." He now sat forward on the chair, his voice lowering. "Just akst yourself—do you know ANYbody, ANYbody who don't do somet'in' wrong now and den? Why, jus' look at yourself!"

"Joey, I just gotta kiss you." Mack leaned over and quickly did so.

"Only t'ing is," Joey went on, after kissing him back. "We give it a little more effort, see? Hey! Jus' like youse—we got it goin' on duh side, see?"

Mack smiled and shook his head, murmuring, "Some genuine article, this one is…" Then, to Joey, "But how did your brother put this all together? That's what I want to know."

"He recently hired a moll who he got duh goods from."

"Yes, but literally not a living soul would be able to find out about me or my sideline business, as you call it." Mack added, "Anybody in my shoes would fear blackmail, quite naturally." (Joe nodded.) "What was said between you both, before he took a whack at you last night?"

"I tol' him if he wuz to try to horn in on your game, you'd have him up duh river like dat…" Joe snapped his fingers. "I tol' him youse wanted me to woyk for yah. So he sez, 'Oh, yeah? So you go woyk for him and SEE who gets sent up foyst—you or me!' Den he takes his poke at me." Joey thought a minute. "Oh, yeah! Den he sez maybe you and me'll have adjoinin' cells wid lace drapes to cover duh bars, so youse can both screw to yer heart's content!"

"Well, that sounds rotten. He doesn't mince words, does he? I'm sorry he had to hurt you."

"Say, I can take it! Duh way I see it is you want me on yer side 'cause you fell in love wid me at foyst sight, and vicie versie—in dis way youse can keep an eye on me, right?"

"Oh, Joe, you really delight me! Yeah, something like that…but we've got to see how things develop. So far, we're hot as Hell for one another and we've got something crazy in common—I'm not sure what, as of yet—"

Joe leaned back in his chair, putting his hands behind his head. "Oppy-sutts contract—every hear dat one?"

A polite voice from the outer office stopped them, saying: "Morning paper, sir. I'll put it out here on the desk?"

"Sammy! It's o.k.—bring it in please!"

So doing, the little man obsequiously made his exit. Mack took the *Herald* and, unfolding it, saw a few headlines down:

RAID ON CLUB INTIME
Prohibition Agents Padlock Popular Night Spot
HUNDREDS OF HIGH-STEPPERS JAILED

He shoved it across his desk toward Joe. "Speaking of which…"

"Yeah, I saw duh paddy wagon comin' almost just as soon as you put me in the taxi. Looks like dose poor saps *never* saw it comin' though."

"But I know somebody who did, Joe—ever heard of The Whistler?"

"Say! Who hasn't? He used to do an act in Pop's old place off Mulberry."

"Did he let on to your crowd about the heat getting put on? Talk of lots of raids?"

Joe thought about it. "Nope, not him." He answered at length. "…but dere's wires into them dry agents' offices somewheres. We don't quite know how."

"Would that you did, Joe, would that you did!" Mack sighed.

"Say, I wish I could quote po'try. Will yuh teach me some?"

"Huh? Oh sure, Joe, stick around—after breakfast!"

Mrs. Rozen, having just returned, answered the outer door. "Breakfast is here, sir! Shall I bring it in?"

Joe took the silk handkerchief from the breast pocket of his borrowed suit, and tucked it into his collar. "I'm stickin', Mack!" Then, noticing Mack still staring at the headline, he said, "Say, I hope dat bad nooz don't ruin your appy-tite…"

"No. No. But I guess—well—I expected it, that's all."

In walked the redoubtable Mrs. Rozen with a box of food. Mack carefully folded and hid the paper from her sight.

"Do you want to go over the Withdrawl Permits now, sir, or wait 'til later?" she asked. It was Mack's habit to begin with these as he had his breakfast.

"Oh, bring them in, Rosie. Mr. Imperio might be interested in seeing how this part of our concern works..."

And then, as Joe masticated away, Mack explained to him, "You must know from your end of the booze business that everybody under the sun nowadays has some reason or another for getting alcohol from the government. A lot of the permits issued are phonies, and so we have to check each one then telegraph each order, individually, to Washington every morning."

"What a pain in dee ass dat must be," Joe commented just as Mrs. Rozen returned with a handful of permits, making short of work them, creating three small stacks.

"The first pile is the genuine article...pharmaceutical companies, hospitals, and so forth...all with justifiable requests for alcohol. But, this second pile here are new accounts—each business—or racket, as the case may be—must be investigated thoroughly by dry agents first. And this last pile—more than a dozen right here before me so far—are phonies. Obvious forgeries for bogus firms which are probably fronts for bootleggers..."

Joe said without any surprise in his voice, "Dem two right dere are my brudder's handwritin'..." pointing to the second pile.

"Moran's Elixir? Cordially Yours Cordial Shoppes? I've had my doubts about them both for some time now..." Mack frowned.

"Yeah, dem two is his bluffs. Don't tell me he's been pullin' stuff off'n youse!" Joe started laughing, having a hard time swallowing his food and suddenly coughing loudly and violently.

"Joe, Joe! This is terrible. Hold on, let me pat you on the back. Don't catch a spasm on me now!" He gave him some seltzer from the siphon on his desk and pretty soon Joe was fine again. "Let's just hold off on these," Mack said, pocketing them.

"You mean you could get him sent up on just dose pieces of paper!"

"Well, just look at what he's gotten...here's 50 gallons, and here's 100 gallons. As I recall, he's been doing this for about four months now. If the prohibition agents went to these places where he cooks it and found it was Bruno and got an indictment on him and then a conviction, well, Joe—he could be doing a ten-year stretch."

"God, would he be mad!—Hey, don't look so discouraged, Mack..."

"But it is discouraging. This whole thing is the bunk! I'll bet you haven't any idea at all how much money went into this whole notion of trying to get America off the bottle, or how underhanded it's gotten!" Mack looked imploringly at Joe, who just shrugged. "Come on with me. I want to take you around."

Outside the garages, two acres of Mack's bonded alcohol distillery, conversion plants and warehouses stretched before them. "All dis is yours?" Joe asked in wonderment.

"Let me put it this way, Joe…all of this is my responsibility. It really belongs to Uncle Sam. Come on, we'll start at the beginning. We bring school kids in on tours all the time!"

As they walked along passing by buiding after building, all painted spanking white, Joe remarked under his breath, "God, I had no idea you wuz such a great man!"

"Well, thanks, Joe. But I'm not great—not at all—there are men who truly defend the idea of Temperance in this country of ours. Men of great honor and principle. About two. The rest…well…they somehow got caught in this undertow from an ocean of booze—just as I have. They may not have wanted to ever do anything illegal at all. But, aw, Hell. And it's rotten, Joey, rotten!"

They had arrived at what appeared to be four towers, side by side, each as tall as church steeples. "These are granaries. This is the whole reason I got into this business in the first place," Mack was afire with his tale. Joe watched him, fascinated. "See that stuff around our shoes here? Grain, Joe…we store it up. It can't be used for anything but the creation of prescription alcohol. That is written in stone."

Joe looked at Mack bending down and letting some of the grain fall between his fingers. "You wouldn't think innocent stuff like this could cause such problems, would you?" Joe just shook his head.

"I never knew booze came from grain. I knew wine came from grapes, 'cause we make duh stuff…but this is a whole new eye-op'ner!" He looked far across the yard. "Is dat duh plant your relly-tives owns?"

"Yes. Leventhals. Those white smokestacks are a familiar sight to all New Yorkers. I get to use their old trucks for deliveries—but even then, I have to buy 'em and paint 'em over. And I get to use some of their staff. That is, in fact, how I got you…or, rather, we got each other."

"My lucky day, pal o' my heart!" Joe cried. "But why do you need 'em at all?"

"Why? Oh…well…Come on, I'll show you how we make the stuff…I'll even show you where we store it, if you promise not to tell." Mack was off again. He had a long and strong stride, Joe noted. Heroic, really. "To answer your question…the preservation and fermentation process is controlled by chemists, which are part of my own staff…but the Leventhals allow me to contract their workers out for regular, unskilled jobs. Now let's go in here…hello, Mr. Weinstock," he said to an employee.

Now they were in a cavernous building with vats on either side as big as bungalows. Quickly Mack walked down the middle, between them. "…some of these are lined with wood, for distillation purposes. The alcohol ferments in those for two to four years before it's ready for bottling."

"What does the stuff end up as, once it's ready for the bottles?" Joe asked, sniffing the powerful odor they gave off.

"We make only drinkable alcohol here. We don't make any for industrial purposes. And we can flavor it in it lots of ways…" Mack gave Joe a wry look. "…as if scotch might cure rheumatism, and gin might help eczema! It's all the same, Joe—it's all just one big drunk!"

"Boy, oh, boy, you sure got duh goods on dis racket!" Joe looked at Mack with respect and awe. "So you wuz able to corner the market, so tuh speak, on legally usin' booze, you might say…but Mack, hold on a minute, slow down…it looks like to me you do not love what you do! Why'd you do it at all?"

But Mack avoided answering—or rather getting to the real point of it all. "Oh, come on, come on…you've got to see this…Mr. Weinstock, let us in to the vaults, please." The white overalled man obliged by taking them toward an elevator.

During the trip down, Mack indicated to Joe with a wink that their conversation had, just for that trip, ceased. "Where we'll now visit is strictly off-limits," he added under his breath.

"Where'd all of dis come from!" Joe whistled low, looking at the seemingly endless, narrow corridors lit by bare incandescent bulbs. From floor to ceiling were thousands of bottles in neat array, some dusty, some packed in straw, all labeled in code.

Mack dropped his voice almost to a whisper. "Just when Prohibition finally went into enforcement, those who were In-the-Know purchased the inventories from the big pre-War distilleries all along the Eastern seaboard…then they stored it all here, with me. Or rather—I guess I should say—hid it."

"Should I akst yuz how dose In-the-Know got hold of it all…and who deez wise-asses were…or are?"

Mack cleared his throat, speaking hardly above a whisper. "Well, you can put two and two together, I am sure, Joe. The big million dollar outfits which made liquor since Colonial times were all closed down by order of the federal government. So, it was the federal government who took control of all of their stuff. Let's say an outfit existed in Jersey that made top notch gin. Comes the Volstead Act. The first big boys in on the take were naturally the senators, and then the lesser public officials. They saw it coming. They had information prior to the general public. So, they just went in and took the stuff in the name of Temperance. But they really took it for themselves. It was like that in every state, in every city up and down this coast. It was a field day. So then they surrendered it legally—back to the government—and I store it for them. Of course, they haven't surrendered it all. They just store here with me. It's theirs, Joe. All theirs. When they want a shipment, I do charge 'em a small fee, and out it goes. Blessed by Lady Liberty herself! They're the biggest of big shot bootleggers, Joe, just the same as Bruno and myself—only untouchable, see!"

"Like who, fer instance?" Joe wanted to know.

Mack named three powerful men in both local and national offices whose names were household words. "But here's the pay-off. You see this whole section here?" Mack waved his hand down an aisle. "This stuff is all the result of what is known as Overage. It's gauged every month, but the gauge amount is always deliberately faked. So we make "over" a thousand gallons of pure alcohol. We report…let's say…a surplus of one hundred gallons, which we are required by law to dump, right outside there in the canal, only, of course, I don't dump it. Look at it all, Joe!" his voice echoed eerily.

"Who controls this stuff then?" Joe asked, agog.

"I do. It's by special request only, you might say. All the blue bloods of America. I am instructed to pad the overage reports. I've got a list as long as my arm and yours put together of those who get the swag!"

Joe not only looked a little discouraged, but confused as well. Mack put his arm around him. "—it's so goddammed hypocritcal, I can't even tell you. Those big-shots in politics have it all over the rest of us. We just can't win, Joe. And as for me—well, they've got me over a barrel, so to speak! I couldn't be honest if my life depended on it!" Mack paused. "But say, listen now—I have to trust you, Joe, and that's all there is to it."

"Say, my brain can't take it all in anyways, so even if I had to rat, I wouldn't know where to begin…" Joe looked at him."You ain't duh type to break duh law, I can jus' tell."

"The worst of it is I've become just as rotten as they are. I make my own stuff better than I ever would for those pricks. Finest around. All those bottles we hauled upstairs last night. That was what you might call Mack Daly's Private Label!"

"Jesus! And Bruno t'ought HE was hot shit!" As Joe held on to him, Mack was very downcast all at once. "Listen, Mack, if you wuz a gangster…I mean a real street guy, everybody'd t'ink you wuz just swell gettin' over like you do big time! I know plenty of guys would sell their souls to be a slick gennul'man like yourself!"

Mack laughed dryly. "Oh, hell, let's just get out of here." He pressed the elevator button. "Sell their souls…that's putting it aptly."

On the way back to his office, Mack was mostly silent. Joe tried to make jokes, but it didn't work.

• • •

The terrace doors of the Armstrong penthouse had been left open all night. Johnnie, the first one up and about, felt a distinct chill passing through the apartment where she lived with Nolie and Elliot. Looking in on Nolie, still somewhere in dreamland, she blew her a kiss and checked to see that her windows were closed. Then she tip-toed into Elliot's room—always looking as if a bomb had been dropped on it—the crooner himself sprawled unconscious, cross-wise on his monkey fur bedspread in mismatched silk pyjamas. No fresh air in here, though it did need some. It had to be the terrace.

Sleepily padding through the silver-leafed hallway, she passed through the sunken living room, remarkably neat for a change. Nolie's particular taste shone here. Not what one would expect of the jazz baby, she had made the place into a modern cottage-in-the-clouds, rustic and comfortably sweet—like a children's storybook.

Up another pair of steps, Nolie found herself shivering through her pegnoir—Elliot had left the French doors all wide open as usual. Out there, tossed everywhere, were saxophones, ukes, music paper, pencils and empty bottles of gin. Closing the doors, she switched on the radio, ensconcing herself on the sofa. Somebody was going on about on and on about the Evils of Drink! Normally, she would've twirled the dial to make sure somewhere over the air waves, Elliot and Nolie were being played. But this particular bluenose made her stop and listen.

"…no great nation like ours will ever be able sustain its noble foundation for very long with the Liquor Fiend kicking in the golden door of her sacred portals! Instructed by our Manifest Destiny to be the brandisher of the Sword of Our Savior throughout this sad old world of ours, we must take up that same sword…that sword which conquered the Devil himself in our Late Conflict, and aim it straight at those who break our laws by drinking, carousing and sinning!"

Whoever this was, he stopped to take a breath.

"Oh, brother," Johnnie muttered, but still she listened on.

"Let us do more than fall to our knees and pray during this most blessed of times!" he continued, more dramatically. "Let us gather up these sinners and, like the swine, so filled as they were with bedevilment, send them to their damnation! My dear friends, in the wee hours of this very morning, a sin nest on our own Great White Way was raided—I speak of a gutter hole known as the Club On Time…"

Elliot's voice hollered from inside: "Turn that damned thing OFF!"

Johnnie hollered back: "You white folks gonna sleep all day!" Then she adjusted the volume, curious to hear more.

"—it is not only the shame of internment and a subsequent jail sentence which those fools now face…not only the fact that—naturally—their lives are ruined forever by going there and thinking they could get away with it…" He was in rare form now. In a leering aside, "…but they could NOT!" A gurgly laugh emerged from the radio. "No! It is their souls which forever shall bear the tattoo of HELL!"

On that note, Johnnie had to pause and whisper to herself, "Wow! This asshole means business!"

His voice was reduced to a melodious but chilling whisper, "Their lives have become a mirror reflection of Hell itself, my friends. Distorted as in a House of Horrors looking-glass. And all because they could not control their desires. Yes! First to drink. Then to drink again, then KEEP ON DRINKING. Then: to sin! Having lost all their self-control, their sense of moral rightness, their notion of what the rest of us would think of them, embarrassing this great land of ours with their drunkenness and their debauchery! Wrecked lives, wrecked homes, wrecked marriages, wrecked families. Then! A Hell on earth. Well…I say—to Hell with them! To Hell with them all!"

Nolie appeared, standing at the threshold of the terrace in one of Elliot's dressing gowns, her hair a tumbled mass of curls, her eyes barely opened, and asked foggily, "Who *is* that guy?"

"Sshhh. He's just wrappin' it up now. We'll see…"

"…so GO AHEAD! Keep it up, you flaming youth, you whoopee crowd, you freaks of nature, you flappers, sheiks and shebas! Our Dear Father in Heaven will teach you that a life without a soul is DEATH in life. DEATH in life! Oh, yes, you will get yours! THIS is Brian Patrick O'Couran. And may Gawd Bless you!"

"That was the most depressing thing I've ever heard!" Nolie yawned, drifting sleepily toward the kitchen to make a pot of tea.

Meanwhile, Johnnie, having spun the dial, delightedly discovered a ditty by Elliot's band and retrieved the morning paper, even though, by now, it was no longer morning.

"He was talkin' about this raid that they pulled…lookee here—front page stuff!—right up a ways from our club, too!" She held the paper up before Nolie.

"We've all got to watch our asses here on in, Johnnie. All we need is to get ourselves hauled into the stir!" Nolie fretted, turning on the kettle "And from the way that wheezer sounded on the het, I'd better run out and buy a file while you make the cake. Did you ever, now I ask you?" With that, she dug through the bread box, producing some stale muffins. "I'll just heat these rocks up. Have some, darlin'?"

"Don't mind if I do. Let's keep it in here so's we don't wake up that pickled monster brother of yours." Absorbed in the news, she turned the pages quickly. "You know, it's really only the tabloids that carry the stuff about you and him. This rag is boring! Oops—hold on…I do take that back!"

Squeezing into the brightly painted breakfast nook next to her, Nolie put the tea tray down, then followed Johnnie's index finger to an important-looking article accompanied by an official-looking photograph of a corpulent, crinkled up face, atop a celluloid collar. "Just look. It's Brian O'Couran! That's the fella we just heard…been appointed as Director of Prohibition for the City of New York. Wonder if Mack knows him?"

Johnnie stared wide-eyed at the picture. "If that ain't precisely the biggest shit-eatin' grin I've ever seen, I don't know what is. Says here, '…a favorite son of Tammany, Mr. O'Couran also is a member of both The National Temperance Union and The Anti-Saloon League, and proudly holds the position of Grand Commandant of the Slaves of Mary. His platform has, as its foundation, the most diligent and zealous of ideologies which he determines will bring about a curbing of our present immoral, modern atmosphere.'"

Elliot now at last appeared at the threshhold of the breakfast nook, cigarette about to be lit, hair tumbled down into his eyes. It was much to his credit that, no matter how dissipated he might be, he always looked good enough to eat. But anyone who knew him well enough would tell you that those looks only went so far.

"What on earth are you two reading?" he snarled. "Stop! Don't tell me if it's gonna upset me…I don't wanna know—I'm too hung over."

"Well, we haven't reached the funnies yet, if that's what you mean," Nolie answered.

Having heard that much, he nodded like an eight-year old might, then made his way carefully out toward the bar, muttering something about the hair of the dog that bit him.

"Elliot!" Nolie shouted into the living room. "You promised if we were a hit last night, you'd go on the wagon again and you lied to us—Again!"

"I know I did, but that hideous article just upset me."

"You didn't even let me read it to you yet…and, furthermore, you got pie-eyed last night and the paper just came out this morning!" Johnnie added, shouting also.

He hadn't heard her. Going out on the terrace, remembering he'd left a half empty bottle of gin out there hidden inside his bartione sax, Elliot reclined on the chaise lounge, drinking it all down, waving to a man in the opposite apartment.

"Hey! Think we could get a tan?" he called out. "Let's get undressed and find out!" Whoever he was, he snorted and walked away.

"Elliot, come inside, you'll catch cold!" Nolie yelled. "This article here is important."

Elliot, now satisfied, bottle sill in hand, reappeared. "Gimmee that paper." He scanned the article lazily. "Was this the guy that was just on the rah-dee-oh?" The girls nodded. "So he's raiding every jernt in town, huh? So does this mean our club will be next?"

"Maybe not. Maybe Mack's got an In with him," Johnnie suggested, tossing her muffin across the kitchen and into the garbage. It landed with a thud.

"Oh...my head...please! Yeah, well just maybe he doesn't, too. I need air, ladies." Out he went once again.

Johnnie said, "He's got bottles stashed in your plants out there."

Both now followed him. Supine again on the lounge, he lifted a new fresh bottle out from under an Atlantic City souvenier pillow. "Has anyone called Mackie yet?"

"No. Should we?" Nolie asked. "He's with that new trick of his...who knows where—"

"Oh, where would he be but at work! Trick or no trick! Say, that fella of his is some hot stuff. Christ, I'm so jealous I could just scream. In fact, I think I will."

Nolie slapped her hand across his mouth. "Don't you dare! You're constantly attracting adverse attention out here!"

He waved to the middle-aged couple across the street, leering out from a penthouse of their own. "And they ask me why I drink!" he hollered to them. "I shall now ring up that lucky bastard myself. Where in Hell's the extension phone?"

"You're sitting on it," Nolie said. Then, she had an idea. "I wonder how Ynez is taking all of this...why don't you call *her* instead—?"

"Yeah," Johnnie added micheviously, "offer her your condolences."

"Oh, you gals are so mean about poor 'Nez. Here goes." The connection was made.

"Honey? Morning or afternoon, or whatever it is. Give me a Hello-girl, please." He waited, then rattled off the Dalys' Great Neck number.

Surprisingly, instead of Alexander answering, it was Ynez herself. Elliot asked: "Is this the home of the kike and the dike?"

"Oh, it's you, Elliot." Ynez's tone was positively poisonous.

"You were expecting maybe Marie of Romania? Were you up, sweetie? We ourselves just crawled out of bed moments ago."

"Mmmmmmm...listen, I can't talk. I've got my masseuse here just now. Then I've got to get my nails done and my hair washed. I'm having everyone come here—to me. I refuse to leave the house today."

"Well, I won't expect you for high tea then, will I, Queen Shit?" (Elliot rolled his eyes.) "So I guess this all means you were up. Why are you getting renovated so soon, Nezzy? You looked more than intact last night..."

"It's just something I have to do," Ynez said, trying to be withering. "One must, you know—things are happening—*you* know!"

"Yeah, I know!" Then, with receiver covered, "Brother...I'll say I know!"

"Never mind. I won't discuss it—with you or anyone...but look, let's change the subject—wasn't last night just a smash, Elly?"

"It was. It was. Especially for my Mackus—bringing Tarzan of the Apes along with him as a date or a bodyguard...or, well, just what *is* he? And then just disappearing that way."

"Oh, shut up. You're not going to spoil *my* day with your mean quips! Why'd you ever call me in the first place? I told you I was busy!"

"I didn't call to talk to you—I called to talk to Mack, you crazy bitch."

"You know very well he's not here—not on a weekday!" she snapped.

"Say, he might be any place at all today—*if* you get my drift. Get with it, will you! He's gone wild, don't you get it?" Elliot shouted into the receiver. Hangovers always had the worst effect on him.

Her voice full of calculated ennui, Ynez replied, "Why don't you hurry up and get drunk, Elliot? You're so much nicer when you're stewed. I don't even know what you're talking about. You must be getting to that stage where people like you have the D.T.s. As far as *I'm* concerned, that greaseball works for Mack and me—I mean, Mack and I. He's putting him on as Help around the house here. To fix things."

They all heard and howled silently. Elliot, pulling the ear-piece away, stared at it intently. "Ynez, wake up, will you. Mack has met someone. This is it. This is...important...you could be history, toots!"

Silence over the wire.

"She doesn't get it, girls!" Elliot informed Johnnie and Nolie who now stopped laughing and looked concerned for Ynez.

Finally Ynez came forth with, "You're making a mockery of me, Elliot Armstrong, and what I'm trying to do here with this marriage of mine! I've told you countless times not to be so mean to me! You're plain good and mean, Elliot Armstrong, 'cause you're a lousy alcoholic who's so wrapped up in himself, you could never get anyone to fall in love with you except those goddammed college boys you seduce who beat the shit out of you afterward! You're just damned good and jealous, that's all!"

"She's got something there," Nolie whispered to Johnnie.

Elliot blinked several times, took a drag on his cigarette then said, "O.k. So go on."

Then Ynez hissed in a terrible whisper, "It's because *you're* in love with my Mackie! It's because you've *always* been! Since the War! Do you truly think I'm as *dumb* as that?" Then she added, "I can say all of this now because the masseuse has gone to get a towel! But I want you to know, and Nola and the Princess, too, that I'm *not...dumb*, that is."

"But you *are*...in love with him yourself, Ynez. And the pity of it is that you can't have him—but I could! In fact, I did!"

Apparently Helga the Masseuse had come back with her towel.

"Good-*bye*, my darling!" Ynez rang off suddenly, her tone changing completely, a death's head smile enveloping her voice, certain that Helga had not heard a word and thought she was chatting with her dear, dear chum, the famous crooner.

Elliot put the receiver back on the hook. "That woman is odious."

"Well…" Nolie looked appeasingly her brother, "…I think everybody's a little jealous of this guy Joe. After all, we've had Mackus to ourselves even during his marriage to her! We all love him in one way or another. We all want the best for him. Except Ynez. She definitely wants the best for herself now that she's got him just where she wants him, and that's that."

"Two years of trying to make that dame see reason!" Elliot grumbled loudly, crossing his arms over his chest and slouching back in his chair. "She always thought everything that moved was having an affair with Mackus and the truth of the matter was, she ran him so ragged since they got hitched, I don't think he even had time enough to pull his own weenie. At least not since the War—when he had the Colonel to deal with…"

Which prompted Nolie to gaze over her teacup, most lady-like, and comment, "Why don't you just get out your megaphone and announce it all over the whole street? Can't you ever keep your voice down?"

Elliot gave her his Number Six Elliot Look: one eye opened wide, the other shut tight in an angry frown. "Ever since we had that one big hit recording all over the air waves, we haven't been able to be ourselves, Winola. We can't even rehearse up here anymore!"

"Oh! Listen to him, Johnnie!" Nolie replied, hoisting herself up on the wall around their terrace. "We haven't ever been able to be ourselves! As if we were ever able to really be ourselves! It's not such a tough trade-off, is it? Just look what we've got, Elliot. Look around you!"

Her brother shrugged, retreating further into the cushions. "Well, everything has its price, he said laughing and skipping," Elliot quipped. "Sure, it was bad enough before fame came knocking on our door, but now it's going to be im*possi*ble. In fact, I now realize that's the real reason why I've so suddenly fallen off the wagon."

Johnnie waved her hands in the air. "Oh! The excuses! The excuses!"

But the phone was ringing and so, Johnnie, in her best maid's voice, picked it up. "Armstrong rezzy-dence. Dey shoo are! An' jes' who shall I say is callin'?" She covered the receiver. "It's those magazine people! Don't you have an interview them them soon?"

Nolie took the phone away from her, a smile and lilt in her voice, "Uh-huh! Yes! Love to!" And so on, and so on. Then hung up.

"Shit!" She whispered. "They want the story of our whole marriage—our first date, our honeymoon, our love secrets! She just asked me point-blank to be ready to discuss our plans for a *family*! Oh, my God! Elliot! Think fast!"

Johnnie said: "I can just see us tryin' to rent out somebody's baby pretty soon and giving its Mama hush money! Why not? As long as the kid's white! Now listen here, you two, sometimes folks like us just get pushed so far they have to do what they have to do. Sometimes you just have to lie your way through it. Like me posin' as your maid. And Mr. D. and his whole phony life. I don't see any reason why we can't just keep kiddin' 'em along for quite sometime. Fact is, we've got to."

"Yes, but pretty soon," Nolie moped, "some way or t'other, somebody's going to find us out..."

Elliot was, at that moment, just too hung over to care and so, reaching for the telephone, he asked, in a sunny voice, "Is Mr. Daly about? It's me, Elliot, Mrs. Rozen."

Mack was there all right. A complicated conversation ensued. Johnnie and Nolie usually disregarded these every morning chats between the two best of friends, but not this time. It seems as if Mack had only just spoken to Ynez who'd told him that she was no longer speaking to Elliot (for the umpteenth time). He then filled Elliot in on the new chauffeur she'd hired, and the fact that he'd also "hired" Joe. And for what purposes...in both cases. Elliot just listened on, his eyes wide, his mouth slightly open.

"Wh-at?" Elliot finally stuttered, then limply bid Mack good-bye. As best he could, he ran Nolie and Johnnie over what had just been said. Mack had filled him in on everything, adding one more piece of news. That he and Joe were meeting with Bruno Imperio on Saturday evening to "discuss certain things."

Having thrown the earpiece down on the cushion, he bolted to his feet and began frantically digging through Nolie's plants. Nolie had already dashed inside to get three glasses, and Johnnie ran for a bowl of cracked ice. Elliot grabbed a handful of it and, putting it on his forehead, murmured: "If you wanna all hold hands and get up there on the railing with me—we can all jump together."

• • • • •

CHAPTER VI

REVERIE

"Allllexander???"

"Yyyyessssssssssssss??"

Alexander could imitate Ynez perfectly. When she wasn't around, he'd put on one of her dance frocks and flounce about, having Mr. D. rolling on the floor.

"Don't make fun of me, Alexander, I'm very nervous just now," Ynez simpered, violently throwing her shoes about everywhere from the bowels of her silk-lined closet.

"I'm not making fun of you, Mrs. D. It's only that when you're with someone as much as I'm with you—" (which seems an eternity sometimes, he was thinking to himself) "—two people like us get to sound alike."

She turned and glared at him. "For Chrissakes, I hope I don't start sounding like *you*!"

Now he was thinking, *What's wrong with the way I sound? At least I'm not trying to be something I'm not!* But he said, "Oh, no, Mrs. D., you sound just like you' from London…or someplace like that."

"I do? I hope I do. Anyway, now listen. On your way back from your class tonight, keep your eyes peeled at the train station for a Latin-looking type of man…"

Alexander looked at her, slightly bewildered.

"You know…somebody with a little…" Ynez wiggled her index finger over her upper lip. Truly, she couldn't remember if he had one or not. A mustache that is. "Or…long sideburns…or…oh, *you know*…anyway, bring him back here."

"Will he give me his name?"

"Oh, yes. It's Reynaldo di Rose."

"You aren't serious, are you?"

"Of course I'm serious. He's going to be our new chauffeur. And after you bring him here, I want you to go right to bed, Alexander."

"Well, what if I gotta stay up and do my homework? I usually do right after class 'cause it's so fresh in my mind and—"

"Alexander. Afterward, go right to bed."

"Yes, Mrs. D...." Then Alexander had a thought: "Is Mr. D. gonna be here?"

"Well, *unfortunatement*...I expect so," answered Ynez, staring at her now broken nail. Where was that manicurist? "See if you can find my other black and gold mule, please. I just broke my goddammed nail in NOT finding it."

As Ynez fairly levitated across her bedroom as if she were in search of a weeping willow to lean against, Alexander asked, "Are you gonna wear that get-up tonight?"

"You mean the ensemble I've laid out on the bed there?"

"Uh-hmmm," he replied.

"Yes. I'm...I'm going to—oh, let's say...put on the *dog* for this perspective chauffeur tonight. I...I...er...want him to be impressed with us...I'd so like him to come and *work* for us. He's very much in demand, you know." (Why was it she always had to explain everything to him?)

"S'okay by me, Mrs. D.—only I hope you wear some coverin' underneath that thing 'cause if you don't your titties is gonna show right through."

"My titties, Alexander, are my business...now find that other mule so I can throw it at you."

He did—right under the bed. Then the phone rang and he had to get into the "big car" and go fetch the manicurist at the Great Neck station.

"—pick up a *Graphic* at the newsstand, will you!" Ynez called as he left. "It should be out by now...almost four-thirty!"

Alexander figured she wanted to see what that columnist who was at the club last night wrote. IF he did write anything at all (what was his name...Walter...something?) He'd danced a couple of times with Mrs. D. then asked her all kinds of questions. Mr. D. would not be pleased if something were to show up in print because of his discretion and reserve. Yeah, that was it; those were the words he always used. But anyway, Alexander thought, driving down Merrick Road, both discretion and reserve would've had their day—after tonight.

"Woooo-eeee!" Alexander piped out loud.

Just up ahead, eating a candy bar, was Chollie Fong. Standing with his kit by his side, at the corner of the station, he waved without smiling. A rare specimen was this male manicurist. Many of the ladies passed him around after Ynez had told them how wonderful he was. Not because he was so good at what he did, but because he could be trusted—whereas female manicurists could not. Whatever you told *them* spread like leprosy. Not so with Chollie Fong, who hardly spoke any English at all, it seemed. When asked by these ladies, who now also passed him, in turn, to other ladies (thus, thanks to

Ynez, making lots and lots of money for him), "Wherever did you find him, Ynez?" she would tell them that Baby had met him in a hospital. He took care of the fingers and toes of accident victims.

Sounded good, yes?

Chollie Fong did keep mum about that, too, big fat lie that it was. For both Mrs. Daly and Madame deVol had met him two years back (although Baby did her own hands and feet) while briefly working at a highly questionable establishment whose most secret clientele included a goodly number of foot fetishists.

Sound good? No.

Chollie Fong had a Chinese sense of the Ridiculous. His laugh was as a wind chime in a monsoon, someone had said—only the monsoon never stopped. Evenso, someone who laughed at everything—deaths, divorces, botched face lifts—was easier to put up with than a gal who wholesaled all you told her over the entire five boroughs.

Today, however, Chollie Fong was not laughing. As he got into the front seat of the Pierce-Arrow, dragging his kit after him and plopping it on his lap, he complained, "What she make me come way out heall for? She better pay me double!"

"You just make believe she has four feet and four hands and charge her accordingly, Chollie. Same thing!" Alexander pulled the car up to the newsstand and unrolled the window. "*Graphic* out?"

He paid for it, handed it to Chollie, and wheeled the big machine around and back toward the Daly house.

The front cover's headline blazed the news about the big raid on the Club *Intime*. Chollie tsk-tsked, and began scrutinizing the inside stuff. The gruesome photos appealed to him. Ladies with their skirts hiked up to here being thrown into the paddy wagon, screaming, weeping; the cops leering.

Alexander looked over at the pages. "Chollie, never mind that—look for a column by a fellow named Walter Winchell..."

"Rarter Rinch-oh? O.k. I do!" He found it and slowly read it to himself. Then, suddenly: "Oh! Mrs. Daree mentioned heall!"

"Bad or good?" asked Alexander.

"Oh! Good! Velly good!" Chollie Fong laughed.

It wouldn't be worth it, Alexander figured, to have him read it aloud...he'd just have to wait for that brief trot from the garages to the servants' entrance to quickly skim it.

Meanwhile, Ynez had gotten out her Sigmund Freud. Until she'd actually heard his name pronounced out loud, she'd called him Sigmund FROOD. It was Annabelle who'd very quietly corrected her at a mah-jongg party one afternoon as Ynez was bandying his name about.

Where's that part about my nerves being all shot to hell over not getting enough sex?

Thumbing madly through the book, she finally tossed it aside and went in search of the nude study of this Latin Threat who was to have his way with her. With one of her many filmy negligees still clinging to her attenuated, boyish form, her hair not yet "up," Ynez Daly, formerly Patsy O'Reilly of Karthage, Pennsylvania, sat before her vanity mirror, propped his photograph up and was at once assailed by a vision of them both wrapped around each other in a fevered clench.

The next thing that happened was Mack walking in on them. Right there on the satin chaise, Mack standing over them, his eyes practically jumping out of their sockets. Somehow, a subtitle had even found its way into this vignette.

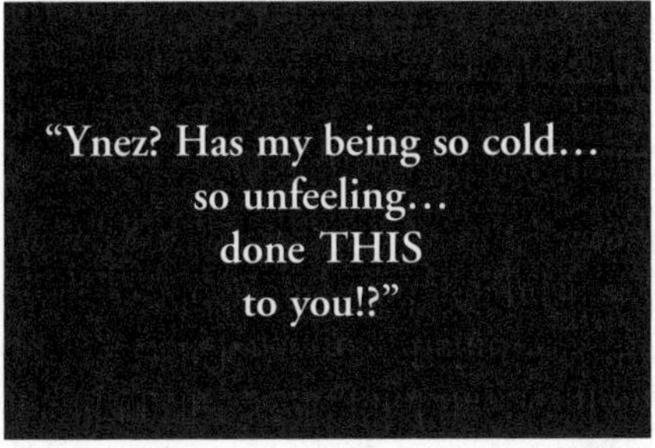

"Ynez? Has my being so cold...
so unfeeling...
done THIS
to you!?"

Twisting around, still clinging to the gigolo as if he were the lattice and she the vine, Ynez saw herself nodding slowly, with tears in her eyes. She saw her husband, her too-beautiful spouse, hands clenched into white-hot fists, turn and storm out. Then, wrenching herself free from the lounge lizard's embrace, she saw herself falling to her knees and crawling, crawling, crawling across the carpet, smoting her breast as she went.

"I wish I'd been in pictures—" she sighed half-aloud. "Gawd! I would've had 'em draped over their seats weeping."

Alas, another dream shot to Hell. "*Well...*" she murmured absently, eyeing her wonderously huge wedding ring, "...it just t'warn't meant to be..."

Looking around her Louis Quinze bedroom, Ynez told herself, in that gritty embittered interior voice which no one ever heard, that she'd gotten pretty Goddammed far, in spite of her unconsummated marriage. She was fast climbing the precarious silken ladder toward becoming a true hostess of the Long Island Set. Nobody had to know that she and her husband had never even "done it"; they seemed so in love. And this question of children. Uh-uh. Lots of professional beauties who worshipped the Uncompromising God of Chic didn't want a kiddy. That big belly sticking out—and all that puking.

"I do love him so...why, oh *why*, did I ever agree to this kind of arrangement?"

• • •

It was back to that: the marriage again. Sobs came forth; unable to look at herself, she turned away from the vanity mirror and closed her eyes. Now, in choking gushes, there it came again. Those convulsive things rising from the darkest place of all. Ynez buried her head in her hands, careening toward the chaise. She hated having this happen again. Yet, there it was...

Back in Karthage where the tracks came to an end—she couldn't ever imagine why they ended there. It always remained the most haunting of images. There she was, sitting on the broken-down steps of the shack in which she was raised. Bad enough—but to have the end of the tracks right next to that hovel!

Well, if that didn't mark one's life forever—making everything around her seem worse. And she was only a kid then! Oh, to have that grim view of life when so young! Even at that age, all she had to do was look around her at those mud entrenched streets, the dingy houses with the paint all gone grey and peeling off; the mountains of shale beyond, stretching for miles it seemed, some still on fire, creating smoke—blackest smoke. Everywhere it hung. Even the sheets upon which she'd slept were never really clean. Everywhere—the acrid odor of coal. So poor. So unsure of any shape which should've formed a child's life. A mother. A father. A home.

And those tracks. The railroad dominating the world into which she was born. Just a little girl all alone, always playing hooky, hanging around the town beauty parlor just to get the smell of toilet water as the doors swung open and shut. Wondering why she had no friends, even among the poorest of the poor kids, like herself. Going down to see the big trains coming into Karthage, stopping and letting off glamourous people stopping to eat at the hotel...never staying for long...who would want to, or need to? The tracks carried them in. Carried them off. Tracks could take you anywhere. They could get you out of there. You could wear a white fox and a hat like a turban with crimped hair and rouged cheeks. You could have porters hold your traveling case as you alighted from the softly lit parlor car. But there you were. Stuck. With nothing but these foolish dreams, right next to the big garbage strewn lot where Patsy, as she was known at that time, would dance all alone, accompanied only by the the tune of the achingly lonely whistle telling her that yet another train had come and gone, and that she was not on it. And probably never would be on it. Stuck, yes, just stuck.

Silly to dance to the whistle of the trains. Yet, for a long time that was the only music she knew—the only form of sweetness in her life.

Whoever that man was who told her, one day, she didn't need to go to school anymore and who took her away from her father—whoever he was...she never knew (to this day) whether to thank him or curse him; whether to hate him or try to convince herself of loving him. She had always thought he was her uncle. That's what he told her, anyway. But maybe he wasn't, or maybe he was. It didn't really matter, because he took over raising her after the terrible things that had happened in that grim shack by the tracks.

Her father was a miner and an awful, awful man. He'd beaten Mom almost to death. There was blood all over the kitchen and when the neighbors came and got her, Little Patsy was shaking from head to toe. Then her Mother, half-dead and hardly recognizable, was put in the hospital in Scranton and some nice Church lady took Patsy to see her. But by that time, she was pretty well gone from being hit on the head by her husband so many times; she didn't even recognize her own daughter. So Patsy decided it shouldn't have much effect on her either. And so she tried to forget ever seeing her mother like that...crazy and off her head...and dying right in front of her.

And pretty soon, she must have forgotten those unbearable encounters. More or less. They wanted to put her father right in jail. He was what they called a dipsomaniac. There was a lot of whispering about what to do with Patsy, because the Church lady said that he'd try to kill her next. So, she didn't care. Put the son of a bitch in there and let him rot for all she cared.

But then, as if he fell out of Heaven, there was this man.

He smelled of Lilac Vegetal, wore flashy rings, and sometimes applied rice powder to his smooth, slightly veined cheeks. He said he was her mother's brother and his name was Al.

He took her to a hotel in Scranton where he worked, and told her that he would never touch her the way some men would. He had a trundle bed in that room all fixed up for her and she slept there, and that little room became Patsy's home for many a year to come. Feeling safe for the first time in her whole life.

She was just over twelve and that was the end of her schooling, the end of her pa and, of course, the end of her ma. But that was just the beginning of Ynez and she came to want to know herself. The day she went away with Al was the day the creature who became Mrs. Mack Daly was really born.

But what about school? Well, he had these dime novels and he would read to her. Then he would ask her to read to him. They had their lessons everyday except on Sunday when he would take her to a fortune teller and everybody would talk to famous people on the Other Side like Beau Brummel or Sir Walter Raleigh. He would take her to the Nickel-ette and the burley-q, too. As far as he could, he would correct her grammar and even teach her some French words which could be used when one wanted to put on the dog. Like "*beaucoup*!"

Al was very, very good to Patsy, and protected her from every kind of danger. He was also—or so he said—cast on The Sea of Circumstance, and though he'd come down in the world, still maintained a great dignity, a wonderful style all his own and a notion that somewhere there were elegant people just like himself who would take him in—if ever he could hook up with them!

When the County People came to see them, trying to yank Patsy away and put her into a Home, he produced these phony papers he'd had drawn up at no small expense which somehow had appeased them. It looked like Patsy was his kid from now on!

He said, "Pal o' mine, we got to stick it as a pair, because out there, life'll get to people like you 'n' me." Out there meant anything which was not part of Al's little world—a world which Patsy was fast making her own.

Sometimes at night she heard him crying softly into his pillow and later on when she heard Mack doing that same thing, he actually caused her heart to almost break. She could feel it inside her, cracking in two. It was the first time she'd ever heard a man do such a thing; although her ma had done it all the time. Way back then. Never imagining she'd ever hear it again. But she did.

When Al was flush, they'd both go to the five-and-dime and buy cheap lace doilies, then come home and trick up their little room with them. Sometimes Al would pinch things, too. Like ribbons which he would artfully tie into her hair and then make her up like a doll. She loved looking that way, and she came to love Al more than anyone. He was just everything and then some to her.

One day she remembered very clearly asking what Al did for a living there, at the hotel. He told her with great difficulty that he was an attendant in the men's room downstairs. But he liked it that way because Patsy was never far, and he never had to go out. Out meant the outer World. Out there. Outside. Al was afraid of getting beaten up; afraid, almost, of everything…out there.

When she started getting her Monthlies, Al told her all about what it was to be a woman, and helped her with everything- his long, shiny nails scissoring up the tea towels which had been thrown away by the hotel for her rags. He told her about the mystery and romance of Love, and how, no matter what Love did to you, to make Love your friend; keep on Her good side. Oh, sure! Love would always turn on you and hurt you. But he also told her that, no matter how many times your heart was broken, you must keep on loving…because that was made life so lovely, and made people who were always in love so beautiful to look at. It was something about the notion that that a patched-up broken heart showed up on your face and made you all-the-more beautiful.

When she went out with him, oh, my dear, they both looked like some picture. Al sewed up her clothes from this and that using what he could find from the cast-offs the hotel guests had left behind. People looked at them in the street and Al would wink at her. He told her that nobody in Scranton really was sophisticated enough to understand them both, and only in the great capitals of Europe would they be appreciated for their hi-klass style.

Once, when they took in a nickel-ette and Al was buying a bag of taffy for them both, a woman whispered to her with tremendous ire, "Little girl, you need to be brought up right!"

To which Patsy said, "I am brought up right! And that man there is my father!"

Then the lady looked really and truly repulsed. But Al minced back and smiled at her, handing Patsy her candy. He was wearing a little lip rouge that day and a big rhinestone horseshoe tie pin. The woman shook her head, then said to him, "I know what type you are!" Suddenly, she spat right in his face, glared at him then turned away.

Yet Al just kept on smiling, taking out his dotted hanky and wiping his face with it. "Don't you mind that sort, darlin', they ain't cultured," he said softly to Patsy. But Patsy found herself shaking all over.

Al squeezed her hand very tightly. People were watching! He told her in a nice, soft, steady voice, "Just hold your head even higher, doll-baby, and walk right on. Come on now! Never you mind!" But behind all of this, she could see that Al was both hurt and angry. More angry than she ever thought him capable of being. She would never ever forget that awful incident.

When she was fourteen, Patsy began to realize that very, very few people knew what Al meant by "cultured." She never thought anything of the pictures he'd picked out of the trash of Sandow and John Drew, naked like Roman statues, all pinned around their little room. She loved it when Al spotted a handsome miner or railroad man and brought him to her attention. "—that's the kinda man for us, dearie," he would tell her, giving her hand a squeeze. But then, as she got older, she did come to see why people thought him so different, and herself so…so…unlucky.

Al told her the human body was a temple. He often said, "Jeez, dearie, if I'dah only been born a female!" He made her feel so beautiful and so protected, and so much a part of their fairyland life there in that hotel by the station. After having been pulled up by her hair in Karthage, well, gee, this might've been a queer kind of life, but to Al and Patsy it was like Paree.

Lying on the bed together, stringing *papier mâché* beads, Al would tell her to imagine she was at Versailles. He'd describe the big white wigs and the big gowns, then jump up and teach her do the minuet all of a sudden. They did laugh a lot together, Patsy and Al.

"I got a notion, dearie, that your gracefulness and the real lady you are turning into might be a Go!" It was time they pulled in a little more jack. And Patsy could do it, too. She wanted to work. So he told her about a fellow who was starting up kooch parlors throughout Northern Pennsylvania and Upstate New York State.

The Koochies were banned throughout the whole country, but due to their popularity in big cities, there was a terrible longing to see them, illegally, of course. And Al knew of this man who had an angle on the whole thing; he would precede the koochy girls with handbills distributed on-the-sly to backroad moonshine shacks. By word of mouth, the place would be filled with fellows liquored up and as horny as Hell, dying to see a female shake herself into a regular fit. They were so starved for this sort of thing, they would not only pay to get in, but pass a hat around to watch her go at it three or four times. Shimmy Shacks were outfitted for the event by means of a wire fence stretched between the audience and the artiste. In this way, if the fellows got out of hand, the artiste was safe...more or less, caged as she was. However, if the sheriff were nearby, then there was Hell to pay. More than a few Shimmy Gals went to the Ladies' penitentiary in Wilkes-Barre.

When the main (and only) attraction hopped from the shay, wrapped from head to toe in a horse blanket, the men at once lost their heads. By the accompaniment of a mechanical piano, a fiddler and some banging on tin wash tubs, she would shake her stuff then run like Hell back to the wagon before those wild bastards mauled her to pieces! And then, it was on to another show! Sometimes three or four a night—and Patsy just loved it.

"But you got be tough, Pat! You might hafta fight 'em off, 'cause you know they got but one thing on their minds!" Al told her with a worried wink.

Patsy told him that she fought her father off for years, and she wasn't a bit afraid. He gave her a pearl-handled little knife to wear in her garter which she came to treasure. So the deal was made. Up to their room there came this real Sport of a gent, with a wax mustache and tong-curled hair. And for the first time ever, Patsy surmised that Al was soft for this fellow. Yes, he was!

Soft for him and acting for the all world like a little lady. They set out some wine Al had mopped along with some dainty (if stale) tea cookies. Al filled the place with flowers he retrieved from a nearby funeral parlor, more dead than alive, but they did the trick! Perfuming their little room with incense, then putting on a suit that he'd borrowed from the tailor shoppe dummy downstairs, he was a regular vision. It was pure black velvet just like coal, adorned only by a floppy bow-tie and a single white paper rose at his lapel.

"But can she shake?" this gent asked Al, just as if Patsy weren't even in the room.

"Shake? I'll say she can shake! Why, who d'you think started the San Francisco earthquake!" Al replied with a kind of saucy look.

By this time, they'd acquired an Edison phonograph and so, with music provided, Patsy went into her dance. Just as Al had shown her, she wiggled her little jugs, gyrated her hips, and somehow gave the genuine effect (for one so young) of a truly hot and all-worked-up girlie.

And she was a hit. "My, my, my, my!" commented the gent.

"Now, don't you let him touch you, darlin', because he'll overtake anything that moves!" Al advised.

Patsy found the impresario repugnant. Anyway, old enough to know what was what, she surmised that Al had a very definite mash on him.

After that, she and Al toured all the backroad gin mills imaginable. He would hide out nearby until Patsy was done. It was awfully rough out there and Al was such a delicate type. Often taking the reins herself, Patsy then went two-forty when she finished her act, eager to put some clothes back on and get away from all those men. Always making sure that Al was o.k.

"I don't like fellas like them, Alberto, I like fellas like you!" Patsy told him, throwing her arms about Al.

Sometimes she just wanted to reach out so much and hug the life out of him. He was so damned good to her! But Al was never much for being pawed, and as she grew into womanhood, he actually put the kaibash on them lying together on the bed. And that made Patsy sad, but also made her love Al even deeper. At the same time, she became more reviled than ever by those men who whooped and hollered after her. Al told her that all he did was put beautiful women like herself on a pedestal and that he couldn't bring himself to topple it. Other men just kicked it out from under women. But not our Al.

In a little over a year, Patsy had done so well with her artistry that they'd been able to move to a little bungalow near Carbondale. But, by that time Al was sick. He coughed up blood and acted valiant even though he was so weak.

Running from the sheriffs nearly every night had made him see that life was much, much more brutally hard than he'd ever wanted it to be. But what Patsy thought really took him down in the end was the fact that the impresario was mean to him. She'd hear him telling Al that he was not the type he liked. Too much like a woman, and why couldn't he be a man! Al would coo, "But *you're* the man, Earle!"

The impresario was nothing more than a money-grubbing bastard. The night Al died, she went over to the rooming house where he was staying and stole his cigar box full of wads of money. He didn't even know it, asleep there in the arms of a handsome miner whom he paid with a watch fob made from Hindu Idol's eye (or so he said). And Al, the poor dear little scout, lay dead in the bathtub back at the bungalow.

She'd always imagined he'd killed himself somehow because there was Al, bled to death in the bath water. But he was always coughing up blood by that time, so maybe he didn't. She never liked to think of Al as having even thought about the taking of his own life. He was so sweet to her. And how could anybody who caused her to dream of the court of Versailles ever commit suicide? she asked God.

And so, one day, not long after Al was put to rest in the proverbial pine box, she actually did board that train out of Scranton with hot tears of rage in her eyes, looking out the dusty window as it pulled away from the station.

"I will never, ever come back here again, by Jesus!" was Patsy O'Reilly's prayer. And since that time, she did not. Nor could she ever even bear to think of it.

Until Mack came along, the only type of man she could ever get close to was a real swish. They were kind and sweet and didn't touch her. But that, she admitted to herself with a shrug, was what really was wrong with her. She just loved fairies.

Mack Daly was not like any man she'd ever met. He had refinement in spades. He was as funny as Hell and he acted like he was all man!

But from the very first, when he would only kiss her on the cheek, he told her the God's honest truth about everything. That's how she learned that the truth, once again, hurt like Hell. And that's how she learned to hate the truth.

"I don't want to hear it, Mack," Patsy, now called Ynez, would whine coquettishly.

"I don't mean to shock you, Ynez, but the whole reason Baby deVol arranged that we meet was to get us both out of the fixes we're in," Mack, sitting so close to her that their shoulders touched, was whispering, his eyebrows bending upward as they did when he touched upon offending or hurting anyone.

"Oh, you could never shock me, Mr. Daly!" Ynez then replied, laughing, hoping to successfully make him just like her—if he only could. They were at a concert of Victor Herbert's music. Never, ever, ever had she seen such elegance! And this gentleman who'd asked her so marvelously—would she mind sitting through it?—oh! he was really taking her breath away, and she said so!

He spoke so softly in her ear, as if an urgency existed: "This may just be all wrong...I'm sorry, but I don't feel terribly comfortable receiving compliments at all from you, although I do appreciate them, of course—well, it seems—awkward somehow...you have to listen to me now. Here it is: I am a queer fellow. I care only for my own sex."

They looked at each other. So close they could've kissed. "I know...but it seems—so—perfect. At least—to me."

Then, finally—intermission. Everytime his knee touched hers, he would pull away. During particularly beautiful passages he would smile at her. It was just killing her. When a march was played, he tapped his feet.

Oh. God. She loved him so. Right then and there.

They rose and he, taking her by the arm, led her out into a far corner of the lobby. "We've seen each other four times exactly now," he was saying. She couldn't stop staring up at him. Home from the War. A real hero! His face tanned by that most perfect month of June. His eyes so much the color of topaze—so soft and so decent! The line of his nose—straight and noble. His lips, full and almost too sensual really…yet speaking volumes of the lover he could be! If only…he could be! The dimpled chin…

"Ynez? Are you following me on this now?"

"I know it makes you nervous when I stare…but I can't help it. How could you possibly be a Jew?"

"Oh, that's beside the point. Well, no it isn't, either, because I couldn't marry a *shiksa* anyway! My family would never have it."

Ynez laughed into the corsage he had bought her. So perfect! Such a lovely gesture! "But we are supposed to get married, aren't we? You said we were."

"Yes, I was thinking of it, I guess, as if it were a real marriage, I mean without the substance behind it. You see what I mean, don't you?" He broke into a big smile. Oh! His smile! Those teeth!

Ynez murmured, "Yes. It's all to be a masquerade. And I know it has to be, because of all you've told me…but…oh, why choose ME?"

"Look. I know, my dear, how much of a perverse thing this must be to you, but if you want everything I can give you…except that one thing…then it ought to work. Baby deVol told me that you wouldn't mind if she related your whole background to me. She told me all about you. Poor kid…but, you see, you're of a certain type, my dear. A woman who really understands and appreciates…well…pansies. You are that type of gal…aren't you?"

Ynez had to laugh again. Oh, the pain of this love into which she was being hurled! "I guess I am. But…it's awfully hard for me to believe that you are…a…pansy…"

The gong was softly sounding. They walked back into the theater and this time, he did not allow her to take his arm, but pensively thrust his hands into his pockets. It seemed as if she had heard him just then reply (as if to himself), "*Well, I am…*" or something like that.

Hardly audible, looking sidelong at him, she whispered, "But I am falling in love with you, Mack Daly, and that's all there is to it."

He shook his head as she looked at him. He was gazing straight ahead. But the profile was quite enough.

After the concert, they walked through Central Park. She had gotten Mack Daly to a point where he really no longer knew what to say.

"Baby introduced us because she believed that, sure, I was that kind of girl—who liked only pretty men, who never enjoyed being made love to because...because of what I'd been through...because I was—all of that. She thought it would be a perfect opportunity to get myself a nice life—finally."

Mack sighed, saying nothing. She sighed, too. "And it's all been presented to me on a silver platter and I really never expected it to hit me like this."

"Of course you didn't..." He went right on talking. " But you're going to be all right. Just give it a chance. Of course, the main thing that Baby did stress was—you could be discreet. Now hold on! Let me make this a bit easier for you if I can, Ynez. It's awfully hard to be discreet when you think you're in love with someone. At least I would think so."

"Have you ever been in love with someone?"

"Well...yes, I have...but what's that got to do with it?"

"Nothing. Only...it was another man, I suppose, wasn't it?"

"Of course it was, Ynez, I've told you so many times now—"

"Who was he?"

"Oh, for God's sake, Ynez, what does it matter?"

"Well...it doesn't, only that...have you had a lot of lovers?"

"No. Not since...the War..." Mack stopped walking. This was becoming agonizing! "I realize if we're to go into this thing, we should feel completely open with one another, but it's very difficult to speak of such things to...a lady I don't know very well...or even, for that matter, to a lady I do know very well, come to think of it."

They both laughed. Mack said, "Oh, Hell..." and went on walking. "You'll get over this emotional stuff pretty soon. Then you'll have mostly everything you've ever wanted."

Now it was Ynez's turn to stop, doing so right under a street lamp. The effect was sublime. "Look, Mr. Daly, it's a sort of mail-order bride scenario, isn't it? I met you because your friend Baby said I was perfect for the job...those were her exact words in fact. I came from a terrible existence, I crawled up and into a very peculiar job, I didn't lie about what I was...Madame and Mr. deVol trusted me—over time—to tell me the fix you were in. We met and you spilled your guts out to me. But I never spilled my guts out to you. Did I?"

"No. No, in fact, you didn't. Not 'til now. And I'm sorry if I've been so selfish about this whole thing." Mack told her kindly. He was so attractive when befuddled! People were watching.

"The few times we've met and talked have been just so...heavenly for me! Well," she added, noticing the moon just over his left shoulder, "—you made every meeting not only like a business conference—but like a date as well! No wonder I'm feeling romantic!"

"Well, that's how it's got to be! I mean…like a business conference! We don't want anyone to know what's really going on here!"

He was looking down, right into her eyes, as if he were talking to a little child. And his voice…so very tender. She could hardly keep from nuzzling up to him. And she needed to, so desperately. To simply be held, in tenderness.

"But you took me dancing at the Ritz, you took me to see the Scandals, you took me to the beach, and now you've taken me for this lovely night out…a concert, a walk in the park. Well just tell me something; here I am with the most gorgeous man I've ever met in life…and…" Now she started to whimper a little. "…He's been so Goddammed kind to me, Goddamm him! Well, what am I supposed to be feeling? How in hell am I *supposed* to act?"

Mack didn't know what to do or say. Turning her back on him, Ynez lifted her face up toward the moon, allowing the light of it to etch a veritable cameo of poignance against the drape of night.

"This won't work, it just won't work," Mack said finally. They walked onward and up to 68th Street not speaking at all for blocks and blocks.

At length Ynez commented: "If you'd only hurt me, I could fall out of love with you…"

"Hurt you? Why would I want to hurt you?" (She shrugged.) He was baffled by all of this."I can't really understand you, I'm afraid. You have a way of acting as if you're being put in a corner, and I think you've got a gift for putting everyone else in that corner instead."

"I know. It's because of Al and the way I've had to get by. You probably will never understand what—what it was like…Well…here we are. *La Maison*! My place of business where I also hang my hat! Thank you, Mr. Daly, for yet another gracious evening." She gave a quick jerk to her head and began to ascend the stairs, waif-like, as Mary Pickford might've done.

Mack, stupefied at her candor and her innate ability of manipulation, looked up at her and said with some difficulty, "We'll talk about this again…perhaps tomorrow if you're up to it."

She turned and offered him a strange smile. Vaguely sinister. Then, turning the key in the door, let herself in and was gone.

Mack looked up at the building. It certainly was a peculiar job she had all right, and a peculiar place to have both Baby and Deucie working! And yet, Ynez certainly was a peculiar kind of a girl! Of course, she would have to be, he reasoned, to go in for something like…like…a marriage of convenience.

• • •

But they did marry. And it *was* that kind of marriage, but by the look of the wedding ceremony itself, you never would've guessed. Not Jewish, or anything at all really, except a Hollywood short subject kind of affair. Ynez in clouds of tulle with a Louiseboulanger wedding gown and cala lillies. And of course there was that ring. Big as a boulder. And Mack, the perfect groom...Everybody bought the whole show outright. Everybody except Elliot (best man), Nolie, Deucie and Baby (maid of honor), of course.

Mack's former C.O., Colonel Connaught, and his daughter Violet, who were also in attendance, seemed to fall under the spell of the storybook quality the ceremony possessed. "May this absolve you of all your sins, my lad!" the Colonel had whispered in Mack's ear during the toast.

Afterward, when he took her to Europe on their honeymoon, there were separate beds all the way. Ynez immediately insisted on pursuing discussions about that particular subject which upon which Mack was adamant—these, evolving almost into shouting matches! They did not have fun.

Elliot finally took him aside and asked him why in Hell he'd wanted to get married at all? Mack very patiently explained for the hundredth time, while calming Elliot down, that to be wed—and to be a government official—went hand in hand. Nolie said it was too bad he couldn't find a lezzie to agree to it. That might've been fine, but Mack wanted a show piece, a diadem on the crown of his new success. *Well, he got one.* All of Mack's inner circle were in agreement on two points regarding Ynez, however: one—she was a truly great beauty and they did make a really breathtaking pair; and two—she was completely, and pathetically, nuts.

Ynez, who had claimed Baby as her confidante, was able to enumerate all she loved and hated about her husband, specifying that what she loved about him, she could also hate. It wasn't his proclivities, as she came to call them, because those were never even slightly obvious, and he never even acted on them. He never gave himself away as a homosexual. Nor was it his relationship to his Jewish family (or absence of them); or his pursuit of this newly invented life of his. It wasn't his increasingly growing fortune, or his incredible big-heartedness. It wasn't his constant attempt to act like an American, when, in fact, he couldn't really act very American at all. It wasn't any of that stuff which both broke and put-back-together that heart of hers. What Ynez fully realized, having known him and adored him for this short time,was that Mack Daly possessed a strange power over people—and one of which he was unaware. Everyone found themselves falling in love with him.

And this could be both good and bad. Because it could get you into a lot of trouble. You would find yourself doing just about anything for him.

Baby agreed. "He's an instrument of Fate. Once you know him, you become part of that Fate," Baby said with her eyes closed, as if in a trance. "—and you don't want it any other way."

Thus, the newly married Mrs. Mack Daly never could stop loving him! In fact, she came to love him *more* and therein, as a Pagan high priestess might, imprisoned herself within the holy ring of fire as a self-sacrifice, forever.

Knowing he could treat her as the other half of his comedy team…as his pupil when it came to which fork to use; how to speak properly; what literature to read. And of course, she grew more and more beautiful as all of it began to hurt…more and more. Just as Al said she would.

She found she could tell Mack anything (and she did). But she could not treat him in a terribly familiar way. There were miles between them, really. She put up with it. She tried to jump in bed with him, jump in the bath with him, jump into some sharing of what he secretly hungered for in men…intimacies. But never would he permit her to cross that line. And he always, always moved his knee away whenever they sat together.

"Tell me, Mackie dear, what kind of man you're attracted to…" This, when they were walking on the beach together, having both been thrilled about the house just behind them, which Mack was in the process of buying.

"Well…I know I've never met him! I can tell you that much."

"…and do you think you ever shall?"

A silence, then, "I certainly hope so. I've always had this idea in mind that goes way, way back to when I was kid. We lived across from Riverside Park. See, I was always kept apart from other boys—I told you how my poor Mother isolated herself from everything. But sometimes I'd sneak across the way to the park and notice these boys who were part of a gang. They were ill-bred, reckless and free, Ynez, free—with each other. They'd meet and talk very rough—and then strip off their clothes and swim in the river—fighting with each other…touching each other. Not even caring. I'd hide underneath the bridge there and watch them the whole day long. I loved them so…I'd go back to Muzzie, all alone—feeling so apart from everything…from other boys, from being an American…from being able to have a chance…at life!"

Ynez watched him, fascinated. His eyes were riveted to the tide as it gently came in. She felt almost a reverence about it all—just at that moment, for here was a memory he had kept stored within him, that had driven him to find his own idea of what love might be.

"…then when the War came and I joined up, I wondered what in Hell I was, I mean—liking my own kind as I did—" This next part was becoming difficult. She was right there with him. "But I got chosen for this special regiment by a man who really changed my life. He told us we were of the same Faith. So…so it became easy for me to accept what was in me, and to be…unified and free—at least there, for a time. It's easier to fight when you're loved by the men around you, and you love them in return."

"But isn't the fighting over, Mack?" Ynez reached out to touch his bronzed hand. He gently drew it away—very gently. Slowly. Never looking her way.

"No…oh, Ynez…it won't ever be over until I find a man, that's all—and not a woman—ever. That's really all there is to it." Mack now turned at looked at their house, a big, wide, serene, ritzy villa. "Isn't it a grand place though?"

It really was. She said delicately, "I only hope it can be a home as well as a house."

Now he turned and smiled at her. It was times like these that she loved him most because so much kindness was in those beautiful golden eyes.

He said to her, in that way of his, "You'll make it a home. You can…because you've never had one. Not really. There it is. You can do whatever you like with it."

Suddenly she felt herself becoming horribly angry. She controlled this (as she could then during those first months) and told him, "But I think of a home as a place of love. That's what makes it a home, Mack, doesn't it? Just…love?"

"Well, I guess that's one way of looking at it. I think of a home as a citadel…closed off from prying eyes!" He then flashed her that smile of his. "I'd like to have a gymnasium in the basement, and a cache hidden somewhere for the Long Island crowd, and a nice library. Anything else you want to do with it is fine with me." Mack paused, then added, "Oh…and roses. Lots of roses…all right with you?" Mack's whole demanor had changed. His eyes shone as he looked toward their house.

Ynez just watched, saying to herself, "Yes. Yes. Of course. All right with me…I've got to be so grateful for all of this. And I am. I really am. Only that—"

He asked her, "What do *you* want to do with it? You know, the sky's the limit!" Still looking toward the house, and not at her.

She could not answer. Not at first. "Could we fill it with love—anyway—somehow?"

He now turned to her. "You could get yourself someone nice and have him over. I could, too…maybe…"

But it was Ynez now who turned away from him, knowing she would never reach that place in his heart, his soul, for which she searched. She would have to go and find—elsewhere—a normal man…yet, someone who possessed everything Mack possessed. Reasoning this out, she then hit upon a tortuous probability—that no one else existed like Mack. Swallowing that, she became, during that first year of their marriage, implacable.

She found an aching satisfaction in fitting herself into the mold which Mrs. Mack Daly had to fit. Apart from Mack's instructions, he was always polite, his voice soft and patient—she thought he might leave her clues hinting at what she ought to do to make him happy.

But to Mack, such things weren't important. And so she began to stitch up this intricate dream—a tapestry of the imaginary life they had together. Yet, every now and then she would prick her finger on her needle and awaken—bleeding. Sobbing.

• • •

Sometime after that first year had passed, Ynez said to Baby deVol, "I was a pretty cheap article, wasn't I?…" (Being cleverly self-deprecating.) "…But I thought to myself, there he is…my husband…he goes by another name, he buries his past, his heritage, his true job—I mean, let's face it, Baby, he's a bootlegger just like all the rest of them…the most high-class bootlegger in this country—"

Baby hushed her. "—*Ynez*!"

"Now you just hear me out, Madame deVol," she continued, holding up an elegant hand. "And he's just one of the boys—like Elliot and the rest from the old regiment. Same perversities…all covered up…those unquenchable urges. Yes, yes, let's call them that! But what lacquer! Thick as mud!"

"Call the boys what you like, but don't you ever forget that you went into this arrangement with your eyes wide open!" Baby could be a little too sure of her own backporch candor sometimes. Ynez felt it was something you just had to put up with if you liked her.

"I know. I know…but the point I'm making is: to Hell with everything, Baby, old girl! To Hell with everything! I'm just a front and why not? I've always hated what I was anyway. And, if I can't have him, I'll just kill myself, that's all!" Ynez let go an artificial laugh, brittle and hinting of some great interior tragedy. She had recently developed this affectation with a throaty voice and a broadening of her "a"s. She waited for its effect.

Baby, however, had a way of rearing up, mid-Victorian school-marm fashion, taking no gaff from anyone. "Mackus hasn't put any limits on you. He's never pulled the wool over your eyes, and he makes sure you live like a queen. You can have lovers, if you'd only get some sense. God knows, other married women do!"

"I can't bring myself to take on a lover…or even a trick, for that matter—because—"

Baby finished the sentence for her. "—because you're so obsessed with HIM. And you're just plain angry, Ynez. You're as angry as any woman can get who can't have what she desires." Ynez started to open her mouth and attempt something, but Baby barreled right on, "I just think Mack made a big mistake in marrying you, Ynez."

As Ynez took the pose of an insulted grand duchess, Baby finished, "Yes, and you can go take a good shit for yourself!"

All of this was taking place on what Ynez had come to call the piazza of the Great Neck house. Just beyond, Mack, Deucie and Alexander were constructing a secret entrance to the cellar underneath their boat house. Mack had especially liked the property because it had this subterranean chamber in a place where no one would ever have thought to look for that special cache of booze for Gold Coast galas.

"Who's up there?" Deucie called from below.

"It's Ynez…come to see what you boys are doing…" Gathering the wide hems of her beach pyjamas about her, she was venturing down the steps.

"Are you all right?" Mack asked. "You look as if you might spit nails…"

"I'm fine. Just fine. It's only that sometimes Baby acts so damned important that I have to get away from her…can I help out any way down here?"

"Sure!" Mack replied; really, he seemed happy that she had offered and had come visiting. "Now, let's see…hold up that light for Alexander—yes, right there beside you…"

Ynez did as she was told. With little comment, the three men worked and noticed her strange expression, wondering if she might burst into tears at any moment.

"Have any of you ever been down a mine?" she asked in a haunted voice.

"Some of the trenches were dug deep like that," Deucie told her. "Does this place remind you of a mine back in Pennsylvania?"

Ynez nodded rapidly, biting her lip. Then, putting the light down on one of the steps, she left abruptly.

Upstairs Mack found her crying hard, unable to catch her breath.

"Oh, hold me! Hold me please, Mack!"

He took her in his arms, telling her, his mouth close to her ear, "I know what it's like. I've got my nightmares, too, my dear!"

"Mack, I hear you. I hear you, all the time."

He pulled her body back from his, staring wide-eyed at her. "You have? I'm so…I'm so sorry…what can I do to help you? I never meant for you to bear witness to those secrets, you poor darling…"

"Secrets?" Ynez shoved him away. A firm desperate action, her eyes never leaving his. On her way back to the house, stumbling along in the sand, she said something…something he could not understand. He called after her, but she went on.

He never figured out what it was she had said, but he knew it was meant not only for himself, but for God as well. And probably for Al, too, wherever in Hell he might be.

• • • • •

CHAPTER VII

THE NIGHT AFTER THE MORNING AFTER

"I wanted to get you in on how this whole operation works, so you can see what I'm up against," Mack was telling Joe as they drove once more out to Great Neck. "What goes on behind the scenes is something most folks just don't understand, I would say."

He let Joe drive and noticed, as they sped along, what an intent listener he was. Throughout the day, Joe had been right on his toes.

"I want yuz tuh know, I ain't gonna peddle dis show-and-tell stuff anywheres," he told Mack, glancing over at him.

"I trust you, Joe."

"Wow dee dow. Along wid 'I loves you,' that's the foyst time anybody ever said that to me! Jeez, I'm proud! Ain't it a shame I can't show yuz off!"

"Well, if we're perfetly discreet, we could get out and go places together. I know a swell queer roadhouse up in White Plains."

"Say! Why do we hafta go way up dere?"

"You have to consider that nite club crowd. Now that I'm out and about, there's always a chance I might be seen. I'll tell you what, someday we'll go up there. How about it? My friend Bootsie Carstairs runs it and he'll just faint dead away when he gets a load of you. It'll be fun—oh...Slow down a bit, Joe, there's a cop following us—" Sure enough, it was so, for the roar of a motorcycle just behind them brought Joe to a halt.

At this, it seemed to Mack as if Joe had turned ashen and actually got a slight case of the shakes.

"Goin' lickety-split you were...oh! It's you, Mr. Daly!" The policeman bent low, pleasantly surprised to see Mack in the passenger seat. "I thought I recognized your machine, for nobody else has one quite like it. Purple as she is!"

"Aw, Mike, we both must apologize. We got to talking business and before you know it, my assistant's foot got a little heavy. This is Lieutenant Reardon, Joseph...Mike, meet my new assistant Joe...um...Joe...Smith."

Without turning, Joe nodded, cracking a fake smile.

"Go on with you both! I'll say I just was lookin' the other way!"

Mack and Mike Reardon laughed over this one. "Yes and I will, too, Mike! Say, how're you fixed?"

"Well, the truth is we got an anniversary comin' up, Mr. Daly. It's our 10th, if you can believe it."

"Aw, congratulations, Mike. I'll send a case around."

"Oh, and you are surely in both our prayers, Mr. Daly, and your dear and beautiful wife, too!" Joe was frozen in his seat and now beads of sweat were forming on his brow. Would this banter never end?

Mack saluted him, thanked him and, thinking it was over, poked Joe hard to start the engine again. But there was more to come…

"—and did you see the papers today by chance?" No, Mack had been so busy he hadn't. "Well, well, well! There's a new District Head of the Prohibition Bureau in New York, you know—shoor, and it's Brian O'Couran himself."

Mack stared intently at Mike's expression. "Oh, yes. I never got to know him, but I've seen him at meetings, of course. A Tammany fellow."

"Mr. Daly, I don't know him neither, but I do know them type of Irish are all ambitious. My Lord, the way he climbed so far so fast and all with the help of his lads! Worse than Eye-talians they are!" Mike gave a wink and started up his motorcycle. "There's a certain type of Irishman that's worse than any Yiddle you'll ever meet as well! And that's O'Couran all right!" Off roared the policeman.

Mack laughed. "Say, he just about covered everything, didn't he?"

"Whew," sighed Joe. "Thanks for helpin' me outa dat one, kiddo!" Joe fell into Mack's arms. "Holy shit! Maybe you'd better drive."

"Sure. Just slide over, don't get out." Mack opened his door, rounded the front of his car and got in, laughing quietly to himself. Joe, mopping his brow with his handkerchief, asked him what was so funny.

"—I guess he's thinks I'm Irish! One thing is damned sure, he doesn't take me for a Jew!" They peeled out and onto the road.

"Are you in that good with the all coppers?"

"Just out here and by the canal. Are you in that bad with 'em, Joey?" Mack smiled.

"Just back dere—" He yanked his thumb behind them, toward the City. "But it don't matter, any one of 'em can smell my kind a mile off. All I hafta do is be within twenty feet of a copper and my blood freezes."

"Not to worry, Joey, as long as we stick, you'll be fine!"

Joey suddenly threw his arms around Mack. "Aw, gimme a kiss! Gimmee a kiss! Jeez I'm lucky!"

As the sun set, the Marmon roadster approached the so-called Villa Hotsy-Totsy. Just behind them, the "big car," with Alexander at the wheel, purred up the drive.

"Mr. D. and Mr. Imperio!" Alexander greeted them as he hopped out. "It shoo is good to see you both! What a day I've had!"

Mack and Joe followed him around to the servants' entrance, Alexander detailing what Ynez had put him through the entire day, and how he had to take the Chinese chiropodist back to the train, then fetched all the remaining copies of the *Evening Graphic* so Mrs. D. could scissor out the plaudits she'd received therein.

"You know she's interviewin' that new chauffeur tonight an's all astir cause the yangyang messed up on her toenails!"

They'd arrived in the kitchen. Mack opened the refrigerator and brought forth three bottles of soft drink.

"I know. And believe me, we'll make ourselves scarce, Alexander…all three of us! You need a nap, and Joe and I are going downstairs."

Then, from far off: "Mackus! Mackus, just wait 'til you see what Winchell—" Ynez's echo-ey tones told them that she was headed toward the kitchen.

"Should I hide?" Joe asked.

Throwing the swinging door open, and hitting Joe on the head, she was there before them, all clouds of perfume and delicate black lace, holding the *Evening Graphic* in her hand as if about to swat a fly.

"Look!" she sang out.

Joe and Mack did as instructed, but Ynez, who had memorized the blurb by now, quoted it to them:

"'*—last night's opening of the Club deVol which was ultra private and ultra swank and just-too-too, my deah, was also this darb's introduction to a New Kind of Animal among the Whoopee Crowd. Ynez Daly, other half of one of the angels of this new watering hole (who dances beautifully, by the by) is one of those new Synthetic types. And, although she was (Synthetic, that is), the gin sure wasn't—best in town, I swannee!*'

"'*Ynez told me she was born during a total eclipse in her parents' castle during a storm at the stroke of midnight on the rocky shores of Monaco. Seems as if Mater and Pater were both royalty from one of those hangnail-sized nations in Eastern Europe somewhere. She does charity work for war orphinks (who doesn't?), presides over endless fetes from her Long Island manse (who doesn't?) and has been asked by the moovies time and time and time again to star. OF COURSE, she refuses. Well, kids, welcome to the world of those who be legends in their own minds! Seems like nowadays, their name is legion! Oh, boy!*'"

As Mack fell into a nearby kitchen chair, she added, "Well, fellas, looks like ol'Nezzie has made the papers!"

It took them all a minute to recover. Mack was the first one to comment, with only, "I'll say you did!"

Then, after Ynez waited for some congratulations, wondering why they were all staring at their shoes, Mack said, "Ynez, that's just awful! Don't you realize he's roasted you? And, my God! Ynez, what he implied about the liquor we served…why, any fool could trace that dig right to ME!"

"Yeah? How do you figure that?" she asked, taking umbrage.

"Because I'm *Mister* Ynez Daly, that's how! Whoever let that guy in is gonna hear it from me!" A pause. "—say! This could get me into a lot of hot water!"

"Oh, you always spoil all my fun. I imagine Deucie and Baby are thrilled by this free plug because it'll bring in just droves of people!"

"Yeah," Mack returned, somewhere between a scorn and a moan, "the wrong kind of people!"

"The wrong kind of people? My friends who came are all in the social register, I'll have you know…not on the WANTED list, like your boyfriend here!"

Alexander tiptoed out.

"I ain't wanted for nothing! Nobody wants me!" Joe returned.

"You can say that again!" Ynez spat.

"*I* want Joe! I want him more than I want my next breath, Ynez! I love him! Don't drag Joey into this! The fact is, this is very serious stuff here! If that booze gets traced to me, I'm the one who's gonna be on the Wanted list!"

Ynez flounced out, throwing the tabloid in his face, leaving the kitchen door swinging and Mack breathing hard. There lay the newspaper on the kitchen floor, and within its pages the photograph of Ramon di Rose in the Altogether which Ynez had so cleverly lifted.

Alexander appeared from the pantry. "Madame deVol's been calling for the last couple of hours, Mr. D., and Mrs. D. refused to talk to her…"

"No doubt about this smear here…" Mack kicked the tabloid with the toe of his shoe, failing to notice the photograph. "God, I'm sorry about all of this, Joe. Let's go down and beat the hell out of the punching bag."

Descending into the gymnasium, Mack told Alexander, "If Baby calls again, let me speak to her. I don't want to phone her and upset her. We'll just make light of it…hah!"

Picking up the *Graphic* and Ramon di Rose's picture as well, Alexander hid them both behind the bread-box before running upstairs again in answer to Mrs. D.'s shrill cry.

• • •

At nine-ten that same evening evening, Alexander Parker wearily threw himself into the Pierce-Arrow to fetch Ramon di Rose at the Great Neck station. It seemed incredible to him that so very much had happened in such a short time and he wasn't sure he felt comfortable with it all. The opening last night was a great success and everybody was thrilled...but along came this Italian dream-boat, and then, on his heels, Mrs. D.'s...*new friend*...no, not really that...what was he? Everything was just so suddenly different, Alexander couldn't help but feel that the best and the worst were yet to come...all connecting somehow to one another—like some truly scary set of Siamese twins.

In the short time that had elapsed, Mack stayed firmly sequestered below, delighting Joe with his Pilates machines, sun lamps...and, of course, his steam room. Alexander had put a typically Mack-style supper on the dumbwaiter and sent it down. Finally, Mack seemed relaxed. Now, stretched out against the leather padding around the boxing ring, with Joe in his arms, both wrapped in white terry cloth robes, he closed his eyes. So did Joe.

"I tol' Bruno I was stayin' the night...it's still o.k., ain't it...I mean, after what happened?"

"Swell. Ssshhhh. Yes. Yes. Yes," Mack whispered. Joe looked up. Mack was smiling.

Upstairs, Ynez phoned Annabelle Harrison at her studio. Before her Big Moment was to arrive, she wanted to let Belle know—all lay in readiness. It was funny, too, come to think of it, that Annabelle hadn't phoned *her* about Winchell's spread!

"I would never even line my cockteil's cage with a rag like that!" Annabelle began, not mincing words. "My dear, that was a mean little essay if I've ever read one. Millicent Maiteland got hold of it from her upstairs maid and read it to me over the telephone only about an hour ago, and I didn't ring you up simply because I've been sitting here with clay all over my hands in something like apoplectic shock! What a perfectly hideous little man *he* turned out to be! I really think Mack should demand an apology in your honor, 'Nez. But, The Power of the Press, my dear...! Oh well, he did say you were a good dancer, which is more than I can say for myself—stepping all over that Italian god's feet as I did...by the way, what's doing there?"

Ynez told her that the boys were chasing each other around downstairs.

Annabelle attempted some cheer: "Well, my pet, in just a matter of time, you'll be chasing someone else around UPstairs!"

Ynez was troubled over Mack's words. "But you don't think what Winchell said will hurt Mack directly, do you?"

"...wellll..." At that, she said she had to go...something about her clay drying up.

Ynez pondered her toes. Chollie Fong's usually steady hand made a mess out of at least three of her tootsies. He didn't really seem to like the pedicure part of today's ritual, she was thinking when she heard Alexander returning with Ramon di Rose. Hastily spraying the room with perfume, she dashed to her chaise and thereupon ensconced herself, lighting a cigarette.

Down in the gymnasium, Mack and Joe also heard the return of Alexander bearing his burden of passion.

"Whaz'at?" Joe asked apprehensively.

"Now, calm down, Joe. It's just Alexander. He went down to pick up Ynez's gigolo friend—see for yourself!"

Mack pointed to the high windows along the opposite wall, covered with Venetian blinds.

"Gotta watch our backs, dat's all, Mack!" Attaining a look-see by standing on the nearby bench, Joe opened two of the blinds and squinted through.

Outside, lit by the large lamps at either side of the portico, Joe saw two figures passing by, obscured by the shrubbery.

"I see Alexander o.k…an' dee udder guy…"

"Typical snake hips type, isn't he?" Mack said from below. "Ynez showed me his photograph."

Joe jumped down, looking puzzled. "Dat about describles it…but, I can't say for sure—I t'ink I might know that mug…"

Mack sat up. "You have the funniest tone to your voice—"

"Yeah. Well, if he's duh same prick I think he is, he sure ain't worth knowin', and he sure as Hell ain't no gigolo."

Just then, Alexander was escorting this person in. "She's up at the top of the stairs, take a left and it's the second door to your left…" Ynez heard Alexander saying, as she was applying her lip rouge for the seventh time that day. She also heard Ramon's slithery voice, low and terribly sexual.

"Right then left then right again?"

"*No…*" patiently Alexander had to tell him all over again.

She then heard him—rustling around just outsdie her door. Cat-like. A pause! Where did he go? Lost.

"Now go left," Alexander was telling him from below. "Oh, just look for the door with the light under it, will you!"

What seemed like an eternity was passing. Then…a soft series of knocks.

"*Entray-vous*!"

The door opened and there he stood, with a bouquet of very wilted daffodils. "*Caro mio*!" he breathed, his white teeth shining like piano keys over a thin pencil-line mustache.

The rose-tinted lights were sufficiently dim so that he looked more dazzlingly swarthy than his photograph revealed…more divinely, dangerously handsome than when she had first met him.

Placing his beret on the delicate end table, he dropped the bouquet into a vase nearby, peeled off his yellow kidskin gloves, deposited them in a ball inside his beret, then knelt before her.

His attire was subtle (a navy blue suit) but obviously cut to reveal his form. There was something, thought Ynez, so mercilessly *erotique* about this man. She found herself hoping, and she didn't know why, that he would not frighten her.

"Would you care for something to drink?" she asked him.

Looking at her in that sexy way, which was suddenly so unsettling, he seemed galvanized by a sudden rush of sex-energy through his whole body.

"I *said*—would you—?"

"—ah! Plizz. Ten t'ousand pardons. It is chust that I am transported by your beauty. But, jhess, what hab you got?"

"A little…absinthe?" Ynez replied. Somebody had asked Mack to hold gallons of it for him and so they had a lot of absinthe. Ramon di Rose nodded, creating on his lips a smile that spoke of unthinkable sins. Ynez rose to fetch some from her own personal cellarette; he followed by barely an inch, now and then bringing his nose close to her neck and shoulders, then drawing it back.

"Oh! That tickles…" she commented. Then pouring the libation into a pair of exquisite little glasses, she proposed a toast; "Here's to us, Signor di Rose! Two vibrating souls beckoned by the eternal animal urge!"

He put his glass to her lips, and her glass to his, switching arms. She had seen that in some movie, too. But did it matter? Sipping, looking at him, she at once was overcome by a delicious shudder.

"What is it, *Caro mio*?"

"It's the sheer *energy* you are transmitting! You must think of nothing but *sex* the whole day long—"

"*Si*, and the whole nigh' long, tew!" He gave forth an unwholesome laugh as she went back to her chaise and, in attempting to seat herself odalisque-fashion, spilled the little drink all down her front.

"Oh, no! no! do not touch it! Plizz, plizz allow me…" Bending forward, he proceeded to lick it off with his tongue, making his way past her lace-trimmed *décolleté* to her breasts. Having arrived, Ramon di Rose became at once enflamed, proceeding toward her nipples.

"Leetle soldiers! Standing at attention! How prrrrrecious!" His mouth leapt from one to the other. Ynez caressed the back of his brillianteened head as he tore the straps away from her shoulders, ripping her velvet camellias entirely off.

"Now see what you've done!" she breathed. Both her little breasts, now having found freedom, sprung upward. "You naughty, *naughty* man!"

During all of this, Mack and Joe had tiptoed upstairs and proceeded into Mack's bedroom. Down the hall, they had heard occasional coos of enchantment coming from Ynez's room. Exchanging glances, they moved on.

The design of the house allowed for a great space between the two bedrooms, separated by the balcony overlooking the foyer, from which ran the curving staircase. Both rooms were aligned, however, permitting the occupant of one bedroom to clearly see the entering and exiting of any party from the other bedroom. This could be arranged by standing at one's open door…or by peeping through one's keyhole.

"I hope she knows enough to keep her mouth shut after that bit in the *Graphic*!" Mack confided to Joe, as he helped him turn down the satin spread. "This business of her having a trick here, whoever he might be, has no precedent—"

"—wha'? You talkin' 'bout Coolidge?"

"No. *Precedent*…Means it never happened before. Still, it all sounds pretty tame so far…and I've got *you* in here, so I guess she ought to have her fun, too, huh?"

"Yeah, sure—hold on, there's Alexander—"

"Joe, get away from that keyhole!"

"He's got a tray of food and a pitcher—"

"Pitcher of ice water?"

"No. No, Mack, a *pitcher*…a photy-graph…now he's knockin' and leavin' it by duh door dere. Now he's lookin' t'rough their key hole just like I'm doin'!"

"Oh give the poor girl a break!" Then Mack thought a bit. "Is Alexander still there?" Joe nodded. "Step aside, Joe."

Mack slightly opened his door and whispered, "Psst! Hey, Alexander! Bring that photograph over here."

Picking it up, Alexander tip-toed across the balcony, all smiles, toward Mack and Joe—by now, also peeking around the door.

"—you never heard such bullshit in all your lives!" Alexander could hardly keep from laughing. "She's got him in there b'leevin' Miss Harrison's gonna do a sculpture of his lousy spic ass naked to the world! Turns out he's done some posin' before…"

Joe picked the photograph off the tray. "Lemmee see that pitcher! Yeah, dat's him all right, and it don't take no genius to see his head's been pasted on somebody's else body."

Mack surveyed the photograph in question. "Say, you're right, it's a cosmograph!"

"Well, I don't know all dem big woyds, but I do know that Eddie is a peanut dick and that set ah woyks don't belong to him!"

"Eddie? Who's Eddie?" asked Alexander.

Mack answered: "The peanut dick at whom we're now staring, apparently, Alexander…my, my, won't Ynez be disappointed…"

"Yeah," Joe went on, as Mack motioned for Alexander to quickly get into his bedroom. "Eddie the Dancer. Woyst yegg dat ever crawled outa Elmira. I wouldn't trust dis rat as far as I could t'row him."

"You knew him from Elmira?" asked Alexander, fascinated.

"We wuz bot' of us joo-vee-nile offenders. I got framed on a shack rap by duh Railroad P'leece, when it was Eddie dat done it. Then he ended up in dere a day or so later for a box job at duh Foundlin' Home where he himself, but a few years earlier, had got left on duh doorstep. Now you gotta admit, dat's pretty low. Anyways, I was always gonna beat duh shit outa him for framin' me, but never could touch him."

Both Mack and Alexander asked why.

"Because Eddie was sprung duh very nex' day by some bleedin' heart who didn't b'leeve he done duh box job. And I was dere for one full, lousy, stinkin' year!" Then Joe added, sitting on the bed, saddened by this memory, "I tell yuh dere is none lower dan Eddie."

Alexander rightly observed, "So this *cucharacha* worms his way into the hearts and homes of the unsuspectin'…"

"—just as he's doing even as we speak," added Mack. Then he asked Joe: "If you were to speculate on what he's doing here, tonight, in there with Ynez…I mean what he's really and truly up to—what would you say it is?"

"*Anyt'ing*!" Joe answered at once. "Anyt'ing and everyt'ing. Doncha see, crumbs like dat find any little piece ah turd they can, then peddle it as a diamond."

"There is truth in poetry, and to put it simply, Joe—you said a mouthful," Mack concluded, grimly. "Now if he read that blurb in the *Graphic*…that is, IF he can read—and puts two and two together—IF he can add—I'm in deep shit, if you'll pardon my French."

Mack flopped back on the bed, his arms folded behind his head, staring up at the ceiling. Alexander took note of them both, Joe patting away comfortingly at Mack's partially exposed thigh, lighting two cigarettes, then passing one to Mack.

Absently blowing smoke rings, Mack appeared deep in thought. But Joe's expression was slowly changing into something which made Alexander genuinely afraid. He was actually growling under his breath: "I'm gonna kill him."

Alexander, hearing this and getting goosebumps, thought to himself: *He will, too.*

Mack turned on his side toward Joe and said, very evenly, very softly, "Wait a while, will you? Let's see what he can figure out from what she lets him in on tonight."

Picking up a pillow, Joe now made his hands into two very dangerous weapons, and plunged them into it.

"Mr. D.?" Alexander ventured. "You think she will tip yo' mitt…about… about…everything?"

Joe was, by then, at the French windows which banked the ocean side of Mack's whole room. "Dis little porch here…does it run clear across?"

"Yes, right over to…Joe! Hold on," Mack bolted up from the bed.

"Lemmee listen in, dat's all." Joe started to let himself out as the wind came in less than gently.

Alexander was at the keyhole. "She took the tray inside and now her light's off."

Mack said: "Alexander, go put your ear up to her door before we go any further…who knows? Maybe he'll be snoring by now."

Easing open Mack's bedroom door, Alexander advanced across the passageway. Bending over, he leaned in—so close to Ynez's door that his ear was touching it.

During this, Mack whispered to Joe, "She'd be a fool if she told him anything. Anyway, except for our closest friends, she'd never let anybody know a thing about our marriage!"

Joe whispered back: "Yeah but you jus' said this whole thing wid' Eddie meant dere was no president—Anyways, look what ended up in duh papers!"

"I'll say—*president*? Precedent, Joe! Precedent!"

Alexander was back. "It seems like in between things, he is askin' her questions. Yet, he spaces 'em out, so as not to appear like she's not a normal lady with normal needs." He laughed a little, then caught himself.

"Such as what kinda questions?" Joe asked, getting frightening again.

"I just heard him observin' that she's very rich and where does they get all the money, and bein' married and so rich and havin' every little thing, why is it she's so unhappy and so un…un…unSATISFIED."

"Oh, God," Mack sighed, putting his hand to his forehead. "So what was her answer?"

"All I heard was them goin' at it again. And if I know Mrs. D.—and I *do* know her quite *well*—she ain't gonna talk 'bout things like that at such a time as this! She wants what she wants an' that's all there ever is to it! Now hear me out, please, Mr. D. He had a copy of that newspaper on him when I picked him up and tossed it in the trash barrel soon's he saw me…then he goes and fishes out that dead bouquet, by the by, while he's pokin' around in there. We *know* he read it! But so did thousands of others! In the mornin' he'll get the rest of of his pay—for services rendered, and then you tell him, Mr. D., that those services are no longer required and then I'll drive him down to the station and that'll be IT."

Joe put his face very close to Alexander's and said, between clenched teeth, "No. *I'll* tell him his soyvices are no longer required, *I'll* drive him down to duh station and then dat'll really be IT."

• • • • •

CHAPTER VIII

MEMORY LAPSE

For Annabelle Harrison and Keys Parker, it was already the beginning of another evening. Still not having slept, they had been existing on nothing more than *joie de vivre* since the night before. The sheer excitement of the club's opening had inspired the eccentric socialite to finish the model she'd been working on for months. Shaping Keys Parker's noble posterior in clay, she paused, looking up at him in front of her. He was finally dozing off and, with a deep sigh, sat wearily down.

"Oh, come on! Let's knock it off for now, darling!" she said to him, being proud of some of the vernacular which he had taught her—injecting it into her otherwise correct speech.

As was often the case, Keys Parker had stayed overnight at Annabelle Harrison's Long Island Studio. Only a stone's throw from the Daly residence, Miss Harrison kept the place strictly as a Get-Away, maintaining her townhouse in Manhattan as well—an inherited piece of property used mostly as an art gallery.

But the studio was right on the ocean—her favorite place to be in all the world. With its second floor entirely removed to accommodate her more enormous statues, Belle had chiseled out the perfect space in which to work, move freely about (Amazon that she was) and make love to her Emperor Jones.

It was here that she and Keys could be lovers, were lovers and loved being lovers. Secluded by a high wall she had erected running around all three sides, they were blissful expatriates, as happy as two Antediluvian giants in their own lost world.

"You still got that myst'ry on your mind, Mama?" Keys asked, rallying and divinating that she was something beyond being merely tired. Fretting, as usual, about others.

Belle nodded, rising to go into the kitchen. There on the table was the very respectable *TIMES*, which lay open to the article concerning this appointment of a man named O'Couran as Commissioner of Prohibition. But, damn it all, she had forgotten to mention what seemed to connect that name and that new appointment to something quite disturbing.

"You remember what I told you about that poor woman I met the other day, Keys—not willing to give me her name? The whole incident just haunts me! Then the initials on her purse—'M. O'C.'—which I'd thought so odd. I couldn't figure out why the 'O' and the 'C' were joined as they were…"

"Do you think this man's her husband?" Keys asked, thinking: *Mama won't sleep with this thing on her mind!* then suggesting, "How's 'bout some warm milk, so's we can sit a spell and try to figure it out."

"I so wanted to tell 'Nez about that poor thing, but with everything going on all at once, it was wiped from my mind…and now, this article…'M. O'C'…I just wonder…" She let go a long sigh as Keys put a pan of milk on the stove. "I'm just too exhausted to figure it out now, though!"

That's how Belle was, Keys thought, looking across the table at her. *What an artist*! *What a woman!* "Honey, after we unearth what's eatin' you, we best catch some shut-eye pretty quick I think." Why, she could hardly keep her eyes open! He prepared a tray and urged her in toward the bedroom.

But once in bed, with nothing coming forth, the warm milk done with, she heard Keys breathing so softly, so regularly—heard the tide softly rolling in—Annabelle Harrison found herself confounded and unable to sleep.

I do wish I could find her—without causing a stir, of course…that poor little thing! she was thinking, staring up at the ceiling, watching the light changing upon it. To Annabelle, who was so rich and so Junoesque, nearly everyone was either "poor" or "little." *Something is terribly, terribly wrong there.*

She also had the somewhat regrettable gift for noticing every detail of life and never being able to erase one iota of it from her mind's eye. Probably, that was one reason she could both paint and sculpt from memory. Yet, she did so fervently wish, just at that moment, that it could all just vanish from the canvas of her mind! *There it was!* Oh, why didn't she remember to tell Ynez? Not only heart-wrenching but…dreadful! Perfectly dreadful.

• • •

She had gone to get checked over. Just a routine thing. Just the other day. Doctor Elizabeth Sutton, a very dear friend, had her office just North of the Brevoort Hotel on Fifth Avenue. It was there they had lunched and, upon returning, both found—waiting to be seen—a most distraught woman.

She seemed in need of immediate calming. While Annabelle stayed in the outer office, she heard the poor woman, by now hysterical, telling Dr. Sutton that she believed herself to be "just full of syphilis."

Elizabeth at once ordered the nurse to go out for an hour and called Annabelle in.

"You might have to help me here!" Such an outburst was hardly routine and the anguished sobs were painful to hear. The woman—a petite and young matron—then physically attacked Annabelle, who was naturally able to restrain her gently. But she would not stop. It was horribly upsetting, watching her fall to her knees, pleading with Doctor Sutton.

"Don't let anyone know, I beg you! I had the most awful time locating a lady doctor! I don't want any damned filthy man inspecting me! Who's this woman? Don't let her know what I've told you!"

"My dear," said the much older Doctor Sutton, with admirable composure and dignity, "it's quite possible that all of Greenwich Village knows of your misfortune by now. You must try and calm yourself. I'd like to diagnose you first—you may not be afflicted in the way you think at all!"

Annabelle helped her up, guiding her to a chair. Leaning toward the woman, Doctor Sutton gently touched her face. "This is my very dear friend, Miss Harrison. She does volunteer work for the Progressive Women's League and I do, as well. There, we have many such cases who come to us believing themselves to be in your state. More often than not, it is a false alarm."

"But I'm a married woman and my husband is a government official! I can pay my own way! I'm sure I've got it…!" At which time she pulled from her purse a wad of bills; it was then Annabelle noticed the monogrammed buckle—"M.O'C."

"What is your name, my child?" asked Elizabeth Sutton.

"I can't tell you—all I want is your help! My damned husband wants to get me pregnant and he keeps forcing himself on me and I've been too sick, I tell you!"

"You're Irish, of course?" the doctor asked, hearing the lilt in her voice, noticing her delicate freckling, and the copper spit curls peeking out from underneath her cloche. She couldn't have been more than twenty-three.

"Yes, and I come from a very good family, too. From Dublin. Dublin proper…and, oh! I want to go back! This country is such a place!—and now I got sick here! From him, who lied and lied and lied to me!" She slumped, folding her hands as if in prayer. "Oh it's a terrible sin to speak of one's husband in that way, but the man is a Goddammed bastard!"

Still fascinated by the unusual monogram, Annabelle recalled what Ynez had told her a while back about Mack's real name (Benjamin Leventhal) and that the name he now went under was really only a *nom de Guerre*, given to him by his commanding officer. Mack had informally received this Christian baptism in 1917, when he was nicknamed MacDailey after the company's chaplain—a Scotsman who had been killed at once during his first week of action.

"…my monograms would've been so much prettier if it had been a bit more Scottish…then I could've had 'Y.M'D.' on everything," she'd continued, tracing

the initials with her fingertip in the air. *"As it stands now, I've got plain old 'Y.D.' which you can't do very much with!"*

"But you would've been known as Ynez MacDailey. And that's quite a tongue-twister!" Annabelle had replied. They'd both had a good laugh over it.

Doctor Sutton was telling 'M.O'C.' that if she proved positive for venereal disease, it would have to be reported at once to the authorities.

"I can't have it, don't you see? My husband is—" But then, she stopped.

"It's the rule, my dear, I'm sorry...you are a citizen of the United States, are you not?"

"Oh, please! This was a waste of my time—I told you—I'm sick and now he forces himself on me to have his baby! He's gotten me dosed for he's full of the curse!"

It was perfectly horrible. Annabelle asked, "*Are* you pregnant? Do you know for certain?"

"Well, if I am, I hope the dear Lord takes both the child and myself when the time comes, because you've no idea the future we shall both face!" Sobbing hoarsely, she staggered from the office out to the reception room, then fled through the door, Annabelle following her.

"See here, you need help at once!" Doctor Sutton called out behind them both.

The woman, turning, cried back, "If it's help I need, they'll put me in The Slaves of Mary! That's where I'll end up!"

"Put you where? Who will do this to you?" Annabelle demanded, holding her by the sleeve of her coat.

"That bunch my husband's joined up with! Fanatics is what they are. Once their shadow crosses your life you are one of the forgotten! Forgotten, I tell you! 'Tis The Slaves of Mary for me, oh to be sure..." she moaned looking up and down the street as if someone were secretly watching her every move.

Annabelle put her arm about her. "Don't jump to conclusions yet, my dear. You may not need a hospital at all. Please let me take you back in."

"Oh, The Slaves of Mary isn't a *hospital*! It's a trash heap for them who are abandoned by the Good Lord! Like me!"

There was no calming her. "Look. Here's my car. Would you like a drink? Come, sit down with me—just for a bit."

Conveniently parked right across the street was her limousine, with the chauffeur still not back from running errands.

"This is terribly kind of you." The little Irishwoman let go a sigh, nestling within its confines. "You're a very great lady, I could tell that right away!"

Well, thought Annabelle, opening the cellarette and preparing a cocktail, at least I've managed to quiet her a bit.

Then, just as she was putting the top on the cocktail shaker, Annabelle heard her distinctly say, "Please don't shake it for me, if you don't mind—*just bruise it*!"

Curious expression. "Just bruise it." Doing as she was told, Annabelle saw the libation working its magic. But even after a refill, no more information could be extracted from this unfortunate Irishwoman.

Thanking her hostess profusely as the chauffeur was returning with his packages, "M.O'C." went to the corner and hailed a cab.

That was it. Annabelle—left sitting there, not knowing what to think or what to do.

JUST BRUISE IT? She had heard Ynez say those same words…JUST BRUISE IT…And then there was the mongram. Some sort of Irish name, of course…M.O'C. Whatever did it stand for…? And why was she so undone? Pregnant, perhaps. Dosed? Hopefully not—and by her husband (whoever he was)! But there was something more there. Horrifying really. What was it?

• • •

Up she got, resolutely going back into the kitchen again, switching on the light. The newspaper was open to the article and there, staring at her, was the picture of this man O'Couran—hardly giving the impression of a monster. Yet, the initials did fit: "O'C."

And she did say her husband was a government official and it mentions, right here…The Slaves of Mary. But Mack has to know this man…he's high up in the same department.

She must remember to tell Ynez at once!

Recradled in Keys' arms, Annabelle Harrison at last fell into a deep sleep. She felt cold to his touch. Maybe it was just the wind. It was Keys who now was wide awake, getting up and shutting the doors which let out into the garden.

Looking down at her face, Keys Parker noted that those patrician brows still had a deep gouge of fretfulness bewtween them. With his finger, he massaged the place where, soon enough, the scar left there by the world's cares retreated. Probably, he thought, now drifting off himself, whatever was bothering her would end up molded in clay sooner or later.

• • •

"If you wuz tuh worry 'bout everyt'ing you got on yer plate jus' now, sweetheart, you'd be climbin' dese walls!" With the moon streaming in, Joe's golden skin was tinted with opaline, holding Mack in his arms, naked and warm.

That same ocean breeze which had chilled Annabelle Harrison was setting the draperies in Mack's bedroom afloat.

"I'm going to meet with your brother tomorrow and find out what's behind his scheme. He won't ever sock you again, mark my words, Joe." Mack kissed the place where Bruno had left his mark.

"Yeah, but he could do a helluva lot more dan sock *you*. I tell yuh, Mack, you gotta go smooth wid Bruno. Hey—do you got a gun?"

"Sure, right in the left drawer over there. But I'd hate to think—"

"Well, tomorrow, let's just bring it along for good luck."

"—whatever you say, kiddo."

"What I sez is—how's about once more, if you don't mind, Mack!"

And so, once more it was.

At exactly 3:51 a.m., Joe awoke to hear someone outside on the stairway. He was naturally a light sleeper, always ready for anything, and always possessed of more than a few ideas of what might happen next…and within these, certain of his own options.

It was that crumb Eddie the Dancer, making like the rat he was, going down to frisk the joint to find anything he could lay his greasy mitts on. He'd probably already relieved Mrs. Daly of her ice, and now was on his way toward the silverware.

Joe put on the bathrobe Mack had given him, went to the drawer earlier indicated, took out Mack's .38, then went right to town.

He was right. It was Eddie, in nothing but his trousers.

"Hey, asshole," Joe whispered through his teeth, catching him half-way down the stairs. Eddie, formerly known as Ramon di Rose, turned. "It's me, Joey Imperio," he continued, noiselessly ending up right next to him and placing his left hand around the asshole's neck in a viselike grip.

Eddie started out with something like a shout—as if he'd seen a ghost—but Joe quickly clamped his right hand over his mouth, still holding Mack's gun in his left. The whites of Eddie's eyes were showing like searchlights. Just as if Eddie were a life-size marionette, Joe lifted him up, carrying him down the rest of the stairs then to the drawing room and past that, into the dining room.

There, he threw Eddie into a chair. Out of breath, Joe said, hardly above a whisper, "Well, fancy meetin' youse here, you shit-faced double-crosser." He slowly let go of Eddie's mouth, now ramming the gun into his temple. "Talk, Senorita."

"I'm straigh' now, Choey! I'm workin' for a dial-a-deeck! I'm here as a chigg-alo, dat's all, Choey. I swear to yew!"

"Well, I jus' fired you, so how do yuh like that, Eddie?"

"How yew got dee righ' to do dat, Choey? What in hell YEW doin' here?"

"None of yer godammed beeswax. What were you jus' comin' down here for, anyways?"

"Choey, I had to take a crap, I swear to yew."

Joe shook him angrily. "That's a goddammed lie and you know it is! She's got a can up there right in her own bedroom."

"No, no! Choey—I don't wanna make no poop noises! I try hard! I straigh' now! I wanna eempress my piipple—my clientz!" (Joe thought about it.) "Why would Eduardo lie to jhooz? Don' we go way back, huh, Choey?"

"Listen, asshole, if I wasn't hooked up to somet'in' dat's makin' ME walk duh straight and narrow and feelin' as happy and as good as I do just now, I'd slam your lousy head in wid the butt of dis rod here, 'cause you got it goddam comin' to yuz. I want you to clear your spic ass out ah here as soon as duh sun's up, you understan'?"

"I cano' do dat, Choey! She's hired me as their Cho-ffer. I got a gig goin' here *permanente*!" Then he smiled, weakly. "She like me, Choey…see?"

"She liked what she saw in that rigged photy-grapht, but when you stripped I bet you anyt'ing she felt let-down about the *real* size of it! Jus' look at you Ed, scrawny as duh pencil dick dat you are!" Joe, looking him over, concluded, "You on hop, Ed? I bet you are! Never mind. What in Hell should I care for?"

"Lemmee take my crap and go back up to her, 'fore she gets suspish! PLEEZE!"

Joe didn't want a scene, or to ruffle any feathers—especially those of Mack's wife. "All I know is dat dere's a terr-lett downstairs in the gym. Come on, I'll show it to yuz an' you better not be lyin' 'bout yer poop!"

With the nose of his gun, he urged Eddie out past the kitchen, toward the door beyond the butler's pantry. It was locked.

"Well, dat's dat, I guess. Wanna go outside, huh, mebee, Eddie?"

"No, no, it's hokay. I don' have to sheet no more, I guess."

That made Joe mad. He whacked him with his knuckles. "Yeah and you never *did*. You wuz about to case duh jernt." They both stared at each other. The nightlight from the butler's pantry illuminated Eddie's pallid, sweaty face. "Come on! Back upstairs wid youse."

Silently, Joe returned Eddie to the threshold of Ynez's bedroom. "Go on in an' *stay* dere. I don't wanna hafta wake my buddy over dis." Eddie slowly opened the door. "I'm gonna be listenin' so do NOT try NUTTIN, see?"

"Whew," said Joe, going back into Mack's bedroom. He hadn't even budged. Poor sweetheart was exhausted. Just exhausted…

Mack's eyes opened and a smile appeared on his face. "Trouble, Joe?"

"No, not really. Dat peanut dick Eddie was out and about is all. He's back in dere now wid duh wifie—I got everyt'ing under control."

Mack wrapped his arms about Joe as he slid the gun under his pillow. "Not *every*thing, I hope—"

"No. Not *everyt*'ing," Joe forced a smile, dropping the robe and crawling on top of Mack. It was now twelve minutes past four.

As they made furious love once again, Ynez had switched on a beside lamp to find that the light in her bathroom was also on and, apparently, her gigolo was enclosed within. She let go a harr-umphh. Ramon di Rose was not at all living up to either his self-promotion or his pictures.

"Ramon? Ramon?"

"Jhes?"

"When you're finished in there…I…I…need to speak with you."

Getting up and tossing on her pegnoir, she pulled a twenty dollar bill out from underneath her perfume tray on the vanity.

He emerged, still in trousers, laughing shakily, nervous for no apparent reason. "Did I awaken joo, passion flower?"

Ynez took his partially dressed form to mean that he perfectly understood what she was about to do. Pay him—some, but not all of what she still owed—and tell him to just…leave. Ramon had lain an egg.

"I guess you know what's coming, Ramon. Here's the balance of your fee, minus a few inches. This whole thing just isn't…well…what I'd really had in mind—"

"Awwwwwww—"

"—no! No, it's not entirely your fault. It's just that…well…I so truly love my husband…and it's just not worth it to me, that's all…" She sat lightly on the very tip of her bed, head bent to the side, her eyes looking down at the carpet.

Having quickly snatched the bill from her hand, Eddie/Ramon proceeded to throw on his clothing. "How'm I gonna get back home?" he whined. "And at dees hour!"

"Oh. *That.* Well, I suppose we'll…just…have…to…*wait.*" Ynez's shoulders fell into curves of despair.

"Lemmee jhoos' ast joo. Whyfore you reject me? Don' I plizz joo? Ain't jhoor huz'ban' not consumatin' joor marriage?" Now almost dressed except for his tie, Eddie looked down on her almost scornfully. He had put the money in his sock and, while bending down, noted her eyes were closed. No tears.

Now those same eyes of hers lifted, burning holes in him. "How dare you imply such a thing! Just where do you get off?"

"But why else do married wimmens seek out men like Ramon di Rose, huh?"

"Listen, this was all just a mis*take*. Why I hired you is just none of your g.d. business. Just please—leave me alone." She stood up with sudden resolve, marched to the cellarette and proceeded to pull out some whiskey. Watching her, thinking he had best say no more or she would demand the money in his sock back, he moved toward the door. She seemed not to notice.

"Could I jus' slipp the nex' coupla hours down'stairs? Wha' time your servan' wake hup?"

"Seven." Ynez tossed down the shot of whiskey. "—there's a half dozen guest rooms over that way—just choose one..." Pointing with a tenebrous finger, she turned from him, cowed by utter weariness, gulping down a another shot. "I just thought it would be so much...*different*...romantic and—oh, *shit*." She was talking to herself.

Ramon di Rose/Eddie the Dancer had gone, silently closing her door.

Shutting off the lights in both her bathroom and bedroom, Ynez dragged her satin spread off the bed and curled up in a ball on her chaise, the bottle in her hand.

Just outside, twenty dollars richer, Ramon/Eddie found himself staring down the hallway which led to Mack's room. As he advanced toward it, he distinctly heard the sounds of ebullient love-making coming from within. The sun was rising and now, he thought, lowering his eye to the keyhole, he might be able to see what this was all about.

"Mmmm. Choost as I t'ought.' Choey! Dat beeg fairy—weed thee huzz-ban'! Ha! Twennie clams is not'ing compare to what I can make on dees!"

Wandering off toward the guest rooms he felt himself salivating, not over what he had just seen, but rather over how he could turn his measley twenty dollars into at least two thousand.

By seven a.m., Ramon/Eddie had left the Daly home. Alexander, searching high and low for the weasel, vaguely remembered hearing an auto slow to a halt outside the gates—then a door slam shut. Apparently, someone had come to get him. Ynez had heard it, too, and rose to see a brown sedan just pulling away from the main road.

Prior to finding him gone, Alexander had knocked on Mr. D.'s door. Opening it, wrapped in his robe, Mack quickly gave an update. There had been some trouble last night; the gigolo should be roused from his sleep with Ynez and Mack wanted a pow-wow but pronto. Then, going to Mrs. D.'s door, knocking and hearing her say in a booze-drenched voice, "He's gone. Gone."

After combing the whole house, checking the silverware, the paintings, and the door to the gymnasium, he then put on his jacket and took the long walk to the boat house. Everything still locked. Everything in order.

So, Alexander decided to let everybody go back to sleep and, promptly going up to his third floor quarters, did so himself.

• • •

Although Mack Daly didn't work on Saturday, Bruno Imperio did. Saturday was the biggest night of the week for a bootlegger like Bruno. It meant a restock for all the speaks he forced into buying his booze, it meant him crashing various and sundry private parties and muscling them to buy his booze, and more than a few deliveries to whorehouses, where he didn't have to force them to do anything.

Up the block from where the Imperio red ink joint lay, Bruno occupied a rambling enfilade of second floor tenement rooms which served as his offices. He still lived—at least part of the time—with his family. But here, offices and living quarters were now combining. As Pop Imperio increasingly lost his grip on the rackets, it was Bruno who naturally began to take over and, in so doing, saw less and less of his mother, Josie. She wouldn't have approved of how he was handling Pop's business.

Bruno toiled his rackets all alone—except for the aid of his newly hired assistant, a moll by the name of Blanche King, who had won the job by way of the information she supplied to him about Mack. This plump jane had 'gone downtown' for some reason which was never made clear to any of the low-lifes with whom she now preferred to run. Possessed of a searing intellect, having come from a good down-East family, and even having had completed three years of college at some large, New England university, Blanche King was in every way a cynical, embittered young woman. Unlikable as could be, she herself would tell you nobody could ever love her. And why?

"Because I don't bullshit around, that's why," she would say to anyone at all. Even if she didn't know them. A foul mouth and a huge vocabulary, well-read by even the blue-stockings' standards, she dressed like a school marm who affected a misguided taste toward the soignee. Replete with horn-rimmed glasses, bushy eyebrows and skin the color of a worm's underbelly, one look at her would tell you that Blanche wasn't quite right.

Her rudeness and her filthy-mouthed candor made her a match for any man. Paid reasonably well for all the illegal work she did for Bruno, Blanche bought books instead of flashy jewelry. She would tell you she liked being all alone—in the company of the only person in the world who could stand her—herself.

In a very short period of time, she had come to know the business of the New York rackets better than anyone else from the Battery to the Bronx. She was irreplaceable, and Bruno was thoroughly ungrateful.

Yet, she had no interest in him either, and let everyone know that it was "all business" between them. Josie Imperio, Bruno and Joey's mother, would not speak to her, and Joey found her homely and creepy. She neither drank nor smoked and, during her off-hours, when she wasn't writing in her diary or eating by herself at the Automat, she was walking all alone with a pocketful of nuts for the squirrels. The only thing in life she loved were those squirrels and Joey, quite naturally, nicknamed her "Squirrely King."

Bruno had someone shadow her once. Maybe she was working undercover for the cops? No such luck. It was Blanche and the squirrels all the way, and that was that.

"Blanche, don't kid me now, are you a virgin?" Bruno asked her following this revelation.

Giving him the finger and a look that would have frozen the entire equatorial zone, Blanche had nothing at all to say.

"Are you planning to stay on with me, Blanche?" Bruno had asked her recently.

"I am, Bruno. Because I *love* my job. Don't you get it, smart-ass?" That was her answer, complemented by that same deadly look.

Bruno's goons all agreed that they had come to fear, absolutely, nobody in all the five boroughs…excepting Blanche King.

On that particular Saturday morning, Blanche sat at her desk sipping her tea when the phone rang. "Who?" It was a man with an accent, asking to speak to Bruno. "I'm sorry, but he hasn't come in yet. Do you care to leave your number?" He did, as well as his name. "Eddie who?" but he had already rung off.

When Bruno did come in, quite hung over, he told Blanche, "That's old Eduardo, a pal of Joe's. They were sent up together when they were both minors. You call him back and find out what he wants."

Well, she did just that. "He wants money, of course," Blanche told Bruno, who was holding an ice pack to his head, his feet up on his desk, a cigarette betwen his lips.

To every normal woman Bruno Imperio knew, he was one deadly attractive hunk. They never said no. He had the beauty of his brother, but it wasn't the nectar of some heathen god— it was his own rot-gut hooch. And whereas Joe was a real comic, Bruno never made you laugh.

"Mrs. Daly, Mack Daly's wife, hired him as a trick last night. He went to their house and she threw him out," Blanche reported, noncommittally.

"She's not so dumb! Did he say Joey was there?"

"Of course. This Eduardo has a tip for you."

"Well, tell him to go to Hell."

"I already did."

Then the phone rang again. "Bruno, it's your brother," Blanche said.

"Well, well, well, if isn't Dead-Above-The-Neck. Heard you ran into an old buddy of yours last night, " Bruno told him. (Blanche lent an ear. Joe sounded sheepish, as usual.) "Sure he did. Called here and tried to act like he was about to provide the goods on your boyfriend there. Naw. Blanche got rid of him. Is Mr. Daly there? Put him on."

From the other end of the wire, Mack's voice was heard. However, at the same time, Joe was trying to explain to him what Eddie had just gone and done.

Bruno let Mack have it. "Tell him to shut the Hell up. What would you expect from a yegg like Eddie anyway?"

Mack told Bruno that a meeting could be arranged for early evening in Manhattan at the Club deVol. Cordially, he also suggested that it would be a chance for Bruno to see the place, and finally be his guest.

Bruno agreed. "As a matter of fact, I'll be in that neighborhood right about then." Hanging up, he looked at Blanche, who had already been burrowing holes in his profile throughout the conversation. "What?!"

"I wonder if that fellow Eddie will start spreading rumours about the Dalys to other sources?" She paused. "Are you quite certain you don't want me to follow up on what he has to report?" (Bruno just kept staring.)

"All right!" Blanche smirked, "You might think you know everything aobut them," lifting her eyebrows in a schoolteacher way, "But if you want to clinch this deal with Mr. Daly, I certainly would use any means at all to make sure it happened. *If I were you.*"

"Well you're *not*, Miss King. So just do your work and don't ask any questions."

Blanche nodded coldly, opened her desk drawer and pulled out a bag of peanuts.

"You going out?"

She pulled on her cloche and put the bag in her jacket pocket. It was time for Blanche King to get squirrely.

• • •

Normally Brian O'Couran slept late on Saturday because of Friday Poker Nights. Since his appointment to the Prohibition Bureau, however, he had been inundated by endless requests for his presence and his opinions, and was, on that post-poker Saturday morning, up early and at work on the telephone.

With an ash tray teetering on the dome of his big belly and a cigar stuck in his gelatinous lips, Commissioner O'Couran lay enormously in his bed.

It was already past noon and he had requested his wife, Margaret, to bring lunch up. He just couldn't seem to unglue his ear from that g.d. receiver.

The hired help O'Couran had extracted from the Old Sod *("Shanty Irish trash who would've died without me!")* had Saturdays and Sundays off, and so the preparation of her husband's gargantuan meal was left to the little Missus.

As sick as Margaret O'Couran was—known as Peggy since a mere lass—she would not let illness ever get in her way. Placing a bud vase on the tray heaped with potatoes, steak, peas and corn, buns, and a beaker of Moran's Elixir—sometimes known as *Moron's* Elixir—she began her ascent upward. Nauseous, dizzy, sweating once again (so indelicate) and praying to the Blessed Mother with every step she took, Peggy was determined to put on a cheery face for Brian.

Halfway up on the landing, she simply had to stop. From above, she could hear her husband talking with someone who evidently was reporting yet another flagrant violation of the Volstead Act. Arriving in their bedroom, she witnessed Brian's eyes looking for all the world like two bloody abrasions on either side of his nose. His cigar rapidly traversed his moist lips from one corner of his mouth to the other.

"Put it down, put it down, put it down!" he ordered, waving his pudgy hand. Then back to the conversation on the telephone, "You don't say! You don't say!" A pause. "Well, if he won't spill the whole thing, rough him up a bit rather than part with any more of *my* money!"

(Oh, why don't they just leave it alone! she was thinking. *Such constant talk of violence and bloodshed! I feel faint...)* Oh, the smell of that food, and that cigar! Surely this must mean she was pregnant. It was now happening all the time. She couldn't eat, she couldn't sleep. And all of this chaos in her house made it worse. Men coming and going all hours of the night, terrible—simply terrible whisperings—it all sounded so dangerous.

She removed the ash tray, placing it on the bedside table with a shaky, pale, damp hand, toppling Brian's collection of holy cards which he had propped up there.

"Now see what you've done!" He quickly gathered them up, just as if they were his winning poker hand and kissed each one. Well, at least Peggy had succeeded in getting lunch up to him. With a swing, His Highness whacked her little ass and replaced the earpiece on its hook.

"Get some meat on yuh, girl! There's nothin' left of yuh!"

Alas, Peggy wished it were so. Ashes to ashes, dust to dust. Blown back over the sea to Dublin. Already she had laid out her things for morning mass tomorrow. There, in the sun parlor, where she now slept with the door locked, out on the wicker couch was her navy blue suit, with its freshly starched, detachable collar and cuffs, her velour cloche with veil, her prayer book and her rosary. If only she could be in church all the time, she was thinking just then. Declare sanctuary, like in *The Hunchback of Notre Dame*, which gave her nightmares for months afterward.

"Where's the *Graphic* of yesterday?" Brian asked. Peggy went into the upstairs bathroom and brought it back in. "Now go to the Winchell column and read me that piece about a certain Mrs. Daly." Dutifully, as always, in a voice devoid of all interest and emotion, she did so.

Without looking his way, she felt him masticating, ruminating, throughout the silence which ensued. "I don't get it—" he said at length, with his mouth still full of food.

"What's to get?" Peggy retorted. "She's one of those Broadway Butterflies, that's all, and the columunist is just making fun of her." *("Fun! How I'd like to have some! Oh, it all sounded so…so…tantilizing…who cared what she was or wasn't? She was out and about, wasn't she? Putting one over, acting like a movie queen…oh, but not for me! Not for Peg ever!")*

"Well, if that's the case, then the whole thing is a mockery. Must be!" Brian took the paper from her and threw it down in something like an infant's fit, leaving his wife to wonder what he had meant by that last remark. "I am sick of these phonies and shall introduce the topic of immorality into my speech to the board on Monday." He chuckled. "Just got a good tip about this Daly and his spouse! Really, every rock you turn over nowadays has some kind of g.d. snake under it! This steak isn't done well enough!—never mind—I'll just have to be constipated the whole day long, that's all." He poured out a full glass of his Moran's Elixir and gulped it down.

Peggy pointed to the bottle. "It's that foul stuff which constipates you, Brian Patrick O'Couran! And you know it's full of alcohol."

"No, but that's what people today just don't get! This in here," he jabbed at the bottle, "is *medicinal* alcohol and is *good* for you. It can't tear away at your system or your mortality as liquor can! Bring me up a nice big piece of that cake you made and drizzle some flav'rin' over it."

Back down she went, still somehow holding back her nausea, now resolved to do so because she was so mad. The "flav'rin'" of which he spoke was from the Cordially Yours Cordial Shoppe and it, too, was laced with alcohol, but this time just to "preserve sweetness." And yet he wouldn't allow any spirits of any kind in the house! Even near-beer! Oh, how she did, on occasion, long for a tilt of the old elbow.

Now, as she cut the cake with efficient and desperate self-control, frantic Peggy O'Couran remembered the toot given her by the nice, wealthy giantess after she had run from the lady doctor's office just last week. How she wished she'd gotten her name—someone to talk to, she thought, ladling out the sticky syrup. Oh! It looked like congealed blood! She fell into the chair nearby and began to helplessly sob.

Wouldn't it be just grand to have a life like that Mrs. Mack Daly has, thought Peg. And here they were, both married to officials of the Prohibition Bureau—and *what* a difference there was in how they both lived! Peggy was slightly cheered by the thought that Mrs. Mack Daly was close to her in that way...both husbands doing the same sort of thing. It would be so lovely if someday they might meet! She wondered what Mister Daly was like. Not like Brian, that was certain! There wasn't a man on this earth like that beast!

"*He is, after all, your husband, Peg,*" Father O'Boyle had told her, "*and you must do three things: Obey Him, love him and forgive him.*"

How she wished that Father O'Boyle would be transferred to another parish. She had given up trying to see him, to talk to him. And, finally, he would take none of her telephone calls; and when she came by near tears, the housekeeper would lie and say he was at a sick-bed, passing her a note to Brian which read: *"Have your husband give us a little extra eucharistic wine this week, won't you please?—I'm always praying for you both!"*

There really was was no one to whom Peggy O'Couran could turn. She had found, quite by accident, while cleaning up around his so-called "den," a collection of appalling, shocking and indecent things...photographs and dreadful objects, concealed in a box behind his smoker stand. But he had lived that way, yes, yes, he'd admitted it—before she'd come from Across. He'd told her about how poor he was down on Coney Island, and how he'd gotten in with this terrible circle of fiends and they'd helped his star rise. Oh, yes! He'd admitted he was once a hooligan! But he'd made a good bit of money out of that kind of work and he told her he'd done it all for His Peg—the light o' his life. He said nothing mattered now but for him to be a good husband, and get his ass over to confession. But he never went to confession, although he was up to the Communion rail every Sunday! And he held onto to those filthy, dirty pictures, those strange depraved devices, and babbled on about how he could go further than anyone would imagine through the help of somebody he called "the Master." Peggy asked him, "*oh, won't you please go and see Father O'Boyle about all this nonsense?*"

And that was when his temper would explode. It was always this one particular subject which would trigger it.

During such occasions, Peg would find herself hiding behind the big armchair in the parlor with their little dog in her arms. Dear little pup. The only living thing who showed her tenderness during those first horrible months after the wedding. Then once, in his fits, he took the little dog up by the neck and threw it across the room, smashing it against the wall, killing it.

So that the neighbors wouldn't know, Peg buried the poor wretched thing out in the back at in the wee hours of the morning. Brian made her swear that it had sickened and died. And everybody would believe it, too—believe anything Brian lied about, because he was so greatly loved, and full o' the blarney. So funny and so good at imitations, and so loyal to his lads with their merciless beatings, and the all the slander and the fiendishly devious ways they got their money…and now she got syphilis from him and was going to have their child.

"Piggy!" He always called her his "little pig." "Where's my dessert!" came his bellow from upstairs.

Her head pounding, she rose and returned to him, cake a-drip with syrup. Just before entering, Peggy dried her eyes with the tip of her apron. She now heard him talking on the phone once again. The Jew working under him with his whore of a wife, thinking they could both prance about! And was he ever going to see to it that both were pilloried. Pilloried, pilloried, pilloried! (He always said terrible things three times just to show he meant them.)

Peggy found herself laughing. Trying to eat that mess, smoke his cigar and continue his harangue all at once—it was really enough to make you laugh. She had to get away from him. Go into the sewing room. Mend a stocking. Anything.

She lifted the tabloid off the edge of the bed and stole downstairs with it. In her little sun-parlor sanctuary, Peggy O'Couran opened to Walter Winchell's column. Oh! what a lady Mrs. Daly must surely be! Would it hurt if she looked her up? Monday, Brian would be gone all day and all night. It was his first official day in his new position. He'd meet everyone, make speeches, and then be roasted by the boys over West Side. She could be gone all day. He'd never have to know…

Feeling God had provided her with courage and an answer, she turned to the plaster statue of Saint Patrick.

She'd have to tell a little white one to Brian but—in such a case—would it truly matter? Mrs. Daly, more than anyone else, could help her out. Advise her, as only a woman of the world, as she was, could! Peggy had to bite her lip to keep herself from smiling back at Saint Patrick, in spite of herself.

• • •

Ynez had remained moodily behind her closed bedroom door. Saturday, past noon already. The Villa Hotsy Totsy was quiet as a pharaoh's tomb. The day-servants, as instructed by Alexander, tiptoed about, sensing that something was not quite the same. Mr. Daly's overnight guest, a strapping Italian man, raised every eyebrow from the gardener to the cook—but no one commented.

Mr. Daly and this fellow seemed blissfully in their own world, and the Master of the House was heard laughing at the other's jokes, genuinely enjoying himself—as he and the Italian man went to play tennis, spent a couple of hours in the gymnasium, ate lunch on the piazza, went off larking to a miniature golf course and finally, just as the day-servants were taking their leave, began to dress for the evening. They had never seen their boss this happy.

Alexander would have to remind the day-help, now and then, that *Mrs.* D. still did not wish to be disturbed. It seemed almost a vacation for them because she was always driving them wild with her unnecessary demands. He did, however, call to her through her closed door; the boys would be going to the club early that evening to see Joe Imperio's brother. No answer. But, finally just before six p.m., she emerged from her chrysalis, dressed to the nines in a poppy-colored velvet number, humming the latest blues song, screwing on a pair of long jade earrings.

Mack and Joe had returned by this time and were already dressed in tuxedos. They stood, surprised by her sudden entrance, in the upstairs hall.

"Oh, hello boys." Both stared at this vision of grandiose victimization. "I poured my heart out to Nolie on the phone all afternoon and now I feel simply swell…really, boys, I do." (*What a friend Nolie is! Listening to that all day!* thought Mack.) "Well, don't just stand there! Let's shake a leg. I am renovated."

Sweeping down the stairs ahead of them, she went for the hall closet in search of her wrap, never making eye contact with a soul above. "I think I'd best wear fur tonight. I hope we'll all be going in the big car."

Poking her head out and glancing upward, she pierced them both with a chilling look. "I'm not going to let the Press make a fool of me. Nolie says it doesn't matter what they're saying, as long as they're saying *some*thing. She said that Winchell was just paying me a left-handed compliment—in a way."

Mack laughed right out loud. "Well, there you are, Ynez. See how things always work out?" *(And Glod bless Nolie for having come up with that one!)* They both came down the stairs, Mack continuing, "We're going to meet with Joe's brother tonight." (She said nothing, adjusting her coat.) "And we should talk about that creature who was here last night…Ynez? Did you hear me?"

With a magnificent lynx cloak about her, she smiled dazzlingly at her husband, blowing him a kiss. "Not now. Not here, my darling—not with *him* here—that's just between *us*…well, do I rate?"

"Like a goyl on a magazine cover!" Joe practically shouted, thrilled at the effect. Then ventured, "But, yuh see, what happened last night involves all ah us…"

Now Ynez laughed—but her laughter was deprecatory. "But how could it?" she asked coldly.

Mack took her arm, guiding her into the drawing room as Alexander appeared from within, all set to go. "Oh—say, Alexander," he said, giving him a sidelong glance, "will you go and tie Joe's tie a little neater?" Then to his wife, "And in the meantime, why don't you have your cocktail in here with me before we go, Ynez?" Then he shot both Joe and Alexander a look which spelled complete co-operation.

"I'm so glad you and Joseph had such fun today," Ynez began, mixing her drink. "I bet you were just like the Rover boys frolicking all over the whole island!"

"Ynez, listen to me. First of all, let me say that I'm sorry things didn't work out for you last night." (She sipped the cockail, not ever looking up.)

"But listen. That trick you had here might be a blackmailer and it's not going to help either of us if both you and I don't stop being so public about our lives—such as they are, I mean—" She still said nothing. He sighed and proceeded, "Joey's brother is a gangster and tonight I want to try and make him see reason…"

"About *what*? You can't make a gangster see *reason*, Mack," she said. "I'm truly *not* sorry about last night because it made me realize how very much I *love* you. That horrible little man! I got around to finally feeling it was all so unnecessary—this sex thing. I don't need it—the way *you* do." Now she stirred the cocktail with her index finger. "Is that why you need to talk to that boy's brother, the gangster? To see if he'll give you *permission* to crawl all over that big goon out there?"

Mack let go an exasperated sound which always went with these conversations of theirs. "Yes, partly. And don't call Joe a goon. But there's a lot more to it. We've got to continue to be friends, you and I, Ynez. I've always told you that sooner or later, this day would come…" He stopped to clear his throat, marveling at how she could act as if she wasn't listening. "From now on we've got to exercise great discretion."

"Meaning what?"

"Meaning just this—" He told her Bruno's intentions, mincing no words.

Then, just as Joe was entering the drawing room, she replied, "Look, Mack, as you know, I survived a life which would have had most women wishing they'd never been born. I'm not scared of any Goddammed gangster! And I'm sure you'll handle all of this mess beautifully. But I might venture to say that you are *hardly* exercising discretion by screwing around with *this* one here" (tossing her head at Joey). "I *unknowingly* brought trash into our house. You did it with *full knowledge* of what he is and what his family intends to *do* to you. And now you come to *me* and tell me you're worried about *us* being shaken down? *Really,* Mack, sometimes you're just an asshole."

As she walked away from them toward the door, she turned. "Well! I'm ready for some fun!—let's go meet this gangster, boys. Now do put your coats on because I can already feel quite a chill in the air!"

• • • • •

CHAPTER IX

SATURDAY NIGHT SPECIAL

At the club, which was still quite empty, Bruno Imperio asked Mack, "Is that your Other Half over there?"

Ynez was talking to Nolie and Elliot, who had also just arrived, off by the side of the stage. She was up to something. Having left the table as soon as Bruno Imperio had entered the club, circling like some gorgeous but famished bird of prey.

"That's her, all right."

"She covers for you then gets her payback by living the hi-tone life, right?" Bruno asked.

"We both pay, believe me, Bruno—you don't mind if I call you by your first name, do you?"

"You're quite a self-invention, aren't you, Mack? You don't mind if *I* call you 'Mack,' now do you? It's a lot better than that kike name of Benny Leventhal, I guess."

Joe, sitting between them, his elbows on the table, one hand holding a cigarette, the other under his chin, grumbled: "Aw cut the crap…let's get down tuh business here."

Mack mutttered, "Well, we have to wait for the deVols, if you don't mind. They run this place."

Bruno said: "Listen, Mack—before I met you just now, I wasn't sure I'd even like you. Over the phone you came across as one of those fake continentals with a high and mighty attitude. However, now that we're talking here, I like you a lot. You've got some balls to have come so far, so fast. This place is swell and it shows a lot of thought and loving care, too. Joe acts calm. He seems to be—well—sort of normal for the first time since he got out of the stir. He had to be tested for inversion in jail, you know, and it screwed him up 'cause on his record he's down as a nut job. He's not much good to me except as a shill."

"Joe is everything to me, Bruno—" Mack countered, looking him squarely in the eye.

"Sure. Sure he is. I've seen pals like you before—when I was up the river myself. And I can tell you both make swell buddies. It seems as if you're really and truly perfect for each other."

Joe spoke up, frowning, "So just tell Mackie what your angle is before we go into this meetin', will yuh pleez, B.?"

"O.k. Just this…since you and my brother like each other so much, we're going to make you part of our family, Mr. Daly."

Mack smiled, nodding his head. "I am honored. Joey speaks highly of your Mother, Josefina…and of your family restaurant. I need a family. I don't have one. Not really—except my friends."

Bruno laughed coldly. "So how does it make you feel to be part Italian, Mr. Daly?"

Mack looked away then lit up a cigarette. He inched closer to Joe, noiselessly moving his chair. At length, he answered, "Just great. But I still don't know what you think you'll get out of this. Now come on, Bruno, you know that moving in on the bonded alcohol business is foolhardy. Don't you see that?"

"It would be as easy as simply going into partnership. Don't *you* see that? You, me—partners. And besides…I've already given you Joe. Now you've got to give me something in return."

"All right. Let's forget the booze racket. What do you want you as fair exchange?"

He jerked his head toward the stage. "Well, for openers—her."

"Ynez?" Mack looked over at his wife.

"Sure. Why not? You know, for such a gentleman, you haven't even introduced us yet."

Mack stood up, caught utterly off-guard. "I'm sorry. Excuse me, I'll bring her over—" and left the table.

"Same ol' game, B.," Joe said to his brother. "You always t'reatenin' the hubbies wid screwin' their wives before you move in on one their bid'nesses."

"So? I'm entitled to it, aren't I? Look what *you're* getting, Brother."

"Well, all I can say is if you t'ink you're entitled to this par'ticlar skoyt, you've got a funny idea of what it is you need." Joe grunted. "Wait'll you get a load a' her!"

And there she was, majestic, dazzling, beside Mack—extending her hand out to Bruno to be kissed. "Hello there—Bruno Imperio, isn't it?"

Bruno got up, shook her hand instead of kissing it, held an empty chair out for her and, when seating her, lightly caressed her bare shoulders.

"Please don't touch me until I know you better," she graciously advised.

"Sorry. I lost my composure there for a minute—because I'm very sensitive when in the presence of beautiful things."

Now people were drifting in. The rolling stage was being pushed back in place and the Armstrongs had vanished behind the curtains.

"They *do* tell me I have a type of beauty—thanks!" Ynez was sphinx-like.

"You've got MY type of beauty, Mrs. Daly. And I intend on getting to know you better."

Ynez was pleased herself. It all suddenly made up for last night. She was creating exactly the desired effect and this Bruno Imperio gangster fellow was pretty breathtaking and obviously a real honest-to-goodness man. "You'll have to ask my husband first, Mr. Imperio."

"Oh, no, I don't."

Ynez was suddenly demure, batting her eyes at Mack, averting Bruno's devouring ones. "Oh, but you *do*."

"No, I don't. You're just his beard. Gals like you work hard and run around without a chain. I don't have to ask Mack here anything."

"—listen, the fact is—I *love* my husband…" Now she looked at him, offering her cigarette to be lit, lifting her shoulders ever so faintly. Taking a deep drag, she looked up at the ceiling. "Our love is the stuff of legends, Mr. Imperio. It is above the dirty word SEX." Her voice, however, was all about sex.

"I have to tell you, Mrs. Daly, that I think you're full of shit. You're living in a dream world—I read that smear Winchell did on you and he had you pegged." No one at the table even breathed.

Ynez looked him up and down. "If you want to screw me, you don't really have to get to know me, Mr. Imperio. You should've surmised that much already, knowing how full of shit I am, as you say."

"I didn't fully realize it until you opened that mouth of yours just now," he replied, hotly angered.

"Oh, you give me far too much credit, Mr. Imperio, considering my mouth is only *one* orifice," Ynez smiled broadly. "I'm just as objectionable with the one between my legs. You'll excuse me now, boys, I think I'll go and throw up." She rose and left the table.

Bruno muttered, "Now I see why women like that only hang around fairies," crushed and hating her. Joe had to smile.

Baby came floating toward them in a haze of chiffon silk posies and cigarette smoke. "We're all ready for the meeting! Let's take this upstairs where we can be private." Introductions were made and they walked toward the back of the club, Baby in the lead. "I wanna tell you, Bruno Imperio, before we go any further—"

Mack waved a warning hand. "Oh, please not now, Baby—he's just met Ynez."

"Well, all I wanted to tell him," Baby barreled right on, "—that if he tries to hurt you in any way at all, I will personally cut him a new asshole." She turned and winked at Bruno towering over her. "Now that ain't so bad, is it?"

Joey whispered to his brother. "Cute bunch, huh?"

"Shut up."

At the top of the stairs, Deucie waited.

Joe whispered, "—got a wooden leg. Don't do so good on stairs."

"Joe, just please shut the fuck up. I'm trying to do business here."

Deucie extended his hand. "—and this must be Joseph's brother, Bruno, right? Well, come on in back and let's hash this thing out—" Clumping into the office, he turned his head with a chuckle. "I take it you've met my wife?" First to be seated, he hefted his game leg up on a footstool.

Bruno remained impassive, his eyes reduced to slits casing the joint, and responded only with a slight nod of repugnance.

The chairs had been placed by Baby in a circle. Mack to Deucie's left, Baby to his right, Joe left of Mack, and Bruno directly opposite Deucie. As soon as they were seated, Mack pulled out a pile of papers from his inside pocket.

Bruno began. "I'm not going to mince words. With what happened to The Club *Intime* last night, I think we all can be assured that the raids are on once again—Business As Usual. You're going to need protection. I'm in the business of protection and I'm going to supply it to you and you're going to supply me with your grade-A stuff."

"Listen," Mack answered, "we don't need protection."

"Well, you will. Have you heard about this new Mick that just got appointed? O'Couran." (Mack nodded.) "You feel safe with him running the show?"

"He works for the same outfit I do…he's in big now with the higher-ups and they're the fellows who pay me to supply them. I don't know how you'd get around that kind of racket. It's the only fairly legal one left in this country!"

Joe shifted in his chair as Ynez tiptoed in at that moment and, finding nowhere to seat herself, pulled the desk chair over to Mack's right. Plugging her cigarette into a long obsidian holder, she waved it about until Mack got the hint and lit it.

Bruno did not even aknowledge her. "You're absolutely right. We think he was put in by the Micks over West Side and we don't even know him or how he came up so fast. But we think he's a step down instead of a step up. Don't you?"

Mack answered, "No doubt about it. If there is such a thing as a step down. We have a formal induction meeting for him up at the Mayor's office this Monday, so I'll let you know. But here it is straight: I can pay you protection money should we need it—and I doubt that—but I can't let my stuff out to you. If you ever got nailed and the booze was traced back to me, all of us gathered here would be put in the big fryer and cooked. Your family would be next, by the way. What the Prohibtion Bureau has been waiting for since it was formed is that one big chance to score hugely. That way they'll put the fear of God into everybody in this country and not one soul will ever take a drink again."

Ynez applauded briefly.

"So then give me a cut in on this club." Bruno passed Ynez a look like he might spit at her then, turning back to Mack, put on an impassive mask once more.

"In return for Joey?" Mack asked, not even surprised.

"Yes."

Joe started to say something, but stopped himself. "I know, I know…shaaat up!…"

Baby, Deucie and Ynez watched Mack do his stuff. Knowing him as they did, they felt privileged to get front row seats.

Bruno continued with specifics: "If you need him, and if he needs you as much as it looks like, Joe can be all yours just by handing me over your share of this jernt, Mr. Daly."

"I don't possess any shares, Mr. Imperio. I lease the building, that's all. This whole thing came about because we're friends, you see. If, however, you were to come in on the club, none of us would want any changes made."

"Such as? Hold on, let me guess: gambling, selling outside the establishment…all that low-life crap—prostitution…" He aimed this last word at Ynez. "Well…you've got to trust me, that's all."

"Well, if I were a person of your calibre, Mr. Imperio," Ynez contributed, suddenly, "I would certainly sell Mack's stuff on the street, charging big-time. And as for a place for gambling—well, you could just use this office here—it's right up over the club. And as for prostitution, you could fire all of the dancers and replace them with whores who would solicit the male patrons then turn their jack entirely over to you. But you'd never think of any of *those* things, would you, Mr. Imperio?"

"Lady," Bruno shook his head in near despair, "where were you raised?"

Mack said, "Listen, Bruno, you've gotten hold of my stuff already and seem to be doing pretty well with it—" He handed him a sheaf of papers. "I don't mean to put you on the spot here, but these are all phony Withdrawal Permits for your rackets. We had them traced to your operations. Look, here's a request for some sort of panacea…Moran's Elixir…and here's one for a chain of cordial shoppes called—"

Bruno was suddenly mad. "Don't throw this shit in my face when I'm tryin' to let you off easy! I could wipe this dump and all you perverts off the face of this town for good, way before the coppers get to it! And don't think I won't, either!"

He was yelling at the top of his lungs, standing, shoving the chair back and over. As it fell, he pulled out his gun, pushed his brother's face against his stomach, and rammed the tip into the side of Joe's mouth. "You want me to kill him right here and now!? 'cause I will. He never was no good to me and this whole goddammed mess has been one goddammed waste of time!"

Mack scowled up at him. "Calm down, Bruno. Joe and I destroyed the carbons first thing Friday morning. Those are from the files of stuff we already released…and without back-ups, they can't be traced. You're in the clear. As for the other creative thoughts Ynez put forward…"

Joe yanked his head free. "Lemmee talk! As soon as he found out who I really wuz, Mack pulled dem Investigation Files on bot' does dumps of yours and burned 'em. He saved us, Bruno! They wuz all set to trace those permits right to yuh!"

"Are you lying to me!?" Bruno now lowered his arm, placing his brother in a hammerlock. "Don't you lie to me, you Goddammed invert!"

Joe was choking. "Let me go asshole! Dis ain't no frame!"

Deucie calmly shifted his wooden leg. "Let the kid go. We're on the level here."

A shot went off, but not from Bruno's gun. It hit the butt end of his pistol, causing him to drop it and spring back with a shout. His gun fell to the floor loudly—not firing—with Elliot's music covering both the mysterious shot just fired and the fall of Bruno's weapon.

Everyone now shifted in their seats, as if the curtain had fallen on the middle act of some truly horrifying play. Mack grabbed Joey away from Bruno, as he moved his Adam's apple up and down to see if still worked. Bruno was baffled and maybe even a little scared—but didn't show it.

Looking around the office, standing in a semi-crouching position, he accused Ynez: "You did that!"

"I did it!" Deucie admitted, raising his wooden leg up off the stool. "See, this one's fitted with a small rifle. There's the hole where the barrel ends just below the heel of my shoe—take a gander."

"Holy Christ! Well don't point it at me!" Bruno jumped back again.

"It's set off by way of a wire," Deucie continued, almost proudly, "which runs up my trousers, then through my shirt, behind my collar and to my ear. When I just scratch my ear like this it goes off and—"

"All right! I got it!"

Mack said, " Now you listen to me, Bruno. You've got to stop hurting Joe like this. You already whacked him in the jaw. Now look what you've done to his neck here!" He paused. "You wouldn't have really killed your own brother over a dozen phony permits, would you?" he asked, his foot moving to hold Bruno's gun down under it.

Bruno replied, hardly lowering his voice, "Listen, I got shit out of this whole goddammed set-up and it is not fair to me at all. Nothing from that bitch of a wife of yours, nothing from what I sent Joe to you for, and nothing what I came here for tonight!"

Baby spoke up now: "Well, you're getting Mack's stuff by way of phony permits—so, that's something!"

"Yeah, but we did that before all of this even happened…"

"—just like more than half of New York, " Mack sighed.

"Well, it just isn't *enough*, Goddamm it!" Bruno spat out, picking up his derby and preparing to leave. "Joe! You come with me! *Now*!"

"Nawww. I don' wanna…"

Mack said very quietly, "Listen, Bruno, you give me Joe and I promise before all my friends here—and my wife, too—that I'll make it more worth your while than any deal you could ever cut with any mug, gang or syndicate in this whole town. But you've got to trust me."

There was a silence after which Bruno let go a deep and weary sigh. "I never did business with a swish before."

Ynez suppressed a noise something like a 'hmmmmf', then muttered: "Well, here's your chance, big boy."

"When?" Bruno had his hand on the doorknob now, slowly opening it. "When do we start?"

Deucie's leg was angled right at him.

"Monday after my meeting with O'Couran. I'll have to see what game he's playing first, then we can get to work. You and I."

"It's a deal."

He left then, putting on his hat, his eyes narrowing with some vast and unimaginable hatred as he took them all in, ending finally at Mack's gaze aimed back at him. Then, lowering his head, almost with a shudder of disgust, he was gone.

A collective sigh.

"Nice work, Deucers." Mack reached over and patted his real leg. "And you, too, Ynez. Thank you. That was, for me, your finest moment."

Tears welled up in her eyes, accompanied by a fragile, silent movie gesture. She stood and quietly left.

Another collective sigh.

Joe was sad. "Gee, I've made a real mess by comin' into yer crowd like dis. I'm really sorry you had to meet Bruno at his woyst…say, I'm embarassed, that's all."

Baby shook her head. "Listen, kiddo, you can choose your friends, but you can't choose your relatives. I only hope you've chosen us as your friends, 'cause we like you a lot. Now gimmee a great big hug." He enveloped her, then she hoisted Deucie up. "Well, Sureshot, shall we go down and join the party?"

Very soon after, Mack and Joe were left alone in the office, with the single desk lamp burning. Mack put the chairs back in place and picked up the phony Withdrawal Permits from the floor where they lay scattered, burning them in the naked lady ashtray.

"Jeez, what am I, a punchin' bag?" Joe had gone to the little mirror by the door, looking at the marks on his neck.

"Come over here, Joey—" Mack motioned to him.

"Jeez, you sure must love me a lot to cut a deal like that wid Bruno. God, Mack, I ain't woyth it." As Joe's head sunk to his chest, Mack lifted it gently, suddenly putting on a frown.

"I know, Mack!—*shhheeet upp*!"

• • • • •

CHAPTER X

OPEN ALL NIGHT

Meanwhile downstairs, Nolie happened to look down at the wedding ring Elliot always made her wear during the course of one of her ditties and promptly forgot the words. Being the pro that she was, Mrs. Armstrong managed to boop-a-doop it and nobody really noticed. But after the set was over, she went back into the dressing room, unable to conceal her agitation. And Nolie was usually a pastmaster at that.

"Those magazine people are out there tonight, aren't they?" Johnnie asked her, wishing the evening were ending instead of just starting.

"Yeah, they're there all right. Now we've got a love song coming up and we have to act lovey-dovey again. Oh, Johnnie, I wish sometimes we could just come clean and screw it all! Does the fact that I'm a wreck show out there?"

Johnnie, dressed up once again as Nolie's personal maid, powdered her girlfriend's shoulders while she fixed her make-up. Nolie never cried, but somehow her eyes, now and then, did get all red.

Quietly Johnnie suggested, "Don't just concentrate on those magazine people! Think of everyone else who's come to see you both. It's all your college crowd tonight—and they just worship you and Elliot. How's *he* doin'?"

"Drunk, but nobody can tell—yet." She patted Johnnie's hand, rising to change her costume. "He's got so much on his mind, though. Our new arrangements, the show Tuthill is doing, how to try and act like he's my husband!" At this they both moaned in unison. "You know, honey," Nolie continued, "he actually told me that the idea of borrowing somebody's baby then paying them off is becoming increasingly attractive. Oops. I forgot to change my hose."

"—and another thing…he's also *bitter*, honey, because Mack is solid with that guy Joe. Elliot is such a responsibility, sometimes I just don't know—"

Nolie tossed off her satin pumps with the metal buckles, sitting down and pulling on her orange stockings. "*—lots* of the time, dear John. He has his pick of every daffodil and he-flapper in this town, but what he really wants is to get married…to a MAN—and who's he married to instead? ME! Oh, God above! Where is he? He'll never have time to change!"

Johnnie helped her tie the bow into her paler-than-pale blonde curls. "Honestly, you look just like a carnival doll."

"Is that bad or good…" Nolie answered her own question: "No. Good." She nodded into her reflection. "—as long as *you* think so. Gotta put more rouge on—" The reflection in the mirror showed Nolie got up as what modern America perceived as a hot young housewife. She even had an apron sewn onto the little gingham dress she now wore and carried a feather duster.

They stood, shocked momentarily, staring at themselves. "You know, it's incredible—you're so white and I'm so black!" Johnnie laughed.

"Ye gods, what a pair. Well, at least we've got each other, hon." Nolie chuckled a little, shaking her head as Johnnie bundled her into her arms. Just then, Elliot burst in.

"Listen to this, gals—guess who's out there? No! I don't mean those magazine people, I mean that lad I made time with in Atlantic City this past summer! He got in with some Princeton kids and brought me this…"

Elliot pulled out a flask from his pocket, unscrewing it. "—and look what's in it!"

Nolie whiffed the lip of the flask. "What is it? Smells nice…"

Johnnie recognized the scent. "It's perfume! It's that smelly stuff all the Broadway queens wear!"

They both pulled off Elliot's white tuxedo while he attempted to splash some under his arms.

"He hated my drinking, but now he's back! I'm forgiven, kids!"

Nolie pushed him down onto the day-bed. "Please co-operate! Yeah! That was why you two 86'd it, if I recall."

Johnnie pulled off his trousers, while Nolie grabbed his next costume—Elliot not helping along one bit. "Awfully sweet of him—you'd better gargle with it, Elly, if you intend on seeing him!"

Elliot swallowed some, hacked it up and spit it into the tiny corner sink. This was nothing new. He had drained both Nolie and Johnnie's collection of fragrances. "Do I? Say, he's better-looking than ever," this, now muffled beneath his attempt to force an argyle sweater over his head. "Where's that Goddammed pipe? When we do the pep number tonight, I think I'll ask him to come up and show off one of his specialties…he was some slick stepper!" Elliot climbed into his plus fours. "Hey, Ynez is out there dancing with that brother of Joe's…way in the back, stuck like a fly to fly-paper—did you both happen to catch that action?"

Nolie replied, "I was a little distracted by those *Smart Stuff* people and this hideous idea of renting out a baby!"

"Why don't we hire a midget instead?" Elliot suggested, finishing his overall effect by slamming a pork-pie on his head. No one was ever sure when he was serious. But he would tell you he was always serious.

Johnnie and Nolie both shook him, telling him to straighten up.

"There's our cue!" Nolie cried.

Grabbing his sister, he rushed out, worrying if his uke was where it should be, with Johnnie following them to the wings.

Sure enough, right down front was the young man who got his heart broken by Elliot in Atlantic City last Summer. One of the many—but this boy was singular. No longer a he-flapper but a he-man, if there ever was one. Right down in front, applauding and beaming with joy as the stage rolled out to reveal a kind of heathen shrine to youth.

"Why he's become just *darling*!" Johnnie observed. "Much more filled out than last year."

She remembered his handle: "Wiggily Jack Wrigley"—a real talent for novelty dancing…double jointed in the pins…and just look at him now! She saw Jack Wrigley's face light right up with the spotlights. Elliot must've made notice of him because he gave a mannish salute during the Armstrongs lead-in to their Kute Married Kouple number, telling their devotees that:

"Life's just bliss with every kiss…"

Then kissed each other on the lips, right onstage.

"Oh, Jesus," Johnnie moaned.

Alexander was passing by. "Have you seen Mr. D. and Joseph, sugar?" he asked his sister.

Having gulped, thoroughly reviled, she replied, "Uh-uh. But just look at that young man out there, Alexander, the one who's all alone, just now grinnin'up at Elly—don't you recall him?"

"Sure…oh, my, my…" Alexander's eyes squinted through the darkness. "—and look over there and tell me who's not on her ownsome—Mrs. D.!"

Everyone had gathered around the band in a crush but in back of it all, Ynez stood with Bruno, encouraging him to manhandle her something awful.

"Honestly, it's just shameful!" Johnnie couldn't believe Mrs. D. carrying on like that.

Alexander, looking at her, curled his lip. "We gotta start in prayin' for these white folks this Sunday, sister!"

"Yes, and please make it eight sharp so Mama won't be cross!" Johnnie was referring to the Parker family's Sunday ritual, with dinner afterward at their mom's uptown. Every Saturday night, Alexander confirmed this with Nolie and Keys—Mack let him take the big car for the day's jaunt to Harlem every Sunday. Gathered 'round the dinner table, Mrs. Parker's children would exchange stories about their crazy lives downtown among the honkies.

Sometimes Mrs. Parker would demand that they stop laughing so hard at the table and elevate their minds—because it was, after all, the Lord's day. Now as to This Sunday—well, Mama was in for a real treat!

The song now finished to a round of whoops, hollers and cheers from the college set. As everyone started to dance, Ynez led Bruno toward the powder room, murmuring profuse apologies for her behavior. But Bruno wasn't buying it. Behind the portieres, she lifted his right hand to her breast and forced it beneath her gown. Since she was never one to don a brassiere, his palm caressed an alert nipple.

"—but you've got to believe me," Ynez was whispering hoarsely. "Can't you see what I'm up against? Everybody's on my husband's side. And nobody's on *my* side. I do want you, Bruno…how could I avoid someone who's *all man* like you?"

"You're a whole fourteen-minute egg, aren't you?" he whispered back gruffly to her, now cupping his hand about her breast, then forcing it further down the inside of her dress. "I know about you and your type…" he offered cryptically.

"Kiss me! Please! Kiss me hard! I can't stand it anymore!"

Bruno covered her mouth with his, forcing her against the wall, grinding into her pelvis with everything he had below his waist.

"Where's that gun of yours? I'd hate to have it go off in my booboo!" Ynez panted.

"It's in my shoulder holster, where I always keep it—"

Ynz blinked. "Oh! Then you mean what I'm feeling *isn't*…oh, *well.*" She responded by devouring him with her arms, her lips—and as far as decency would allow—her whole body. A man passing on his way toward the room marked "Gents" gave them the eye, commenting: "Whoa Nelly!"

She pulled away, breathing heavily. "It's been so long…*I can't help myself*!"

"That's all right, babe. I said I know your kind. You're that type."

Bruno had been drinking rather heavily by then, courtesy of Ynez. He attacked again with his hands reaching down, down, inside her pretty French creation, until she heard RRRIIPPPP. He had torn her bodice practically off. She tried to make him realize it by holding his arms in place. It was no use.

"Now *look* what you've done! Well! You'll just buy me a new one!"

"The Hell I will, with all your husband's money—"

"Oh shit! My straps are broken! I'm degraded!"

"Impossible! Come on outside then…I've got a big touring car…"

"Listen, all I need is a needle and thread! Oh, get your paws back where they belong!"

"Come on with me—" He was forcing her now. She was beginning to get a little scared. "—we can climb in the back and go at it. Put the side curtains down and nobody'll be the wiser."

"Why, I'm falling out of this thing, you big *beast*!"

He was by now pulling her toward the coat check, as she wrapped her arms over her breasts, attempting to make a graceful exit. Fortunately, Baby was way back in the kitchen.

"Never mind my fur…I'll get it later…just go past Keys or he'll—"

Before she could finish, they were outside where the redoubtable Keys presided over a line of society swank. She whispered desperately, "Bruno! Behave! I *know* these people—oh, *do* act like a gentleman!"

There on the sidewalk, only a few feet from those waiting to be let in, he turned toward her, seemingly enflamed by the fact that, at last, for some inexplicable reason—he was to have her. "I'm crazy-hot to have you, and you feel the same way about me, goddamm it. Now stop acting like something you aren't! Come on!" He forced her along with people staring, murmuring.

On the same side of the street as the club, parked toward Sixth Avenue, was a huge deep-green Packard touring car.

(Exactly the kind gangsters drive. Bullet proof and outfitted with tommy guns, no doubt! Ynez was thinking.)

"Get in—and get that Goddammed frock of yours off!" Bruno ordered. She had goose-bumps and was relieved to find the interior a shield from the wind which had risen. Bruno efficiently dropped all the side-curtains as Ynez pulled off what was left of her gown, lying down, breathless,upon the seat. There was plenty of room—Bruno was quite right.

He was on her immediately. Pulling off his jacket, ripping away at his tie, she stopped at the shoulder holster.

"—I'll get that," he growled.

"Put it away! Throw it in the front seat. It frightens me!"

He did so. Angrily tearing his trousers asunder, Bruno lifted her up as she submitted to him, hoisting her skirt, opening her legs. With this, utterly relaxed in her nakedness, she smiled, cat-like, up at him.

"Take it easy, big boy…what's gotten into you ever so suddenly?" she whispered.

"I hate you," he replied.

Squirming about, licking her lips, lifting her arms over her head then finally dropping them about his neck, she pulled him right over her, inviting fast penetration.

"You're some twist, know that?" His eyes, through the darkness of the auto, were like some powerful animal's. He was just as rough with her, within those few remarkable moments, as she'd figured he would be. *I can take it,* Ynez was thinking to herself. After all, he was big and made of steel just like Dempsey. He was mean and low, too. But handsome as Hell.

The thought occurred to her that he might grab her neck and choke her to death. Gangsters were known to do those things. But the very word GANGSTER made her feel so unnaturally unleashed; she found herself clawing him, biting him…making him suffer.

Maybe, she thought then, *I might grab his neck and choke him to death instead!* Mack might like it if she did him in! "I'm not through with you yet, Mr. Imperio…" she hissed into his ear.

"Don't! Let go! You're hurtin' me!"

Ynez had developed certain techniques upon which she now complimented herself. After all this time, she still remembered a few neat moves.

"Oh, *Chhhaaaariiissst!*" He collapsed back, breathing hard, sweating, swearing, like a man who had become lost in a devouring jungle—gaudy, but volatile in its strange claustrophobic beauty. Having found himself a clear path out of this undergrowth, he was, just then, despising the place and himself for becoming lost within it.

He rudely pushed her away with a growl of repugnance. "You lousy bitch!"

The eisenglass at every window in the Packard was, by now, steamed up. Ynez remained still, looking him over, hardly blinking, not even attempting to cover herself up, unashamed at the manner in which Bruno had used her body. Legs still fully opened; her breasts, high and illuminated by the nearby streetlight, looked opalescent. Her lips, a moist vermillion pout, let go a cutsie-wootsie sigh, then got right down to business, rattling away in a thoroughly business-like tone.

"Now you can do something for *me*. Tell me how you found out about the kind of marriage I've got…"

"Gimmee a minute here, Goddamn you!"

"Leave your gun right there in the front seat, Mister. Tell me now, Bruno, my new all-man lover. Just do that much for me…if you…um…*like* what's going on here. After all, there's no reason why we shouldn't continue our special friendship, *ne c'est pas*?"

He started to dress. "All right. Here it is—you used to work at a place called *La Maison*, didn't you?"

"Yes. Two years ago. Before I was married."

"It was a whorehouse, wasn't it?"

Ynez lifted her head languorously and laughed, not answering his question, her index finger making curley-cue's all over her breasts. "Say, listen, hot shot, you've got to run me over to one of those Broadway dress shoppes that are open all night. My poor gown is in shreds and it's got your goo-goo all over it!"

"Hold on." He found his keys. "Get in front. I've got to open the windows. Put this lap rug over you. *Well*? Was it or wasn't it a whorehouse?"

"No. It wasn't. Not at all, in fact. If I told you what it really was, it would probably just go over your head. But if you're implying that I worked there as a prostitute—you're way off, brother."

"Well, you sure screw like a high-octane whore, so I thought that this *Maison* place must've been a ritzy brothel."

"Well, you couldn't be more *wrong*, Mr. Imperio," Ynez answered. "Say! What's the rush?" He was driving like mad, weaving in and out of after-theatre traffic.

"I've got to see clients…so…you weren't ever a whore…and that place wasn't a whorehouse?"

"No to both, Big Burly Bruno. It was a *Maison pour les Voluptuaries*. And it was completely an undercover operation—unknown except to The Initiates. The only reason it got closed was because of the dirty bookstore on the main floor. I don't see how *you* ever found this out!"

Bruno looked confused, like he didn't want to go into it.

"—anyway, I heard about you marrying our boy Benny Leventhal, maybe as an arrangement of some sort…" He lit a cigarette and offered one to Ynez, who refused it.

"Only Egyptian, thanks." Intent on pursuing this further, she leaned forward now. "How did you ever put two and two together? How did you figure out Mack's inclination?"

"I told you already. What does it matter?"

"On hearsay, then, you pointed your brother in Mack's direction to bring him to ruin by making my husband fall for him?"

"Yeah. Here's one open. Take this dough and make it quick."

"Bruno! I can't go in like this! *You* go in and pick me out something in black, no bows, a little hip swag maybe…these shoppes have nothing chic ever, but with black you can't ever—"

"*Jeeeesus*! I bet you drive that Jew fairy of yours nuts! Look at you, lying there with your goddammed tits out like you didn't care!"

"—get me a size six. And NO trim, please."

He grumbled, opening the door and snatching the keys from the ignition.

"So, anyway, do you think my Mackie really is *falling* for your brother?" Ynez now sat up, fixing her hair in the rearview mirror. "Or do you think your brother's just working hard and doing a good job of it?—or could it be both?"

"I'll tell you in a sec. *Chhhhhharriiisstt.*"

Ynez snuggled into the lap rug. It wasn't chinchilla, like *their* big car had, but it was cozy anyway. She rummaged through the glove box, finding a bottle labled "Moran's Elixir," and tested it by puttting a little on her finger.

"Medicine," she concluded, squinting to see the bonded alcohol information on the back. "Mack is simply *every*where!"

Bruno returned and threw a black, rayonette number in her face.

"This'll do," she said, examining it. "Thanks."

He peeled out, tires screeching. "So—to answer your question. I DON'T CARE. I don't CARE if my half-witted brother and your pansy husband are sweet on each other or NOT, see? Got that? All I care about is getting Mack Daly's *alcohol*...now what's so difficult about *that*!"

"Well, if that's *all there is to it*, fine! Say, I guess I will take one of your ciggies after all—are you taking me back to the club?"

"No, I'm takin' you to gay Paree! *Of course* I am! What am I supposed to *do* with you? I've got to get to work here!"

"Oh, take me with you, Bruno!—downtown dives, taxi joints, blind pigs!—as long as there won't be any shooting—"

Bruno laughed heartily. "You've seen too many pictures, sister, and if I did take you with me, you'd be bored to distraction."

Ynez looked up, pursing her lips. "So now you're taking a run-out powder on me! Well, I like that! "

Bruno said: "Get out."

"*What!* You're not even going to walk me back to the club?" He shook his head, reaching for his gun, then adjusted the holster within his jacket. "—well, at *least* take me around to the back alley. Talk about ignominious!"

"You know, sometimes you act like you might be sort of intelligent! I *told* you—I'm *busy*. Now get *dressed*."

"—this had better be only the beginning, Mr. Bruno Imperio!" he heard her say from underneath the new frock as she put it over her head.

Dressed and alighting from the Packard, Ynez found herself a block from the deVol.

"You make me sick!" Bruno yelled from inside the car.

"I'm the best screw you've ever had!" she shouted back then, realizing what she'd done, looked guiltily about. "Gimmee a kiss goo'm'bye..." she pouted.

He did as he was told, leaning out the window. They kissed then, placing her lips to his ear, Ynez traced its line with her tongue. Hoping the effect was a success, she added, in an efficient voice, "I want you to tell me all you know about Mack and me—"

"Well, I want *you* to tell that goddammed mockie that he'd better surrender several thousand gallons of hooch to *me* pronto—or else. Got that, Mrs. Daly?"

He roared off. Ynez stood there, very cold, very confused. She walked quickly up to the club and down the alley, pounding on the delivery doors.

Upstairs in the office, Joe, looking out the window, told Mack, "It's dat wifey of yours—breakin' down duh door. She musta bin wid Bruno."

"I should've thought as much," Mack said, sighing. "Still, I guess after last night, she had to take what she could get—I'll go down and let her in."

There she was, her hair askew, in some new get-up. "Oh! *Mack*! Thank *Heavens*! I'm *freezing* out here...but I'm glad you came to my rescue. Listen, I've *got* to talk to you...*alone*..."

As they went down the narrow corridor passing Alexander and Johnnie on the way, Mack, by means of sign language, told Johnnie that the Armstrongs' dressing room was going to be "in use" for a a short time. By the important evidence of Ynez's wholly altered appearance and the look on both their faces, she understood perfectly.

Ynez closed the door and barricaded it with her body, as Mack stood waiting before her. She told him bluntly, "—all right. I let him screw me...and Mack! It was *terrible*! Oh! I felt so *cheap*! So cheap!"

"Ynez, so what?You got what you'd wanted at last."

"Listen, my pet, just call me Mata Hari! I'm thinking of becoming a double agent—isn't that what they're called? I got him to admit to *more* than a few things."

"—such as?" Mack lit up a cigarette.

"Such *as* that Joe is really *playing* you, Mack Daly, for a sucker. He's working you every inch of the way!"

"—go on."

A pause. "—*well*? Doesn't that shock you?"

"Just go on, Ynez."

Realizing she was getting nowhere, Ynez quickly recounted what Bruno had told her about *La Maison* and the "leak" regarding their marriage.

Mack responded, "Well, all I know is he got it from some gal whom he hired. After all, Joe was perfect for the part—and Bruno loaded him into the cannon just like at the circus, and shot him my way!"

"So you don't trust him, do you?" Ignited by this, Ynez drew closer to her husband, taking the cigarette from his lips.

"...it's not a question of trusting him, Ynez. The fact is we're in love with each other."

"Ha! Ha! Ha! Not *that* again! Now the feeling has beomce *mu*tual!" she teased childishly, uncoiling her body, her face now close to Mack's, his own cigaret hanging from her lips. "Well, get this—Bruno is falling in love with me! *Me*, Mack Daly!"

"Fix your face, Ynez, your lip rouge is smeared everywhere."

She went to the make-up mirror. "I won't say I could *love* a man like that. I've obviously got better taste—" She shot him a look over her shoulder. He let go a weighted sigh. "—but I do need sex. And, oh, my darling! He does service this ol' libido—and howsky! It was somehow really *glorious* to just let myself turn into such a—"

"—don't say it! I get you. Listen, Ynez, Joe and I are leaving now—going back home. Do you you want a ride?"

She turned, bracing herself against the make-up table. "I hope to God he's not moving *in* with us!"

"Ynez, do you want a ride or not?"

"Well, *no*. In fact, " she lied on, "Bruno's coming back to get me. He's renting a suite at the Astor for us…I'll be over there if you need me…he's just gone to rob a bank or kill somebody or something."

"All right, Ynez."

He left.

Nolie, Elliot, Johnnie and Wiggily Jack Wrigley found, upon entering the dressing room, who else but Ynez—slouched over the vanity, head buried in her arms, a bottle of gin at her elbow. Having wept angry tears, her mascara had made her eyes great hollows.

All three were stopped short by this surprise and, as she raised her head, hair-do askew, murmuring a lady-like "—oh! *So* sorry," Elliot introduced her to his last-summer's flame.

"Wriggs, I'd like you to know the Wreck of the Hesperus."

She didn't even acknowledge him. "—can I stay with you folks tonight?" she whined. "They've *left* me here! Left without me!"

This was not what Elliot had foreseen. Jack Wrigley (known to all as "Wriggs") was to be the guest of honor for an overnighter, and not Ynez.

"Ynez! Whatever happened?" Nolie asked, nearly laughing.

"Don't answer that…" Johnnie interjected. "—it might take too long—and they're not finished out front yet."

Elliot was trying to make Ynez understand by repeatedly inclining his head and eyes toward Wriggs in quick jerks. Ynez, who had informally studied silent film acting, got the message. "Oh, all right then, if it's a full house! I'll just stay upstairs with Baby and Deucie."

She attempted to rise, but faltered. "Sorry, old pal, I emptied your gin…"

"Good!" Wriggs said, then took a step back, embarrassed.

"Won't someone please help me up the stairs?" Ynez was playing it for all it was worth. "I will!" Wriggs now took a step forward, gallant youth that he was, however embarrassed. "What stairs? Where?"

Elliot pushed him aside. "—thanks anyway, boy scout, but never mind…you stay right here."

"We'll help you, Ynez, " Nolie volunteered. "Come on, old girl, up and at 'em!"

"Oh, you darlings! There, there, you've got me now—oh—this damned dress…too big! I've got hold of my boobies—wouldn't want to expose my breasts to this young man here!" Tittering, she was hoisted aloft. "I just had the most terrible experience with that brother of Joseph's. Such a low-life gangster!" she was saying on the way out, Elliot pushing her, "…but I had to do it—for Mackie!"

Elliot slammed the door on the three ladies.

"Gangster? What gangster?" Wriggs asked, completely confused by now.

"Pay no mind, Wriggs! That woman is under the care of a Freudian doctor—sorry, I mean *Froodian* doctor. Whew. Let's sit and start all over again…"

"*Do* you really want to start all over again?" Wriggs asked, also sitting on the studio couch.

"No, no, no. Not that. I mean, that's not what I meant. I meant, let's start the whole thing of us coming in here and pretend we never witnessed…what we just witnessed. Not you and me…starting over again. I mean…not that we ever could or would…but…"

"But what?" Wriggs had that infernal all-American smile on his face the entire time.

Nervous, Elliot fidgeted. "But what. What? Well, it's good to see you, Wiggly Jack Wrigley!" Elliot scratched his head, lit a cigarette and leaned forward, elbows on his knees, trying to give the impression of the rising star he was.

"No more of that 'Wiggly Jack Wrigley' stuff for me, Elliot. I did that turn in vaudeville and found it a sordid and cheap world. Now that I'm working at Princeton. I'm…"

"Oh, you're going to Princeton now?"

"No. *Working at*. Not *going to*. I do work full-time there, though. In the athletic department. However, sometimes, they let me sit in on classes and I'm broadening my education."

"—as well as your chest!" Elliot commented.

"Well, all of the fellows there and even the profs have been very, very good to me."

"I'll just bet they have."

"No—not in that way, Elliot. There's nothing like that kind of thing going on…nothing sordid or decadent or indecent," Wriggs stopped, carefully assembling his phrases in that mind of his. "I admit, I've been pursued by certain types, you know what I mean…and, yes, Elliot, young women, too."

Elliot's heart was in the process of melting. "I'm sorry if I made you uncomfortable by asking you to come up and do a solo with us," Elliot said.

Wriggs had declined, of course, waving it off, blushing, taking a step back. "No more of that for me, Elliot," Wriggs said, smile fading, quietly definite.

"No more…of—anything—for you?"

"As I said, I've had you on my mind *a lot*. Everywhere I look it seems you pop up—music stores, newsstands, malt shoppes…and if I don't see that face of yours, well, I hear your voice on the rah-deo, it seems."

"Gee, thanks." Elliot felt his heart melt.

"I've also had it on my mind that we had a grand time this past summer. And I've thought a lot about your drinking, too, and how that was what really came between us."

"Oh, my God, don't tell me you've come here tonight to save me from the Demon Rum! Wriggs, please! Don't tell me you've turned into a…a…*do-gooder*…"

"Elliot, you're still, to my way of thinking, a grand fellow. But since I saw you last, I've been inspired by Socrates and Plato and the Spartans!"

(Oh boy! Elliot was thinking. *—up on the soap box with him!)*

"And," Wriggs continued, even more serious, "—there is a different *kind* of love between men which is higher and finer and nobler than—that other kind of love certain men of a depraved nature only lust after."

"Wait a minute. Wait a minute…Before we go any further…does this more noble kind of love include *sex*?"

"Of course—sex! YES! Sex, by all means."

"Oh! Good! For a minute there, you really scared me…whew…move over while I let you feel my pulse—" Elliot transferred himself to the studio couch, placing his arm over Wrigg's lap.

"Now let's be serious here for a moment," Wriggs said, looking out of the corner of his eye at Elliot, but leaving his arm right where it was. "I was hoping you might think about us two getting back together…"

"Tonight?"

"Say, I'm already up past my bed-time. Every morning at five I'm up for my three-mile run. Since I've been working for the Athletic Department, I've become a great follower of Bernarr Macfadden, you know."

"Oh, God—you and Mack!" Elliot grumbled.

"Who?"

"Oh, my best friend Mack, remember him? He was bitten by that physical culture bug years ago."

"Oh, yes. That strapping man with the winning way. I only met him. Never got to know him." Still Elliot's arm lingered, now about to go into action and about to grab Wrigg's thigh.

"Well, I'm sure you'll have a lot to discuss with him…all that noble fairy bullshit."

"Now, now, Elliot. My philosophy has taken me out of the doldrums and lifted me into the realms of highest hope! Just think of those Spartan heroes of the glory that was Greece, loving each other with such…magnificence!"

Transported, Wriggs looked out at seemingly nothing, but Elliot knew he was picturing something sensual and began to nuzzle closer, raising his arm up, caressing Wriggs, trying to get him to relax.

Wriggs went on, passionately, "I can picture myself with some beloved chum in some great forest going at a giant oak with a couple of axes! Naked and singing!"

"Naked and singing! Naked and singing! Naked and singing!" Elliot echoed. "But what about the poison ivy and the pricker bushes?"

"Oh, that's right, those friends of yours who own this club here once had a naturists' colony, didn't they? Didn't you tell me it never got off the ground because of the bug bites?" Wriggs had landed, now looking into Elliot's eye, touching him.

"Amongst other things, yeah…Come on, come on. Flop over me. I don't have much more time before I have to go again!"

"But your crowd has the wrong idea of it all, Elliot! It's not about whoopee, it's about—say, *your breath smells of gin.*"

"It does? How about that!"

But Wriggs had sat up. "Everything always was a-o.k. with us, Elliot, except the drinking."

Calling to mind yet again that he had promised everybody he knew that he would go on the wagon if the club was a success—and it certainly was—Elliot replied, "Well, you know what? Made a vow, which I didn't keep—that I'd climb on the wagon. But now that you're back, Wriggs, I WILL keep that vow, kiddo."

"—you said that last time, Elliot," Wriggs looked him squarely in the eye as a football coach might.

Springing to his feet, Elliot began to strip off his costume, jubilant suddenly. "No, siree! Raise my right hand! oops—" It had gotten caught in the sleeve of his shirt.

"Do you really and truly *swear* this time?" Wriggs continued, also standing there like he was ready to catch a forward pass, a smile slowly lighting up his face once again.

"Honest Injun." Elliot also smiled, and that was the smile of a star. So Wriggs, quite naturally, melted.

"God, you look fetching in your BVDs…" he hoarsely sighed. "I'd forgotten just how grand-looking you were, Elliot!" Suddenly grabbing his favorite crooner and long-missed heart-throb, Wriggs caught him in a bear hug, grabbing Elliot's ass with both hands.

"Hello, fellas!" The girls were back. Wriggs released Elliot like a medicine ball.

"Winola?" Wriggs offered, his voice slightly shaking, "Jonquil? How is…your–um–patient?"—for want of something better to say.

"Oh, just fine," Nolie answered, smiling cheerfully. "She's always just *fine*. Now I have to change, so why don't you step out?"

"Elliot," Wriggs said, clearing his throat, "I'm going back to my crowd now—good-bye…"

"Wait! Come home with me tonight! Are you nuts? You will, won't you?"

Wriggs nodded with vigor, looking like he might faint, opened the door, went out, closed it, opened it again and poked his head in, this time with a charming grin, then closed it again.

Elliot looked at them. "Well, I must be out of my mind but I told him I was stopping drinking. I did. And I am."

Both girls said nothing but merely stared. Nolie, ready to pull another gown over her head, diverted the subject: "Let's hurry so we can sit with the magazine people for a while before we have to go on."

"You both don't think I'll make it, do you?" Elliot muttered. They just looked at him.

But Elliot was floating on air. He would take Wriggs out to Great Neck the next day (on Sundays, with Johnnie at Mrs. Parker's, Elliot and Nolie drove out there) and show him off as being Back in the Fold Again. Mack might not even remember him, but would certainly be impressed with his wholesome-homo outlook! *No more booze*, Elliot told himself. He would need everybody's help on this. But with Wriggs in his life, it wouldn't be difficult…or at least *as difficult*…that all-American was going to be just the right medicine. Nolie had Johnnie, Miss Harrison had Keys, Mack had Joe, Deucie had Baby, and Ynez had…?…*poor* Ynez.

Anyway, now he had Wriggs. He would write better ditties, sing in a better voice, play better stuff, arrange better arrangements, and feel he had something to defend when he had to constantly lie about being married to his sister…and now lying about when and how a baby would soon come along? Piece of cake!

Moments later, Elliot ecstatically churned all of these thoughts about in his mind, as he turned on the 150 percent charm when greeting the folks from *Smart Stuff* magazine at their ringside table.

"We felt," Nolie was saying to them, having gotten it all down pat, "the career of a jazz orchestra manager and his wife was just too much for raising a family. Touring the country! My goodness! Buses and trains! One night here, another there! What kind of life would that be for a snook-um-wook-ums, now, I ask you that? And so, we set aside the past few years to firmly establish ourselves as hits! And we're so blest to have so many fans, and so many nice things being said about us, we do think the stork might just be hovering nearby in a year—or so!"

Johnnie, passing by and taking it all in, decided to go outside and talk to Keys. She'd also broken out in a cold sweat.

"Then do you and your hubby," the plump, utterly thrilled interviewer was asking in a breathless trill, "believe in the modern idea of a 'planned marriage'?"

Elliot answered, "Do we? Say, we always plan everything."

• • • • •

CHAPTER XI

NIGHTMARE AT NOON

When Baby found Ynez curled up on their new davenport at five a.m. Sunday morning, she covered her with a blanket she'd knitted for Junior years back, then swore several times under her breath and turned in.

Deucie, who had just finished putting that night's profits behind the toilet, asked, "Whadda you make of it, honey?" half-asleep himself.

"Well, we both witnessed her antics with that crumb Bruno after our meeting. She must've gotten him to screw her, then he dumped her..."

"Finally! But I figgered that would happen..." Deucie answered thickly.

"Me, too. " She was as good as in dreamland.

"Honey?"

"Yeah," Baby foggily replied. Maybe he had A Great Thought. They frequently came at dawning.

"—he didn't dump her. He set her up. Used his other weapon: his dingdong."

"You're right! The son of a bitch! And she's too Goddammed vain to realize it."

"—we gotta watch out now...You know Ynez, darlin'!"

Baby saw it all in a flash and decided not to skip her prayers as dog-tired as she was. Ynez, however, was wide awake as a result of this conversation, having heard everything. And as she lay there, she began to think again of all that had brought her to the life she had come to lead.

• • •

She'd been having an awful dream, so it was just as well. Ynez rarely dreamt, yet when she did, it was always in black and white and she was always the leading lady. And it seemed to her that dreams did nothing more than dredge up the past. Dreams were never, ever, what they'd been cracked up to be.

Because now, there she was, laying wide awake, tortured once more by her life just past...neither dead nor buried. She had, of course, found the events of that evening obviously disturbing. Ynez hated to relive any parts of her past; she didn't like them, and this was not without good reason. *La Maison*...now how did Bruno get hold of that bit of information? That was what triggered the goddammed dream, of course.

Ynez had awakened with a start and at first didn't know where in Hell she was...then she remembered. God! Another night on a couch! This time, the deVols' spanking new parlor set sofa! Oh! How her lovely lean legs ached—curled up as they were! The sun was coming up. Oh! She was simply crazed with fatigue!

Why attempt to get back to sleep at all? She toyed with the cigarette as memories of those days just before she had actually met Mack were already falling upon her like a gigantic, damp, wilted gardenia.

Even her most recent past—being her marriage to Mack—could not live up to what she had hoped life might've offered her. It was hardly, she decided, the stuff of which dreams are made!

And, prior to that—those years right after the War, when she had, at last, gotten herself to New York—so alone and so broke—they had not *at all* been what she'd hoped life would be like.

Yes, that was it...so much of it had been so very disturbing that—finally—she had tried, and succeeded, in convincing herself that It Had All Never Even Happened. But still...there it was...right before her. *La Maison.*

And yet, that was how she had met Baby—and thence, Mackie. Where would she be now if she hadn't not gone to the curious bookstore upon the Countess' prompting, that January day of 1925?

She'd been dancing at the Beaux Artes on 40th Street and had heard of a fortune teller who lived right upstairs. No mere woman, at that. A countess, who was a professional clairvoyant and told you things that were unaccountably true!

And so, Ynez's dream was about the Countess. Once again. Ynez always held a secret horror of the Countess; she felt someday she might end up like her. Everything the Countess stood for...everything she, in fact, *emitted* (the scent of her cigars, the overpowering odor of tuberose and Chinese temple incense, the medication with which she smeared her poor, strangely withered hands) all were permanently filed in Ynez's olfactories.

It seemed so very long ago...when she'd gone upstairs, just before work, to have a reading with the Countess. and without her even knowing it, Mack Daly had passed her—right in that very corridor! Talk about Fate!

He was just leaving, following his session with her—and Ynez was just arriving. They had glanced at one another. Into each other's souls really, Ynez had always thought. And then, he was gone.

It turned out that the Countess had actually known Mack's Father (whom she always referred to as "The Baron," Mack said). Ynez found that out later, Mack having assured the future Mrs. Daly that no Jew living under the old empire could ever have been a baron—his Father most of all—but Ynez clung to the title and felt somehow, by reflected glory, that she, herself, was royal by marriage. That part of it was nice. It had made her act dignified at least.

But the Countess—she really was a Somebody. This fabled and perhaps deliberately strange oracle truly could claim to be of the nobility. Part Russian, part Magyar-Hungarian, she had married a member of the ousted Serbian royal family, thus receiving her title. She had also predicted Ynez's marriage to Mack before Ynez had even met him! The Countess knew him well and adored him.

"Who was that man out there?" Ynez had queried upon entering. "He's the most beautiful thing I've ever seen in my life!"

The Countess said nothing. But a little way into her trance, she tossed a scarf over her crystal, looked across at Ynez and became very matter-of-fact.

"This is what you must do, my child—if you wish to know him," Xacha intoned. "Go and see a former nurse who works at a place on 68th Street which caters to private and exquisite theatrics for those of particular sensibilities. This woman will give you a position, and introduce you to a man named Benjamin Leventhal—the son of a very dear old friend of mine from before the War."

"But what about that man I just saw in the hall? And what's a former nurse doing at a place like that?" asked Ynez, aflutter.

"She is taking care *of the sick*, of course," the Countess answered. "And the man who you just saw is not one, but two."

She handed Ynez a visting card upon which was printed the information the Countess had just told her, exposing the peculiar flesh-like gloves she wore, looking for all the world like thin layers of human skin, complete with porcelain fingernails.

Withdrawing her right hand back beneath its voluminous sleeve, the Countess told her to ask for a certain "Madame deVol" and that Xacha herself had recommended her...and to also stress that she was not only a dancer, but a woman *of a certain type as well.*

Why, Ynez, boldly asked, could not the Countess introduce her to Benjamin Leventhal herself? And *what* about the man in the hall!

The answer was a shrug and in her ghostly, gritty voice, the Countess replied simply, "One coin has two sides, does it not, my child?"

Ynez had to admit that, yes, it did.

It wasn't until quite a while later that Ynez learned of Mack's deference and loyalty to the fabled clairvoyant. Baby told her that he'd paid for her passage to America and had set her up at the Beaux Artes through his two friends, the Bustanoby brothers. And also that everything she had every told Mack Daly had so far come true.

And when Ynez, so shocked, so scared—for what reason she could not find—had asked Baby, "Even *me*? Even that he'd marry *me*?" Baby had replied, "Well, you're married to him, aren't you?"

It always bothered Ynez. How, like ships, they'd passed in the night (well, it was actually 3:45 in the afternoon—but still), how the Countess had the card ready, there, on her table.

She vowed she would never see her again. She never wanted to dream of her again. But always, she did dream of her, and somehow felt she *would* be seeing her again.

And so, Ynez arrived at the house on 68th Street, as she was told, having taken a bus up Fifth Avenue, frozen to the bone in her three-year old cape. Finding it to be a Georgian style mansion, apparently uninhabited except for the street floor which held a shoppe for books, she saw but one sign which read: "RARE AND PRECIOUS" swinging in the wind.

Was this man Benjamin Leventhal a bookworm? And who, therein, was sick?

"I am looking for Madame deVol," Ynez said to the prim relic of Victoriana at the desk. "Countess Xacha Obrenevitch sent me. I am a dancer and a woman *of a certain type*."

"Ah!" said the man. "Would you please come back here, Mam'zelle?"

Following him, she noted how he kept staring at her feet, and looked up quizzically at him.

"Ah! You have no galoshes? It may snow again soon…" he observed.

"I…I didn't want to spoil my ensemble…"

At the back of the store, behind a heavy calf-skin portiere, was a small chamber stacked neatly with files, some of which were in French, others in…Latin, perhaps? Just ahead, a stairway.

"Go up. Please. She will be somewhere in the nether confines…" He waved his hand but did not lift his glance from her feet.

Ynez found herself on the actual first floor of the mansion, at the back. A powerful aroma of *chypre* hung in the air. Not a soul about. The room was hung in deep red velvet. Just like a funeral parlor!

Ynez was seized by a moment of panic. *This* was no place to shimmy! And where were all the sick?

"Hellooo?" she called.

"Hello yourself!" A voice said from somewhere beyond. Following the voice, she encountered, for the first time in her life but hardly the last, Baby deVol.

In the third room toward the front, opposite a truly imposing sweeping stairway, a woman of small stature was supervising some workmen as they covered the floor in black carpeting. The whole room was, in fact, black. Even the windows had been hung in black velvet. At each corner was a huge jeweled torchere like something out of a Theda Bara movie. The floor she walked on was deeply cushioned. This was no ordinary rug. It must've been for those who were sick—muffling all the noise.

Ynez repeated the purpose of her visit.

Madame deVol, looking her over, smiling politely but not warmly, whispered for Ynez to follow her.

Incredulous, standing there in the marble hallway, Ynez looked Madame deVol over. This gal was not like any nurse she'd ever seen!

Baby deVol asked, taking the Countess' card, "Yes, but what *kind* of certain type are you, exactly, dearie? We've got lots of certain types here."

"A novelty dancer. I do the shimmy."

"The legal or illegal shimmy?" Madame deVol asked instantly, for some reason a little nervous.

"Well…I can really let go, if that's what you mean."

"So much so that you've been arrested? Be honest now."

Ynez held her head high. "I've never been arrested. But if you must know, I *can* go that far. I consider what I do ART."

"Good girl! Let me shake your hand. Myself, I'm a progressive…my husband is, too. Not Bohemian, but more the European type. We spent time in France during the War and got inspired there. We don't believe in free love, but we do believe in the idea that we're all only human when all's said and done." She winked and smiled. "Would you like a cup of tea? It'll warm you up…"

Ynez had no idea at all what Baby was talking about at that time.

Yes, she would like tea, and so Baby led her into an office directly behind the black velvet room. It was there Ynez got her first inkling of What It *Was* All About.

"Can't take your eyes off the etchings, can you?" Baby smiled. "Have a seat and I'll fill you in."

Behind the desk was a small gas burner with tea things. Baby put the kettle on, then sat behind the desk. It was littered with a dozen or so black cambric masks, some of which were turned the wrong way and said something written in white ink in French.

"Has there been a masquerade party?" Ynez asked.

"No, no, no, my dear. These are for memberships. See, each one has the name and contact person written on the back. Go ahead, hold it up to your face!"

Ynez did so, then pulled it away. The writing had disappeared!

Baby was gleeful. "That's invisible ink, so nobody can trace the folks who patronize this dump! It responds to the warmth of your skin. "

"—but you said there was a contact name as well as a patron's?" Ynez asked, turning the mask over in her hand, amazed.

"Sure, a *Liaison.* That's a sucker who is paid off dearly to let the patron know when there are soirees. That's what they're called '*liaisons*'...everything is very contintental, you know. They're sworn to absolute secrecy! That's the only way word can get out—or else we'd all be hauled into the hoosegow. But don't worry!"

"I'm only worried about a regular paycheck. Is this *steady* work?" Ynez asked, picturing an occasional strip-act once a month or so.

"We're going great guns most every night. But a lot depends on what kind of act you can get up. Seems like you've gotta give it a little twist—if you get my drift. Dirty shimmy or no dirty shimmy, you're going to have play up to our clients' odd little quirks in order to make dough around here."

"Is this a whorehouse?—because if it is, you can count me out!" Ynez registered raised eyebrows.

"No, honey! Keeps your socks on. Although we do, in fact, have some rooms upstairs called '*Salons des Assignations*' where people can go...but they pay for the room, not for the girl—or boy..."

"Boy?"

"Yes, we employ young lads here, as well. Did the Countess send you for your dancing or for your imaginative flair?"

"What?"

Baby laughed again. "Water's boiled."

While making the tea, she continued on, "I used to be a damned good nurse—during the War, but I couldn't find a thing to bring in the jack—'til now! And in some cock-eyed fashion, it's my way of helping people!" She let go a throaty laugh. "These folks here are pretty regular sorts, though—once you get past the fact that they're all pree-verts. Say, where are you from anyway, honey? What brought you to New York? The truth now, kiddo! I've met all different types in my time"

Ynez briefly told her everything.

"—and you didn't want to get into the Follies or something like it? Something legit?" Baby was bringing a pretty arrangement to the desk...an Oriental tea set with matching cups and saucers depicting naked men and women wrapped about one another in odd positions. "This is worth a fortune, but I couldn't find anything else."

"—as far as me going legit, honestly, I wouldn't know how. I can't follow steps, things like that. I guess I could pass for a showgirl, though."

"You sure as hell could! You're stunning!"

"But the kind of dancing I do means steady work. I can peel off as much as they'll pay me for, or I can leave it on. I was doing my stuff at the Beaux

Artes and doing all right, too, but they're cleaning up Broadway, as you must know…I have to be careful—" The tea tasted lovely.

"Do you turn tricks on the side?"

"Never. I'm a romantic. I'm in love with gorgeous things and people. I can't help myself! I'm stubborn that way, I guess."

"In other words, you don't really like sex."

"—well!" Ynez paused, tea cup about to touch her lips, somewhat wounded by Baby's candor. "The fact is, I find most men to be brutes…all the ones who've gotten the best of me, anyway, and there were more than a few! I can tell you that because you're a nurse. Afterward I just wanted to slap them! Sometimes, I even did!"

Baby laughed loudly. It was very surprising. "Good for you, darling! But, say, you don't like your own kind, do you? You know…a Daughter of Sappho? I don't myself but, you know, honey, I have to ask you these things. I hope my approach isn't too clinical for you."

"No! This is kind of fun! No, I don't. I'm attracted only to pretty men…like Valentino or Gilbert or Rod La Rocque!" (*Or that man in the hallway back by the Countess'!)*

"Know any?"

"Chorus boys…" Ynez admitted, with a shrug.

"Like 'em?"

"I love them! We have so much fun together…but of course, they don't like me, not in *that* way…"

"Well, this set-up here is only for those sorts with special tastes, Miss O'Reilly. In fact, almost anything the traffic will allow, IF they can pay for it…and the *couvert* is pretty steep, believe you-me! We have lots of gents who would love to see the real shimmy—as it should be done—and who'll pay a lot for it as well. But you've got to take it all off, honey! Every stitch!"

"But I don't want any of them touching me now! I've had it up to *here* with those grabbers!" she pointed a gray-gloved finger at her lovely penciled brow.

"Well, you see, that's the beauty of it. They never WANT to touch you. If they do—well, whatever it is makes them tick just fades and dies. Oh, you'll have to audition for our board…they have a very correct and rigid pecking order here. Bring a phonograph record and go into it…we could probably pay about one hundred dollars or so a performance…and I mean PER only one solo number."

Ynez's eyes opened wide. "You can't be serious! For one single dance?"

"Yessirree! We'll rig up some kind of costumes for you—a bit of lace—a tassel or two. Peel it, and then just make sure you roll around the floor somewhat toward the end. They seem to like that lots…oh, and by the way, do you know what a voluptuary is?"

"—I thought it was a dusting powder company."

"Far from it, my dear." Baby then explained to her, almost as if she'd memorized it from some book on abnormal psychology, what the word embraced in most of its forms.

"Oh, *that*. That's nothing. I knew all about *that*. Just didn't know what to call it."

Baby then told her that the Board met this coming Friday afternoon. Could she be ready? Could she ever!

"Good. Do you like shortbread cookies? Here…"

Baby brought forth a tin box with the brand name of LEVENTHAL BAKERIES in elaborate scroll writing on it and, opening it, let her choose from the dainty assortment therein.

Ynez then said; "Oh, that reminds me, the Countess told me to tell you I oughta meet up with a man named Benjamin Leventhal."

"She did! Well *he's* not a member of this *Maison*, although he does have proclivities. He's our best friend, my husband's and mine. She must be thinking about—mmm…well! I'll see just what I can do. I think he'll see something in you!"

"Is he a 'butter and egg man' looking for a dollie?" Ynez asked, thinking how luscious the shortbread cookies were, and taking yet another.

Baby had to laugh at that one, too. "He's more of a bread and *booze* man looking for a beard." Ynez laughed, too, but didn't really get it.

After she had gone, Baby took the back staircase to the third floor where Deucie was supervising the latest exotic installment to the house. It was his duty to report to a group of four men in black robes and masks once weekly, receive his orders, and then see that they were filled.

There in the middle of one of the bedrooms, a glass floor had been placed, surrounded by a gilded balustrade, and now the workmen were putting on the finishing touches. Below, one could see—directly underneath—a bed.

"I'm afraid when they gather 'round they'll steam up the glass and won't be able to see nothing!" he muttered as she marveled at the very idea of Deucie thinking of an imperfection like that.

Baby waved the visiting card before him. "Listen, the Countess sent this stunning kid around who's a filthy shimmy dancer and might be right for our Mack."

"What makes you think that?" he replied, looking at his blueprints, now considering the idea of electric fans in each of the ceiling corners of the room.

"She's not normal," Baby answered efficiently.

"Well, she might just GET normal when she casts her orbs on Mackie!" He paused. "Actually, electric fans might just do it…small, quiet ones. Anyway, it's worth a try. Not the fans, the shimmy kid. He'll never find anybody on his ownsome. Gotta be introduced. The Countess is awfully psychic, hey, Babe?"

And so it was arranged, about three weeks into the very early spring of '25, that they meet Mr. Daly. Their best friend would never ever go to a place such as the one where Baby and Deucie had now found work and yet it was Mack himself who tipped them off to the place.

Within only three weeks, after an audition held at the stroke of midnight, before the "board" in the black velvet room, Ynez had impressed them (whoever "they" were: all wore heavy black hoods) enough to move from her Hell's Kitchen rooming-house into the fourth floor of the *Maison* upon Baby de Vol's suggestion.

Once installed, she and Baby became fast friends, sewing fringes and taffeta rosebuds onto her undies, sharing simple suppers. "Will Mr. Leventhal want to see my act?" Ynez asked, a little too excited.

"Now, hold on a minute, honey. This man is not meeting you for THAT. He's a rare type. A real he-man who only likes other men. Real men. Get me?—and only and exclusively men, see? Many, many ladies fall for him 'cause he's such a swell gent. Oh, listen, you talk about a matinee idol—wait'll you see Mack Daly!"

"Who's he?"

"Oh. He's one in the same with Benny Leventhal. Mack Daly is…well…it's like his nickname, see."

It was then Ynez remembered: one coin, two sides.

"Well, everything you're saying's not making it any easier. I've always dreamed of some sweet beautiful man falling for me. It's in my every damned prayer!"

"Yes, and that's what worries me. Anyway, he will be here tomorrow night, for your seven veils number. But remember, when you get carried in on your palanquin by those four naked fellas, he'll have eyes only for THEM, and not you, darling!"

"Well, what's the point then? I know we've been over this and over this but—ouch!" Ynez had pricked her finger with the needle.

"The great thing is," Baby replied, dipping her hanky in the glass of water beside the bed, "—you couldn't ask for a better way of life! Here, wrap this around that. It's bleeding…And when you meet him, remember—he's looking for *a certain type of woman.*"

"Yes—an arm-piece."

"But one who'll leave him alone and see it his way! Why, honey, what you told me about the way you've come up—!"

"—the hard way, Baby."

"Sure! But you're just perfect for this kind of life."

"Well, in fact, I always want queer men to love me! Oh, I hope I don't fall for this guy!" Ynez sighed. Yet, already that tormented and terrorized heart of hers was conjuring up what might be...if only...

"Darling, in that case, you're just setting yourself up," Baby said to her.

Always setting herself up. And now, with a real he-man. Well, so what? At least he was *all* man, wasn't he...more or less?

Baby was wide awake when Ynez lifted herself from this meditation—putting on the coffee, singing one of Elliot's new tunes. Plopping the sateen sofa cushion over her head, she feigned sleep. How her head pounded and her stomach churned! The pungent fragrance of Bruno's perfume mingled with his all-man sweat had stuck to her skin. As nauseating as Ynez found it, she also relished it, deciding she might not bathe until very, very late in the day.

• • •

At the Federal Building first thing Monday morning, Mack heard several speeches and then went with other major prohibition officials to the Central Park Casino for a luncheon hosted by Mayor Walker. It had been especially dried-out for this occasion, and chosen perhaps by Hizz Honor himself with tongue-in-cheek.

He sat to the right of Brian O'Couran, the new commissioner, who sat, in turn, to the right of Jimmie Walker. It was evident from the very first moment the mayor had opened the meetings, that he just wanted to get the whole thing over with and go and have a drink. Now the luncheon, with its acrid tone, absent of all and any humor, dragged on. After O'Couran's opening speech, done in typical Billy Sunday fashion, a kind of saintliness swept over the men gathered there.

Mack looked nothing like those who surrounded him at the large, round table, and shared his jaunty style with only the mayor himself, who, now and then, would look over at Mack and roll his eyes in boredom.

As they were finishing dessert, Brian Patrick O'Couran spoke for the first time to Mack, who had been waiting for some kind of acknowledgment. When the final course arrived (Boston creme pie) he had not so much as made eye contact with this new man in charge. O'Couran, throughout the meal, had spoken to everyone but Mack Daly, and Mack contented himself with craning his neck either in front of or behind the commissioner to make small-talk with Walker instead. In this way, it could be said that Mack did, after all, enjoy himself.

He and Beau James had something in common—they shared the same tailor and very nearly the same sense of humour. The mayor also admired Mack's taste in women, notably Mrs. Daly.

That was what brought O'Couran to look with a superior smirk at Mack, his head tilted almost sideways, resting in the pillows of his chins, and demand: "Your wife, Mr.Leventhal! Tell me about your wife, now! If Hizz Honor thinks of her as a great beauty, she surely must have to be kept on a rope!"

Mack answered that the only rope Ynez was kept on was a rope of pearls. Mayor Walker laughed heartily. O'Couran continued: "—and I'll bet you indulge her every little whim, don't you! "

Mack answered that he could no longer draw a line between whim and necessity when it came to Ynez—she herself was the epitome of whim, but also absolutely necessary. The rest of the men at the table now started listening to this repartee.

"And so you must be a very, very happy man, Mr. Leventhal?" O'Couran pursued, speaking louder now.

Mack's eyes took in the entire table. He answered honestly: "I'm the happiest I've ever been in my life, Commissioner. What a perfect life I have and now a perfect job as well—with you at the rudder steering us through dry waters at last!" At that, all gathered applauded. Mack suppressed a smile; he was thinking of Joe.

"I thank you for that, Mr. Leventhal. "O'Couran made a little seated bow, letting his eyes flutter, implying that he was truly touched.

The Mayor then took it as an opportune time to stand and propose a toast (consisting of iced tea) to Brian Patrick O'Couran. "Let's hope from here in on," Jimmie Walker concluded, "that all of us can be as happy as Ben Leventhal is right now, on nothing stronger than iced tea!"

Sitting down, Walker reached over and patted Mack on the shoulder. "Thanks for helping me out there. This event is as dull as ditchwater. Now let's hope we can end this thing and get back to our girlfriends!" Hizz Honor was again taking the day off.

As O'Couran was saying good-bye to Mack, he leaned in toward him and whispered, "I'll be wanting to see you alone at your earliest possible convenience."(Mack looked at him in subtle bewilderment.) O'Couran went on, "—the fact is, I've heard there's some pretty dirty stuff goin' 'round about you, Leventhal, and I only hope to God it isn't true."

Mack felt his blood run cold. "There's no time like the present, sir," he answered.

O'Couran consulted his pocket watch. "I'm afraid not. As busy as you'll grant I am! After ten tonight it'll hafta be..." He was insistent.

"All right..." Mack thought it rather a peculiar hour, but demurred. "Just name the place."

They were walking together toward the exit from the park. Behind them were three newspaper men waiting to speak to the Commissioner. "Meet me at eleven tonight at 'The Patch' on Tenth Avenue...do you know the place?" Mack nodded. (Peculiar hour. Peculiar place.) "I'll be upstairs. I still keep an office there, you see." O'Couran waved him off, turning to the gentlemen of the Press all grins and backslaps.

Mack went at once to the plant in Brooklyn, where Joe awaited him in the back of the garages. Here, he happily went about his new job—supervising the overhaul of some old bakery trucks into delivery vans for booze.

"Whadda yuh t'ink about dat!" Joe proudly displayed his handiwork, now having donned cover-alls, holding in one axle-grease covered hand an Orange Crush bottle and in the other, some drawings made by Deucie.

"Swell, Joe!" Mack jumped inside the back of the truck just completed. "No rattles, and no broken bottles, huh! Just look at that padding!"

Joe and the trustworthy Abie, who had been discovered some days before in perfectly sound shape collecting junk, had spent the morning rigging secret panels around the sides and back of the truck, all lined with second-hand mattresses. These, Mack had acquired from Abie who bought and sold almost anything as long as it was used. Between these they had fitted shelving to hold as many as nine dozen bottles.

"Then you close up the panels over 'em and nobody's the wiser!" Joe demonstrated. Deucie had done it again.

"Benny, tell me somethink," Abie said to Mack who was paying him in cash at that moment. "How many more mattresses you think you need, huh?"

"How many more hotels are in bankruptcy, Abie, old pal?"

"Oi! I get your drift!" He started to walk away, pocketing his money. Then, at the doors to the garages, he called out, "—saw the Vheestler last night, Benny! He needs to talk mit you!"

"A request from the Whistler?" Mack turned to Joe. "This is a first. " He and Joe sat down at the edge of the truck.

Sunday evening, after the Armstrongs and Jack Wrigley had visited Great Neck, Joe had gone home to visit Mama Josie. He had not seen Mack since this moment.

"What do you make of it?" Mack asked.

"I never heard nuttin' like it! How was yer meetin' wid the Mick?"

"Well, first off, I missed you like Hell. Thought about you every minute. Next, he wants to meet with me tonight, at that Irish dive called the Patch."

"Dat's a den ah cut-t'roats, Mack—oh, wait!" Joe turned, going on his hands and knees to the back of the truck and returning just as fast, balancing a large paper bag in one hand. "Look. Ma made yuz some cavvadeels and some peppers on duh side! She put some of her own gravy in a jar here for yuz, too. I know yuz just ate, but—"

"Boy, smells great—makes me hungry all over again."

"Ma wants tuh meet yuz. She sez yer duh only t'ing tuh come along what's ever done right by me. 'Course," he added, "she t'inks we're only pals and 'You Know'!"

Putting the bag aside, Joe swung himself over Mack, hugging him, planting a kiss on his lips.

"Let's go up and have this in my office and call Bruno. I must tell him about this meeting I've got with O'Couran tonight."

Proceeding in that direction, Joe, holding the prize cavatellis, said, "I t'ink Bruno's idea of protection might come in handy tunnight, after all, Mack."

Picking up his private line, Mack reached Joe's brother at once, with Joe bending an ear. "I've got Joe on the other extension, Bruno…listen—" Mack then reiterated the Commisoner's inferences and told Bruno the place they were to meet a few hours later.

"That's been a sink-hole of scum since the days of Boss Tweed," Bruno informed Mack. "I don't know why he's asked you there, but you'll come away in one piece thanks to Joey and me, after which I shall elicit from you what I've got coming." Bruno's voice was full of confidence. "I think that goddammed bog-trotter knows more than you might imagine."

It was arranged that Bruno and Joe follow Mack by foot from Forty-second to Forty-fourth Street, certain that he would shadowed by O'Couran's thugs. Fanning out from the building itself would be a league of Irish cut-throats who, by a certain sign language, could tip one another off. In this way, some of those who entered the Patch never returned. So, staying well behind, Bruno and Joe could proceed through the alleys, around to the back of the building and sneak up the fire escape, waiting outside the window where O'Couran had his private digs. They would not be far from Mack at all times.

Satisfied with the arrangement, Mack told Joe that they had better locate the Whistler at once. But Joey wanted to dine on Ma's food first, and so both repaired to the employees' kitchen just as the next shift of guards was going on duty.

As Joe was finding a pan and lighting the gas jet, one of these guards motioned to Mack from outside. Joe saw them talking through the window, then Mack returned.

"Joey, go on and get everything ready. I've got to run outside the gates—there's a man who fits the Whistler's description being held there. I'll be right back."

Joe called after him, "Ain't dat funny, dough—we wuz just speakin' of him!" He watched Mack break into a graceful run through the window. "What a man!" he observed, stirring up the cavatelli.

There, just outside the gates, was the Whistler. It was still daylight, but the high barbed-wire fence cast a eerie shadow over the poor man. He was breathing hard, and looked ill.

"Blackie! Come on in—through that gatehouse. I'll open it up for you."

The Whistler could not even greet him, and his wheezing was painful for Mack to hear. "Get him some water, please," Mack told the gatehouse guard. "Come on in, solider."

Blackie drank it down then looked up at Mack and reached out to take hold of his arm, bringing him closer.

"Tell that guy to get lost, will yuh!" Mack did so. "Don't say nothing. I'll be o.k. in a bit, but just let me get this off'n my chest, old pal!" He smiled, but it was fraught with terror. "Now listen tuh me, 'cause if there's been one true friend I've had since we all got back, it was you, sir, and I want you to know what you can do to save yourself from all of this…"

Mack nodded.

The Whistler began, looking straight at him, choosing his words carefully, enunciating every syllable. "The reason they closed down the 68th Street place wasn't because of the litt-er-chure. It was because of a murder. It was all O'Couran and his gang who was behind it, and it was a big cover-up because of what happened that night. Then, so that they couldn't throw together a case out of it, his boys did something to the body."

"What!"

"I don't know what happened to it, but next thing you know O'Couran had the money he needed to put him into office as commissioner!—for one reason and one reason alone—to get you! He's gonna wreck your whole life, soldier! You just wait and see!"

Mack started to say something but Blackie, by now so agitated and wheezing again, lifted up one of his gloved hands. "Now lend an ear! You tell him you know how he got that money— from someone sellin' body parts!" He looked around him, desperate. "I know he did, 'cause…well, I just *know*, that's all. I'll try to locate that butcher, yessir!…and then you've got the commissioner!" Blackie issued forth a hollow laugh.

"But Blackie, who was murdered?"

"—they cut off her feet…can yuh believe it! They cut off her feet—the Goddammed devils! Now they'll come for me next, because…" He was wracked with a sudden spasm of fear, and began backing off down the stoop of the gatehouse and outside, his trolley making creaking noises which echoed between the buildings.

Mack went to hold him, but Blackie whispered, "Let me go. God help me! I've…I've said enough! "

Standing at the door to the gatehouse, Mack called after Blackie who, turning, began to whistle. The piercing sound—so haunting and so death-like, filled the air.

"Blackie! Blackie!" But the beggar turned the corner toward the canal. And still the whistling lingered, even though he was gone. Mack ran back toward the employees' kitchen.

"What happened to youse! What's wrong, Mack?" Joe left the stove and held him.

"O'Couran had somebody murdered up at this 68th Street place where Ynez worked. He had the body cut up. God! I feel like I did back in the War!" Joe led him to the kitchen table and sat him down.

"I don't know, Joey, I feel like I saw Death just now! And heard its voice as well."

"I got no idea what yer talkin' about, Mack, but I t'ink I'm about tuh get goose-bumps!"

"Well, don't let go of them, Joey. When I tell you what the Whistler just told me—you're going to need 'em!"

• • • • •

CHAPTER XII

THE PATCH

Before going to the Patch, they stopped to see Baby and Deucie at the club—closed, because it was Monday.

"What's the serious looks for, fellas?" Baby eyed them, escorting Mack and Joe into the parlor of the upstairs flat.

Deucie had been working on a telephone system for inside the building all that day. During his tinkering he always wore a carpenter's apron and a green celluloid visor, and came away from his chore in just such a costume.

"Say, sorry we didn't show up to Great Neck yes'tuh'day. But we'd had just about enough of Ynez—'lo Joseph. So we told 'em we were just too damned tuckered out. And we were, too! But, Hell, Mackus, we made a bundle on Sayre-day night! Whadda we s'posed to do with it?" Deucie had articulated himself into his armchair, lighting up a cigar.

"Well, let's hope we need it to pay off Commissioner O' Couran with! I'll find out in a couple of hours."

As Mack went over the arrangement for later that evening, Baby got a little uneasy and held up a fist. "Joseph! You won't let anything happen to our boy, now will yuh!"

Joe had seated himself on the sofa next to Mack (moving off the arm of the same, at Deucie's aside, "She'll kill yuh if you break that sofa!"): "Say, I'm an expert at dis kinda t'ing, Mrs. dee Vol!" he answered.

Baby chortled. "Oh, I'm sure you are, my darling—and you can call me just plain Baby." She turned to Mack, her pencilled brows knit, "Mack, what happened at that official meeting of yours today? Now, don't leave out a thing—"

After he had delivered himself of that, Mack went over everything the Whistler had told him, ending with the strange murder.

Deucie spoke up first: "The gal in question was one Lady Lucky Lee. We both called her UNlucky Lady Lee, because she seemed tuh bring trouble in there from her first day. She was a dimmin-ah-tive Chinee of the Mandarin class, with teeny bound feet. But we never knew she got murdered…"

"—that's how we met Chollie Fong, the chiropodist," Baby put in. "He saw to those little paws of hers.That was her act, see."

Deucie continued: "She did all sorts of unnatural things with her feet. Lotus Feet they calls 'em. You never knew a pair of feet could travel in and out of so many places." Swallowing hard, he removed the cigar from his mouth. "Act'erly, it kinda made me nausee-us."

Baby took up the tale. "We had to put her down in the cellar, which was originally tricked up like a chapel out of the Inquistion. Deucie kinda converted it to Buddhism, and she had quite a following. She had Chinee phonograph recordings playin' and it always got noisy down there. Her clients got carried away, you might say."

"I don't get what she did wid her feet," Joe murmured.

"I'll tell you later," Mack patted him. "Was she on the level…I mean, she wasn't working for any Fu-Manchu outfit, was she?"

"Mackus," Deucie gestured holding his hands out. "She was no chop suey Chinee, no sir. She came by way of the fellows who owned the place. Lady Lee did justice to her name. She was a real Lady."

"I do think she might've banged the gong though," Baby added. "'Course, with the Ornamentals, you can never be sure. Chollie Fong would know more about that. Anyway, she was a tiny thing, and always walked around using two canes, on accounta her feet were so small, as well as bein' her meat and potatahs."

Deucie continued, "Small! Say, they was microscopic! She was there just less than a month, suddenly disappeared. Then before we knew it, we had an injunction slapped on us for sellin' dirty litta-chure, and WHAM they closed us down. She once said—in kinda broken English, mind yuh—that she was goin' back tuh Frisco to work there."

"Yes," Baby added, "and that was when Ynez, having no place no go, accelerated the notion of getting hitched up to YOU, my dear old friend!"

"I never heard a thing about this until now." Mack shook his head.

"Say, you got any sody pop?" Joe asked Baby.

As she went into the kitchenette, she continued with the tale, "No reason you should. We had freaks like that comin' and goin! And what do you know but she just up and left one night, as quietly and as lady-like as she came. Carried out in her sedan chair to a waiting motor coach." Opening the bottle, she added, "Nobody ever thought she was murdered! How and where and why, for God's sakes?"

Mack began to frown. "And nobody ever found out who ran the *Maison*?" Both Deucie and Baby shook their heads. Mack took a swig of Joe's Orange Crush. "Did she live in the upstairs quarters along with Ynez?"

Deucie and Baby looked at one another. Deucie then recalled, "Just for a couple of nights, it seems." He paused. "Yessir! I do recall now."

"Then Ynez must've known her—briefly, of course," Mack added.

Baby shrugged. "Possibly. Lady Lee didn't waste any time though—got herself some sugar daddy like *that!*" She snapped her fingers, then sat back down lighting a new cigarette from her old one.

"—'cause after we closed…five a.m. most nights, mind you, she'd get into that sedan chair and be driven off. You had to marvel at that car, too, because it had big side doors openin' wide that accommodated her conveyance."

"Who toiled her up and down in that t'ing?" Joe asked.

"Oh, she had a couple of goons, no doubt paid for by her sugar daddy. Now I don't know if this patron of hers was a yangyang or not, 'cause everybody wore masks from the time they entered, of course—"

Mack said, "Two lackeys carting her around, a custom made car…she wasn't doing too bad! I marvel at how she found a rich guy with such rarefied tastes so quickly!"

Joe shook his head. "I got it all t'ru my bean but the big woyds. And, really, I don't get the attraction. A Yella midget with feets the size of a tot's who did strange t'ings wid 'em?" Joe was overcome laughing and excused himself, going into the kitchenette for another bottle of soft drink.

Deucie now speculated, "—and we were instructed never to ask any questions, of course. So we didn't, natcherly. The only thing I can figger is that her sugar daddy was in with the Micks somehow. Mebbee he paid 'em off to croak her before anybody found out what a pree-vert he was!"

"Isn't Deucer a genius though!" Baby winked at him. "—but you say the Whistler put the finger on O'Couran?"

Mack shook his head. "No. He merely said O'Couran was behind it all."

Joe returned with his soda pop. "—maybe I could find out more from the moll Bruno's got woykin' for him—Squirrely King I calls her. She knows when Alphonse Capone took his last crap."

"Well, be careful, sonny," Deucie warned. "You never know who or what's behind these kinds of rackets. And if you have to use this stuff against O'Couran…if it comes down tuh that…you'd best OWN the info first, Mackie."

"Meaning I only let Mack know and nobody else. Sure I will." Joe grinned broadly. They were firmly in his territory now.

"Sonny," Baby raised a wagging finger, "when my man says 'be careful' he means it."

Mack, having thought a bit, then offered, "First we go to Chollie Fong…Baby, how about if I spring for a manicure and a pedicure?"

"As long as he's got 'Was my Face Red' in stock, you're on!"

Before leaving, Mack instructed Baby to make her own appointment.

Tidying up, Deucie yawned and turned to his spouse, "You know, for somebody to buy a couple of teeny weeny feet—well! That somebody would hafta be a pretty sick ticket, honey."

Baby replied with an enthusiastic "Hmmmmm!" Deucie, rolling away, went on, "Now if I was enough of a pree-vert to want to buy a pair of hacked off Lotus feet...I'd say I couldn't live without 'em." (Baby, in a higher octave: "Hmmmm?")

By this time, running the bath water as she undressed and staring down at her own feet, Baby was almost repulsed. "Just imagine stickin' your dogs in places where they shouldn't be. And the Hell of it is—gettin' paid for it!"

"What was that, honey?" Deucie yelled from the parlor, unable to hear her over the running water.

"Oh, nothing..." Then addressing her feet, "Christ! I'm afraid I'll never feel the same about you two again!"

• • •

"G'wan up dose steps! He'll be awaitin' you."

If there ever was a real low-down dive, Mack thought to himself, this was it. He had been admitted to a putrid smelling, dank room, having gained entrance by rapping with the tip of his cane on an iron door—then, by shoving his business card through the peephole.

Before him, Mack perceived through the gloom, a rickety staircase, and a hundred pairs of miserable eyes which told of despair, murder and insanity looking back at him.

Mounting the rickety steps, he gazed below. Every type of degenerate, scrapping, yelling, swearing, out cold, or suffering delirium tremens, writhed like bloated snakes. There were more than a few sots who had fallen down on the sawdust floor. And there they stayed, surrounded by their own vomit, as their cronies staggered or fell right over them. A shamefully degraded old woman was sitting off in the corner singing "Kathleen Mavourneen." No one listened. The place stank of every kind of human excretion, and Mack had to hold his breath until, by knocking on the only door ahead of him, he gained entrance.

Two big Irish fellows, lantern-jawed with rum-blossomed noses and a half dozen bruises on their faces, slumped at the entrance. Just ahead, at a varnish-bare desk, stood O'Couran. To his right, amid heaps of papers in disarray, a cheap lamp of colored glass; to his left, a cracked statue of the Blessed Mother; beside it, a medicine bottle. In the center, his eyes glassy, a bedeviled smile on his lips, the Commissioner stood, hands on the desk, fingers splayed. Just behind him, a window, a torn drawn shade, and a glimpse of a fire escape, which Mack knew held Bruno and Joe.

"You alone, Jew boy?" O'Couran growled.

Mack bowed slightly. "I am."

Huffing away, O'Couran sat down, waving the thugs off. "—well, here it is. This was what I sprung from! And I still go back to it when I have to. Like returnin' to the scene of the crime, you might say! In its stinking swill, I often catch a glimpse of my sad and forsaken soul!" He laughed an unearthly, bitter laugh.

Mack apparently was not going to be asked to be seated, because there was no chair in sight. With his hat in one hand, his stick in another, he remained relaxed.

O'Couran, cocking his head to one side, regarded him through one open eye—the other remaining shut, almost as if he were taking aim.

"I'll not mince words, Leventhal. Your wife, a strumpet and a kootchie gal, capable of monstrous deceptions, hired a spic lounge lizard to service her. He has come to me with information which I intend to use against you—if necessary..."

"—as well you could!" Mack said quietly.

"You deny nothing, of course."

"Tell me what I am to deny before I attempt it!" Mack smiled only very slightly.

"This apparent gigolo has told me you are indugling in sodomy with an Eye-talian gangster who has a record proving that he is an invert...among *other* things...and that you are in on a speakie on 46th Street. In my new administration, it is, of course, out of the question to keep you in my employment. Queer fairy that you are! A gangster to boot! And, of all things, a bootlegger as well!" He let go a triumphant laugh.

Mack, remaining impassive, repled, "I deny the fact that I am a gangster, first off."

"If you, as a government official, are in any way connected to any public place which openly and brazenly purveys liquor, then you are, in fact, yes, of course...a gangster."

It did give Mack pause, but it also made him also want to laugh. "What do you want to know about the club, Commissioner? I'll tell you everything, naturally."

"I want to know *every*thing—naturally."

"I lease the building and offer it rent free to my friends who run a private club from that address, and live on the third floor. As a gesture of friendship, I give them various kinds of alcohol which they stock in their home. I realize that the transport of the Alcohol Without Permit is interpreted as a crime unless, of course, it is sanctioned by the head of the bonded plant which lets it out. In this case, it is myself, making, distilling or storehousing it." Mack was utterly cool. "—so I thought it might be all right."

"—and do you sell the stuff to the public there?" asked O'Couran, his eyebrows lifting, his mouth a scar of smug superiority.

"I myself don't. Once the product leaves my plant, my work is really over."

"Listen, Jew boy, you and I both know that since Prohibition went into effect and you got that plant up and running over there in Brooklyn, you've been supplying everyone from the governor to the senators to the mayor himself with your stuff! You can't deny it because we're both in the same racket here and we're speakin' plainly about it now!"

"I can't deny it. I was ordered to do so from the very first, and have always obeyed my superiors. If I were to stop supplying them—for some reason—they wouldn't like it at all, I should think."

"Now you get this *straight*," O'Couran said between his teeth. "I hate queers and I hate Jews and I hate men that always button themselves up so goddamned neat they look like they got no dirt underneath their fingernails. Consequently, I am going hate you, on what I have recently heard. And even if I had not heard it, I would still hate you *on principle*. I wonder at how you wormed your Goddammed fairy mockie way into the racket you've got going! I'm telling you here and now, Leventhal, as I get bigger and bigger with this new job of mine and get more men on my side, *I'm going to ruin you*. I'm going to wipe up the Goddammed floor with you, see that! You may think you're untouchable because of Who You Know and who needs you right now. But I can change all that! And I will, by Jaysus, I will!" He was smoting his chest and had turned purple.

"Well, you're the boss, you've got every right to," Mack said. "I can't stop you. How can I help you?"

"Oh! Smart-ass kike, is it now! Let me begin by telling you that I want your overage. I want it all, and if you breathe a word of it to anybody in the Bureau here or in Washington, you're finished."

"Well, that can be arranged. Your department will just pay off the gauger to lie about the increased number of gallons we produce each month. He already has to lie anyway. We can just produce more."

"You're *usin'* that overage, aren't you—instead of dumpin' it in the canal as you should!"

"I'm stocking it. I was told to do so."

"Well, you'll now double the amount. In other words, your gauger must now report some sort of accident or leak in the vats or something, equal to half of what is reported. Then you put it aside for me, see!" He was calm now, but breathing hard.

Mack thought about it. "All right, but—then what? Shall we deliver it someplace? We can't hide that much stuff. But…if perhaps you have a cutting plant—?"

"Meaning what?!"

"Well, I'm sure you intend to dilute your share with some sort of…'kicker'?—in order to make more profit."

O'Couran looked as if he might jump over the desk and choke Mack to death. "What I do with the stuff is my own G.D. business!"

Mack said, "Oh, come now, Commissioner, this whole prohibition thing is a dirty joke to every citizen of this country! All it does is turn people who've never had a drink in their lives into lushes, because they think it's so smart to break the law. And as for all of us—on the inside—it only paves our way to Hell."

But O'Couran didn't crack—he had been deep in thought. "Quit the preachin'. I got a plan here, Yiddle. You want to know what I'll do with my batch? Well, I'll tell you. I am not lettin' you off easily now! You and I are going to op'n our own company."

"Go on," Mack urged placidly.

"*Sure*. You'll put up the money…and I'll run it. Some falterin' thing which uses spirits…you must know every one in the East! We can just go on using the owner's name. Help 'em out a bit, then buy 'em out!" Then he thundered, "Come on! Hop to it! Think of one!"

Mack pointed to the bottle on O'Couran's desk. "How about that one right there? Isn't that a bottle of Moran's Elixir? They order from me, as you probably know. They're not doing so well. Down to only a mere trickle this past month. I can speak to them if you wish."

O'Couran lifted the bottle, just having been emptied. "Ye Gods, the stuff is so good for you, too! Keeps me going! Of course, there's such a tiny trace of alcohol in it—just for preservin', I would have to put considerable kick into it." He now squinted to see the manufacturer's name. "'Tis somebody right here in New York City! Sounds perfect. We shall use it as a front! YOU do the leg work, Jew boy, report back to me by week's end and I might not tell on you!"

"Be happy to—and I thank you, Commissioner. I'll see that this new—er—project is up and running in no time."

O'Couran stood up. "If you let me down for even a minute, or if you allow any of the big boys in on this, or if you do not do EXACTLY as I say, you may be sure that I shall stop at nothing! *I've got the goods on you*! Remember that!" His voice now rose—quivering, hollering, "Now get the hell out! I cannot stand the sight of you!"

He threw the bottle above Mack's head and it broke against the cracked plaster wall opposite. Mack turned, after having ducked. Amid the mess, he saw, hanging off a nail from that same wall...a pair of very small Chinese slippers.

That was enough. He beat it out of there, down the stairs and out the door. As planned, he met up with Bruno and Joe back on Forty-Second Street. They kept on walking only a short distance, saying nothing until hailing a cab.

Inside, going downtown—"You wuz followed, Mack," Joe said.

Bruno told the cabbie to go to their place on Houston and Mack said, "Only to the end of his block. I noticed them turning back. Did you hear what went on?"

"Every word," Bruno said, staring straight ahead, eliciting a wry laugh. "You're either the luckiest or the cagiest son of a bitch I've ever known! Anyway, if you can pull this off, I'll be greatly impressed. He'll be brewing up stronger stuff than that elixir for morons like him in a month! I just can't believe it!"

Mack said, "Neither can I! If that bottle hadn't been on his desk! I hate to think...but, just remember, he means to profit from the reformulation."

Joe was also amazed at what he and Bruno had overheard. "He t'inks yer gonna buy our Moran's Elixir comp'nee outright—for him!"

"There isn't any Elixir in Moran's Elixir, Mack," Bruno shook his head, smiling. "It's just an inventory of bottles with that name plastered on them which get filled up with my stuff cut from yours—as if you haven't figured it out by now. God! That Mick's in for it. We've gotta find some way of making it look like he's King Shit, though."

"Listen, Bruno," Mack said. "I have no interest in being a part of any of this—other than supplying the surplus amount. It looks like you'll be turning over your so-called company to me, and I'll have to give it to O'Couran. He'll only have to re-staff it. I'll supply him directly with alcohol, but keep right on filling your permits as well."

Joe proudly patted Mack on the shoulder. "Youse is one smart boyfriend!"

Mack shrugged. "I just got orders from the top. What else can I do?"

As they headed across town, Bruno seemed to Mack a changed man. "It's a deal then. A swell trade for Joey here! And I won't screw you, Mr. Mack Daly, don't you worry. We could maybe come to even like each other someday."

"Well, I hope so. You'd like that, wouldn't you, Joe?"

Joe eagerly nodded. "Yeah, and maybe I'll get beat up less."

"We'll make that part of the bargain, Bruno. O.k.?" Mack was serious.

"Sure," Bruno reluctantly agreed.

Mack had parked the Marmon in front of the deVol. Getting out of the taxi with Joe, he said, "I'm taking him away from you again, Bruno—hope you don't mind."

Joe and his brother said their good-byes in a friendly fashion, Mack standing aside. He divinated that they got along best when they were partners in pulling a job—such as the one just accomplished. Joe, it seemed, had thoroughly enjoyed being a part of climbing up the fire escape and interloping with his big brother.

In the car, letting Joe drive again, Mack found himself marveling at his cheerful response to anything illegal, and how, now more than ever, he seemed to belong to a way of life which to Mack was entirely strange.

"—an' pretty soon you can meet my ma and my cousin Sal, an' my Aunt Maria an', an' Fat Tony an'—"

"Joe, I'll be glad to meet them all, but I don't know if they're really going to accept me," Mack said sensibly.

"Yeah, they will! They'll understan'...you'll be surprised! You got Bruno impressed wid youse. Say, you was so smooth! Now my famb-lee'll be in duh chips 'cause of dis job here, and we owe it all to youse! Boy, how did I get so lucky!"

Mack settled back in his seat, resting his head, tipping his hat over his eyes and patting Joe on his knee. He then told him about seeing the Chinese slippers.

"You said you'd tell me what kinda t'ings she did wid her feet later. Is dis later?" Joe asked.

"The question is what kinds of things *somebody else* did with her feet once they killed her. Of course, her body is missing as well. Years ago there was a racket going down on Coney Island which used to...but—" Mack drew a deep breath then shook his head.

Joe shook his head. "Jeez." A pause. "You gonna ever tell me or not?"

"Better wait until we know each other a little better," Mack grinned, emerging from his deep thoughts and pinching Joe on the cheek.

• • • • •

CHAPTER XIII

WHEN THE WHISTLING STOPPED

Ynez thought better of telephoning Bruno that Monday night. Anyway, she could not imagine what to say to him. Did words count? Hardly. Sparked by the frenzy of passion she had known, a wild hunger for more sex burned within her.

Searching the Manhattan telephone book, she had found a few Imperios listed—but no one with his first name or initial. Remembering that his family owned a restaurant, she looked there as well, finding nothing. Finally, she decided on chewing Nolie's ear instead.

"I'm so afraid he might do something terrible to Mack—so I wanted to get on his good side, by letting him have his way with me."

"Yeah…I'm here. Go on." (Nolie was apparently eating something and listening to the phonograph rather than paying attention to Ynez.)

"So you're listening, of course…" Ynez rambled away. "Hello? Noles? Ah! Well, I'm afraid he might call me up and have to see me again," she lied. "He considers me his twist, you know."

"You mean you don't like him?—you don't find him attractive?" Nolie *must've* been listening. She was, at least, following along.

"Oh, but he was a *brute* to me. But I *had* to do it—even though I felt so de*graded* and hated every *minute* of it. But now, you see, I have the ad*van*tage. I can get things out of him which he otherwise wouldn't tell a soul—unless of course they were gangsters themselves."

"*Or* gun molls."

"Who, *me*? My dear, I don't think of myself as a *gun moll*," Ynez half-tragically murmured. "—and yet…"

"…and yet you've been called a lot worse. Oh! Say, I've got to run."

"Wha—? But! Nolie! Hello? Hel*lo!*"

Tuesday morning at 1:45, just as Mack was heading back to Great Neck with Joe, Ynez finally did hear from Buno, who called her from Downtown.

There on his desk, he had found a note from Blanche King. In her typically fastidious manner, she had written:

11:08 p.m. Monday
Augusto phoned to tell you
Whistler run over and almost killed.
Body was crushed & he's now near death
He said to tell you blame is on us and
to clear it up right away. —B.K.

Bruno was speaking slowly and deliberately to Ynez. "Do you know who I mean—the Whistler?" he asked her, his voice all-business and chilling.

"Yes, yes, of course, everybody knows Blackie. But is he…still alive?"

"I'll find out. He's at St. Vincent's—I've got somebody over there who'll tell me everything. I'll call you back."

Sittting up in her bed, in total darkness, she was paralyzed by this news. Just as she switched on her beside lamp, the phone rang again. Her heart leapt.

"He won't last much longer. They slammed him up against a building. He's all mangled they said…keeps calling out your husband's name over and over like he has to tell him something. I don't know what."

"I'll tell Mack when he gets in," Ynez heard herself say in a small voice.

"You tell him I'm going over to the hospital myself."

"I will," she murmured.

He had hung up. For what felt like hours, but was not more than fifteen minutes, Ynez remained immobile. When she heard Mack's latch key turn in the door, she rushed to the top of the stairs and shouted out the news, finding herself, for no apparent reason, standing there crying.

Below, both Mack and Joe stood dumbfounded.

"We're going back. If Bruno calls again, tell him we're already on our way," Mack said, turning to leave.

Ynez rushed down the steps, her hair in braids, pyjamas causing her to look like anything but herself. "—he might be dead by the time you get there, Mack!"

Mack started to say, "Who would do such a thing to a poor soul—" when the telephone once again rang. Mack picked up the extension in the foyer.

It was Bruno. "Mack, listen, I'm at the hospital. They're going to pin this on my gang. There's a detective here…"

"Is there a phone in Blackie's room?"

"—he isn't in a room…it's a ward…and there's a Helluva lot of reporters and coppers here…he's going fast, too. Everybody was shovin' to get a look at him. I closed the curtains around him. I told him you were on your way."

"Can you get that phone over to his bed—at least I can speak to him!"

There was a pause. Bruno answered that it was too far away. Then, "Hold on—" he said, and the sound of the receiver dangling, hitting up against the bare, white wall was heard. Joe and Ynez stood close by Mack, not saying a word, barely breathing.

Now the sound of the receiver being lifted up was heard. But the voice was not Bruno's. "Are you Mr. Mack Daly?" it asked.

Joe knew at once by the tone, his ear close to the receiver…"A cop!" he whispered.

"Blackie keeps callin' for you, Mr. Daly—you know what he wants? He's on the way out, I must tell you. Hold on." Mack looked at Ynez and Joe, sensing what was to come next. "Mr. Daly, I am sorry to tell you that the Whistler has just passed on."

"My God—no," Mack whispered.

"I imagine you were one of those who kept care of him…everyone was so fond of Blackie. This was a rotten thing to do to a guy like that."

"Is there anything I can do?" Mack asked, his eyes closed, his voice hoarse.

"Sure. But not just now. Why don't you come down to headquarters. Tommorrow will be fine. 6th Precinct." He gave his name and said goodbye.

Crossing the foyer, Mack sat on the stairs, his heads in his hands, Joe and Ynez standing over him. "I did this to him," he said.

As Joe and Ynez both held him, Mack gently rocked to and fro. If there was one thing Ynez could not bear, it was to see Mack cry.

It was an odd arrangement—Joe on his right, Ynez on his left. Both cradling him in their arms. In that horrible instant, however, it did not seem at all awkward.

"I'll call Deucie, Mack. He'd want to know," Ynez said.

Calmly, she went to the phone and began placing a call to the deVol's, hearing Mack sobbing, her heart breaking.

"Aw, stop, Mack! Stop! You couldn't help it!" Joe cried out.

"He can't stop Joe," Ynez whispered. "Just let him go…he can't stop."

• • •

Later that morning the papers had the story:

WHISTLER DEAD!
BELOVED ONE-LUNG CITY MASCOT
SUCCUMBS TO GRISLY MURDER
ATTEMPT ON HIS LIFE!

"At eleven o'clock last night, the famous hobo who brought a lilt to our hearts by whistling from a hole in his lung, sobbed his last song at Saint Vincent's

Hospital. Calling out the name of an old Army pal, this gallant veteran of the Late Conflict was found in an alleyway on West Tenth Street, the victim of a deliberate hit-and-run—presumably by a large commercial vehicle. With The Whistler having been pinned against a wall, it seemed that the truck slammed up against him at considerable speed.

"There was not much left of Blackie the Whistler. Sobbing in anguish, left in a pool of blood, this legless hero must've managed to cry out for help—but too late. Within only a few hours, he met His Maker, surrounded by those who knew him only by his smile and his whistle, but who loved him like a son or a brother.

"Police are investigating the possibility of his ties with the Underworld, and his presumed work as an informant therein..."

Johnnie finished reading the article and looked up from the tabloid at Elliot, Wriggs and Nolie, who had just succeeded in reaching the deVols. They had also only just read the story, Baby reporting that Deucie was taking Blackie's death like a trooper.

Elliot, Nolie and Johnnie were numbed. Wriggs knew nothing of the Whistler, but understood by their sorrow and shock how much he was loved. Nobody could sleep, and so they waited until after eight a.m. to telephone Great Neck. No answer at the Dalys'—not even Alexander.

"He's probably down there at the hospital," Elliot reasoned.

"Call the police. At least find out," Wriggs suggested, wandering alone out onto the terrace. Overhead, a drape of black clouds hung, rain plummeting down. It was so dark that morning that almost every light in every apartment was on. Then the telephone rang, causing the four to jump.

Johnnie answered, taking Nolie's post as she went for a cigarette. It was Alexander, coming through the wire in a strangely quiet, cautious tone.

"What's going on, Alexander? Where is everybody!"

"Well...things are all on pins and needles here. Before they all went into Manhattan, Mr. D. instructed me not to answer the telephone on any account," he began.

"All of them?"

Alexander told his sister that Joe and Ynez had gone along also.

"Mr. D.'s not in any trouble, is he?" Johnnie asked. There was a pause.

Elliot had to know: "—Is Mack all right?"

Alexander, realizing he was addressing the whole Armstrong household, replied, "—if he is in trouble, he's smart enough to get himself out of it."

Taking the receiver away from Johnnie, Elliot said, "What's that supposed to mean, Alexander?"

Nothing at all came across the wire.

"Alexander?"

"I'm right here—"

"All right. I don't want to put you on the spot. As long as Mack is in one piece. Tell him—when you see or hear from him—to call us after four today. Tell him we have to meet with the producer for our new show." Hanging up, he let go a deep, long sigh. "I won't do it, but I wish I could."

"Drink?" Wriggs replied, "Not on your life, Elliot!" following him back out into the living room.

"Gee," Elliot commented bitterly, "how'd you ever guess!"

"Well, don't be sarcastic! I'm just here to help, you know!"

Elliot's heart melted as Wriggs sneaked a comforting kiss. "I know. I know, kiddo. Oh, boy, do you get to me! I wish you could stick around here for keeps. Think how dry and divine I'd be then!" He snuggled up to Wriggs. "Why don't you just move in?"

"I'd sure like to, Elliot, if you'd have me.You need a fellow like me at times like these." There, in the middle of the living room, they held each other tightly, Wriggs suddenly thrilled by Elliot's invitation. Then Nolie reappeared almost completely dressed to go, reminding her brother, "You'd better shake a leg! And Wriggs, we've got to get you into a taxi so you can catch your train to Princeton."

Elliot remained stationary in the middle of the room, his arms about Wriggs, leaning on him. "I just wish we could crawl back into bed and pull the covers over our eyes, that's all. Mack tells Alexander everything, and the rest of us nothing. What's *he* got to do with the Whistler's murder, anyway?"

Johnnie, shuffling Elliot's new music charts into his briefcase, said, "He helped him get along, just as he does every one of us."

At that, Elliot went to finish dressing with Wriggs in tow. "Come on, I've got to give you something of mine to wear."

"Johnnie," Nolie said, "hold down the fort, sweetheart."

"Yes *sir*," she answered, saluting, then hugged her.

In a flurry of painted raincoats—courtesy of some loyal fans—Nolie and Elliot finally left, with Wriggs in one of Elliot's get-ups, feeling quite smart.

As soon as a they had gone, Johnnie went about getting herself dressed. She had planned on meeting her brother, Keys, at Miss Harrison's Murray Hill townhouse, to help arrange her up-and-coming exhibit. With such terrible news, and Mr. D. feeling so sad, Johnnie felt like crawling back into bed herself. Such a nasty day to go anyplace! But, perhaps, she thought, it might soon stop raining. As she was donning a practical jumper, she heard the house phone ring. Had they forgotten some of their score? It often happened.

"—there's a man down here who says he's a private investigator."

Johnnie at once fell apart. "But—Mr. and Mrs. Armstrong just left!" she managed to say, quickly assuming her maid's voice.

"He says he wants to come up anyways. Says he wants to see the place," the switchboard girl reported.

Johnnie thought about that one. "Does he have…a search warrant?"

There was a brief discussion on the other end. "No. He just wants to talk to their help."

"Their help? You mean *me*? Why *me*?"

A pause, with more discussion. "He wants to question you about somethin'. He just showed me his badge."

What could she do or say? Was this connected with Mr. Daly? She'd have to put on her maid's uniform but fast—"All right, I guess so." Hanging up, she wriggled into the black taffeta dress, tied on the apron, pulled the cap over her uncombed hair, rolled on some dirty hose, stuffed her toes into her patent leather slippers, daubed on some lip rouge, and prepared herself for the worst.

At the ring of the doorbell, she took a deep breath, and opened it but a few inches.

A man, whom Johnnie later described as a pie crust before the filling went in it, stood unsmiling, asking if this was the the Armstrong residence, and showing his badge. She allowed him entrance—wondering if she should. Wasn't there a law against this sort of thing…rubbernecking about from his place there in the entrance hall!

Then he turned to her and asked, in a bored voice, "As an employed domestic here, I wonder if you might answer a few questions?"

"Do I have to?" Johnnie asked.

"No, but if you choose not to, it won't help your situation—or theirs any," he replied as if walking in his sleep.

"Well, let's try just one to start off and see if I feel like answering it." Johnnie replied, standing there, watching him step down and peer into the bedrooms—all the beds unmade.

"All right: here we go. What's *really* going on here, sister?…and I mean really."

• • •

Ynez and Joe had first been dropped off at Houston Street before Mack went on to St.Vincent's alone. From the hospital, he had gone to the morgue, following right behind the police. Now, standing before the Hell's Kitchen tenement where Blackie had lived, Mack felt he ought to explain himself to the officer assigned there.

"I would like to be as much a part of this investigation as is possible," Mack said.

The young man, Detective Sergeant Becker, removed the pipe from his mouth in order to reply, gestured with it, and nodded laconically. "Why not?"

Mack felt uncomfortable in this rookie's presence. Not more than twenty-three and possessed of a brand new, tough, cynical attitude, Becker was giving the impression of seeing right through him.

"...because of my friendship to Blackie, you see," Mack attempted, as two other cops in uniforms were given the nod of approval by the sergeant to enter the building.

"Yes. That's natural. You're the gent who gave him money to live. You work for the booze patrol, don't you?" Becker asked. Mack nodded. "Sure. I looked you up when we heard Blackie calling for you. Fact is, I have nothing to say about it, sir. As a government official in your particular position, you can certainly call the shots, up to a point, unless—or until—you're implicated in the case."

"Sergeant Becker," Mack answered, "I am here to help in any way I can. He was a good friend—that's all."

A search warrant had been obtained to scour the pathetic space in which the Whistler had dwelt for possible clues, with Mack following the procedure of the investigation to its present stalemate.

Inside, Blackie's little nest was as neat as a monk's cell. It told of nothing more than the life of a lonely cripple who got by as best he could. The glimmer of happiness in that single room, lit by a cellar window and a kerosene lamp, were stacks of song sheets, an old gramophone and some phonograph records.

"What made you both such good friends?" Becker asked Mack, thumbing through the song sheets bored and disinterested.

"Well," Mack answered, "we have a mutual war buddy, and he brought us together...I guess I felt sorry for him, that's all. I liked him a lot." He could not erase the image of Blackie on that slab.

"He must've memorized all these ditties...apparently, I guess, people gave these to him—and the recordings as well."

"Everyone was very good to him," Mack said as the rookie named Becker quickly filed through the records, then promptly threw them all in a nearby coal bucket.

"There's nothing here, let's go." Becker was so sure of himself.

They were outside now. It had stopped raining but the grim neighborhood, the meanness of the afternoon light and the unsettling warmth, upon which hung the stench of garbage, surrounded them.

"How often did you give him money, Mr. Daly? Regularly?" Becker had a baby face with eyes rimmed in long lashes and an expression which was contrived to give the impression of somebody who couldn't be fooled.

Mack answered, "Just whenever I'd see him. About once a week, in fact." They walked back to Mack's car. "Would you like a ride?" he asked. Becker declined.

"Just one last thing, Mr. Daly. I think it was grand of you to pay for the funeral and the grave plot for him." Becker leaned down to look at Mack in the driver's seat. "Can you think of anyone who would smash him up against that building like that?"

Mack had already started up the Marmon. "I can't imagine that kind of anger aimed at Blackie. Not him. But whoever it was, they must've wanted him dead in the very worst way."

Before parting, Becker told Mack that he would remain in touch, meaning that he did not fully trust him—and Mack knew it. But he had more to think about than Sergeant Becker's long eyelashes and the facade of his cocksure manner.

A specific time had been set for Mack to arrive at Bruno's office. There was still time as he sped down the long stretch of those Manhattan blocks, sensing that Alexander might be worried. Parking in front of a corner drug store on Eighth Avenue, he located a telephone booth.

"Mr. D.!" Alexander picked up at once, after the connection had been made.

"Fill me in, will you, please? I haven't much time." (He relayed that the Armstrongs wanted him to call after four.) "I've got to go downtown and get Ynez and Joey. Then, I'm going to try to get in to see the Countess."

Alexander said, "Not that spook-chaser! Lordy! Things must really be bad if you're lookin' her up!"

Mack opened the door to the booth and, half out, added, "I just want some earthly information. Please don't worry, will you?"

Mack was not one to go in for messages from the Beyond; this was a real emergency. Something Mack had just seen the Sergeant throw in that coal scuttle made him think of his old and mystical friend.

Would Blackie be alive now, Mack asked himself, had he not placed himself in such a treacherous situation? Those phonograph records were not fox-trots or novelty numbers. They were something Mack couldn't imagine the Whistler owning, or even listening to. They were recordings that had to be ordered only by mail, dealing with the Spirit World. But why would someone like Blackie have them? Of all the people Mack knew, the Countess alone would hold the answer.

• • •

Meanwhile, Ynez was not at all comfortable with the way Blanche King was looking at her—the other woman's eyes raising and lowering from the pages of illegalese with piercing rapidity. Fortunately, Ynez had donned a hat with a wide, swooping brim and half-veil, in keeping with her new Mata Hari image. She felt that Blanche was making every effort to look right under that brim, finally rising and going to the other side of the desk to have a cigarette then open a window. She mustn't have approved of Mrs. Daly's perfume...or perhaps the fact that she was up there in Bruno's office at all.

"Want one?" Blanche asked Ynez.

"Thanks, no—" As Blanche lit up, Ynez turned her attention to Bruno, who was sitting at an opposite desk. "You've been a very naughty boy, not even sending me orchids or ankle bracelets."

"What books have *you* been reading?" Bruno shook his head, then his glance went past Ynez to Blanche. "You can go and fix up those new Moran's Elixir papers with Sal and then do a title search on the 68th Street property."

Placing the papers in a briefcase, donning her coat and hat, and reaching for her paper bag full of nuts, Blanche loped to the door. "Fine. I'll be back. It's been a pleasure, Mrs. Daly."

Joe, who had been taking it all in from his position on the sofa, commented, "Don't let Squirrely get to yuh, Mrs. Daly."

"Hadn't you better start calling me 'Ynez'? I mean, after all—aren't we partners in crime now, among other things?"

She walked toward the window and sat on the sill, her foxtails hanging about her elbows. With crossed legs, she lit up one of her own Egyptian blends, inhaling deeply. "You know, Bruno, that gal Blanche is the most miserable human being I've ever encountered. I swear I recognize those weird eyes of hers. I wonder if she worked as a liaison at *La Maison*?"

"She acted like she'd seen you around, too. I guess it takes a mob girl to know one!" Bruno noted, laughing under his breath, shuffling through the phony Moran's Elixir company papers.

"Say! Are you going to be sweet to me or not?"

"When you keep on showing me your legs up past your garters, I've got no choice!" Walking toward her, Bruno stradled her then, gazing down, smiled.

Joe asked, "Gee. Wonder where Mack is?" Unable to think of anything else to say, he watched Ynez wrap her arms around his brother. "I'm gonna go downstairs and get some chewin' gum."

He thought it best they be left alone, and as he rattled down the stairs, Joe again concluded how "girl stuff" always gave him the creeps.

Going to the corner of West Broadway to get his favorite Beeman's Pepsin Gum, he picked up a copy of the *Sun*. It featured news of the Whistler's murder, and as he glanced over the pages, also of another slaying.

"Holy cripes!" A small article reported that Eddie the Dancer, once known as Ramon di Rose, had been shot and killed just the evening before. He had to read it twice, his lips moving slowly. Then, looking up, he spotted Mack rounding the corner, parking below Bruno's office.

"MACKIEEEE!"

Suddenly, he was a kid again, running to the car. "Jeez, where wuz yuh! I feel like kissin' yuh right here out in public!" Joe slid in beside him.

"Aw, it's great to be missed, Joey. Let's save it for inside the hallway. What're you reading?"

"Only dat Eddie duh Dancer was also killed. Finally! Same night we wuz up at duh Patch. So at leas' my ass is covered. Want some gum? Where wuz yuh so long?" Joe closed the newspaper.

Mack put his arm around him, looking deeply worried. "Joey, I'm sorry. I didn't mean to be so elusive."

"—is that like exclusive?"

"Yes! It is, in a way! But I'm exclusive only to you, pal. That poor guy Blackie—God! It all made me so sad…" Mack looked up at the windows on the second floor. "—I guess it's o.k. to leave Ynez there a bit longer."

"I'd say so. Dat's why I'm down here instead of up dere."

"I see. Did you expect that Ramon di Rose character to get croaked?" Mack asked Joe. "You don't act very touched by his passing, I must say!"

Joe tilted his head to one side. "Aw, you just don't get it yet. See, he was a yegg, and yeggs is always on duh lam somehow or udder. He had it comin'."

"I'm sure Ynez will feel the same way, too," Mack responded dryly. "And just how are she and Bruno coming along?"

With a gesture that told Mack they were an Item, Joey replied, "Mack, he's bin totally straight wid her. He don't want no complee-cations to get between himself and dis new deal we got goin' here. He means to do dis t'ing up right and do it big if you aksts me. Only t'ing wuz, Squirrely and 'Ynez'—she said I could call her dat now—dey didn't hit it off at all—not dat Squirrely would ever win any votes in a pop-a-larity contest, but dere was somethin' in duh way they looked at each udder."

He then told Mack that Ynez believed Miss King was among those working up at *La Maison*, disguised under mask and robe.

"Could she be a yegg as well?" Mack asked, to which Joe threw his head back, laughing.

"Tomatahs ain't yeggs, Mack! Only punks!"

Mack let that one go, then said, "Listen, I want you to come with me back up to Hell's Kitchen and do some garbage picking, then on to see an old friend of mine."

"You pickin' t'ru duh trash for clues, right?" Joe at once understood.

"Exactly, Joe. We'll just quickly pass by. Then you're going to meet a genuine clairvoyant!"

Joe put his hands up in front of his face. "Oh, boy! Another big woyd! I ain't akstin' dis time—whatever she is, if she's a friend of yers, it's fine by me…"

In mere moments, they were back in front of Blackie's dump and, sure enough, the ash cans were being placed curbside by a glum-looking ten year old boy, himself covered with soot. Right on top of one can sat the pile of phonograph records.

"Dese 'em?" Joe asked, hopping over the passenger side door.

"Yes. Grab the bunch, Joey." He did so, then blew off the ashes before putting them on the floor of the Marmon. "We'll bring those up to show the Countess," Mack added.

"Now what is it dat she is exacklee again, Mack? I didn't quite catch it all duh foyst time."

"Oh. She's a clairvoyant, Joey. That's a person who can see into the future."

The Countess was "At Home" every afternoon from eleven until four. A sign on her door read "IN SESSION" so Joe and Mack waited a couple of minutes.

A dignified couple opened the door to leave, and standing behind them was Xacha.

"Benjamin! What kept you! I knew you would come. Ah, and this must be your heart's desire! Your celestial gift from the gods! No! Do not tell me your name! I knew you at Luxor in my second re-incarnation! You are Ko-reh-amun, aren't you!"

"I yam?" Joe felt like it was Hallowe'en.

Escorting them in, she at once launched into a monologue about the Death of the Whistler, as they sat in chairs opposite her table. As Mack listened intently, Joe, holding the recordings in his hands, took the Countess in, galvanized by her pale violet eyes that seemed to burrow holes into one's very soul.

The Countess, tilting her head, said wistfully, "—you are quite beside yourself, Benny, my poor boy. Did you know that Blackie had gotten himself into some very nasty business?"

"I really do feel responsible—" Mack replied reverently.

"Blackie was going to die very, very soon anyway. He had fallen under the spell of a quack doctor who was about to attempt an operation—putting new limbs on him!" The Countess' kohl-rimmed eyes narrowed marvelously. "IF you can imagine such a thing!"

"Indeed I can, Countess. A racket like that one was going great guns down on Coney right after the War!"

"Poor Blackie bought the entire ruse in exchange for working as this doctor's informant. You see, the charlatan went in for the carriage trade—and their purses as well!"

"Do you know where the doctor is?" asked Mack.

"Do I know where he is? Do I know where he is! Of course I know where he is! Didn't he talk me into fixing my poor hands just a year or so ago! Just look what he did to them!" She removed her paper thin kid gloves. They were much worse than before. Joe's eyes widened.

She continued chattering, "He's everywhere and nowhere, my dear boy. I understand from your friend Bootsie Carstairs—who's been taking monkey gland serum, though I advised him not to, that he's most recently gathering a flock together! A veritable cult!"

"What?" Mack was aghast.

"Yes! People who are apparently interested in becoming perfect human beings through—oh—just all kinds of hoo-doo hokum!"

"But of course he's not winning over anyone, is he?"

"My dear boy, I have a client who got away from him just in time—else she would've been wearing her face for a hat, it was just that lifted! I cannot, of course, disclose her name, but if she can find him, she will expose him and sue him for whatever he is worth! At any rate, he is somewhere in New York, of that I am quite certain."

"Have the authorities been informed? Apparently he's been getting away with this for years."

The Countess looked at Mack as if he were an imbecile. "Really, dear boy, come to your senses! A man so fiendishly cunning will elude all efforts to be brought to justice! And furthermore, as they say nowadays, there's a sucker born every minute!"

Joe just loved her for saying that. How could such a regal lady be so down to earth?

She now stared at Joe and he stared back, eyes even wider. "This young man has the eternal beauty of Orpheus—or Adonis; a martyred gladiator at the Circus Maximus! Close those beautiful orbs of yours and drift with me, for just an instant, into that arena which enfolds both the past and the future!"

"Go ahead, Joe, she's telling you to close your eyes. It's o.k.," Mack whispered.

"Jeez. O.k. Watch my back now."

The Countess' eyes closed slowly. Her voice became dreamy, poetic. "Nothing will ever separate you two. Not even death. Yours is a devotion written in the stars. You have come to love this man at your side because without you and the great and noble heart that is in you, he would die. You are his flame in the darkness which will surround him, and you will never ever falter —though the winds and the rains be harsh! You will always be, past the life plane, one with him through all his sorrow, for all eternity."

There were tears in Mack's eyes as she finished her trance. Joe could not utter a word.

"And as for you, my dear Benjamin! What is this you have come to see me about? I seem to sense your concern about...discs."

"Yes, yes, Xacha, phonographs records...privately issued perhaps, with the label Opus, dealing with esoteric mysteries. Joey, show them to the Countess."

Xacha would not touch them, but only stared as Joe held them up before her.

"But don't you see! I have already answered your question. These recordings are often sold to people by fakirs—like the quack doctor whom I just mentioned!" Xacha sat back in her ornately carved and gilded chair. "Some of them promise cures through self-hypnosis, through communicating with Indian guides—some promise to ease pain by way of bringing the lost souls of Atlantis right into one's drawing room!"

Mack looked over at the records. The sleeves in which they were placed were without information, and even the labels themselves were blank circles hand-inscribed with numbers.

"What name does this doctor go under—do you happen to know?" asked Mack.

"He is as known Dr. Sloane...or Soames, is it? Yes! Soames!"

Then Mack asked the Countess about the murdered Chinese girl.

"I did in fact see an exquisite Oriental little thing who worked at *La Maison*. She was brought up to see me in the most marvelous sedan chair, encased like a little doll!"

"That fits!"

"She spoke perfect English, too. I told her that she was surrounded by simply indescribable danger. And she said to me, 'Oh, yes, I know! I am trying to get back to my home in San Francisco, you see...'"

"She never made it—" Mack said.

"No, and I knew she would not. Was she—?"

"Yes. Murdered. And partially dismembered."

The Countess took a deep breath, then shook her head slowly. "Be very, very careful with all of this, Benjamin. When one is able to lift oneself up on a certain cloud and glimpse at Heaven, one must always watch out for an ill-wind. In its blast is the power to topple."

A knock came at her door just then, making Joe nearly jump from his seat. "Alas! My next client..." The Countess stood up, followed by Mack and Joe.

Kissing her lightly on the cheek, Mack pressed more than a few hundred dollar gold pieces into her silk-encased hand. "Thank you, Xacha...and bless you."

As she swept toward the door, she turned to Joe. "Don't I get a kiss from you, too?"

"Yes, Your Majesty!" and Joe obliged, feeling her patting his bottom.

As they left, two giggling young shoppe girls were let in, giving the fellows the eye. The Countess whispered in a sigh, "Ah well! I cannot discriminate! We are only souls, here in this life plane, imprisoned in temporary splendor…or misery!"

Going down the hall, Joe was full of questions, practically jumping up and down. " Jeez! am I impressed! I was breakin' out in a col' sweat, dat's how scared I was! What happened to her hands? Jeez, they looked awful!"

"Looks to me like this mad doctor did one of his treatments on her. She was always self-conscious about them, but now they're totally ruined—poor darling."

"What wuz wrong wid 'em in duh foyst place, Mack?"

"Oh. When she was in India, the Countess materialized the goddess Kali at the behest of the Maharajah of Kikarrou. He at once keeled over dead, then her hands caught fire."

"India! Kali! Ma-hah-ahahah!" Joe shivered visibly, not even having to know what Mack was talking about. "Boy, lemee tell yuz, we're sleepin' wid duh light on tunnight!"

As they approached the roadster, he asked Mack why he had paid the Countess in gold pieces. "Oh, she now only accepts gold or silver, Joe. She's pretty sure something terrible is going to happen to the stock market next year."

• • • • •

CHAPTER XIV

OF VISITORS AND VICTIMS

Nothing in this world could've kept Deucie deVol from going down to the crime scene that morning. Baby soon saw it his way, at first telling him he'd just better leave things up to the police. But there she was, right beside him, in a taxi bound for West 10th Street.

With Deucie giving directions to the cabbie, they alighted at Tenth and Seventh Avenue.

"Why do you think it's over this way?" Baby asked him, trying to angle her umbrella so it sheltered them both.

"I b'leeve there are businesses farther west…loading dock, trucks, that sorta thing. Come on, darlin'—looks to be lettin' up."

Because of the ignominious status of Blackie the Whistler, none of the papers had reported the precise address of the killing. When at last they reached Ninth Avenue it was merely drizzling. As Baby looked up at the clouds, she heard her husband say, "There it is. That's where they got him," and felt a chill overtake her. Looking to her left, she saw a long, narrow driveway with a police barricade across it. Not a soul stirred; nary a copper was present. Deucie limped at remarkable speed toward a loading dock where the heavy downpour had washed away some of the blood.

"I didn't imagine so much blood," Baby said, taking it all in. "—and with all this rain…why so much blood?"

They both bent close to the place where Blackie had been smashed up against the loading dock. The entire platform, sheltered partially by an overhang, was covered with blood. There was blood still clinging to the vertical portion of the loading dock, and blood on the tarred pavement around it.

"—far too much blood," Baby said again, shaking her head.

"How do you figure, honey?" Deucie asked, now running his pen knife between the concrete and the iron edge of the dock. Baby, frowning deeply, just shook her head, then assisted her man in getting up the stairs to the surface of the loading dock. He had something on the end of his pen knife.

"What you got there, hmm?" she asked him.

"Looks like some threads is all," he replied, and wrapped these carefully in his handkerchief.

Ahead were two steel doors, with a larger one at their center that had panels which folded into one another. They were all locked from the inside.

Now it had stopped raining entirely. Deucie and Baby managed their way back down the stairs, around to the side of the building, then onward to the front, which was on Ninth Street. It appeared to be abandoned. Both looked up at the five-story building, with its steel-shuttered windows. A wooden door at the far corner toward the East side of the city had before it a sturdy gate, also locked. Noting a mailbox rudely nailed to the inside of the door frame, Baby hastened to wiggle her fingers toward it and successfully lift its lid.

"Feel anything?" Deucie asked.

"Oh, yeah. Nertz! If I can only grab onto to it!" Some forearm acrobatics yielded nothing.

"Here, I'll use my cane." Deucie pulled the lower third portion of his walking stick off, revealing small set of tweezers operated by a screw at its top. Inserting the cane into the mailbox, lowering it down into the confines thereof, then, as his tongue moved all about his mouth while operating the little instrument, he pulled forth a scrap of paper.

"Whadda you make of it, Baby?" Deucie asked. Both read it again.

"Looks to me like somebody got stood up!"

The note, written in pencil on a small, plain sheet of paper, said only this:

"Waited for over an hour.
Don't ever forget me.
B."

Deucie neatly folded it and put it in his handkerchief along with the threads. As they headed for the subway, Baby noted that whoever wrote the missive had very flowery penmanship.

"Man or woman?" Deucie asked as if he were playing a game with her.

"—well, I would have to say a very feminine type of man, or a very masculine type of gal. With very good taste in foolscap. The paper is from a small notebook—the kind with those tiny pencils attatched. Very thick stuff. Imported…expensive." They walked on in silence.

"Anything else you might wanna add?" he asked her as she helped him down the steps to the IND.

"Maybe. But I've gotta think some more. How about you?"

"Oh," Deucie said, as the Uptown train roared into the station. "Me, too, but we're prob'lee thinkin' the same thing anyway."

However, on the way back Uptown, Deucie spoke not at all.

• • •

If Ynez had only truly read the papers instead of just looking at the pictures, she might've recognized the name of the woman who was telephoning her on that most sombre of afternoons. And, if she had only paid attention to what Bruno and Mack had been talking about up at Bruno's office, she might've been alerted to the telephone call she was now just receiving. As it was, having been booted out, Ynez was feeling distinctly *left out.*

"I've tried to reach you numerous times without success, Mrs. Daly," came the voice over the wire. That Irish accent was enough to make Ynez drop the ear-piece back down on the hook! The Brogue always made her think of those immigrant coal miners back in Karthage who manhandled her with their dirty mitts!

"I'm sorry, but I'm so terribly upset today! I simply can't place you! You'll have to leave all your information with my social secretary—"

Alexander shot her a weary, weary look. Would she never stop?

"—but I just did speak with him, Mrs. Daly, and it's you I must talk to, Mrs. Daly. Your husband works for my husband, Commissioner O'Couran!"

"Who? What?—oh. OH!" It finally registered.

Ynez had decided to bury herself in the opulent confines of the drawing room, where she drank one cocktail after another, wept and whimpered on-and-off, blew her nose ceaslessly, thumbed through fashion magazines and listened to the radio. She had only one thing on her mind and it was driving her wild: Bruno. How could she be falling in love with such a monster as that? He'd actually given her the bum's rush!

She had to get Alexander to drive all the way into town to fetch her. He and Mack were going to talk business, he'd told her. And he just didn't have time to play around...maybe later, he'd told her. She left, tail between her loins.

At first she'd been simply furious at him—but Bruno had at least promised that he would drive out with Mack and Joe and spend the night with her! Keep hoping, old girl! she told herself. Well, maybe!...It wasn't *quite* a promise...*still*...

Alexander had tossed the telephone her way, so he had no choice but to pick it up. "What'd you want?" Ynez had asked, with a yawn in her voice.

The woman on the other end of the wire told Ynez that she was a great admirer of hers—having read that grand article in Winchell. She wondered if Mrs. Daly had been asked to join the Women's Temperance Union yet?

"*What!*" Ynez nearly choked on her cocktail.

A ripple of Gaelic laughter came from the other end. "I know! Me, too! Not that I've got my elbow forever at a tilt, but I do like a little spirits now and then and I'm not afraid to admit it either!"

"Are we supposed to join! I mean, is it required?"

"Well, it isn't a bad idea, Mrs. Daly, being that our husbands are both doing what they are doing! There's a meeting coming right up!"

Ynez made mumbling sounds. "Well…my social calendar is *so* full just now. Do I really *have* to?"

There was a pause from Mrs. O'Couran. "Oh, well, I shan't blame you if you decline." Now, an even more awkward pause. "The fact is, Mrs. Daly, I simply wanted to meet you—in person."

(Could this be something about Mack and the awful mess he's in? Ynez thought. *Perhaps I should meet with her—I might be able to find out something…)* "I guess it could be arranged. But as I said—my social calendar…" she now answered.

"Oh, please, Mrs. Daly. It's very, very important—" her voice said with an urgency and a desperation.

(Hadn't they just been talking about what a perfect shit somebody with a last name like hers was? Someone who's getting Mack into awful trouble?) It all was coming back to Ynez now. "—all right," she said cautiously, "but it's difficult to say when I'll be free."

"Are you free this evening?" Again, that truly touching ache in her voice.

Ynez had to think about it. "Where would we meet? I wasn't planning to come into town. We're way out in Great Neck, you know." (*Perhaps Bruno might come by and take her off to a small hotel somewhere!*)

"I might see you just after supper by taking the train out. I just live in Forest Hills." A certain ray of hope was now penetrating Mrs. O'Couran's odd sense of the imminent.

After ringing off, Ynez hollered for Alexander. "Listen, you've got to go down to the station and pick up this Irish lady at 7:30."

Alexander shook his head in despair. "And you know I'm gonna ask you—how am I supposed to recognize her?"

"Red hair and freckles, stupid."

"Check."

• • •

As soon as the detective left the Armstrong apartment, Johnnie changed back into her jumper and headed not for Miss Harrison's townhouse in Murray Hill—but for the rehearsal hall instead, going in search of Nolie and Elliot.

Fortunately, they were returning from lunch. Spotting them with a few of the band members walking back up Broadway, she hopped from the cab and breathlessly cried out, "Hold on! I've got to talk to you both. Alone. Right now, too. And I don't mean maybe."

Elliot told the boys from the band to go on ahead. Standing before Johnnie, who was a real wreck, they felt her shock.

"Just let me get this out. Don't talk," she continued. "Right after you left, a detective showed up asking all kinds of questions."

"What?!" both Noilie and Elliot gasped.

"Now wait. Hold on. He was hired by Jack Wrigley's father."

Elliot slapped his hand over his heart. "I'm fainting."

"Now wait. They think that Wriggs is up to no good again. You know, falling by the wayside. By 'they' I mean his folks—and this detective, too. They think he's crazy for Nolie, not you, Elliot."

"Me?" Nolie squeeked. Then thought a bit, "Well, that's not so bad. Do they think he's just pestering us by hanging around?"

"This detective didn't say. I told him that Wriggs wanted to learn the music business, and was simply just fascinated by it all. I told him you both saw talent in him, and thought he might fit in with the orchestra someday. I told him that you both insisted he finish his schooling first."

"Schooling? What schooling? He's a towel boy, for Chrissake!" Elliot scowled. "And furthermore, he can't read a note of music!"

Nolie jabbed him with her elbow. "Oh, Elliot! She had to think fast, that's all! You did a good job, too, honey. But we'd better tell Wriggs about this right away."

Johnnie continued, "—the main thing is this detective didn't figure anything out, I'm sure of that. When he saw Elliot's bedroom, I told him it was the guestroom where Wriggs was sleeping…alone, too."

Both Elliot and Nolie let go a sigh of relief, Elliot shoving his hands in his pockets and shutting his eyes. "—see. It's over! There goes my big moment. Then you ask me why I pick up sailors."

Nolie and Johnnie felt a bender coming Elliot's way—fast. They hooked their arms in his and walked in the direction of the rehearsal hall with Elliot's head bent low.

Nolie said, "When he phones later, he'll no doubt let us know what happened to him on the home front. Poor kid." The girls didn't know quite what to say. Elliot had been so happy…and now…

"Oh. I need a drink," Elliot muttered. Their grips tightened.

"Elliot, please. Don't. We'll get this final song down and we'll be done in no time," Nolie softly urged. "Talk to the kid when he calls. Things may not be so bad."

"So bad? I think he's moving in with us, for God's sake! This is really a mess. Obviously, he went and told his parents and they set this dick on us!"

"Oh, don't jump to conclusions," Nolie said. "Maybe he hasn't gotten that far yet. He probably went right to the campus."

"Elliot," Johnnie said, "I thought about all of that. I don't think he's said a word. And I don't think he ever would. Let me see if I can locate him at the Princeton Athletic Department. I'll tell him to—well—just be prepared—that's all. Will they let me call long distance from in there?"

"Sure," answered Elliot, unconvinced. "But I still need a drink."

"Wriggs will never speak to you again if you go on a toot, Elliot Armstrong!" Nolie was hustling him inside by now. "We'll just get to the bottom of this and you'll go right back there and croon your tonsils raw."

• • •

Mack had stayed on at Bruno's office to finalize the Moran's Elixir deal. Joey, in the process of running back and forth from the restaurant, had turned the desk into a dining table, piling it high with food for the last fifteen minutes.

"All this for me!" Mack inhaled the scrumptous aromas. "You want to get me fat, Joe?"

"Ma sez you gotta eat, 'cause yer under a lotta pressure just now. Come on—siddown. We always have meals like dis when t'ings get rough. It's how we talk."

Joe pulled out a desk chair for Mack, pretending he was a hi-klass waiter just as Squirrely King walked in and was reluctantly asked by Bruno if she wanted to join them.

"Why not?" Blanche sneered, pulling out her own chair, and very properly unfolding the checkered napkin then placing it on her lap. "I'm so famished, I feel like my last meal came from my Mama's left tittie."

Mack marveled at the chasm which existed between her foul mouth and her correct demeanor.

"I got a Victrola up here if you want to play those records," Bruno pointed to a niche at the end of the room. "Maybe what we need is a little dinner music."

As both brothers dug in, and Blanche oh-so-politely cut her sausage into the tiniest of pieces, Mack cranked up the machine and put on the first record.

A mellifluous voice with the ring of an orator began:

"There you are right now, sitting before your phonograph wondering what can possibily be offered by me to make you feel better. Well, I'll tell you, my friend, the only way to change that world out there is to first of all begin by changing yourself!"

"Eat! Eat!" Joe called to Mack, motioning him to return to the table. "Dat stuff's all bullshit anyways—"

Mack did so, munching thoughtfully, listening intently.

"Let's start by smiling! Feel those muscles at either side of your mouth lifting! Lifting! Lifting! Up into a wide grin! One! Two! Three! There we are!"

"Hey, have some more rigatonis! Don't be shy, Mack!" Joe heaped his plate full.

"Shut up, Joey!" Bruno said.

"Don't you see, my friend, how, by counting our blessings, we can create a list of all the good things we have around us to build on! What's that you say—you don't have any blessings to count? Now! Now! Don't we have the sunshine? Don't we have the the stars twinkling at night? And...don't we have our dreams? Please turn the record over."

Blanche held up her hand. "You want to hear the other side, don't you?" she addressed them all.

Joe answered loudly, "No!" while Bruno, masticating away, shrugged, and Mack answered, "That's the first in the series...let's go to the last one. It's number five I think, Miss King. Let's try side two."

Blanche rose, turned the record over and gave the machine a crank.

The last lesson was now concluding: *"...and here is the most important point of all to remember! When things get you so terribly, terribly, down, and you fully realize that there's absolutely nothing you can do about what they now call The Blues—because you feel simply trapped in a life which was not of your choice—not of your making—and you truly have no future whatsoever at all—then! Then is the time for a quick call for help! What's that you say? Your telephone has been disconnected because you couldn't pay your bill? But that is no reason not to find us! You can always, through one of our living guides, locate us! Remember our little secrets! You and I are pledged to work together—to change your entire life experience for the better! I am here! Now! For you and with you! But you ask...where? Where, O Great One, dost thou dwell? By only reaching out to a Living Guide will you be brought to me, Thy Master! Go now, if you are still so terribly blue! Contact a Living Guide! And if you feel at all that I was in any way able to help you—uplift you, and change your life for the better—ask your Living Guide how you, also, may become One—like They!"* An organ played.

"Mack," said Joe, "he lost me."

Blanche got up and switched the phonograph off. Then, returning to the table, she asked, "Did someone give you these records, Mr. Daly?"

Mack told her they were left to him by a friend who had passed away.

"Do you find such messages uplifting?" she continued.

"This kind of thing seems to be in the air right now...mystical cults and that sort of thing," Mack answered. "But it seems a bit...well...suspect somehow."

Joey looked up from his plate. "It's a lotta bullshit is all."

Blanche spoke up at once. "But for those who are in despair, for those who are one of Life's Lost—surely—?"

Bruno looked at her narrowly. "Do I detect a soft spot in that heart of stone of yours, Blanche King?"

She rose haughtily. "I'll just finish my notes now, if you don't mind," and went back to her desk as Joey cleared the plates.

"Oops. And have I offended you, Miss King?" Bruno asked her facetiously.

"No," she answered, carefully averting his glance. "Not at all."

"We still got zepps and espresso!" Joe called out from across the room, putting coffee on a small kerosene burner.

Mack noticed Blanche's sudden change and wondered if she herself might've been one of Life's Lost, and in deep despair as well. "I'm sure Mr. Imperio meant nothing by it, Miss King, it's only that sometimes desperate people who have no sensible recourse would naturally end up seeking out a man like the one on these recordings." Then he added carefully, "Have you heard of the work of a certain Doctor Soames, Miss King?"

Bruno, Joe and Mack were now looking right at her as she tidied her desk, eyes downcast. She seemed to react as if jolted somehow but, shaking her head, whispered coldly, "Never. Why do you ask?"

Joe, returning with the zeppolis, answered in Mack's stead, "Oh, he's gotta have a toot' pulled, dat's all."

Mack got it. The idea was don't trust her.

• • •

While Alexander was once again down at the station, looking around for yet another of of Mrs. D.'s visitors, the phone rang again. Ynez picked it up, hearing Annabelle Harrison's voice.

By way of Keys telephoning the Armstrongs, she had gotten word of the Whistler's murder. "Oh, and by the way," Annabelle continued, "only as a sidelight, my dear, but it's been simply *haunt*ing me! I met this poor woman the other day and I'd meaning to tell you all about it. I've come to calling her simply 'M.O'C.' because of the monogram." And she then proceeded, finally, to tell her all about the unfortunate meeting itself.

"*What*?!" Ynez was incredulous. "—but! But—it's the same woman…Mrs. O'Couran! She'll be here in only a few moments! How did she find me? Why, by my newspaper article, of *course*!" Ynez answered herself. "My dear, I've no idea *what* she wants! But she's gotten syphilis from her husband, you say? And she's going to have a kid on top of it? And he's going to have her put away in some sort o f…*asylum*!"

Annabelle calmly provided, "Darling, you've got to be a friend to her, that's all. She's a *pathetic* thing. She just needs someone to *talk* to! That husband of hers—Commissioner O'Couran—is a *very* unsympathetic character, I would venture!"

"What? But am I safe with her in my house?"

"*What?* Oh!—there's my darling Keys! We're running off to the studio. I'll ring you up then, muffin." And that was that.

At First Ynez was void of any thoughts at all, standing in front of the tall mirror beneath the stairway in the hall, looking at herself in black chiffon trimmed in white at the collar and cuffs. Looking further into her reflection she saw in her eyes a sudden sense of inner resolve.

"I can do something with this, even if she *is* nuts," she told herself. "I'll be a friend to her, all right. And find out all I can."

Hearing the big car pulling to a halt, she went to the front doors and opened them wide. Toward her toddled a plainly Irish lass, barely smiling—obviously wracked by nerves.

"Mrs. O'Couran! I am Mrs. Daly, but you must call me 'Ynez.'" She swept the demure thing inside, as Alexander walked behind them, going toward the kitchen. Just ahead, in the drawing room, he had set out tea and cookies for them both, as instructed.

"Oh, and isn't this grand!" Mrs. O'Couran whispered as if she had entered a church. "You've no idea how much I admire you, Mrs. Daly, I mean, rather, *Ynez*...what a backdrop for a lady like you! My, my!"

They sat, and Ynez, taking the role of a sob sister, told her, "Well, *I've* certainly had *my* ups and downs. Oh! The things I could tell *you*, Mrs. O'Couran!"

"Make that Peggy, please, Ynez."

"Peggy, it is! Tea, my dear?"

"Wellll—I don't suppose you've got any spirits at hand, have you?"

"Oh, you've just no idea...what'll it be, Peg?"

Peggy O'Couran thought a martini would fit the elegance of her surroundings. Ynez, pulling open a modernistic cabinet to reveal a well-stocked bar, commenced to make a shaker full.

"Oh," Peggy O'Couran cooed, "—and you've got such graceful ways with your cocktail things...I notice you bruise rather than shake! A woman after my own heart!"

Two hours later, at nine o'clock that same evening, both women had polished off two shakers of martinis, and were more than agreeably drunk. Whenever Peggy got sloppy over her days back on the Old Sod, Ynez got sloppy about her days back in Monte Carlo (never revealing the truth). When Peggy wept about her loneliness, Ynez wept about hers (real tears, but fabricated stories of how Mack was always working so late, leaving her alone);

when Peggy laughed helplessly about her Uncle Liam's pranks in Dublin, Ynez laughed helplessly over her Uncle-the-Baron Roland's pranks upon the Riviera, squandering their millions.

Finally, Ynez placed her hand upon Peggy's little knee and had to know, "But whash wrong, Peg? Whash really eating away at yoo?"

And at that Peggy O'Couran opened the flood-gates and told Ynez everything. "—and thash why I had to shee you inshtead of any ol' lady doctor! You're so cosmopol—cosmopol—oh, *Hell*...such a woman of the world!"

Ynez was not so drunk that she was incapable of remembering everything said henceforth, down to every grisly detail. She helped Poor Peggy along. "But firsht, you little shweetheart you, you've gotta fin' out if you really *are* gonna have a kiddie-widdie! Then, you got to get that social disheez taken care of! Then, you gotta divorsh that son of a bitch you're married to!"

Peggy wept again. "But the poor wee one, Ynez! What if it's born with the disease!"

Ynez staggered to the bar to prepare another round. "You don't know 'til you got the FAKCSH!—oh, oh, oh...there's waysh...there's waysh. Sssshhhh!" Ynez looked about as if the walls had ears, then winked. "I'll help yuh!"

"But, Ynesh, do you think I should have it taken care of if I really have bin *dosed*!" Peggy stopped, her bleary eyes wide, beseeching. "You know what I mean?"

"—shurr I do!" Ynez poured out two more martinis, sniffling. "But you don't wanna get scraped unless you have to, Peg!"

"OH! And I'll go to Hell for shoor if I'm reduced to that! But I'd rather go to Hell than to the Slaves of Mary, that's for shertain!" Peggy cried.

"The *wha*—?"

"Oh, it' such a joke! A joke, I tell you! A private hoshpital, they call it. Well, it'sh how they get rid of 'em! Indeed!" Then: "What *time* is it? I've got to be home to Brian! I told him I was over to the convent helpin' out the nuns! Now look at the condish-un I'm in! He'll beat the Hell out of me!"

Ynez rose and hollered for Alexander. He at once appeared, being just around the corner, listening the entire time. "Take her out to Forest Hills, but first fill this shaker up with coffee. *Make sure she drinks it.*"

Alexander, marveling at how so-suddenly-not-soused Ynez was, helped her put Mrs. O'Couran back together, then practically carry her out and throw her little self into the big car.

Left alone, Ynez went at once to her bedroom, peeled off her frock, thence to her bathroom, in search of an aspirin. Oh! How her head pounded all over again! That *woman!* And that truly despicable *hus*band of hers. Well, perhaps, her own life wasn't so bad after all. The telephone rang and she rushed to it, hoping it would be Bruno. But of course he would never call…

"Hello?" a deep voice said.

"Bruno! Oh, *Bruno*!"

"Ynez, it's *Mack*, for God's sake—don't you know my voice by *now?* Listen, Joey and I are heading out to White Plains—to Bootsie Carstairs' roadhouse. I think he can help us. We'll be staying overnight."

"You're not coming back here then?"—sitting down on her chaise, ovrcome with a sudden need to have Mack there…to talk to him about her visitor. "Mack, I just had a most *peculiar* visit from Brian O'Couran's wife!"

"How on earth—?"

"—she told me all about him…" Ynez then filled Mack in. "And so, the poor thing is pregnant, she thinks she's got the syph and on top of that he wants to have her committed to a crazy house! She asked me if I knew anybody who could take care of her pregnancy to avoid such a thing…*you* know what I mean."

"Say, that's a shame. But it's the perfect lead-in for getting Bootsie to tell us who this quack doctor is. I'll ask him if he knows of any doctors who are a bit shady."

"—you've found out more horrible things, I suppose."

"Yes. Unfortunately, lots more. By the way, when you were back at *La Maison*, did you ever get to know a Chinese gal named Lee?"

"She was around, but our paths never really crossed. I think I sent her to see the Countess, though. I did know she had a sugar daddy and he put her up somewhere—then she was gone. Why?"

"Listen, I don't want to scare you. We knew all of that. But—well, you'll be all right on your ownsome for a night, won't you, Ynez?"

"Of course I will, you needn't worry about me," Ynez answered, pouty, feeling left out. "But Where's Bruno? Maybe he'd come out and keep me company!"

"Oh, he's busy fixing up his cooking plant for the Moran's Elixir change-over," Mack felt a mixture of pique and self-pity coming in waves across the wire. "Say, I'm awfully sorry, Ynez. If you're feeling so alone, why not go stay with Annabelle?"

"Oh, she doesn't want *me* there—she's got Keys. And besides, they're working on that new exhibit she's got coming up." Ynez, feeling dumped all around, looked at her clock. "Oh, well. It's after ten. I'll just go to bed, I guess."

They both rang off, with Mack expressing concern, apologies and excuses about how what he was now doing might save them both from scandal and ruin. But it all boiled down to the same thing—he was gone! And gone for the whole night with his flame, too. While Ynez, her head aching far worse, threw herself back on her chaise, lit a cigarette and wondered why Mack had said, "Listen, I don't want to scare you—"

Whatever had happened, Ynez then wondered, to that little Chinese thing? Rising, she went to her vanity and rummaged through her drawers until she found a worn, little silk fan. Lady Lee had scrawled a telephone number on it. What if Ynez simply rang her up? It was a Manhattan number, and so she asked the operator to place the call. Soon enough there was an answer.

"Hello?" (With great hesitation.)

"Lee?" Ynez queried. "Is that you?"

There was a pause. "Lee is not here. She is dead." Another pause. The voice was taking on a personality. Distinguished, most likely British. It was clear that he had first entirely disguised his voice, for some reason. "Who is this, please?"

Ynez faltered. "Oh—I'm terribly sorry—just an acquaintance really..."

"From what circle?" the voice demanded.

"*Circle*? Oh, it was years ago...thank you—good-b—"

"—Did you know her from a certain house on East 68th Street, by any chance?" The voice was cold, like a gravedigger's.

"No, no. We met through her chiropodist, that's all." Ynez had to think quickly.

"The redoubtable Mr. Fong, then..." the voice said. "Have you lovely feet?"

Ynez removed her mule and took a look. Still in hose, but through the veil of silk, they did look quite good. "Well, they'll do, I guess...don't tell me you're a shoe salesman?"

"Not *quite*," the voice replied and Ynez got gooosebumps.

Ynez heard Alexander returning. She was so relieved! "I've got to ring off now. It's been swell talking to you." She absently placed the ear-piece on its hook, hearing Alexander coming up the steps. "Oh, thank Gawd you're back! What*ever* took you so long?"

Alexander answered, "At this hour, the local trains don't come any too often, and I couldn't very well just leave her there. She was gettin' very nervous about what her husband was gonna do to her once she got back home! He must be some kinda demon, let me tell you! And another thing, she kept lookin' behind us, mumblin' about bein' followed." As was Alexander's habit, he unconsciously went about straightening up her room. "What kinda man would do that to his wife?"

"Mack's boss, Alexander, Commissioner O'Couran. And he has done awful, *awful* things to her, apparently!" She held her hands up before her eyes, resting her head back on the pillows. "But I'm going to have to become her chum so that I find out what they're going to do to our Mackie next!"

"Say, your phone was off the hook, yuh know!" Alexander held it up, listening, hearing a distinct click. "Whoever it was just heard every single thing you said, Mrs. D.!"

"Well, I couldn't help it! Anyway, it was some creep is all."

"Creep? What kinda creep!"

"Oh, Alexander! You do try me sometimes! Now don't look at me that way, Alexander. You're scaring me!"

• • • • •

CHAPTER XV

BOOTSIE

The Tumble On Inn, Bootsie Carstair's queer roadhouse, was not what it seemed from the outside. A gloomy and grand Second Empire mansion on the road to White Plains, it was a Mecca for fairies only. Patrons of the inn came there, as Bootsie Carstairs said, "to loosen their corset stays" and just let themselves go. Rarely did an evening pass when every bedroom in the place was not filled with men of all types and all ages, consorting illicitly. On the main floor, an eight-piece Negro jazz band ragged, as a drag queen, dressed up like 1890s belle, provided the entertainment. Any "normal" being who might've wandered in by mistake would quickly get the idea, and run for the main road—fast.

Mack had arrived with Joe, causing quite a stir. Bootsie's patrons were of every class, from longshoremen to florists—from clerics to chorus boys. When Bootsie Carstairs and Orchid, his new and evanescent young beau, threaded through the crowd to see what all the commotion was about, Bootsie commenced to shriek with joy at the top of his lungs.

Like the world in which they lived, Bootsie and his amanuensis, Orchid, were of the hothouse variety of swish, enslaved to the secret world of camp. Their dress and manners imitated the style of the mid-Victorian Era with perverse exaggeration; they matched the mad decor of the Inn perfectly, and lived as only those pansies reckless enough to advertise themselves for what they were did dare to live. Bootsie and Orchid were either adored by their own kind—or completely shunned.

Mack absolutely and fearlessly adored Bootsie Carstairs—corseted, rouged, painted, bewigged and dressed to the nines like a pansy version of Diamond Jim Brady. The old queen merited from Mack a deep bow, and a kiss on the hem of his lavander frock coat.

"OH!" Bootsie screamed. "Is that all I get while you're down there?" Placing a pudgy, beringed hand under Mack's chin, he lifted his lips up, kissing him with a loud smack. The crowd went crazy.

Gazing for the first time upon Joe caused him more theatrics. "But! *But*! You're not real...You're not *real*..." Bootsie kept saying over and over. Orchid, leading them to a private dining salon draped about with portieres, indicated with a toss of his head that Joe had yet another an instant admirer. The drag queen, from up on the small stage, was flirting outrageously with him.

"Joey, I think she wants you for a duet—" Mack told him.

"Say! I'm game!" Joe hopped up on the stage, producing an ear shattering cheer.

Over the din, Bootsie told Mack that Joe was just precious.

"I'll say he is, Boots. But wait'll you hear all that's happened since we met." And then Mack told him—almost everything—leaving out his interest in the so-called miracle doctor.

"*But of course*, Daly! Love is a cruel teacher! What else matters but love? *Nothing*, my dear! *Nothing*. Look yonder at dear Orchid. I would die without him!" They had only just met a couple of months before and the lad, looking for 'a situation,' promptly moved in with him.

It seemed as if this far younger man now ran the place, while Bootsie happily held court. There was Orchid, bartending, waiting table, waving to them from across the room, handsome-to-tears, joyously overworked.

"He's such a *dear*, my hothouse flower is!" Bootsie grabbed Mack's hand. "You must *listen* to me! All of this which is happening to you and this young *god* of yours is worth it—every single *tear*, every bead of *sweat*, every *centime* thrown to the peasants, every little spat, every smile, every *goose-bump*! Because you are both *so so so so* in love and because you are both cursed and blest by being *queer*! Stick to him no matter what, Daly. In the end, it's all that will count."

"Thank you for that, Bootsie," Mack replied reverently. "And you are so in love, too, it appears."

"Yes! But, Daly, I am *old*! Old! Old as Methusalah. Fame came late to me, and the wonder of it is—it came at all! Had it not been for you, Daly, I would not be here right now!" Then, he became instantly pathetic. "Daly, I've got to confess something to you! I've gone and pissed away all the money I just earned from decorating your club!"

"Do you need a loan? I'd be happy to—"

"No, no, no—it isn't *that*." Bootsie struck a most classical pose. "But tell me: do you think it's helped?"

Mack at first wondered what he was talking about. Bootsie looked no different at all. Then, he remembered: the monkey gland serum…"Have you been seeing that miracle doctor who was treating the Countess?" Mack felt like a heel leading poor Bootsie on this way—but he had to.

"Mmmmm…once a week. Violently ill after the treatment, Daly, but, oh, my—*le transformation veritable* in one's vitality! Oh—if I told you! I can go all night now! Hard as if I were twenty again! And my skin…just *feel* how firm!"

Bootsie lifted Mack's hand to his face. Underneath the thick powdering and the stubble, it felt just like the face of any sixty-year old man.

"Do you have any money left?" Mack was blunt, because he was so concerned.

"Well, it always keeps trickling in…somehow. But! Well. He tells me if I stop these treatments, I'll just go back to feeling—and looking—like an old piece of *shit* again!"

(Mack was thinking, *He's got the poor old dear completely duped, whoever this guy is!)* He asked him, "Is he terribly expensive, Bootsie?"

Bootsie nodded. "Oh, God, yes. Each treatment is a thousand clams, Daly." Then brightening, "But I *do* look years younger…don't I?"

"You look in top form, Bootsie! Better than ever," Mack lied, as Orchid brought drinks and *hors d'ouevres*. "Orchid," Mack grinned up at him. "It's clear you're making my dear friend supremely happy!"

Not over twenty-five, Orchid was an exquisite angel out of a pre-Raphaelite painting—not at all like the he-flappers up and down Broadway. He breathed a thanks. Yet, those long lashes, casting shadows on his pale cheeks, suddenly fluttered nervously. Something behind his perfectly beautiful face now told Mack that Orchid was worried about Bootsie Carstairs.

Lifting his limpid eyes to Mack's, he asked, in a sylph-like voice, "You're both staying the night, I hope, aren't you?"

"If you have a room available," Mack said.

Bootsie held up his lorgnette. "*What*? Well, if we haven't, I'll throw somebody out on their asses just to have you and your he-man lover under my roof! We do have so much catching up to do, my darling boy!" Putting his arm about the wraith-like Orchid, he said, "This is quite an ocassion, sweet child. Seeing Mack *sans* that infernal *fake spouse* he got himself hitched to!"

Joe, onstage with the chantoozy, was accepting applause.

"Never knew Joey had such a good voice!" Mack laughed, clapping along, as Orchid left to serve more drinks.

Bootsie asked, *tres droll*, "And how does that *hideous bitch* you're married to get along with this new love of yours?"

Just then, Joey came back beaming. "Pretty good, ain't I?"

"You can have a job here anytime, my *jeunesse doré*!" Bootsie, giving him a violent goosing, told him, "Now go up there and do an encore or I shall never speak to you again!"

With Joey gone, Mack tried to stop laughing and answer Bootsie's question about his hideous bitch of a fake wife. "Joey has an older brother—Bruno—handsome devil…but the genuine article when it comes to being a mobster. He and Ynez have hit it off!"

"Well! A clear cut case of *la même chose*! Keeping it all *en famille*, eh?"

Bootsie continued to pursue his morbid interest in Mrs. Mack Daly. "Still, I can't imagine her ever getting over *you, mon ami*..." Mack lit Bootsie's long cigar. "I suppose I should do the old *mea culpa* and congratulate her! I rather imagine she's greatly modified since she's now getting serviced?" Mack simply lifted his left eyebrow in response. "*Au contraire*, hmm?"

"Oh, you know how she is, Bootsie!"

"Yes, but she does *mean* well! It was such a shame we got into that tussle over the deVol project, Mack. I do truly adore her. If there is anything else she'd like done to your home—slipcovers...or—something!"

"Well, in fact, you might be able to help out—this miracle doctor whom you see—would he, by any chance, have an associate who would be able to help a woman who doesn't want to have her baby?"

Joe returned once more, by now positively jubilant, finding Bootsie staring at Mack wide-eyed.

"Wha's wrong?" he asked, sitting down and gulping the rest of Mack's soda.

"*Joseph*!" Bootsie commanded. "Seal up those ears of yours! Your divine beloved here has just told me that his wife is *enciente*!"

"How could dat happen so quick!" Joey was just as surprised. "Unless she was foolin' around wid' someone before Bruno!"

"No, no, no!" Mack waved his hand in the air still laughing. "Listen, both of you. *Ynez* isn't pregnant...I swear! She's not! She wouldn't lie about a thing like that! It's a friend of hers who's in trouble."

"Oh, my dear Daly," Bootsie hissed. "*Je regret*! But I just can't help!" he said with finality. "Not that I wouldn't—but my doctor is not taking any more clientes, you see."

Orchid came to the table, just catching the end of the conversation. "Some lady needs to get taken care of—pregnant—is that it?" he asked in a whisper, then asked Bootsie slyly, "Your doctor *does* do that kind of thing, doesn't he, Boots?"

"Orchid! *Please*! My doctor is an *artiste*, not a coat hanger man!" Bootsie cried, at once jumping to this mysterious medico's defense.

Later on, in their room, Joe and Mack discussed this conversation, which, typical of Bootsie, was ended by the pronunciation that such a matter gave him the vapors and he insisted on changing the subject.

Mack explained, "So you see, Joey, what we're looking for is a way to uncover the whereabouts of this Dr. Soames character. Bootsie is one of his patients, and so was Blackie."

"Yeah, now I get it," Joe nodded. "—but how do you figger dis bone crusher has anyt'ing to do wid O'Couran an' duh moyder of dat midget dere?"

"Because right after Deucie came home, I looked into having him fitted for a wooden leg, and even some possible alternatives. We located a man who was supposed to be able to graft a real leg onto somebody who'd lost one. Baby was dead set against such a thing. You know, she's a nurse. But Deucie was kind of desperate and insisted. So we went down to Ocean Drive on Coney Island where this so-called doctor had his offices in somebody's basement."

"Dis next part ain't gonna give me bad dreams, is it?" Joe nestled closer up to Mack, hearing a certain tone in his voice.

"Well, it's not exactly *Goldilocks and the Three Bears*...just listen—at the time—1920 it was—there were lots of wounded veterans all over New York. Not only were they physically damaged, but had undergone terrific mental strain as well. I myself was going through all kinds of legal issues trying to get the business of making booze for the U.S. government to work for me."

"Dat ain't so scary."

"—everybody had these crazy ideas about making fast money in any way they could once the Volstead Act became national law. Fellows were applying for permits left and right! One racket required alcohol permits for the preservation of body parts. The idea was if you lost something, there was another one around to replace it, see? Anyway, turns out it was this doctor who owned the racket." Mack saw Joe making a face. "Joe? You see what I'm talking about here?"

"Yeah," he said slowly, covering his manhood with both hands and shuddering.

"You can imagine how many gallons it would take to preserve an arm, for example. But anyway, these poor soldiers were so desperate they would go down to Coney to this—well—this sort of miracle grotto, I guess you'd call it, and get hypnotized, and have that part of them, which had lost something, placed in a pool of alcohol which carried a slight electrical charge. Then this so-called 'expert' would try to stick it back on. He had to be this Doctor Soames fellow."

"I wish I didn't akst you to 'xplain it all!" Joey was shivering by now, but Mack held him closer.

"Well, I'm almost done. So, Deucie and I took one look at the whole thing and turned around and left. We never met the doctor himself, but was shown the set-up by a suspicious assistant. I feel pretty sure Brian O'Couran was part of that horror show. Through the Irish mob, he might've diverted some of the alcohol used down there for bootleg liquor, and probably also took in profits from the racket itself. The idea was that you were hypnotized into this state of mind where your body would go numb and respond magically, attatching back to itself the part that was missing. You know—like grafting a plant. They had some guy in there with his arm missing, and somebody else's plugged back into the socket. It didn't even fit right. And—well—you can just imagine the rest. Joey? Hey!"

Joe had, by then, hidden his head under all the pillows.

A faint knock came at the door. "It's Orchid," was whispered from the opposite side.

Mack, wrappping the bedspread around him, opened the door to find the young man standing there in an extravagant kimono with a baleful look on his pretty face.

"Please excuse me, Mr. Daly, Mr. Imperio. But I must simply talk to someone." Mack let him in, as Joe's tousled head emerged from the bedding.

"Hey! How yuh doin', pal?" Joey greeted Orchid.

"Oh. I'm so *distrait*...Bootsie is ill, Mr. Daly—*très malcontent*—from what he ingests...the medicine which that Doctor gives him. And I don't know what to do! He believes that I won't love him because he's old, but I don't care! That horrid man has my poor Boots wrapped around his finger. He's a murderer, my dears! If this woman whom you know needs an abortion you might locate him in that way. I don't know where he's got to since he left—" Orchid's sad eyes lifted upward, past the ceiling to the third floor of the inn.

"You mean Bootsie had him staying here, at the inn!" Mack exclaimed.

"Oh, yes, for only a night though. Then, off he went—just as mysteriously as he'd come!"

Joe sat up and grabbed onto Mack. "You don't mean he was stayin' up in duh attic?"

Orchid nodded.

"Did he leave anything? Have you checked?" Mack asked.

"No. I couldn't be bothered. I tell you he's killing my Boots!"

Mack then asked, "Do you think we could go up there now and have a look-see?"

"Of course."

Joe almost jumped under the matress itself. "Oh no! Uh-uh! No siree! You ain't gonna get me up in no attic lookin' for no nut job like dat!"

"Well," Mack tried not to smile. "Would you rather stay down here all by yourself?"

Leaping out of bed and reaching for his dressing gown, Joe followed Orchid and Mack out into the hallway and toward the attic stairs. According to Bootsie's wishes, the entire place had never changed from gas to electricity. One gas sconce had to be lit to get up the attic stairs, then all three tip-toed into the third floor of the mansion.

There, in a smaller hallway, Orchid again lit a gas lamp. Gesturing to the right, he whispered, "This is Bootsie's atelier here," Orchid opened the door. "And over there is the room wherein the medico stayed." Faintly, the glow of the gaslamp also illuminated Bootsie's studio." Minerva! Look in there! The place has been rifled!"

With Orchid leading, and lighting yet another lamp, it proved to be true. Sketches were tossed everywhere.

Joe said, taking it all in, "Some wise guy toyned dis dump upside down—and for a very good reason!"

Orchid was horrified, bending to pick up the sketches and put things back in order. "But why! Why would anyone steal his designs!"

Mack looked about the large garrett space. The contrast to the rest of house was startling. Everything was ultra-modern. "Other than you and Boots, does anyone else ever come up here?"

"No one has been up here except his doctor. It was he who did this deed, *naturallement*! He did it!"

"What's missin'?" Joe asked, also helping Orchid make order out of the chaos.

"Oh, I can't tell you that now. I'll check everything aganist our files tomorrow." He sighed, turning. "Well, anyway, he stayed right over here—the doctor who did all of this." Crossing the hall, he opened the opposite door from which emerged powerful fumes such as one might smell in a hospitial.

Mack cautioned quickly, "Don't light that lamp. We might all get blown to bits. He must've been using ether in here. Did he see other patients up here as well?"

"No," answered Orchid, pushing the door open to allow some light to come in. "Only Boots, of course."

Meanwhile, Joe was carefully lighting a match. "It's o.k.," he said. "That smell's comin' from duh bed dere."

Orchid lit the gas light at the side of a dresser and another overhead. The room was furnished with a heavy walnut bedroom suite, wallpapered in cabbage roses, and hung with heavy velvet draperies.

"God, this looks like the room Lincoln died in," Mack commented, beginning at once to look about.

"Prollee smells like it, too," Joe added, throwing the bed covers back. "Whew! He musta bathed in duh stuff! At least he had duh decency tuh make his bed up before leavin'."

Orchid, searching the drawers of the bureau and dresser, found them to be entirely empty. "He brought only two bags with him and, oh, he was in a great rush to get up here and *en couchant*, then get to work on my poor Boots."

"What sort of fellow is he? Can you describe him?" asked Mack as they searched on.

"Oh, perfectly. He was tall, about fifty I should say, dressed terribly *à la académique*. Wore *pince-nez*, and resembled in every way possible nothing more or less than a school teacher, come to think of it!"

Joe was on his hands and knees, looking all around and undereath the bed itself, as Mack turned the dresser scarves back. The room was entirely void of its guest's imprint.

"Could be any face in the crowd, I guess," Mack murmured, shaking his head.

Orchid, now stripping the bed, finding nothing at all, told Mack to check the armoire. Nothing there but a few coat hangers which tinkled as they were shoved aside.

"I found sump-in," Joe said, running his hands beind the seat of a tufted slipper chair in the corner. From its confines, he pulled out a small tie pin and went with it to the center of the room. There, under the hanging light, he lifted it up, holding it by his thumb and forefinger.

"Well, what do you know!" Mack patted Joe on the back. "Good work, Sherlock!" He took it carefully from Joe and asked Orchid, "But does it belong to you, or to Bootsie?"

"No. It's much too new. Although we do wear them. It's also too small for a man's cravat. I think," he said, now taking it from Mack, "it's a lady's stick pin."

"Yes," Mack answered. "For a stock. Used for riding. And you see the decoration—thirteen. See that, Joe?"

The small stick pin had, as its ornament, the number "13" in gold not being less than one half inch in diameter.

"Must have sump'in tuh do wid a gambler, yuh know, dey either love it or hate it, duh number thoyteen."

"A lady gambler?" Mack raised a brow, inspecting it closely. "Very good gold. Must be a custom order. Looks to be pre-War."

They continued searching, but found nothing else.

As they finished and went back down to the second floor, Orchid, whispering once again, suggested, "It might've belonged to the former owner of that chair. Everything we buy for this house is second hand."

"May we hold on to it?" Mack asked.

"Oh, please do. Now I must get back to Boots, before he gets suspicious..."

"Orchid—" Mack called softly to him. "How will you explain his studio being gone through?"

"I won't. I'll get up early and clean it up, then let you know if anything is missing." Thanking them, and blowing kisses, he levitated down the long, wide hall into darkness.

"How do you think that stick pin got there, Joe?" Mack asked as they climbed back into bed. "That was awfully smart of you finding it!"

"I always look in places where people might drop stuff, and never t'ink to reach down into. Now since you akstes me, it had to get flipped from a case mebee, like it was stuck to duh top of a jewel box, and when it was opened, it went flyin' and ended up down inside ah dere."

"Maybe it was given to the good doctor as a momento," Mack mused.

"Yeah, or mebee 'cause one of his patients had no dough left from bein' shooken down by him so much!"

Mack looked at Joe's perfect profile, somewhat comical now, because he was staring at the ceiling, lost in thought. Their eyes met. "Joe, if you had stayed down here, that clue never would've been found, you know that?"

"Yeah," he answered. "Well, yuh gotta t'ink duh way deez crumbs t'ink, yuh see, Mack. And it don't hurt none if you come from dat ellie-ment, needer!"

• • • • •

CHAPTER XVI

RUSTIC RAMBLINGS

The former Commanding Officer of the Army of Charm regiment was an alcoholic, yet dignified, pederast named Calvin Connaught. A decree had gone out to his Flock every year since the end of the War—comprising those veterans of his old regiment that his birthday be ritualistically celebrated by a reunion.

A pleasure dome had he erected to be the Mecca of the veterans' pilgramage known simply as his Lodge nestled into a mountain, and reflected upon the blue waters of a lake named Caisson. No mere lodge, but rather a huge log and stone affair in the Adirondacks, surrounded by acres of forest land, populated by some dozen dogs and one brow-beaten beau named Huck.

This was the Colonel's lair, his year-round home and his entire universe as well.

It was to this rustic castle that the former military hero had retired, weighted with decorations, remembered in every important historical annal, constantly toasted and roasted, the subject of more than one or two books of fiction. This was his citadel from whence he gazed upon the crumbling of Western civilization like the god Wotan, growing year by year more reclusive, more apocalyptic, more dyspeptic and more than just a wee bit nuts.

Having naturally grown from out of the rich soils of Edwardian England's nobilty, this one-time blossom of heroic British manhood still wore his arrogant beauty with aplomb, still carried himself regally, and was, in that year of Our Lord 1928, still something to gaze upon in wonder. Not a single soul would ever guess that deep within him there lived demons who milled away at monsterous fears, obscene fantasies and epic desires producing strange yearnings for pain and cruelty, eliciting from him ectastic laughter laced with tragic shouts of howls and shrieks.

Colonel Connaught was known to have never done a single wrong. Never had he lied or cheated or stolen. Never had he besmirched himself by dishonoring the Code of the Gentleman which was bred into his very bones. But Colonel Connaught had killed thousands upon thousands of German men and boys from 1914 to 1918. Killed and killed again without ceasing. And for these thousands upon thousands of sins, he believed that he had to pay—thousands upon thousands of times over. He was, somewhere deep within himself, never completed.

Now, his kept-boy, Huck, tried valiantly and with pure, selfless love, to fill the aching void which had become him. Before that, during the Fighting, it had been Mack. And Mack still haunted the Colonel. And not a day passed wherein his whole being did not throb for him. Nor did a week pass when the Colonel would not take pen to paper and write to Mack Daly, pouring out his maledictions. Mack alone could make Connaught feel better about himself, what he had done and what was eating away at his very soul.

This annual affair of his birthday, a week-end of drunkness and debauchery, was strictly limited to the homo variety of paganism which Colonel Connaught demanded be an exact replica of those revels celebrated when on leave. But eight years had passed since the lads of his regiment had come Home. Some now dared to decline his invitation.Others went simply out of loyalty—or guilt. A few went because they, like the Colonel, were still fighting the war, still rasing Hell and still possessed of a wildness which they could not quench.

For Elliot, Deucie and Baby, their reason for attending was utter and unquestioning loyalty. For Mack Daly, it was a complicated and ever troublesome collection of feelings. Because Mack had been the Colonel's "boy" and had never stopped being loved by him; he always let Mack know it, hammering into Mack's heart that brand of tortuous anguished adoration which the Colonel deified. Mack felt he owed almost everything to Connaught, or more simply "Calvin."

Only Mack was allowed to call him this, his Christian name, and after all, hadn't the Colonel named him "Mack Daly"? Wasn't this name a sort of baptism into the life he now lived? Mack revered the Colonel but he feared him, too. Not for his well-known temper, or his thundering judgments against almost everyone around him, no—he feared him because the Colonel was himself a weapon. A weapon he turned upon himself, over and over, making you stand there and watch. Like a public execution. One might wince, but one could not, somehow, look anyway.

And Mack had witnessed that same execution over and over since first the Colonel had stripped him naked and brutally thrown him down upon his cot and had his way with him.

Now that the time was nigh, Mack, Deucie, Baby and Elliot had to make plans for this execution Northward, letting nothing stand in the way and going about it exactly as if they were devotees of some Eastern, self-immolating diety.

Always put in charge of this long trek, Mack oversaw, with nonchalance, its scheduling, the buying of presents, the packing of potables and libations. And, for the last couple of years, he had also to invent things for Ynez to do while he was away, because she was never invited because the Colonel hated Mrs. Mack Daly with an almost unearthly hate. Baby was the only female ever to grace the three day affair, and that was only because of her unique place as their priestess-nurse. She knew how to take care of the sick.

Upon returning from White Plains with the #13 stick-pin wrapped in his handkerchief, and the desciption of the strange doctor committed to memory, Mack had found his ornamental spouse wringing her hands and walking in circles. Briefly, she told him she had missed him terribly and that Bruno wasn't very much in evidence. She was lonely, that was all. Or was it more than just that?

"Oh, I must feel your arms around me! Please!" she commanded, shrilly, tossing a note-pad upon the bed upon which she had scribbled everything Mrs. O'Couran had told her.

Her husband complied, and heard her whispering in his ear, with a shade more tenderness, "Ever since you met that dago gorilla our lives have gone right down the crapper!" (Mack murmured how sorry he was.) "Now it's just *all business*! And what a *nasty* business it is, too!" Tearing herself away from him, Ynez careened down upon her bed, beating the pillows with her fists. Mack picked up her notepad.

"Now, now, kiddo. Very kind of you to take notes, though," he said, sitting down beside her. "We've simply got to see this thing through, Ynez. We'd be in much worse trouble if we hadn't met up with the Imperios—don't you see that? O'Couran would've moved right in on me and I'd be in jail now—and where would you be?"

She turned her lovely face from its satin hiding place. "I'd be right down there in the kitchen baking you a cake with a file in it! Oh, Mack, even though we never ever made love, we still had such a peaceful, happy life." (Mack decided to leave that one alone.) "You see? I've written almost the entire conversation down there. I'm a good scribe, huh?"

With Ynez at his heels, they left her room, going down the stairs–Mack, never taking his eyes off her notes—and ending in the library. He pulled back all the draperies, letting the light in. "Why so dark in here?" he asked. "Why are the curtains closed all over the house?"

Ynez answered. "Oh, it's been so…so…sunny lately, that's all."

"It has?" Mack replied, absently looking over the neat spread of newspapers Alexander had placed on the library table. Every date was in order since the aricle had appeared in all the papers proclaiming Brian O'Couran's ascendency to his new office. "You did a very good job, Ynez. Now what's this place called the Slaves of Mary?"

"Oh, it was mentioned along with O'Couran's honors," Ynez replied. "Here it is," she said, pointing to a particular article. "—says that he's one of the chief officers of the Slaves of Mary."

Mack shook his head. "Now what in Hell's the Slaves of Mary?"

"A crazy house!" Ynez replied. "Belle told me that when Elizabeth Sutton saw Mrs. O'Couran at the her office in the Village, she'd made mention of it then, as well—with the same sort of horror in her voice I heard when she was here for Tea."

"Ynez," Mack put down the newspaper and held his wife out at arm's length. "You're a perfect darling for going along with me during all of this!" She virtutally sagged in his arms.

"But what is it, for God's sake, Ynez! Have you given up on Bruno all together?"

"It isn't Bruno...oh, he'll do I suppose." Ynez stalked the library in search of a cigarette. "At least my libido approves. It's...oh, it's...never mind, sweet thing. You just go get ready for your reunion, and I'll—"

The phone rang and somewhere in the house; Alexander picked it up. Appearing at the library door, he announced with a smile on his lips and Mack's Army kit in his hands, "Mrs. D.! It's big brawny Bruno!"

A shudder of joy passed through her as she thanked him and went, as if floating on air, for the library connection. Mack returned Alexander's grin, and left her there to help Alexander finish packing.

Alone, she purred, "Oh, you *do*? Oh, *shall* we? Yes! I promised I would! Oh, you *will*! Oh, swell!"

Upstairs, as Mack and Alexander were packing, Ynez entered in a tizzy. "Mack, can you spare Alexander? Bruno and I are going to Annabelle's gallery! He wants to *buy* something of hers! Can you beat it? I've got to look my most fetching."

Alexander, as amazed as was Mack, commented, "Now I've heard everything! Mr. D., can you pack your own stuff? I' ve got to get her lookin' like High Culture!"

Both sailed out, exuberant, leaving Mack with a much needed laugh. He went about smoothing out his old uniform, replete with putees, canteen, and even his old helmet. Whatever, he wondered, would Joe think of this whole jaunt up there? The weekend which was now upon him would take a great deal of explaining! And his relationship with the Colonel—that would take some explaining, too.

• • •

At that same hour of the morning, Nolie Armstrong had gone to get the mail at the main desk of their building. Rarely did they receive fan mail there because it all went to the recording studio. Only bills, bills, bills, and the usual supply of magazines which lately had been filled with articles about the two lovebirds. These Nolie dutifully clipped and pasted in numerous albums, sometimes wanting to just cry. But on that particular day, looking over the half dozen they'd just received, she considered it a passable way to spend a peaceful afternoon with her Johnnie. Thank God those boys would be gone for the entire weekend! With Wriggs moving in, the place was in chaos.

Yet, upon rifling through what proved to be invitations to new speak-easy openings, a few Broadway revues and cocktail parties, Nolie came across a very official looking yellow envelope. On the upper left hand corner was the name of the management company of their very own building.

What was up? Never ever had she been late on the rent. Wandering back into the elevator, with the ever nosey elevator girl Millie scowling and watching every move she made, Nolie inserted a bright red fingernail under the flap and opened the envelope. She had to read it twice to believe it.

"Bad news, huh?" Millie asked through her adnoids.

Pale as a sheet, Nolie tore back into the elevator and up to their apartment.

"*Now* what?" Johnnie had to know, turning toward her as she was trying to make sense of the luggage Wriggs had strewn all about.

"We're getting evicted. Thirty days." Nolie handed Johnnie the letter.

Without a word, Johnnie read it quickly, then said, "This is precisely what we do not neeed."

Nolie just shook her head and sat down hard, staring out at the terrace and the skyline of the City just beyond. In the distance, the boys could be heard whooping and hollering, apparently having a pillow fight intead of unpacking for Wriggs. Something fell and broke with a loud crash. Nolie looked dazedly up at Johnnie. "But at a time like this, could you expect anything else?"

• • •

According to the plan, Mack and Joe arrived at the Club deVol promptly at seven-thirty a.m., and went at once to the third floor flat.

"Nobody is ever ready on time, Joe. Not like you and me. So we're going to have to help them along a little."

True to his prediction, they found Deucie, his tongue moving all about his lips, maneuvering a ribbon around a box wrapped in blue polka dot paper, under which was a pipe rack the Deuce had lovingly carved himself. Baby was in the kitchenette filling up an ice chest, folding sandwiches in waxed paper, swearing and singing out loud all at the same time. Even though Alexander had already packed a hamper for the trip, you simply could not refuse Baby's chicken sandwiches. They competed with his home-made pies every year.

"Well, don't you two look sporting!" Wiping her hands on a dish towel, she hugged and kissed them both. Indeed they did, dressed in plus-eights, golf caps and argyle sweaters. "We've just got to close up, and then we're set. Deucie, aren't you gonna say hello?"

"Hello, you two," Deucie sputtered. "Cripes, I can't tie a bow to save my life!" Baby took over. "Just lemme get my grip, is all." Limping and wheezing into their bedroom, he returned with several carpet bags (tied together with a head scarf) and his Army duffle.

Joey had noticed that Mack had also brought his along. "Why youz guys bot' takin' dose?" he asked.

Deucie explained simply, "Well, Joey, when we're up there, we all have to act if the War never ended. Even the Babe has to get herself up in her old nurse's u-nee-form again. You'll probaby have a private first-class get-up waitin' for you!"

To himself Joe pondered aloud, "I gotta wear a u-nee-form and I wasn't even in duh war?"

Mack, heading downstairs with Baby's bag and one picinic basket, turned. "What was that, Joe? Something about our uniforms?"

"Do I hafta wear one, too?" Joey asked, helping Deucie with the rest of their luggage.

Mack drew close to him and said under his breath, "We'll talk about that later. We'll make it all fun, Joe. Fun, see?"

Fun, yeah, fun, Joe thought to himself. Well, just so long as his uniform didn't reek of mothballs the way Deucie's did just now. You could smell it coming right through his grip.

"All set to go!" Deucie grinned, trying to hide his excitement. "Good thing we don't still have that canary that died on us last year, 'cause Baby would ne'er cease to worry about it all entire time we was away!"

Baby, who had gone to the bathroom for the third time in the last half hour, stuffed a roll of toilet paper into her knitting bag. "Mack, I must tell you, I'm back to polishing my own claws! I did call up Chollie Fong, just as you asked, and he's leaving town. Seems as if he's headed out to Frisco to be with cousins, or else he's already there. I got a bit of news though…Anybody even remotely involved with what went on up at *La Maison* two years back has since vanished. How's them onions?" She proudly displayed her fingernails.

"Well, they look most fetching, Baby, but what does he mean exactly?"

"Well," Baby replied uneasily. "I wasn't quite sure, but he did tell me that Deucie and I had better be real, real careful. In fact, he mentioned Ynez in that breath, too."

"Well, let's not get into that now. I've got a few theories we can talk about over the weekend."

Mack and Joe now put on their hats, as Baby locked the door to their flat.With Joe grabbing the ice chest and the bag full of presents for the Colonel, and Mack assisting Deucie, they headed for the door.

"I'll want to check the club again before we go, fellas." Baby clattered down ahead, all high heels, parasol, picture hat and ring of keys. That was the way she was. No stone unturned. And with Elliot putting Nolie in charge of the band they could still count on drawing the crowds. Johnnie had been elected to manage the place in their absence, with Alexander manning the cover flat.

As they were passing the back entrance to the club, Joe intercepted Deucie's worried look. "Don't be noyvous, Deuce," Joe told him. "Bruno's got duh bot' ah youse covered all around. O'Couran's gonna get what he wants, so he'll leave yuz alone." Baby hurried out from the back entrance, having locked up the club, to begin arranging their effects within the car.

"You sure you told Alexander where we keep the key to the cover flat, Deucers?" She looked warily across the street at the window which was always manned by one of Mack's Army buddies, absent as well, for that vet was also going up to see the Colonel.

"Honey, you know Mack told us that he'd even written it down on the blackboard in the kitchen for him!" Deucie wheezed, insisting on helping pack the trunk, even though he wasn't able to do much.

"Let's up-and-at-'em, kids!" Baby cried, wrapping her veil about her and opening her parasol. Off they went to fetch Elliot and Jack Wrigley.

• • •

As soon as they entered the Armstrongs' apartment building, Joe told Mack he felt a distinct chill from both the doorman and the girl at the desk.

Alighting from the elevator there in the lobby, Nolie fluttered before them in a state of barely supressed panic. "I was waiting for you. Watching from the terrace. Get in, quick."

On the way up, Nolie slipped Mack the eviction notice.

"Did you tell Elliot yet?" Mack whispered, having glanced at it, passing it to Joe.

Millie the elevator girl was smiling in a smarmy sort of way. She knew! (Always was a jealous five and dime flapper!) Landing the trio with a jerk on the top floor of the building, Nolie grabbed both Mack and Joe and hustled them out into the vestibule behind an urn. All lined up before the door to their apartment were boxes, velises and and trunks.

"He ain't takin' all dat shit for duh weekend, is he!" Joe cried.

"No. No," Nolie answered nervously. "Wriggs is moving IN just as we're moving OUT! Listen, I'm not going to tell the boys. It'll spoil their whole trip—although Johnnie knows, of course."

Mack agreed. "Wise child, Nolie. Because Elliot would spoil it for all the rest of us, dragging this news up there along with him." Mack expected anything from Elliot and always got it.

"This is all the result of a detective coming up and snooping around. Jack Wrigley's folks hired him it seems. " Nolie was talking so fast, it sounded to Joe like a Victrola on the highest speed. "'cause he's a minor...here...with us. Happy, though! Elliot's happy. Not drinking! Just having fun. LOUD fun." Elliot and Wriggs could even be heard out there.

Mack said, "Yes, but this kind of hoopla has gone since the day you moved here, Nolie. I'm really surprised they waited so long."

"Sure! Wild parties 'til all hours, band rehearsals half the night, Elliot running around the terrace naked as a jay bird. Then, this detective poking around! Sure! What would you expect?" Nolie looked as if she might cry. Mack removed his cap. Joey handed him a lit cigarette, which Nolie took from him with shaking fingertips.

"But I ask you, Mack, are All Of The Above very good reasons to go and really throw people out on the street?" she whimpered.

"Sad to say, but it appears so, honey. Now look, while we eject your boys from this chaos, you go on ahead and ring up the management—let's see what we can do..." Mack suggested. "Go right in there and drag the hall phone out here, while we do some organizing."

Nolie gulped, opened the door and squeezed through it, as Mack and Joe entered, picking their way through Wriggs' half opened trunks and suitcases.

"I sez we jus' leave 'em behind!" Joe snorted.

Entering the living room, he slid across the polished floor almost falling over backwards, then bent to pick up what was all over the place—clippings for one of Nolie's scrap albums. Pages from the past, he realized, looking them over. And what was this—Mr. and Mrs. Daly as newlyweds! Joe shoved them under Mack's nose.

"Well, well...look at dat date! Two years ago! God, Joe, our anniversary is coming up soon!"

Joe snickered. "So's ours...one month tuggedder! And before yuz knows it!" He then pointed to the people in the group photograph, naming them off. "Dere's Mr. and Mrs. deVol, an' Elliot and Winola...jeez, the wifey looks like a movie actress!" His finger moved across the photo. "Who's dem?" he asked, pointing to a dignified man and a plain Jane type beside him.

"That, Joey, is the Colonel himself! The one you'll soon meet. And the woman beside him is—or was—his daughter."

Joe absently picked up a pair of socks and some underwear in one big motion with his left hand, while still holding the wedding picture in his right. "Was or is? Wha' happen' to her?"

"Nobody knows. They never got along—Violet and the Colonel—I guess she went back to England."

By now Elliot was presumably beginning (at last) to pack for the weekend, and emerged half-dressed, holding a gladstone bag, all apologies and kisses. Down in the car, Baby had started a crossword puzzle and Deucie had opened a Police Gazette. They knew what to expect. It was the same every year.

Elliot gestured, taking in the mess. "Joe, if you'll help me, we can figure this all out. Mack, that stuff in the corner is for Wriggs to take, and this bag is mine."

"I'll start down," Mack said, taking the velise, hoisting Wriggs' up as well, and using it as an opportunity to slip back through the half-opened front door. He arrived just in time to hear Nolie numbly replying, "Yes, Mr. Klipstein, no, Mr. Klipstein, but Mr. Klipstein, oh, Mr. Klipstein…" Then breathing a choked goodbye, she turned to Mack, who closed the door tightly "They hate us over there, Mack. We've gotta get the Hell outta here. Fast."

"Well," he said philosophically, "I'll think of something, Nolie. Just wait 'til we get back."

Now Joe could be heard rapidly losing his patience. "So what if yuh can't find dee udder one! Yuh don't need dat many pairs ah shoes! Yuh know, it ain't pullite tuh keep people waitin'!"

Johnnie was even heard to scream out, "Jack Wrigley! Are you ready or not! Mr. and Mrs. deVol are downstairs collectin' dust!"

As Mack entered the elevator with his burdens, again enduring Millie's withering glances, Nolie re-entered the apartment, making some very strange faces at Johnnie meant to symbolize despair.

"We'll be so sorry to see you go," Johnnie was commenting to Elliot, picking up his uke, saxophone, the presents for the Colonel and shoving them—and him—out the door.

"This is all my stuff right here, I think," Wriggs waved his arms around a pool of small boxes bound together with neckties.

"Here, I'll get 'dose! You finish gettin' dressed!" Joe ordered and left, kicking the front door closed. At this point Mack, returning from downstairs, encountered Elliot on the way out.

"Hold the lift! What's eating you, Millie?" he asked, as the eleavtor doors closed.

Inside the apartment, it appeared that Wriggs was finally telling the girls goodbye. Then Elliot showed up again, beaming, perspiring and disheveled. "All ready to go! Won't the Colonel go wild over our boyfriends, Mack!"

"Oh, no end wild, Elliot," Mack raised a testy left eyebrow. "We'll have to have a little talk with them both before we get there" (under his breath). "O.k. you two! Over the top!"

It seemed as if he had them both as good as out the door when, as if out of nowhere, Joe's voice was heard from fourteen stories below.

"MACK! MACK! HURRY THE CHRIST UP, WILL YUZ!"

"Oh, God, that's all we need," Nolie wailed, but by that time Elliot had dashed onto the terrace and, leaning way over the balustrade, was yelling back.

"DON'T YOU WANNA COME UP AND RELIEVE YOUR BLADDER BEFORE WE GO?"

"WHAT'S DAT MEAN?" Joey was heard to shout back.

"COME UP AND GO PEE, YOU DUMB ASS!" Elliot shouted down to him.

Mack quickly ran from the vestibule to the terrace in record time, grabbing Elliot and waving like a shortstop to Joe. Pulling him in, he panted, "Never mind that now, Elliot! We'll be stopping soon enough! Joey doesn't know what a bladder is!"

The girls, beside themselves, helped Mack push Wriggs and Elliot out of the apartment and into Millie's elevator.

As soon as they hit the street, Joe came at Elliot with his fists bared. "Who you callin' a dumb ass!" he growled as the doorman took cover behind the potted bush.

Wriggs, taking Elliot's side, loudly cried out, "He didn't mean it! It's just a turn of phrase!"

Mack got in the middle of it. "Apologize to Joey, Elliot, please, and let's get OUT OF HERE," he demanded, attempting to control his own voice, but not, he suddenly realized, doing very well at it. Looking up at the building, he saw several dozen heads looking out.

"I was just trying to be funny, that's all, Joe!" Elliot admitted, his voice going up in the range of a tenor.

"Hah!" Joe retorted, coming closer and snorting at him. "Yer funny all right!"

Now Elliot screamed, "Well DO you have to pee or don't you!"

And by now, lots and lots of the tenants were at their windows. A small crowd of pedestrians was gathering around them, keeping their distance, but fascinated nonetheless.

"I DO <u>NOT</u>!" Joe hollered back, turning and then having a thought. Serenely he said to no one in particular, "Ackshully, I do all of a sudden."

Mack took off his hat, running his fingers through his hair. "Oh, God! Well go on up there and make it snappy please, Joe. Please."

Then it seemed it was Baby's turn. "I'd just better just go up there, too, and make sure everything's all set for the club with the princess and Nolie while we're gone."

"Awwwww," groaned Deucie. "This year it's *worse*!" As Baby was rising, he took her arm. "We went over this stuff a million times, honey! You gotta quit worryin'!"

Joe had started to run in, but then ran back out.

"Now what?" Mack asked wearily.

"I don't gotta pee no more," he answered proudly.

In climbed the four of them, with Elliot insisting that his saxophone and ukulele go in the backseat with him, and Wriggs holding on to his Brownie camera set-up, case and all, for dear life. With Elliot shrieking good-byes and waving a big white scarf in the air, the car took off with screeching tires, Mack apologizing all over the place for such a speedy exit.

Back up in the Armstrong penthouse, Nolie had collapsed in Johnnie's arms. There was no money with which to move. Elliot spent it as fast as they made it. And, after all, no matter where they went to live—wouldn't it just end up being a repeat of what they now were experiencing?

Johnnie couldn't think of a thing to say to help her. After several moments, she did come up with a little something. "Well, look at it this way, at least we have the place all to ourselves for three whole days, sugar."

"Yeah," Nolie sighed. "And that leaves only twenty-seven more in which we have to find someplace else to cage the four of us!—whilst we beg, borrow or steal the money to do it with. Meanwhile I'll be plotting to murder my brother and his boyfriend."

• • • • •

CHAPTER XVII

SO NEAR AND YET SO FAR

About twenty or so blocks South of this upper East Side crisis point stood Annabelle Harrison's Murray Hill townhouse. It was to her elegant and dignifed place where Ynez and Bruno had gone with the intention of the underworld figure purchasing one of Belle's statues, and also help to organize her latest exhibit. Whenever possible, Ynez wanted to be both away from her Great Neck house, and also with Bruno—not just for the sake of satiating her passion, but for protection, too. And it was extraordinary that he had asked to go with her to look at Annabelle's work. What had gotten into him?

As they stood before the door of Miss Harrison's place, he was, just at that moment, wondering the same thing about her. "What in Hell's gotten into you?"

It seemed ages before Annabelle herself appeared, thrilled, with open arms, into which Ynez melted with a deep sigh of relief.

"Don't blame me, Miss Harrison!" Bruno quipped as they went into the gallery. "I haven't done a thing!"

But the change in her was very evident.

After looking at all that was, just then, being so artfully arranged by Keys and Alexander about the space, Bruno said, "I'll take that one, there," indicating with a nod of his head a two-foot high bronze of a satyr.

"What about the one of me?" Ynez asked, crushed. It stood right next to the satyr.

"I can see you naked anytime, toots. This just gets to me. It even kind of looks like me!"

As Bruno peeled a thousand dollars in cold cash from his money clip, Annabelle laughed. "It certainly does! He's a naughty little fellow! Thank you, Mr. Imperio. All the profits from this show of mine go to my artists' collective. You're the first one to see all my new work and the first to make a purchase!"

Bruno had a smile that melted every woman's heart. Too bad he couldn't use it more often. He apparently was very pleased by the attention he was getting, the art he had just bought, and the fact that he had come with Ynez to see Annabelle Harrison's exhibit going up.

Uncertain of whether or not he would even stay on, Ynez asked him, "Shall we linger for cocktails, B.?"

"Need any more brawn around here?" he asked Annabelle, watching Keys and Alexander moving pedestals about and hanging the orange velvet draperies.

"I'll say we do! Some of these statues weigh up to three hundred pounds. We can certainly use your muscle. And Ynez," she added, seeing a slightly more cheerful look on her face, "I always appreciate your exquisite taste."

"Darling, I'll do anything! Anything!"

Stripped of his suit jacket, Bruno had at once gone to town helping Keys place the lovely chrome-plated figure of Mrs. Mack Daly up on its pedastal. Annabelle led Ynez to some packing boxes, where she helped her—absently unfolding some of the velvet draperies with a desperately meloncholy look.

"Ynez, my darling, what *ever* is wrong—you know very well Mack himself will buy that statue of you!" her friend whispered.

"Yes and I'll just have him use it on my tomb!"

Bruno yelled from across the gallery, "Oh, would you just can that stuff!" In his rolled up shirtsleeves, he did look like a work of art himself.

Keys got a chill. "Your tomb? You fixin' to up and die on us, Mrs. D.?"

"Maybe..." Ynez whined, barely audible. "But I'll be all right. For a time. As long as I'm not...*seen*...too very often."

"Ynez," Bruno strode over her way. "The idea is you've got to be seen a lot, or else how can we find out who's trailin' you, for God's sake!" He then addressed everyone. "See, she's being shadowed. All the way over here she was looking out the back window!"

Annabelle's eyebrows rose. "Shadowed! How *ghast*ly!"

Ynez waved her hand in the air. "No, it's all right. But it's better that you're kept in the dark about all of this, knowing nothing of what I'm now in the middle of. I so want to spare you kids my personal terror."

"*Ynez*!" Annabelle was by now truly concerned. Removing her smock, she lit up a cigarette and pulled Ynez down on an ottoman. "This is no time for histrionics! *Are* you in trouble or *not*? If someone is following you we want you to *know*. We're here to help you, silly thing." She turned to Keys, who was massaging her shoulders. "Aren't we, darling?"

Bruno gestured helplessly. "Somebody keeps driving up to her house. Same car. Circles around—then leaves. All hours of the day and night."

Ynez rose, wandering to the tall windows which looked out on a lovely back garden. Dressed in wispy grey chiffon, with huge grey pearls about her swan-like neck and at her ears, she was looking most poetic. "I can only think that—" She could not even finish. "It's all frightened me so. That's just it, really!"

Now turning and standing at the other end of the gallery, her hands pressed togther, her eyebrows at tragic angles, she continued: "I asked Bruno if he would come out to Great Neck to stay there with me this weekend—but he's so terribly busy with this new business Mack's let him have. You see, I need to be *protected*! Joey protects Mack but who protects li'l Nezzie?"

Alexander piped up, "I'm tryin' to, Mrs. D. And I seen 'em, too, drivin' slowly right past the house oftener and oftener!"

"Maybe I'll have to just skip town," she concluded in a montone.

Bruno made fists. "Oh, will you stop it! It doesn't matter where you are—creeps like that'll find you!" Then he added: "When you're scared as shit, you always have to put on an act, don't you? To cover up how you really feel!"

There was an awkward silence.

Belle reached out her hand toward Ynez. "Listen, pet, you've got to report this to the authorities."

"How *can* I? Now that...Well, you *know* what I've become!" Looking at Bruno, then back at Annabelle, then to Alexander and Keys, she murmured, "But, I haven't told Mack yet. Perhaps I should've."

Alexander piped up, "It all started the morning you dumped that gigolo. I was up! It was the same car that came and got him down by the road."

Ynez shrugged, tears sprouting in her eyes.

Bruno, turning to Belle, said under his breath, "She's drivin' me wild. When I get those jerks I'll wring their necks!"

"I truly think they're out to kill me," Ynez said, suddenly rising and walking toward them. Taking Belle's place on the ottoman with both Keys and Belle standing watching her, she urged Bruno down beside her. Having left her purse there, she dug absently for her cigarette case. Opening it and drawing forth one of her own blend, she let Keys light it for her, scowling—as if internally scolding herself.

"All right. Here it is," she began. "There was a little Chinese thing back at that unspeakable place called *La Maison*...you know, the one that was murdered. When Mack was up at Bootsie's, he asked me about her over the phone and I remembered a little fan she'd given me with her telephone number on it. So, I rang up the number and got this strange creature on the wire. Afterward, I was in such a state, I neglected to ring off properly and this horrible man must've heard me talking to Alexander. By now, they've put it all together...that I worked there, and had a passing acquaintance with this 'Lady Lee'—and that my marriage to Mack was arranged, if you want to call it that. *They're* the ones who are watching me. All the time now. I feel their eyes on me everywhere. Always." Quickly, she glanced over her shoulder at the tall windows.

"Oh, shit,Ynez, why in Hell didn't you tell me this before!" Bruno cried.

Belle sat down beside her. "But *who*! *Who* are these people!"

"The ones who ran that place, I think—the owners of *La Maison.* Voluptuaries. Decadents. Not just swishes or daughters of Sappho or Bolsheviks or even modernists—but terrible people like the scum of the sewers—only rich…so rich they could indulge themselves in any kind of debauchery! They're not simply New Yorkers or even Americans. I think they come from very old, corrupt families going way back to ancient Rome or *Babylon*!"

Bruno got up. "Jesus H. Christ, you've seen too many movies!"

Keys asked reasonably, "But what do you think they want—these folks who are out to get you?"

Ynez shrugged, then stated methodically, "They will question me on how much I know, of course. O'Couran, the nite club, my marriage—such as it is. Probably using ancient Chinese torture in a some dungeon somewhere. They'll torture me because I won't tell them! I won't! Then, they will rape me repeatedly and toss me on a boat bound for Shangai. I'll be the victim of white slavery, that's all, and end up in a leper colony on Pago Pago."

"Where's that!" Alexander asked, enthralled and horrified.

Belle hardly knew what to think. "Darling, these things don't actually *hap*pen, do they?"

But Bruno stated plainly, "Sure they do, Miss Harrison. They happen right here in this city—everyday. Don't kid yourself."

Belle gestured. What did she know of such things, after all!

Ynez looked down on them both. Drawing herself up imperiously, with her head lifted high, she whispered, "You have no idea what I've seen first-hand working there at that terrible place. Don't forget, I performed my dirty shimmy for them, covered by nothing but the ceiling." Now, she was not acting. "Those people behind their masks had the most hideous look in their eyes! Their fingers just *covered* in diamonds, always grabbing at their crotches, ripping their clothes off, crying out in ecstasy…some of them using narcotics as stimulants. Then, being taken out in fits by those servants who lurked about! Crazed, frothing at their mouths!…*Je*sus! I'm *scared*, that's all. Terrified for my very life. And that's no exaggeration!"

"Did Baby deVol witness all this kind of thing as well?" asked Belle.

"Both she and Deucie were always around, but they never were allowed into any of the rooms, as was I." Ynez stopped for a moment. "Well! I had to make a living! It seemed to me, at first, that the patrons were mostly observers, somehow enslaved by their own obsessions…"

"Voyeurs, they're called," Bruno put in smartly. "But that couldn't have been all there was to it! You can't make a good buck by letting people just stand around and watch and whack—" He stopped there.

Ynez bridled. "Well, in *my* case that's all they did! And I gave 'em a good show, too. Some people don't want you to touch them, you know. Or to *be* touched. The folks who worked there did things to them*selves* most of the time. They were just…just…performers…but some of them did offer various types of pain. Whippings and such."

Annabelle was fascinated. "You don't think they're starting up a new *house*, do you—and want you back in their employment?"

Keys frowned at her. "Belle! Be serious!"

"I *am*! Maybe they just want to *talk* to you about it…in private, of course. How else could they convey such…an…opportunity?"

Alexander spoke up. "Yeah! Sure! Next time we see 'em, let's ask 'em in for tea."

Ynez brightened slightly. "But maybe you've got something there, Alexander. Bruno, you might just be scaring them off. Next time I see them, you hide and I'll go right up and ask them what's shaking. Then you rush out and grab 'em!"

"I'll grab 'em all right."

Keys said quietly, "Alexander and me'll protect you, too, Mrs. D. We don't—any of us—imagine you're exaggeratin', it's only that we have to make believe sometimes that the world out there can't be half so bad as it really is."

"Oh, but it is…it is. " With that, Ynez grabbed her purse and left the gallery.

In the foyer, pulling her furs about her shoulders and cramming her cloche down over her head, she quickly made for the door. Bruno, on her heels, found it slammed in his face.

"Jesus! What a dame! Let her go! Let her go!" He turned back into the gallery as Keys, Belle and Alexander met him.

But just outside, a tan colored sedan, parked right across the street, stood in wait. Ynez froze in her tracks. In the driver's seat was that same man she had seen sitting in that very same car, right in her very driveway. And next to him, the smaller man. Both nondescript.

Tossing her head, she made believe she had forgotten something. Turning back to open the door again, she found it locked. Pulling the bell, she grew frantic. Bruno, fuming, yanked it open.

Indicating what lay behind her with only a slight eye movement, Ynez directed Bruno's eyes toward the waiting sedan. Jumping down the steps two at a time, running across the street and pulling his gun from his shoulder holster, he swore loudly. But the sedan took off, wasting no time.

Alexander, Keys and Belle came to the open doors, looking out.

"Put that gun away!" screamed Annabelle. Bruno, from the street, ordered everyone, "Get the plates and the make!" Ynez seemed as if she might be on the verge of collapse, falling into Alexander's arms.

"1927 Packard sedan!" Keys answered.

"2244-54 NY!" Alexander chimed in.

Belle was breathless. "I can draw their faces from memory!" She dashed back inside, as Bruno ran from the street up the steps catching Ynez in his arms.

Ynez gasped, "—oh, God, Bruno. I need a drink."

"You did good, babe." Bruno gave her a gentle clip on the jaw then wrapped his arm about her waist. "I've got her now. Go get her a toot, Alexander." Then he said, softly but firmly in her ear, "Listen, you've got to tell me everything if you want me to help you. I know you're holding back."

Belle had gone into the gallery to fetch pencil and paper with Keys, while Alexander went for the cellarette. There, in the foyer, Ynez, looking up at Bruno with frightened eyes, murmured, "What? Whatever…do you mmmean—?"

"Just the truth. Nobody else has to know. We've got some very hot irons in the fire right now, kiddo. You don't want to endanger Mack's life, or Joey's or mine…or worst of all your own! What's up with these birds followin' you?"

"Bruno, I would never betray a particular friendship which Mack holds sacred. He wouldn't ever speak to me again if I told a single living soul what I'm fairly certain is really going on here." Turning from him, she quickly accepted the shot glass Alexander was holding for her and downed it in one gulp.

Belle came from the gallery with a large sheet of drawing paper upon which were sketched two faces, with the make and year of the car, and its license plate number scrawled in the corner. "Here we are. Isn't this the way they looked?"

Her voice shaking, Ynez mumbled, "Yes. That's them all right."

Alexander, who knew Ynez better than she knew herself, realized in that instant that she knew those two faces very, very well. He intercepted a look from Bruno. She would tell him, all right. For Mrs. D. was as scared as Hell.

• • •

Elliot, strumming on his uke, had gotten everybody singing at the top of their lungs. With the tonneau down, Baby wrapped up in her traveling veil and mole skin coat, Deucie was crammed contentedly between his wife and the crooner, whose legs were tossed over Wriggs. They made a hilarious quartet. In the front, with Mack at the wheel and Joe beside him, the pilgrimage Northward was turning into the best of any trek so far.

"I will now sing the dirty version of 'Nagasaki'!" Deucie announced.

"With this mere wisp of a boy next to you?" Baby played mock serious.

Wriggs laughed out loud. "Go ahead, I'll cover my ears!"

As Deucie hit all the wrong notes but got all the lyrics right, Joe covered his ears instead.

"Joey! Be polite!" Mack batted him. "It'll be your turn next. You get to do 'O Solo Mio.'"

Already clearing his throat, Joe assured Mack, "You hoyd me up at Bootsie's. I got a slick voice! Maybe Elliot'll put me on the rah-dee-oh."

But before Joe could begin, Baby pulled out her knitting bag, making certain the roll of toilet paper was within. "Boys, I hate to tell you this, but I've got to iron my shoelaces at once— sorry!" Baby had become weak and wet from too much laughing. "Can't we stop just ahead at those cabins there?"

"Sure we can...anybody hungry yet?" Mack was slowing the car down as they approached a motor court.

Parking next to the pumps, Joey proceeded to fill the radiator with water as Elliot and Wriggs unpacked the hampers and Baby ran, lady-like, in the direction of the outhouses.

Deucie, spreading the map out on his lap, observed, "Looks to me like a good three and half hours more. Mack, as many times as we've made this hike, I swanee, I've never enjoyed muhself this much."

Even though Mack could, by now, certainly make the jaunt without the aid of a map, he knew Deucie relished being the navigator. "Deuce, let's get you out and stretch that leg of yours." Mack helped him up and out of the back seat.

Hobbling away from the pumps to light a cigarette, he asked, "Mackus, it ain't none of my beeswax, but have you had a talk with Joey about the Colonel's ways with you?"

"No, I haven't, I thought we'd put the window up and let you folks in the back play What Color Am I Thinking Of while I discuss it with him."

"—and that kid there. He's just a pup!" Deucie smiled. "We gotta prepare him for what's in store, too, yuh know. "

"Yes, but I'll leave that to Elliot. I'm sure when the Colonel sees our fellows he'll of course want 'em." Mack shrugged and smiled grimly. "That's always been his way."

At around four o'clock, while waiting for a train to pass a railroad crossing, Wriggs, Joe and Mack put up the tonneau. It had gotten chilly by that time and Elliot, asleep in Baby's lap, was covered by the fur rug.

As Mack climbed back in the cab section of the car—this time on the passenger side because Joe was aching to drive as usual—he cranked up the separating window.

"We like a little fresh air, don't we, Joe? Still won't get there 'til seven, you know!" Mack told him.

The oil-slicked road lay ahead like a bucolic roller coaster. Everywhere about them were lush fields, cows, horses, sheep and vast combinations of barns, stables and silos. Now and then, people would wave at them, marveling at the great hulking machine roaring by. Joe and Mack both never failed to honk back.

"Jeez, I wonder if they know we're queers!" Joe mused.

"They could be pretty queer themselves, Joe. You just never know. Takes all kinds, as they say. " (Mack hoped this would work as the opening strains of what he was about to spill.)

"Just smell dat country air!" Joe sang out. "Gosh, does it ever makes me horny!"

"Well, there'll be plenty of time for that, my boy. Just you wait—"

"Say, Mack, d'yuz t'ink we can go skinny dippin'?"

"Oh, I'm sure we can do that, Joe!"

"You...you don't imagine duh Coynel'll mind if we don't wear our bay-dinn soots?" Joe was thoroughly excited now. He had brought an outrageously tight one made of some shiny white material he was dying to show off.

"Oh, he'll just eat it up, Joe. You can even strut around the house with it on. Right inside! The Colonel favors exhibits of the form divine!" (Joe giggled as Mack cleared his throat.) "Which brings me to a subject I'd like to talk over with you." He looked at Joe out of the corner of his eye. "O.k.?"

"Shoot, sweetie!"

"Well, Joe, I want to tell you about the Colonel. Now, I know I did let you in on a little bit of what he was all about during the War, but I really must tell you...well—tell you what actually makes him tick." (Joe nodded excitedly as Mack was thinking that everybody loves a good war story or two, so it might not be all that bad after all.) "The Colonel was able to organize us fellows into this regiment because of his connections with the British. Connaught—the Colonel—is a Tommy, you see. Also, he'd fought since the War started, and by the time America entered, he was already quite the hero. So he was offered our bunch because we were part of the AEF...and all of us, of course, wet behind the ears, as they say."

Joe took his eyes from the road and gave Mack a big, cheerful wink. "Gotcha!"

"Now, at first, all of us weren't of the homo type persausion. Some, as he would say, were just walking the fence. Some were—well—not at all interested. Beautiful-looking guys, but as straight as shooting arrows. Well, he got rid of them but fast! And the others, the fence-sitters, well, he convinced them that they were really queer and no short work of it, either!"

"You mean he jumped 'em?"

"Oh, yes, Joe, he did indeed 'jump them,' as you say. In fact, he jumped all of us. Down to the last man. And he kept right on jumping us, too, Joe, all through the whole goddammed foolish war."

Joe nodded. "We had a warden like that in the stir. An' you couldn't say no, neither!"

Mack let go a sigh of relief. "There! You see! I guess life is pretty funny. Anyway, he still does—every year we get together." Mack tipped up his hat, looking squarely at Joe. "That is…jump us."

"Jeez. Well, yuh know, I'm a Cat'olic, Mack," he murmured reverently.

"Sure. Of course. But you do see that he expects Elliot and myself to comply…with getting jumped, as you say."

Joe's voice got very low, as he sped up considerably. "Yeah, but you're my boyfriend and Elliot is dat kid's boyfriend. You ain't gonna let him do a t'ing like dat!"

"No. Of course we're not. But there's more to it, you see."

Joe had to think about it a while. Finally he came forth with, "So what yer sayin' is dis Coynel of yers is gonna expeck dat kid back dere and me to hop in duh kip wid him, too?!"

"Yes, Joe. And maybe both at the same time, too. Slow down a bit, Joe."

"Oh. Oh. Oh. Wellll. I jus' don't t'ink so, Mack. I mean, jeez, I'd do anyt'ing in duh woyld for yuz, but you're my fella, see, and I'm your guy! We're jus' gonna hafta talk to dis here Coynel of yours."

"Yes, but, well, it's not just simply him. All of the fellows up there really tend to let themselves go at these clam-bakes, Joe."

"I'll slug 'em, dat's what I'll do!" (Mack made a "hmmpph" sound.)

"I won't have any fun wid all dis orgy stuff goin' on! Hell, I don't even know deez guys. Yuh know, Mackie, I ain't like dat! Jeez, Ma 'uld kill me if she ever t'ought I was in a orgy!"

"I completely agree with you, Joe. But I truly believe we're going to have to handle this whole thing very delicately. See, everybody runs around naked and everybody gets all carried away, too."

"You tellin' me it was like that durin' duh war!"

"—when we were on leave…*yes*." Mack shifted in his seat. He was waiting for what was coming next.

"You mean you got into deez orgies wid all your buddies!"

"Well, that's the other part of what I must tell you. I guess we went over how I was Calvin's favorite—the Colonel, I mean—he got me when I was an innocent. Nineteen. I never had been with a man—or a woman—before Calvin. I mean, the Colonel."

"Everybody's gotta start somewheres," Joe reasoned. "Wid me it was wid Cheezy LaBotta in de alley back of duh rest'rant."

"Yes, but I'll bet you and Cheezy are finished with each other now, aren't you?"

"Oh, God! Dat was so long ago! He's dead anyways."

(Mack hardly knew what to say. Poor Cheezy! But Colonel Calvin Connaught was very much alive and still considered Mack his paramour. Still had possession of him—or so he thought. It was only once a year, but this year was going to be different.)

"Joe, I have no intention of letting Calvin—the Colonel—intrude upon our happiness."

"He'd just better not! Say, I'll have a l'il talk wid dis Coynul Calvin Connaught if yuz wants!"

"No. No, Joe, I'll see to it myself. But the other part of this has to do with the rest of the fellows. You'll be swatting them off like flies!" (Joe went, "Phhhhtt!") "—and so for that matter will our young friend in the back seat."

"D'ya t'ink Elliot'll behave himself?" asked Joe.

"I don't really know. Between the boozing and the sex parties that go on up there! I just hope that Wriggs isn't too shocked."

"Yeah, but what about Mr. and Mrs. dee Vol! How dey gonna stomach all ah dis?"

"Deucie and Baby have their own cabin, quite deep in the woods. They just love it there. Of course, they've always been aware of the hi-jinks—but they're good sports."

"Good sports! Jeez, I hope I don't knock somebody's lights out! I'm a good sport, too, but only to a pernt!"

Mack put his arm around Joe and leaned in close to him. "Joey, you're my whole life."

"Me, too, Mack. But I'm what dey calls the puzzessive type."

Mack was now driving. Just as the sun was setting, he turned down a narrow dirt road. The big car climbed—higher and higher. As the trees clotted either side, sweeping up against the doors, a mammoth gate made of timber and boulders came into view. At either side, lanterns glowed softly in the twilight. It was open, revealing an even narrower road stretching farther upward still, lined with tall, precisely trimmed pines at either side. As they slowly made their way in, a tingle of excitement filled the air.

"Wait'll you see this place, Joe! It's as big as a castle, only all made of logs and stones—it's like Valhalla."

"Who's she?"

With the sun setting behind it, Connaught's lodge loomed before a Maxfield Parrish sky. Baby was heard to murmur that every time they approached the place it took her breath away.

The Colonel's grand retreat was a rambling, vast and rustic mythical citadel, with one great turret in the middle, from which a sturdy shaft of oak rose, displaying a huge American flag flapping in the wind. All made of timber and seemingly prehistoric stone—so big were these rocks—it was wonderous, heaving out of the mountains and forests. A dozen cars of various types were parked about a swollen veranda which circled most of the house, canopied with striped awnings dotted with ferns, wicker chairs and kerosene lamps. Past this, a stable yard connected to the main house, topped by cuploas. More awnings, descending from every window, balcony and porch, gave off a gentle rustling sound. Beyond this, a gramophone was playing "Keep the Home Fires Burning" and deep masculine laughter could be heard.

Mack honked the horn, and soon enough the main doors swung open as a score of dogs roared out. Then, framed in the light of an overhead lantern, stood Connaught himself— a towering man, masterfully built, smiling and slowly rasing his hand in a salute. In riding breeches, boots and an open flannel shirt, he fit the style of his home perfectly.

Joe could see that he was not young anymore. Weathered and tough as nails, here was a man with whom nobody trifled. His black hair streaked generously with silver was not worn short as might be expected, but slicked straight behind his ears. The Colonel's eyes, an intense blue, shot through the dusk, taking in every face with a piercing intuition, sizing up the two newcomers, and looking, finally, with absolute adoration at Mack. His noble head spoke of an ancient and aristocratic lineage, sitting on broad, muscular shoulders, telling of a man who was ripped with muscle.

Striding toward the car, he smiled in a manner that spoke of many victories yet too many heartbreaks. Elliot helped Baby out first, then Joe and Mack—emerging, stretching—then Wriggs, in absolute awe of both man and manse. The blue light of the late Adirondack afternoon etched Colonel Connaught's virtual mightiness against the golden luminesence of the last rays of sunlight.

He began to speak, but could not. Tears filled his eyes.

Behind him, trying to round up all the dogs, was a lanky young man of about 27. Dressed identically as the Colonel, with unruly chestnut hair, smiling shyly at the guests, he nodded, then went at once to take the flag in. Wriggs was feeling just then as if his dreams of the noble and heroic homo had all come true. Joe also took it all in, and being the true Italian that he was, and remembering every word he had not so long ago heard, thought he might start getting a little jealous.

"Well, if it isn't the Last of the Best!" Connaught said at last, taking Mack into his arms. Mack was tall, but Connaught even taller. "Godamm it, but you're a sight for sore eyes! And who's this!"

Mack carefully said, "This is Joseph Imperio, Colonel. He's the one I wrote you about."

Connaught's hand went out to shake Joe's. The tough charm born in the trenches revealed itself. It only made him more attractive. Silently, the Colonel smiled, nodded. Joe did the same. No words of greeting were exchanged. Turning then to the only female traveler and guest for the weekend, Connaught picked her right up off the ground, hugging her.

"—my darlingest of sweethearts, Baby!" Swinging her around, he made her laugh and hold onto her hat.

His attention then went to Deucie, and the tears which he had held back now fell down his cheeks. Deucie threw his arms around him, patting him heavily on his back.

"It's o.k., Colonel. I'm still here. And in one piece—more or less."

"Sorry. Sorry, there—" Connaught muttered. "Just glad we're ALL still here, that's all."

Baby was ready with her hanky, as Deucie turned away. He never wanted anyone to see him cry.

And then, to Elliot: "Oh, you beautiful bastard, you! Never writing me a single line! Now who's this chicken here? The son you and Winola were supposed to have had?"

"This is my new and only boyfriend, Jack Wrigley. He goes by the handle of 'Wriggs.'" Elliot was clearly nervous. Joe had never seen him this way before.

"Sir!" Wriggs cried out, as Connaught caught him in a rough and apparently painful handshake.

By this time, the lanky lad who had taken down the flag was at Connaught's side, still beaming. "And this, my new recruits, is Huck, my slave, my Mother, my savior, my nemesis and my whole heart and soul!"

Huck nodded, farm-boy fashion. "Please tuh meet yuh. Joe.Wrigley. Mighty glad yer here and welcome!"

Baby, kissing him on the cheek, caused him to be overcome with embarrassment. "Why, Huck! You've sprouted into a man since we saw you last!" Whatever he had been the year before this youth had plainly left behind. He had the look of a hard-working outdoor sort of fellow completely unaware of the sex he exuded.

Everyone grabbed some piece of luggage, with Connaught leading them toward the house—all the dogs at his heels following devotedly. Slowly, the front doors opened, yielding an outpouring of men dressed for the country, smiling, waving and calling out the names of Mack, Elliot, Deucie and Baby. This was evidently the real army of charm.

Then came several more behind them. Two blind men, led by another, possessed of a face like a saint. One in a wheelchair, with no arms at all, another, like Deucie, with a cane. Joe realized that these were the casualities of Mack's regiment. The rest were whole, apparently in good health—but some of these appeared to have never truly survived the war inside themselves. It was written on their faces. They had a sadness about them, even through their smiles, a few of them struggling to hold back their tears.

Then, for no apparent reason at all, Joe felt like crying, too. But a chorus of laughter and jubilant foul language made him at once feel welcome. The weary travelers found themselves almost being lifted up by a sea of embraces and brought inside.

Joe looked at Mack. He had never seen him like this, and reached out and touched him because Mack also appeared to have tears in his eyes, giving him a slow smile. "It's all right, Joe," he whispered.

Awkardly Joe stood in the huge great room, letting Mack now and then introduce him. All about were momentos of the Great Conflict, hung from even the rafters. Everywhere there were banners, photographs and etchings, artillery shells.

Wriggs whispered to Elliot: "It's like a war museum!"

He found himself before a huge fireplace over which hung a painting showing one soldier saving another's life. There was something so disturbing about it, Wriggs found himself thinking. One doughboy in the other's arms, being lifted from a trench. Their bodies entwined, their uniforms ripped from them, revealing their bodies smeared with dirt and blood. The savior's face so close to the dying soldier's he seemed almost to be kissing him. He turned to see Joe looking up at it, too, as both became surrounded by the Colonel's guests. He had never felt anything like it before. His heart beat faster, as he was trying to make sense of it all. These men were his heroes because they had fought for and won freedom. The fact that all of them—down to a single man—were queer, gave Wriggs an awed and reverent feeling.

Staying at the Colonel's side, Mack, accepting hugs and even kisses, was called "MacDaily" by everyone. Then Connaught reached out, suddenly putting a hefty arm about Joe's shoulders, roaring, "Don't want you to feel left out, gorgeous! City boy, hey?"

"Yessir. You got it."

"MacDaily good to you?"

"Oh, swell, sir. We get on just peachy, yeah."

"Say! You are a fine figure of a man, Joseph, and I'm going to like you!" (hugging him even tighter now, running his hands all over Joe). "I want to introduce you and—Wriggs, is it? Yes! Wriggs!—to all my ladies here! I call 'em my girls, you see. Now I know you shan't remember their names, because each one has at least two or three—like our MacDaily here—but no matter!" He then stood apart and his voice became like a foghorn. "All right, you Floradoras! Let's have roll call!"

Joe was deluged by a bewildering amount of names. Each man gave their real name as well as their nickname.

"Vernon, sir! But they call me Hortense!"

"Matt, sir! Known sometimes as the Horse's Ass!"

"Lawrence, sir! He calls me Big Bertha though—"

The Colonel boomed, "Because he's got the biggest prick in the regiment!" Then to Baby, "Forgive me, dearest—"

Baby hollered out, "That's o.k.! I bandaged it up once, don't forget!"

After roll call, there was bugle call. Everyone marched into a long dining hall with a trestle table in the middle. There, grey and white uniformed servants stood at attention, as others brought out tins of food which looked to Joe like slop. Mack sat at the Colonel's right, Joe next to him. Baby sat at the Colonel's left, then Deucie. Far down the column of men were Elliot and Wriggs.

The Colonel then recited a poem that Mack traced to Kipling, and gave the go-ahead to dig in.

Passing before him, Joe saw a stew of meat and potatoes, a big container of beans, and a basket of hard tack. Just like in the army, thought Joe glumly, who was already missing his Mama's ziti and meatballs. Wine was even served in tin cups, but at least the very best and in various varieties—one concession that was being made because the Colonel loved to drink. Mack took special note that Elliot passed all the wine up, elbowing Wriggs proudly.

Huck, who didn't seem to be sitting anywhere at all, was supervising in the kitchen, sweating profusely as he dashed back and forth. Joe noticed him looking his way more than once. Most of the fellows were giving him and Wriggs a pleasant but lengthy passing glance.

Scanning the table, it soon became clear who was part of the regiment and who was not. It was obvious, by a certain befuddled look—a kind of resignation, combined with baffled enjoyment—that all the rest were obviously the boyfriends and not part of the old regiment at all.

The soliders among them immediately began swapping stories, usually at the top of their lungs, howling with laughter. As it developed, all of the ones who had been married were, by now, either divorced or separated. Mack was, Joe surmised, the only fellow (not counting Deucie) who had remained wed.

Soon enough the conversation came round to the men who'd brought along these boyfriends. In all, there were a half dozen of them, with their sweethearts sitting beside them. Every single one of the boyfriends were younger, too, Joe noted—even Wriggs—and Elliot was certainly the youngest guy in the original army of charm.

"I hope this isn't boring you, Joe," Mack whispered to him as Joe caught Huck giving him a wink while passing from the kitchen.

"It's a new 'speerience, I'll say dat much! We had crowds which got rowdy at the rest'rant before, but nuttin' like dis!" He looked over at Baby who was overcome with hysterics at some off-color joke the Colonel had just told her.

Wriggs now caught Joe's eye. Smiling, he shrugged. Cute kid, Wriggs. "Are all deez guys gonna end up doin' each other, Mack?" Joe asked under his breath.

"It all comes down to a small group of very naughty fellows. You can pick 'em out if you look closely."

Joe was no stranger to picking out bad guys. Going up and down both sides of the table, he spotted seven men with intensely roving eyes and probably very dirty minds. Three of them had buddies by their sides who were all, Joe observed, trying to fit in.

"I'm t'inkin' it's duh ones over dere, and down dere, and over dere—"

Mack grabbed Joe's finger. "Now you know it's not polite to point! Don't you like those beans?"

"I just wanna know—where's duh spaghettis?" Joe laughed.

After dessert, which unfortunately consisted of terrible apple crisp, more wine was served. A rolling cart displaying brandy, cognac and after dinner liqueurs was wheeled in, replete with a choice of cigars and Turkish cigarettes. Some of the old regiment were getting pretty tipsy by now and even louder. Wriggs was being undressed by many eyes farther down the table, cuddling close to Elliot whom he made sure passed over the libations enitrely "Remember that goddammed hill we took outside of Neuilly!" the Colonel shouted. This brought on a defeaning affirmation. "Ladies! We are all of the same faith!" He wobbled to his feet and held his tin cup high. Now quite drunk, Connaught raised his other arm into the air then brought it down led by a big fist. BAM! Everything was sent skyward.

"Duty! Duty! Duty! Duty! Duty! Duty! Duty! Duty! Duty! Duty!" they all yelled out, so rapidly and so firecely that Joe couldn't make any of it out, and Baby, laughing away, stuck her fingers in her ears. Everyone picked up their dessert spoons and banged them on the table to the rhythm of their cry.

"Duty! Duty! Duty! Duty! Duty! Duty!"

Joe thought they were all nuts by this time. "What's dat mean!" he shouted in Mack's ear.

"It means we all must do our duty, Joe," Mack shouted back, obediently banging his spoon along with everyone else. "Which means, well—you can guess, I imagine."

Afterward, Joe had a lot of questions. He and Mack were put in a spacious room paneled in knotty pine and decorated with homespun furniture. As he looked out from his window, he could see the Caisson Lake with a full moon reflected upon its ink black surface. Into the apparently ice cold water, some eight or nine men were now headed, all naked and joyously screaming obscenities.

"We don't hafta do stuff wid a bunch of 'em like dat, do we, Mack?"

"Not tonight, but if you want, there's a whole group going in at dawn, no matter how cold it is, right after bugle call." Mack yawned deeply and, naked himself, stretched out in bed, savoring the soft mattress and the quilt over him.

"You mean we all hafta get up wid duh bugler?" Joe shook his head, now making muscle man poses in the dresser mirror. "Do you t'ink I look as good as duh rest ah deez guys here?" He slipped off his BVDs, posing again.

"You're the most gorgeous piece here, Joe, just as Calvin said." Mack was barely able to keep his eyes open. "And no, you don't have to get up. But I do. Tomorrow the uniforms all go on. Then it's mess, then out to the woods for our drill, then we go on maneuvers."

"You kiddin' me?"

"I wish I were, Joe. Look in the wardrobe. I bet the uniform you're supposed to wear is already hanging there. Oh, you don't have to go with us, but for his birthday party, the uniform is required."

Joe pulled it out from the wardrobe. "Well, looks like it'll fit me o.k., but it's kind of beat up."

"Oh," said Mack, looking over toward it. "I think that was poor Wilbur's. Got run over by a tank."

"What! I ain't wearin' dis!" He tossed it back. "Jeez. If yuh aksts me, dis Coynel's still fightin' duh war, Mack." Joe now climbed in beside him, as Mack let go with a sigh of weary affirmation. "How comes Mr. and Mrs. deeVol beat it out so quick?"

"Oh. Because things always start happening right about now. You know, they're not interested in such—stuff."

All kinds of noises were emerging from downstairs.

"Dey're downstairs doin' it in da front room like dat?"

"Take a look..."

Joe got up. The bedrooms were all situated around a balcony which encompassed three sides of the Great Room. Almost all of the kerosene lamps had been extinguished, except one on the stairway, one at each corner of the balcony, and one on the center table of the Great Room. Looking down, Joe could see what clearly was a wild orgy in progress.

"Jeez," was all he said once more, softly closing the door and getting back into bed with Mack. "I couldn't make out duh Coynel nor Elliot an' Wriggs down dere dough. It kinda looked like a a plate full of rigatonis."

"Wriggs would probably kill Elliot if he went in for that kind of thing. But believe me," Mack added, "he used to be going at it all weekend, and right in front of us all, too."

"...but you wuz duh Coynel's favorite...you only stayed wid him?"

Poor Joe. Mack engulfed him, kissing his neck and cheeks, his forehead and finally his lips. "I never felt like doing that sort of thing, Joe. I'm too much of a romantic. But until you came along, yes—I had to sleep with the Colonel every single year we came up here."

Joe asked slowly, "—what wuz it like?"

Mack yawned. "Joe, aren't you beat? We both drove so far today...oh, all right. It was strange, Joe. Calvin is a sado-masochist."

"I t'ought so." Joe nodded wisely.

"Joe, do you know what a sado-masochist is?"

Joe bit his lip. "Sure, it's, it's—what exacklee is it, Mack?"

"Well, it's someone who finds intense erotic pleasure from giving or receiving pain, Joe."

"Gotcha! I used tuh know some coppers like dat. Whaz up wid dat shit, Mack? I hope he didn't hoyt youze, cuz if he did—!"

"No, no. I had to make him feel pain. Oh, it got to be very boring. It had gone on for years. God! No wonder I couldn't find a real beau for so long!"

"It was a lotta woyk, right?"

"You said it! Whew, am I exhausted!"

Joe caressed him. "Just lie dere. I'll make yuz feel swell."

As they made love, a knot from the wood panelling fell to the floor. They had left a candle burning and Joe, hard at work on Mack, failed to notice it. But Mack didn't. Through that hole he saw an eye—wide open. It was the Colonel's eye.

Mack was too tired to wonder if the spying episode would be mentioned in the morning, and too much in Heaven to care.

• • •

Wriggs was becoming nervous. Elliot said he had to go and use the bathroom, which was down the hall from Mack and Joe's room. He'd been gone more than twenty-two minutes as Wriggs timed it, checking his wrist-watch constantly. It was a fine thing that Elliot hadn't touched alcohol, had expressed disinterest in what was going on downstairs, and had made love to him so wonderfully as soon as they'd closed the door.

But where had he gone? Opening the door, Wriggs at last saw Elliot approaching, naked of course.

"Sorry. I'll tell you about it," Elliot whispered. Wriggs started to say something, but Elliot put a finger to his lips. "Don't. Just wait. I had to go see the Colonel. He's got Harold and Wally in there with him."

"What! Where's that guy named Huck?" Wriggs asked, shocked.

"He went to talk to Baby and Deucie. Huck's been with the Colonel for over a year now, so he knows what to expect. But…well, I told him he was in here with us."

Wriggs sat down on the bed. "*What*? You told the Colonel that his nice young man was in with us having a love triangle! Why did you tell him *that*?"

"Why are you wearing pyjamas when everyone else isn't?" Elliot asked.

"All right, I'll take 'em off…but wh—?"

"Because Huck is very worried about him. He told me so when we were all doing dishes—"

"Oh, yeah, why did you guys have to all do the dishes when he has all these servants around?" Wriggs asked, pulling off his bottoms.

"It's part of this ritual. We did it in the Army, so we do it now. I know it's crazy, Wriggs, but you've just got to understand that this is a yearly reunion. Once a Goddammed year. That's all." Elliot jumped on the bed suddenly. "Just never mind any of this!"

"Elliot! This means we're going have to lie for Huck! What'll we say?"

"Your body drives me crazy, do you know that, kid?" Elliot was all over him. But Wriggs was all business.

"Elliot! Do we have to say all three of us had a sexual party!"

"Yeah. Come on, just let me…let me…"

"No. Now, Elliot, what's so wrong with the Colonel that we have to lie? I don't know if I like this—" But Wriggs was helpless when in Elliot's arms.

"How can you bring up that Victorian-help-an-old-lady-across-the-street stuff when everything's so SEXY here!" Elliot was on top of him by now.

"Elliot, please just tell me. And what's that old uniform hanging over there for?"

"You have to wear it tomorrow."

"Well, it's too short in the legs. What in Heaven's name is wrong with the Colonel!"

"You mean why is Huck so worried? Oh, drinking, for one thing. And depression. Just like me before I met you!"

Wriggs gulped. "Elliot, you're my dreamboat." For a while, neither spoke. Then, coming up for air, Wriggs returned to the matter at hand. "I don't want to have to tell anyone we had Huck in here! I can't picture myself doing that sort of thing, really. I'm too young yet!"

Elliot threw his head back and laughed. "You had all of my old pals dripping wet for you, kid. It's that innocence of yours that drives 'em wild."

"Oh, ye gods, Elliot! Don't stop!"

"I love deflowering you, Wriggs! Who needs booze when I've got this ass of yours!"

"Elliot, I'll make it a point to speak privately to Huck tomorrow. Perhaps I can help him. After all, look what I've done for you."

"Get off that soap box, please…Oh, boy, oh, boy, oh, boy…"

• • •

After talking with Deucie and Baby, Huck took the trail back that led toward the main house. He hadn't meant to stay so long, but they had insisted. Both Mr. and Mrs. deVol were such grand folks. He felt, now, as he loped along, hands shoved in pockets, a sense of his heart being lightened. It was so late now. Way past three a.m. All the crazy goings-on by the lake and down in front of the fireplace had probably run their course.

Aren't people really just animals after all, Huck thought, now swinging an old stick he'd picked up, walking more slowly, filled with awe at the beauty of the night. So many stars and such a brilliant moon! Huck loved the country and never wanted to leave it. He loved their horses and mongrel dogs and soaring pines. He loved the Colonel so very much, he couldn't live a moment without thinking of him and how he needed all of his love. Huck devoted his every second to him. He worried far too much about Calvin (whom he called "Cal" of course), but he couldn't help it.

Looking up, he prayed out loud. A prayer that his man would get better. A prayer for a miracle.

Now, at the crest of the knoll which allowed him to see the big house with only a few lights still burning, the cabin where Deucie and Baby now soundly slept, and the old monastery past the stone wall…he realized that everyone had a much bigger world than his own. Those handsome fellows Mack and Elliot had brought with them, with their stylish clothes and big city ways—they didn't know what to make of all this! And he didn't really know what to make of them, either. But he so wanted to make friends. He had no friends at all, except for Calvin. He wondered what each of them felt about their men. Those queer fellows from the cities called their man "my lover" or "my beau" or "my boyfriend"—but to Huck, the Colonel was HIS MAN, and that was all. And that was enough. Even though, recently, Calvin had become so sad and so strange…so very strange. Every time that odd little man showed up and they both went into the library with the door closed, and all Huck could hear was terrible yelling…awful accusations…then angry weeping.

Across the field, past the old stone wall, Huck now noticed what must've been the glow of candlelight from the chapel at the monastery. With the moon behind those clouds, the eerie light through the mullioned windows glowed like fresh blood staining the night. He figured those candles went on burning for days and nights with peoples' prayer attatched to them. Wretched, desperate people. He'd seen them, when they'd gotten loose. He'd found that bunch over there to be very un-neighborly, especially that man who came to visit. There was no reason to act as they did, just because they were taking care of those crazy people. He wasn't sure what exactly they did do over there to help poor folks like that, but felt it wasn't good for Calvin to have the place occupied as it was. It seemed to upset him terribly, ever since he got that land back because of MacDailey's helping him out. He should've just let the property go. But, for some reason, he couldn't and Huck never could figure out why—or what was behind it all.

They'd put barbed wire on top of the old stone wall, and planted trees all around the place. In fact, the only way you could ever look over there was to reach the top of the knoll, upon which he was now standing, in curious wonderment, and take a good gander.

At that time of night, the guards weren't out. *They must be sleeping, too,* Huck thought. The moon was out fully now, resplendent, victorious. Huck could see the wrought iron sign they'd put up at their gates. Funny how those gates had such big locks. And what a peculiar name was emblazoned on them—SLAVES OF MARY, Private Sanitorium.

Huck got a chill and walked home faster.

• • • • •

CHAPTER XVIII

OF TOWN AND COUNTRY

Every once in a while, Bruno acted almost human. Staring at him, as he, in turn gazed at the statue of the satyr which he'd just purchased from Annabelle, Ynez considered how she might even fall in love with him a little, if he weren't such a bastard prick. There, on the sofa in his offices, she watched him, fascinated, moving the staute about until he found the absolute perfect place for it. Centering it on top of a low bookcase, his hands caressing the base gently and with tremendous respect, his eyes soft and almost dream-like, Ynez marveled at this change in him.

"That was so kind of you to buy it, Bruno."

"I just liked it, that's all. Maybe I'll go for some modernistic paintings next, who knows?"

The late afternoon sun was filtering through the half-drawn shades. They were alone. Blanche had something to do once again and had left early Friday afternoon Mack was gone to celebrate, Northward. Already she missed him so terribly. There, with Bruno, she felt safe from those terrible people whom she had encountered first-hand. She felt almost as if she had begun a whole new life as a gangster's moll. He would protect her—she just knew he would—and she didn't quite know why…other than the fact that he and Mack were now partners and he didn't trust a single living soul for even a split second.

Bruno stood away from the statue, admiring it. He hadn't even heard her.

"It looks o.k. there, huh?" he said.

"Swell, my pet. It's just a pity you don't have some grand digs in which to put it!"

"Everything in time. When Pop goes, I take over," he answered, still looking at it—smiling, Ynez thought, a bit satyr-like, himself. "I'm gonna be the only gangster with an art collection to match the Louvre!" They both laughed. He went and sat down beside her, taking a lighted cigarette from her lips. "No. You wait! I'm serious! I've got dough rolling in now thanks to things working out with Mack, and I should reward myself. You know, I'm not stupid, Ynez."

"Who said you were! I only said you were a nasty unfeeling son of a bitch, that's all!"

Bruno looked down at the carpet, grinnng even now. "Well…I've put up with *you* this long, haven't I?"

"Say! And I'm damned good at what I do, too!" They both laughed again and he drew her close and kissed her on the forehead. "Bruno, Annabelle considers you quite a phenomanon. A tough guy with exquisite taste…still, I don't think you'll ever change—going around scaring people the way you do."

"Listen, *I'm* damned good at what I do, too, you know, and don't you forget it!" He paused and kissed her again. Ynez was enjoying herself immensely! "Besides, I don't scare you like those dopes who are shadowing you do!"

"Bruno. Please stay close to me."

"You know I can't do that, sugar. Not the way you want."

"I don't want to go back to Great Neck tonight, Bruno. I'm so terribly scared!"

"Well, if you'd just tell me what's up, I'd maybe help you out a little–"

Now wrapped in his arms, she allowed him to feel her breasts, urging his hand lower, opening her legs, tossing off her shoes.

He growled pleasantly, rubbing her nose "—oh. I know what you're trying to do. But I can't keep you here. And I won't go to a hotel. Not unless you tell me, that is—"

Ynez sat up, pale, looking at him with brows knit. "I don't know what you could possibly do about it. I'm not even supposed to know anything about it." (Bruno was standing his ground.) "Oh, all right! Well, here goes—you know how Mack is always doing everything for everybody?" He nodded. "Well, during our first year of marriage I heard him talking to Colonel Connaught about some sort of property transaction. Apparently, the Colonel had purchased a parcel of land and it was overtaken by these people who had no right to it. The property went into bank foreclosure because Connaught couldn't keep up his payments. So Mack bought it from the bank for him. This was entirely done over the phone and it went on for days until it nearly drove poor Mackie wild. Anyway, Mack thought that these people should vacate this property up there, since it was now his—but they refused to leave or pay a dime to rent or lease it! I asked him about it and he wouldn't tell me. So I dropped the matter. Then I found out that the Colonel was completely under the thumb of these people! Squatters, really."

"How did you find this out?"

"Oh. I went and read his letters."

"That he'd written to Mack?" Bruno sat up, now really intrgued.

"Yes. I just wanted to know what had gone on before Mack and I were married. In his letters,the Colonel wrote that once Mack bought the land outright, he would start a nudist colony on it. And Mack was trying to find something for the deVols to do at that time, so it rather seemed like a plan. You see, there was an old building on it. But the folks who were occupying the place would simply not leave! Finally, these people told the Colonel they'd pay cash to lease the place, but they never did. Not a penny. So, Mack still owns it—legally—and they've set themselves up on it. Still. To this day. And the Colonel just lets them stay there. And Mack ends up out of luck—as usual."

"Sounds like a dirty deal, all right. Who are these assholes anyway?"

"I never could find out. And anyway, Mack got a letter from the Colonel telling him to never mention it again. So, of course, Mack just let it drop." Ynez shrugged her shoulders.

"And Mack continues to pay the taxes on this property which he can't make use of because these mugs have something on this Colonel Connaught guy?" Bruno was putting it all together.

"Yes. And Mack is absolutely loyal to him. It's deep in the woods of the Adirondacks. I've only seen photographs. Never been invited up there."

"The nudist colony racket is rotten. Seasonal. So what happend to the deVols since that scam didn't pan out?"

"Next thing you know, Deucie and Baby end up running the place where I met Mack, here in the City—*La Maison*. The Colonel himself got them hired! Mack went and asked him. He was positively desperate to get Baby and Deucie some work, and that was all that materialized."

"So," Bruno slowly said, "this Colonel guy heard about the place here in New York from…who? The people that moved in on the land Mack had bought for him maybe?"

"—oh, Bruno, please, I don't want to go on."

"If you leave me hanging like this, Ynez, I'll wring your neck!" Bruno grabbed hold of her, but let go at once. It made her laugh a little, but she was clearly most upset by unravelling the tale, apparently for the first time ever. "O.k. Now listen. This has been haunting you for years, right?"

Ynez nodded, looking away.

"Do you think the Colonel was behind *La Maison*? Is that it? Isn't Mack up there now visting this nut job?"

"Bruno…Mack and the Colonel were, at one time, lovers. I never asked what went on, but I've always believed that their relationship caused Mackie to, well…*withdraw* as he did for years. Mack always worries about him. In one of those letters to Mack, he said something like 'I'm buckling under because all of this is breaking my heart in two…'"

Bruno, holding her by her shoulders at arm's length, asked, "But how does this all tie in with those creeps we saw today?" (She looked away.) "You *do* know them, don't you, honey?"

She began: "Something happened once at *La Maison*. I had finished my act, and was going up to the third floor to bed. It was past five in the morning. The place was emptied out. Only four of the patrons remained. You must remember, Bruno, every one of them wore masks. Always. The orchestra had left, the servants, the rest of the artistes. Baby and Deucie were closing up and I heard one of these patrons saying, 'We'll shut off the lights and lock up, you two be on your way.' And so they left as well."

"These must've been the owners—closing up themselves."

"Yes. Left alone, I heard one say, 'Let's go someplace where we can talk.' I thought nothing of it, shut the door and got ready for bed. My little room was in the attic, at the back, and looked out on the old carriage house behind the building itself. There was a mews where many of the cars parked. In this way, they were completely hidden from the police. I had put off my light, and heard some arguing going on below. Then, it stopped. From the back of the place, there were two ways of leaving the house. One was an underground passage through the kitchens into the carriage house. Must've been an old cold storage. The other, simply by the kitchen door. It was by this way that these people—the owners I believe—made their way out to the mews."

Ynez paused, took a breath, then went on, rapidly. "Well, out came a woman in a long opera cloak and mask, and got in a car with a tall man. They put the side lamps on within the car, then there was an exchange of money—oh, a lot of cash…a great wad of it…from the man to the woman. She took it, dashed from the car, handed it to another man through the open window of his car parked there, and jumped back in. This other car, carrying two men, rolled down the mews, then drove away. But their car stayed—the car with the woman and tall man in it, with the lamps still lit. The tall man was in the driver's seat and had by now removed his mask. It was *positively* Colonel Connaught. He was at our wedding. I'd only met him then, but you could never forget his face. He has a sort of ravaged look. At any rate, he was very, very upset. In fact, so upset he was sobbing! Can you imagine a war hero like that sobbing so horribly? I lifted my window and heard him say, 'I'm so sorry, my dear! Please, please don't despise me!' He just couldn't even drive! So the woman removed her mask and, well—it looked like a woman, but then, it took off the wig and it was more of a man than a woman. And it was clearly, too, a man's voice. Both had British accents. I heard this person say, "You shall never be without my devotion to you"—in the most evil tone! She—or he—hauled the Colonel right out of the car and then beat the shit out of him!"

"—left him there?"

"Oh, no, picked him up and tossed him in the back seat then drove off. I remember thinking what a powerfully built man the Colonel was, and yet he allowed himself to be thrown around just like a marionette!"

Bruno nodded, letting go a sigh. "Who was this freak that had it all over this colonel?"

"I think it was Connaught's own daughter, Bruno. She was with him at our marriage. I guess they were on better terms then. Very butch. Easily could pass as a man."

"—he's married—this Colonel—or was?"

"He must've been. Before the War. I'd asked Mack about this daughter of his, and he said the Colonel wanted *nothing* to do with her."

"Now let me sort this out." Bruno leaned back on the sofa cushions. "And let's have a good stiff shaker of cocktails while we're at it. The wheels of my devious mind are turning. Who knows? Maybe I can work it so Mack isn't sucked in by these creeps and get a new racket going up there in the Adirondacks in the bargain!"

Ynez rose to make the cocktails and light the lamps. This was working wonderfully, too. She might elicit a stay—over at a cute little hotel—if it got much later. Afterward, he'd order up from his parents' restaurant. Oh! That marvelous food! Ynez felt safe and a little more in love every minute. Bruno was going to save Mack. They were already partners, and certainly had that O'Couran prick by the balls now.

"Here you are, my darling." She brought a tray with glasses and a shaker and placed them on the table, sitting beside him. "You're not going to let these hideous people get me, are you, Beefy Bruno?"

"What! You just watch me! So you think one of them in the car today was the Colonel's daughter…posing as a man?"

"Yes, but she seems to have *become* a man somehow in the interim. Didn't you see her mustache!"

"So who's the other jerk then?" He poured out the drinks.

"Another disguise. That one is certainly the same person Annabelle and I met when we went to to find a trick for me—before I met you, my darling. It was a bogus domestics agency called Dial-a-Dick. I think Belle realized it, too, as soon as she made that sketch. But of course, she wouldn't say anything with everybody about."

"Both of 'em drags, huh? Working for some syndicate that had too many Hallowe'en parties as kids. It's all part of a dress-up fascination and then it gets into sex and then they go nutso and that's it. Stopping at nothing."

"Bruno! You're a *constant* surprise to me. What a psycho-analyst you are!" She raised her glass in a toast to him.

"Don't make fun of me. I'm a helluva lot smarter than you." He was defensive now. Maybe even a little hurt. She had to hurry to make up for what she'd said. "I'm *not* making fun of you. I truly mean it. What do you make of it—these ghouls trying to kill me?"

"Well, it wouldn't be a senseless killing." He laughed. "They want you primarily to rat on Mack, see. Because of the kind of marriage you've got, and how he rigs his business. They'll get all of that out of you, then they'll kill you."

Ynez sighed. "Grand! So it's O'Couran on the one hand, and these creeps on the other. Well, I never! How'd I ever get myself into this!"

"By marrying a pansy, you asshole, that's how." Bruno paused, sipped his cocktail then winked at Ynez. "But if you hadn't—you never would've met me! See how lucky you are. Plus, these nut cases never bargained on Big Bruno. I'll take care of 'em."

"—oh, you absolute darling brute, you!"—kissing him hard and long. (They'd never gotten along this well! What had happened? Mack was gone! That was it! He had her all to himself.)

"Listen. I'll bet you dollars to doughnuts that O'Couran is behind 'em, sweetie."

Ynez blinked. The man was quite simply a criminal genius! A goddamed criminal genius. More cocktails. Ynez sat up, excited. "—all right. Because of his connection with Unlucky Lady Lee. I can see that. He must be in on lots of different rackets. But I *don't* see how it all connects up."

"Oh, it doesn't yet, but it will! And we've got to get him, Ynez, and we will, too. Him and his whole bunch."

He looked at her—in his marvelous eyes, an expression of sex mixed with fretfulness.

"What's in it for you, Burly B.? Take over this depraved vice racket? Get his list of people to shake down? I don't like that very much."

"There's really no money in that funny sex stuff. If you run a perfectly ordinary whore house, you can always do much better. The kind of crap these lunkheads purvey takes money and time and, well, you know something, it really takes mugs who have something very, very, wrong with 'em, come to think of it!"

"All right!" She was loosening his tie, sliding her left hand beneath his shirt, undoing his trousers with her right hand. "I promise I won't be scared if you tell me that their bark is worse than their bite. *Let's use me as bait then!* I don't care!"

"O.k., but later, babe, later. Here, let me pull that thing of mine out for you. Come 'ere." He yanked the neckline of her blouse down.

"I'll do that part. I don't want you to rip another one of my Paris frocks all to Hell, now do I?"

(This was perfect! She was foreseeing going two times around with him, then leaving him exhausted completely. THEN she could just collapse right up in the office there with him.)

"Oh, you're such a mess, Ynez Daly," he whispered in her ear as she opened her legs, stradling him, allowing him to massage her there, kissing his chest, his nipples, his stomach. "I figure even if I screw you twice everyday for the next fifty years, you'll still be the most sexually frustrated bitch in all New York." He let her pull off his trousers and BVDs. "Get the shoes and socks too, please."

"Yes *sir*," she hoarsely whispered, now only clad in garters and hose. "But you make me that way, Bruno."

"Get up here. Come on. Give it to me. What? I do not make you that way, toots. The fact that you're married to a fairy makes you that way. Get with it, will you? Where's your brains?"

(So it *was* Mack, after all. Bruno took what he wanted and he wanted all of it. Ohhhh, was this man ever good. All man. Brawny and beefy and brutal and big all over, and a bastard to boot. But Mack was still her great love. And even though Big Beefy Bruno was way up inside her just now, she still missed Mackie and thought of him every minute. Well. At least every *other* minute.)

• • •

Up at Connaught's lodge the very next day, Joe, Wriggs and Huck were sewing the seeds of buddyhood. On that fine, warm morn, this trio had stripped off their shirts and set about doing chores out-of-doors. Because their men had gone from drilling to a "mess hall" breakfast, then on to maneuvers, the boys had found themselves left to their own devices, and naturally gravitated toward one another. Huck was piling wood around the side of the house, with Wriggs and Joe helping.

"Sun up 'til sun down, this is how I keep my mind clear!" Huck was telling them as they tossed the logs to one another. "I got so many chores, I don't know which end I'm on first."

Wriggs agreed, catching a log in mid-air. "The place shows it, too, Huck, but you need some hired hands around here."

"I know it! But we can't afford nothin' no more. It's just me and the Colonel, and he's so crazy lately he ain't suh good's he usta be."

"My pop's off his nut,too, Huck," Joe said, tossing two logs at once up on the porch. "I know how it is. When do yuh get time tuh read all dem books dough?" Huck had shown them his mail-order collection of books on depression, psychosis and other mental aberrations shelved in the library.

"Oh, after dark," he said. "Don't do no good though. My man won't see nobody to gitt himself helped. Thinks he's right as rain."

Wriggs suggested, "Well, Elliot and Mack should speak to him, I think..." stopping to wipe his brow with his handkerchief. All the boys were sweating now, standing about gleaming in the sun.

"Oh, that'll never do. My man—he's too proud. Thinks he's just God's gift, yuh know. Well! Just one more cord, and then I got to go help with lunch."

Joe looked at Wriggs, and Wriggs at Joe. "If dere's anyt'ing we could do tuh help yuz...I mean wid the rest ah yer chores. You got a houseful!"

"Naw," said Huck, sitting down on a log. "Most grateful to yuh fer what you done so far! Now, yuh see, I got some time to spare." He brightened. "What say we take a dip?"

Wriggs and Joe were more than in agreement, and so followed Huck down the path to the lake. Before them was the Caisson, long and narrow, peaceful and inviting. It was then that he told them the Colonel was going to put the lodge up for sale.

Joe shook his head while removing his trousers. "Say, dat's a cryin' shame. Swell place like dis. Youze sure don't look broke at all."

"He's gone through his money like wildfire," Huck said, stripping naked. Wriggs was doing the same, but Joe seemed to want to keep his underwear on.

"Perfect day for us fellows to take a swim!" Wriggs was saying, "Just like the ancient Greeks and the Hellespont!"

He and Huck stood proudly displaying their physiques in the early afternoon sun, admiring each other's bodies as Joe was turning crimson.

Wriggs loved it, though. "You've got a strapping shape there, Huck, and one which I must admit I admire! Come on now, Joe, aren't we all men here! Remove those things," he urged, slapping him on his back.

"Aw, o.k.," Joe muttered, grinning sheepishly.

Huck blinked twice when Joe was fully stripped. "God, Joe, you've got a whanger as big as those logs we wuz just pilin'!"

"Never mind dat, it's mortifyin'," Joe said, following them into the water. "Say! I want yuz tuh bot' know, I can't swim a stroke...so don't leave me!"

The water was like ice. Joe had only put his toe in before he turned around and headed back. "Joe! Joe! Come on!" both boys called, now waist-deep in the lake. "It just takes gettin' used to!"

"Aw jeez," he sighed, turning back. "I guess I'm just a sissy is all." It took him almost ten minutes before the water reached his waist, and by that time, both Wriggs and Huck were finished with their swim.

"Joe! Just relax and dunk yourself in," Wriggs urged. "Here, I'll hold your hand." Wriggs caught Joe, as Huck cupped water in his palms and dripped it over Joe's chiseled but goose-bumped shoulders.

"Don't ever say yer a sissy, Joey," Huck commented, admiring all those muscles. "Yer built like a brick shithouse."

During the course of this ablution, Joe quite naturally got aroused.

"Jeez. Now look at me. Stiff as a board down dere."

Soon enough, the three half-immersed bodies were touching beneath the water's surface and making no attempt to separate from the hard, smooth feelings of touching at once.

"Aw fellas, fellas!" said Joe. 'Now yuz got me goin'!" He turned and hurried out of the water, glistening there on the shore, doing all he could not to stroke himself, taking in both Wriggs and Huck, who were trying not to laugh.

Coming toward him, they each mirrored what had become a problem to Joe, but didn't seem to be bothering either Huck or Wriggs at all.

Wriggs dropped down on the grassy shore beside Joe, still standing, still wanting to touch himself, and now doing all he could not to touch Wriggs. Huck came slowly behind him and soon lay down beside Wriggs.

"Come on, let's just lie here a bit and soak up some sun," Wriggs suggested, shifting his body closer to Huck's.

Huck looked up at Joe. "From this view, Joe, you look even better. You got some legs and some ass, that's fer shoor."

"Aw, you guys got me crazy now. I didn't plan on dis. 'Xcuse me, I'll jus' go behin' dis tree here and whack off."

"Wait! Don't!" Both Huck and Wriggs hollered, and pulled him down on top of them both.

That was all Joe needed. With terrible thoughts of Mack finding out about all of this racing through his head, he joined his two new friends in a fondling party. Sinking first to his knees, then becoming engulfed in their bodies, Joe couldn't help but let his animal-self emerge.

"I can't say no! Youse bot' are so beauty-full," Joe nestled between them, working his way toward an explosion.

"This is perfectly *all right*," Wriggs assured him, one hand on his manhood, the other around Huck and Joe. "As long as we don't do anything."

Huck, however, was getting a little too adventurous for Joe. "—Huck! Huck! Once I start, I got no control over myself!" Joe breathed, now, true to his warning, becoming almost uncontrollable, looking down at his own body and the other two which were wrapped around each other's and his own.

Joe had reached the point of abandon. Huck, so enthralled by all of this, was unable to say much. His lanky physique, already browned from being naked in the sun throughout that especially warm Spring, was sandwiched between Joe and Wriggs.

These big city boys certainly got him going, too! It was plain that Huck had wanted Joe from the moment he'd met him, because he kept crawling over Wriggs, trying to lick him. But Joe had never seen anyone quite like Wriggs without clothes. He was so smooth, so well-defined, like some of the swimmers he'd known back at reform school. Somehow, Joe now ended up in the middle, facing Huck. Wriggs got on top of them both and everyone became lost in each other's bodies.

"Jumpin' hop toads!" Huck yelled out. "Watch me gush!"

Wriggs fell over Huck's body, pressing himself against his glossy stomach. "Oh! Hold me! Joe! Huck! This is it!" Wriggs body, covered with water, sweat and semin, now slid around theirs. All their muscles strained to give him pleasure.

Now Joe let go. "Mama mia! Fongool!" Both Wriggs and Huck went for Joe, covering his mouth with theirs, attacking him everywhere. Then, panting, exhausted, the three lay with arms wrapped about one another.

"I will, of course, tell Elliot," Wriggs managed to whisper, still smiling and dazed.

"Mack's gonna kill me."

"My man don't mind. So long as it's only this par-tikkler weekend and once't a year. 'Sides, all we did was let go of our juices! We didn't screw nor put our mouths down onto our tools nor nothin'."

"Yes, yes, yes," Wriggs, patted Huck on his thigh, where his hand just happened to be resting "But we wanted to! And now that the great veil of our heroic manhood has been rent, we will want to approach these pagan altars once again."

All Joe understood from what Wriggs had said was the word "rent" and at once connected to the fact that the Armstrongs, Nolie and now Wriggs himself, were getting evicted. What did that have to do with all of this, he wondered?

As they washed themselves off and began to pull on their underwear, trousers, shoes and socks, Joe's mind was elsewhere. And here he had just heard that poor Huck (who was very, very attractive and a swell guy, too) might have to leave the wonderful big log mansion where he and the Colonel lived.

Suddenly, Joe looked across to the islet, where, about forty feet away, he spied someone. "Hey! Who dat over dere!"

"Maybe some of the fellows," Wriggs saw someone there, too, hiding behind some trees.

"Naw." Huck looked toward the islet, frowning deeply. "They're way up in the mountains. It's those folks from over next door…they're always watchin' us."

"I hope dey didn't see what we just all done!" Joe exclaimed.

"Oh, I bet they did," Huck said, who was almost dressed, and never wore underwear anyway. "They're awful pests. Come on, let's go…"

As they began to leave the lakeside, Huck, who had at once become pensive after Joe noticed someone watching, said, "They're the ones who's buyin' our place off'n my man."

At the luncheon "mess," where Joe was increasingly becoming bored with the horrible food, he told Mack about the Colonel's having to sell the lodge.

"Oh, Joe, that's really too bad. Why, it'll break his heart. This is his whole world here!" Mack put down his fork. "Where will they both go? What will they do? Why, up here, they can live like noble savages. They can't go back out into the real world. And what about the dogs and all the horses—and Huck loves his gardens. Oh, this is very, very, sad news, Joe."

"Yeah, well I got more sad news for yuz, Mack." Joe leaned in and whispered in his ear. "Wriggs and Huck and me went down to duh lake and we went swimmin' naked and den we all beat off." Mack burst out laughing so loudly, the boys at the table, along with Deucie, Baby and the Colonel, stopped eating, with food lifted in mid-air.

"Care to share the joke with us, MacDailey?" the Colonel smiled over at him.

"Joe wondered when we were having spaghetti!" Mack covered him smoothly.

Later on, with everyone retiring to their rooms for a brief siesta, the Colonel ordered Mack to meet with him privately in the gymnasium.

"And just because you cavorted down at the lake with your two new friends, I want you to know that I won't allow Calvin to have his way with me, Joey," Mack told him with a wink, changing from his uniform into a tank suit.

"What am I s'posed tuh do while yer gone!" There was no chance to answer, because Elliot appeared at the door looking most upset. He entered, glumly. "Well. Wriggs told me what happened..."

Mack took him by the arm. "Elliot, close the door. Joe told me as well. That's why I was laughing during mess."

"Laughing? Do you think something like that is funny?" Elliot's eyes grew large. He was out of uniform, sporting a cream silk shirt and trousers. His hair was tousled and he looked sullen.With Joe near the window about to open it, Elliot sat hard on the edge of the bed, his elbows on his knees, glaring at him.

Joe knew at once why. He was getting blamed. "It just happened, thas' all. We wuz all swimmin' and naked. And it jus' happened. Nobody t'ought it up foyst."

"Do you realize the beauties I am passing up to have Jack Wrigley in my life!" He shook his head firecely. "I've got 'em throwing themselves on me. First I don't drink, then I don't fool around, then I go and fall in love...what a sucker I am!"

Mack sat down next to him. "All of the boys up here are horny as hell, Elliot. It's always been like that. It's a once a year thing. You take three young marvelous guys like your Jack Wrigley, the Colonel's Huck and Joey here and you put them into a setting like this. Well—what would you expect to happen!"

"I would expect them all to control themselves!"

Joe turned from them swiftly, staring out the window.

Mack continued, "We never did. It wasn't expected of us. And now, even though we've got our boyfriends up here, it's still somehow expected of us."

"Well, what does that have to with anything! We've managed to say 'no' and they should've, too."

"But if we were in the same position as they were in earlier today, do you think we could've said no then—at that moment?"

"Mack, I've controlled myself over you ever since you married Ynez. I've got it hot and heavy for you to this day. I guess I always will. You never forget your first one. But I've managed to deal with it!"

Mack put his arm around Elliot and drew him closer. "Yes, but I've helped you along the way. With our three graces here, nobody helped them! They just helped themselves to each other!" He paused. Elliot's head hung low, and Joe had turned to listen. "Just drop it, Elliot. Wriggs is a sweet, wonderful kid. He's all for you—you know it and so do Joe and I."

Elliot now hardened. "Well, I don't think he should've moved in so soon. You never know what he might drag into our apartment some night! Then where would we be?" Mack stole a look at Joe, who responded in kind.

"Where indeed!" Mack replied, as Elliot looked at them both.

"Is there something else going on which I should be party to?"

Joe pointed at the sky through the open window. "Oh, look, a airplane!" But it didn't work. Joe turned to see Elliot was staring intently at Mack.

Mack rose as a knock came at the door. "Only that I'd really like to see you and Wriggs not let this thing come between you, that's all, Elliot."

It was Wriggs himself. "Oh, there you are—" he said, downcast. "I hope I didn't make a mess out of everything, Elliot, that's all I can say. I've said I'm sorry, and I mean it."

"We'll talk about this. Mack and Joe have talked, so I guess we'd better talk." Elliot went past Wriggs out the door, then waited for him in the corridor.

Standing there, hangdog, Wriggs awkwardly said hello and goodbye, then followed Elliot down the hall as Mack gingerly closed the door behind them both.

"Now wait'll Elliot finds out dere gettin kicked out!" Joe whispered.

"He'll use any excuse at all to take a drink again...did you really see an airplane?"

"Yeah, circlin' and circlin'. Hey! You ain't leavin' right now, are yuz!"

"I've got to see the Colonel and just get it over with, Joe. This won't take long, so just sit tight."

"Aw, gimmee a kiss! I'm noyvous!"

Left to his own devices, Joe sat for a while and watched the airplane circling overhead.

"It's funny," he said to himself, "it don't go in one direction ever. I t'ink we're bein' watched." He then went in search of Huck.

The Colonel had been waiting for Mack in the lodge's gymnasium for a full three minutes. Checking his wrist-watch constantly, hitting his palm with his fist and pacing nervously back and forth, he reacted when Mack entered by closing the doors behind him, as if a shot had gone off.

"There you are, solider! By God! You've kept me waiting! Christ almighty, just look at you!" Lunging at Mack, he crushed him in a great embrace and covered his neck with desperate kisses. "Oh, you don't how I've missed you, MacDaily, and how I've dreamed of you!"

Mack patted him, pulling him away, looking into his eyes which told of a man who was very much on the edge of a dark ravine. Drink, depression, old ghosts from the War and his terrible lust for men had at last gotten to him.

"There, there…it's all right now, Calvin. Let's just sit down a bit…got your pipe?"

Connaught twirled about, confused. He laid it on the matte of the boxing ring, with his pouch of tobacco. "Jesus! Hiding on me again!" Grabbing it up in his hand, he sat on the bench beside the ring, with Mack next to him. Mack filled the pipe up, as he had all throughout the War, lit it for him, giving it a few start-up puffs, then gently put it in his mouth, noticing how his jaw was shaking—yet, only very slightly.

"I need you, MacDaily. Need you more than ever, old dear!" he said, placing a hand on Mack's knee and leaning upon him.

"I think a change would do you good. Why don't you and Huck plan to spend some time out in Great Neck this Summer?"

"Oh. Well. You see, old dear, it's awfully tough on me.Traveling any place these days. Don't like to leave my camp! I alway feel somehow—well, somehow so godammed different from the rest! Feel like everybody's always judging me. Don't know if it's worth it really. But let me feel your fine body, MacDaily! Oh, God! Please hold me tightly, old dear."

"How can I help you, Calvin?" Mack asked simply, as he felt his former commanding officer quivering in his arms.

"Help me! My God, man, whatever makes you think an old soak like me needs your help! Just look at me! Have you ever seen me in better form, I ask you!" Connaught drew back and pounded his chest as Mack sighed. "I'm still a beauty, aren't I, MacDaily? Aren't I?"

"I love you, Calvin. I always have and always will…" Mack found himself struggling with his words. "From now on, I promise we'll see more of each other."

"Yes. Yes. It's that damned tradition of marriage we nancies must bow to! And now you've got this Italian fellow in tow. Oh, my God, and he does love you! Worships and adores you just as that goddammed foolish wife of yours does…still hanging on!"

"Ynez is a true friend to me, Calvin—"

But the Colonel rose up, thundering, "Don't give me that mallarky! You got married because *I* was married! Don't tell me! You followed in my footsteps thinking it would cover your sins. Well, has it!"

"Are they sins?"

Connaught turned to him, his eyes large. "In my case, of course they are! You know what happened to my wife Isolde. "

"Yes. But that was long ago, Calvin and…"

The Colonel sat again and, as if the weight of his past was crushing him, cradled himself in Mack's arms. "There is no such thing as long ago. Nothing ever really dies. Death never releases itself anywhere except into our souls. It burrows within us and devours our bodies and our pricks all too soon," he muttered pathetically.

"Calvin," Mack said hardly above a whisper, "all this…this haunting of your self. It's doing you no good. Just look around you at all of us who worship you. And Huck—he's so devoted."

His eyes met Mack's. "Huck, yes. And all of my lads, too. Yes, of course. But devotion isn't always such a fine thing, MacDaily. My daughter is devoted to me. Devoted to seeing me driven mad. She won't let go of me or leave me alone. You see! There's a sin if ever there was one!"

"Where is Violet? I thought she went back to England—"

"No! No, man! She's been here the entire time!"

Mack was shocked. "Here! In the States?"

"Yes, in the States!" Connaught was bellowing again. "Of course in the States! But here! Here! On my land—actually, on your land…right over there, in fact!" His thumb jabbed past the doors.

"What—you mean your daughter has taken up living in that old monastery I bought for you?"

"Of course she has, man!" Connaught stood, tearing at his scant clothing. "She's been over there for two years now!" Connaught stood up. "But I don't want to talk about it anymore. I want to make love to you! Desperately."

Mack began to realize that there was no way out of this one. "Calvin—"

"Pull out your cock, man, let me get my goddammed mouth over it! I'm wild to see it, don't you understand!"

By now, the Colonel had sunk to his knees, burying his head in Mack's crotch. Then, Mack heard terrible sobs. Choking, aching sobs.

"Oh, I can't…I can't! I'm being eaten away by all my sins! I know you've found happiness in that Italian boy…what am I doing?"

Wearing a one-piece tank suit like Mack's, he began stripping it off frantically. Now, with the suit about his ankles, he groveled at Mack's feet, placing them upon his chest, as if he wanted to be crushed by them. With his hands gripping, vice-like, Mack's legs and thighs, he slashed away at Mack's shorts, trying to shove his hands up and inside them, growling like an animal, yet sobbing, too.

Although Mack had so often seen him in states of self-deprecation before, it was always—in the past—like play. Now, it had become horrible. Running his fingers through the Colonel's mane of hair, Mack bent down, lifted his face up and kissed him gently.

"Stop. Please, Calvin. Just stop—for your sake, and for mine—we've all been through so much—"

The Colonel now seemed to gather himself together a bit. "Yes, yes, I know we have…I'm so sorry…but something has to be done about Violet. I simply can't go on with this relationship she's heaved upon me."

"But as your daughter, I would imagine it's all right if she stays over there. I don't really mind if…"

Now he rose to his knees, his hands folded as if in prayer before him. "But she's slowly driving me mad, I tell you, old dear! You have no idea what she's doing to me. Oh, God!" he cried out. "I wish she'd just run a bayonet through my heart and get it the Hell over with!"

• • •

Deucie and Baby, throughout this epic scene, were doing a little exploring. Relieved of maneuvers, they had hatched a plan, beginning innocently enough over their morning coffee as a mere inquiry among themselves.

Whoever was occupying that property upon which they were supposed to manage a nudist colony? Toiling back to their cabin after breakfast, both noticed, standing on the knoll overlooking the place, that some changes had been made in the old Gothic manse, and it now seemed to have been turned into a prison of some kind. But hardly at all, through the thicket of trees since planted, could they make very much out.

"You know that cane I designed that goes up like a periscope?" Deucie asked Baby. "Well, sir, I brought it with me, don't ask me why. Got a funny feelin', that's all. What say we go on back and get it?"

Baby shook her head. "Honey, you stay right here. It's too much for you. I can get it, and be right back."

While she was gone, Deucie, leaning up against a fallen pine and having a smoke, heard some terrible screams echoing out over the woods. They came from across the stone wall. Breathless, Baby returned with the specially made cane, and was told about the hollering.

"Somebody's in trouble back inside of there, sweetheart," his eyes narrowed. "I'd like to get as close as possible to get this thing to view what's up over that wall."

"I'll help you. Just let's don't break both our asses."

And so the deVols scrambled patiently and as quiet as two Indians down the knoll, into the hollow beneath it, and then up on the narrow precipice that held the high stone wall.

"Barbed wire," Baby observed as Deucie was preparing his cane to transform into a periscope. "Maybe they've got wild men in there."

"We'll see soon enough, darlin'."

Having removed the rubber end of the cane, he now pulled out a telescoping metal shaft with an eye-piece on a tiny hinge. This he bent and held up to his right eye. The other end of the cane, which was made at a right angle, had already been prepared by removing a tube which concealed a powerful lens.

Baby held her breath. It seemed as if Deucie had nothing to report when, all at once, she heard what must've been the front gates opening and a car passing through.

"Automobile just drove in," Deucie reported. "Some big fellas runnin' to meet it. Look like thugs. Two people gettin' out. Both fellas. All talkin'."

Baby strained to hear, but the wall was too thick, and the distance from the drive too great. Deucie was breathing hard, saying nothing. "Anything else?" she whispered.

But before he could answer, there was something of a commotion. "Grab her! Grab her!" was heard clearly from across the wall. Then a woman's voice was heard, hoarse and screaming.

"You'll not put tape over this mouth! I know what you are and I know what you're all about!"

Baby heard a horrible whack.

"One of the thugs just hit this poor little lady," Deucie reported.

"You'll not get away with this! These people in here aren't sick! You're the ones who are sick!"

More shouts of "Grab her!" and "Get hold of her!"

There were more screams.

"Oh, muh Gawd—" Deucie whispered. "Oh, muh Gawd!" now truly stunned.

"There, see! I don't care! You can't fight like a man because you're as much a female as I am and you always shall be, too!"

"Take her away—" came the utterance, growled in reply.

"Quick, hon, take a look at this—" Deucie handed her the periscope.

"What in Hell?" Baby squinted into the eye-piece. "Well, did you ever?"

"Isn't that who I think it is?"

Now, an airplane was slowly descending in the direction of the property.

"It's gonna land inside there," Deucie whispered.

"I'm getting a good look at that face now. That little lady's been taken inside. Did you see her face?"

"No. Her hair was all over the place. Let's get outta here before we get put in there!"

Deucie returned the instrument to the inside of his cane and, with Baby's help, made it down the embankment. But he was wheezing and sweating profusely. Baby grew alarmed.

"Honey, you can't make that hill. We'll have to go around this way…"

"But that's their private road! What if we get caught?"

"I saw 'em going to meet the airplane. Come on, we've got to chance it or I'll end up a widow."

Hobbling out toward the private road, they found themselves at the main gate to the property.

"'Slaves of Mary, Private Sanitorium,'" Deucie read the sign. "Now, if anyone else drives up, our gooses are cooked!"

"Well, at least you're on flat land, and we can stay in back of the trees here. Soon enough, we're bound to hit the main road and then maybe we can thumb it back to the lodge!"

At last reaching it, and stopping to rest at a most welcome tree stump, they again heard an automobile approaching. This time, however, it proved to be Huck, navigating the Colonel's old touring car. They waved him down.

"What in thunder you folks doin' way out here?" he asked, helping Deucie up and in, as Baby cleared a space for them both, the entire back seat having been filled with vegetables from the farmer's market.

"Well, just call me Mata Hari, Huck!" Baby quipped, handing Deucie the bottle of birch beer which Huck had offered her.

"Yuh know," he said, putting the car back in gear. "It's awful dangerous out by that private road back there. There's guards all over carryin' rifles!"

"Never mind that, sonny," Deucie waved his hand. "Whadda you know about the Colonel's daughter?"

"He ain't got no daughter no more. She went and turned herself into a son," Huck replied with a strange note in his voice.

"O.k. Then whadda you know about his son!"

"All I know is he's an awful lotta trouble. And I hate him, if that matters any. Like to kill him if I could ever get muh hands onto him."

"All right, sonny," Deucie pressed on. "Now just why is it you'd like to kill the Colonel's…er…son?"

"I don't mind tellin' you folks 'cause of how close you are to the Colonel. But that relative of my man is just rotten. Man, woman or beast, or all three rolled into one! He's done things to my Cal the divvil himself couldn't even think of! He's the cause of my Man's entire decline. And he'll have him in the grave before long. That's just where that relative wants him, too. Pushin' up daisies."

"That's just what we thought," Baby nodded, giving Huck a pat on his strong, bronzed arm. "But what made her want to masquerade as a man all of a sudden?"

"Oh, it ain't no masquerade. Not no more! At first, it mighta bin. But I seen her with her clothes off! She's got almost all the equipment of both sexes now."

"What!" Deucie gasped. "A freak ah nature?"

"Hold on, Deuce. Huck, did you see breasts and a you-know-what on this offspring of the Colonel's?" Baby asked, with a medical kind of tone to her voice.

"Well, sure, and if she didn't show it off! She's got a fully developed whang tool, Mrs. deVol, and yet a set of jugs just like any lady! The only thing she lacks is balls, if you'll pardon my bein' blunt, but I know you're a nurse so I can say things like that."

"Hmmm," Baby pondered. "I wonder if she's a hermaphodite?"

"No, I think she's Episcopalian," Huck answered. "'cause that's what my man always said he was."

• • • • •

CHAPTER XIX

BIRTHDAY BOY

At 1:30 Saturday morning, Alexander Parker looked from the window of the cover flat to the sidewalk below. He had noticed the same car driving by the club four times already. Each time, it slowed down and a face was seen looking up at him from the passenger side. There, parked directly in front, was that same automobile.

Two men got out in dark overcoats, which he thought odd because the weather had become so unseasonably warm. He heard them entering the front door to the stairway below, then making their way up the stairs of the two-story building.

This door was always kept locked, and housed below the cover flat was a cobbler shoppe. He stood before the bolted door to the flat waiting for them. He knew there was going to be trouble. And he was terrified.

It took only twenty minutes to beat him to such a degree that he was almost dead. Bleeding from wounds inflicted on his head, his eyes, his nose and mouth, he'd somehow managed to let the chair fall over the floor buzzer which Deucie had put there in case of an oncoming paddy wagon, signalling, of course, a raid on the club deVol.

Alexander would not answer their questions, saying nothing at all except, "I work for Mr. Daly and I'm loyal to him." He had repeated that phrase more than a half dozen times until, finally, one of the men violently picked him up and threw him across the room.

Then, both of these men started in on him. Kicking him over and over, whacking him across his face, then tossing him back into the blood smeared corner of the little room. Alexander did not fight back because he felt certain that Keys, right across the street, would at once come to his aid.

But Keys was inside the club, quelling a fight between two drunks. It was all planned that way, in order to distract the person across the street—who just happened to be Alexander.

Feeling his ribs collapse, and a gush of blood mixed with vomit coming forth, over his nice new suit which Mrs. D. had just bought him, he felt he was done for. He was missing some teeth, his eyes (he was sure) were shoved from their sockets into the very back of his head, his whole body was throbbing. It had gone too far for him to rise up and fight back. And the truth of it was, Alexander Parker was no fighter.

He had never even offered so much as a verbal retort to those who'd made fun of him throughout his life. He just would take it all, as he now did, sure that God would spare him, as God always had, somehow or other.

Mr. D. loved Alexander and God had brought them together, and that intercession had saved Alexander and his whole family. He would never tell on Mr. D. or his wife. He would never say a thing against them, no matter what. And he had let the floor lamp fall right on that buzzer. Somebody was sure to come up and save him from dying.

Across the street, at 2:11 a.m., Johnnie, sitting in the upstairs office going over that night's take, had heard it go off. Putting on her coat, she raced down the stairway, out and into the alley, then, carefully, to the sidewalk. There wasn't a sign of the cops anywhere. Looking up and across 46th Street, she could see one light burning in the cover flat where Alexander had been stationed. Everything looked all right. He'd brought some of his school books up there with him, and was probably doing some studying by the desk lamp. There was no other lamp burning.

But even though things looked all right, it didn't somehow feel that way. So she stood, staring for a moment more. Then, she saw a shadow passing before the window…no, two shadows. Was someone up there with Alexander? Clearly, Johnnie had seen two silhouettes. On their heads were fedoras and Alexander never wore a fedora in his life.

There were two men up there. And where was her brother? She ran across the street, pausing before the building, immediately noticing that the lock on the door to the staircase had been broken. Pulling it open, she began to climb the stairs crying out her brother's name The door at the second floor landing was ajar, and just as she was about to enter the flat, the two men stepped out and, with horrible smiles on their faces, gestured just behind them.

What Princess Johnnie saw caused something like a howl of anguish and terror to come out of her. Grabbing her, they dragged her within, kicking and screaming. Then, realizing what had walked directly into their trap, they both let go with beast-like groans. What a piece of black ass she was. What a stroke of luck, too. The larger of the two men cradled Johnnie's head in his big hands, almost crushing it.

"That's gonna be you, eightball, if you don't tell us what we need to know," he whispered in her ear.

Johnnie was a match for any man. She sent her left elbow straight at his stomach, and kicked the other man in the crotch. At once, she was beside Alexander, taking what was left of him in her arms.

Behind her, both men advanced, and following the same technique they had used on her brother, kicked her repeatedly, beginning with her face, one holding her fast. As the other bent low, grabbing her arms and twisting them behind her in a vice-like grip, he ripped the bodice of her dress off.

"Want the privilege of a white man's cock?" he growled, drooling as he spoke. The one who watched stopped him. "Not yet with that stuff," holding her fast as she attempted to break free. "First, we gotta know things, and right now, too—or else you'll be sorry!"

"Let me go! I don't know what you're talking about!" Johnnie screamed, defiant, wiping the blood from her eyes.

"Sure you do. You're in with them. Come on, dinge, spill it!"Johnnie managed to sit on up her haunches, then struggled up to let go with a kick. Now it was the other man's turn to hit her with a brutual slap which knocked her back down to the floor.

"Is that Jew a fairy—that Mack Daly? Does he fuck his wife or is she a lezzie? Answer!"

"You're talkin' to the wrong gal about lezzies, you dirty honky prick! Let me go!"

Alexander was now slowly becoming conscious. The man who had offered her his unspeakable 'privilege' left her just long enough to whack her brother again in the head with the side of his shoe, laughing.

He then turned on her, "So you're one of 'em, too, huh?"

His compatriot yelled, "I said never mind that! Whadda you know about the Dalys!"

Johnnie felt she might pass out, but fought to resist. Coughing up blood, she answered, "I don't know anything about them!"

The more controlled man continued, "Yes, but you work over there at that speak-easy! Is that kike a queer or not? Answer!"

"I don't know what you want and I don't know what you're talking about!" she screamed.

The other grabbed Johnnie by her neck, yanking her head back. "You know all right. You're part of that nigger-loving crowd and you're the type who'll do both sexes, aren't you? You filthy, dirty coon!" He slapped her with the back of his hand across her already bloodied eyes.

Alexander moaned, calling out his sister's name. "Johnnie…Johnnie—"

"Who's Johnnie? Answer!"

Johnnie's eyes were both bleeding by now and she let go an angry, piercing sob, kicking and twisting about.

"Let up on her or you'll not get a thing out of her," said the other.

The man who held her down now let go, and Johnnie managed to first get on her hands and knees, then crawled to the wall and pulled herself upward. She paused...naked to the waist, blood streaming down from her head. One of them went for her breasts, but Johnnie kicked him in his left knee. The other, yanking her around, threw her with a cry of rage and triumph across the room. Advancing the few steps it took to reach her, he bent down, tearing her dress nearly off.

Gasping for breath, he again asked her: "Is that Jew a fairy and is his wife a lezzie and a whore? Answer! Answer! Answer!"

Johnnie looked down at her nakedness, and with trembling, blood-covered hands, attempted to pull her dress back together. But the man standing over her kicked her arms away, falling down on top of her until the heat of his foul breath made her bleeding wounds sting. Opening his coat, he began to remove his trousers.

"Tell us right now or you will regret it. We have ways. And we know of certain types who go for black meat, too. "

"Stop that right now!" the other cautioned. "Don't say no more. Don't try that stuff. Get dressed," he ordered. "We'll take her downtown and see what they can do with her. Maybe they'll sell her and we'll get a cut!"

Johnnie uttered a curse upon them both which neither expected any woman of any color or persausion capable of even knowing. And she paid for it, too.

Alexander, hearing her screams, regained consciousness. "Johnnie! JOHNNIE!"

The men had left. Johnnie's coat, her shoes and a locket which Nolie had given her—ripped from her neck—lay broken beside him on the bloody floor. But Johnnie was gone.

• • •

By the time Johnnie Parker, bound and gagged, had been thrown into the car parked in front of the cover flat, the festivities marking Colonel Connaught's birthday had reached their height.

Throughout the late afternoon, Huck had worked with the servants on the birthday party arrangements for that evening. Night had fallen, and every one of his guests now gathered around the long dining room table, each outfitted in their old uniforms as if ready for some unknown, unnamed battle, as if this celebration would be their last before going Over the Top to die.

Soon fireworks illuminated the vista behind Colonel Connaught, like bombs lighting up a battlefield. In his eyes, a strange look emerged as he stood over his birthday cake, all his medals glistening, a breathtkingly beautiful vision of super human will.

He was fully back there again. It was 1917. Standing amongst his men, hands on his hips, rakishly assuming a stance of triumph, smiling and laughing, basking in the adoration they were offering him, feeling the War had never ended.

Every glass was raised and after he was toasted, a rousing cheer went up. Distantly, through the tall trees, the merriment of this celebration had unsettled the inmates of the Slaves of Mary, and their crazed hollers echoed eerily over the mountain, like the cries of the wounded and dying from out of the trenches.

Mack and Joe, having gone into town to ring up Ynez and check on the club, had made it back in time to change and appear at these ceremonies. They went right to Baby, now dressed in her regulation field nurse's outfit, standing apart from the men, at a pretend Red Cross station just off to the side, feeling slightly ridiculous.

"We had to go into town to make a telephone call, " Mack conveyed in her ear over the cheers being offered to Connaught. "Elliot said you and Deucie wanted to speak to me?"

"I'll say we do. Did you check to see if everything at the club was running smoothly?"

"Yes. I spoke to Nolie. It's a good night and everybody loves her."

"How about Alexander across the street?"

"Johnnie was just going over to relieve him when Nolie and I were talking. Oh. There was a fight between two drunks at the club, but Keys took care of it. But listen, I also spoke to Ynez. I first rang her up in Great Neck, but she wasn't there so I found her at Bruno's."

"—and?"

"She and Bruno think we should head back early tomorrow."

"So do I, Mack," Baby looked up at him.

"O.k. by me!" Joe put in, who was really having a terrible time.

Baby, nodding with comic earnestness, which told Mack she wasn't in much of a party mood either, began to say something, but was upstaged by a loud roaring cheer at a burst of fireworks.

Taking her arm, Mack moved with Joe toward the Colonel. Deucie, Elliot and Wriggs were all standing at the Colonel's right, and aknowledged Mack with a collective look which told him they all wished the whole thing were over and done with.

Someone pushed a knife into Mack's hand, indicating that he should in turn take Connaught's hand in his. Every year Mack had done this, only this year it seemed almost frightening to him…the knife, blazing in the light of the sputtering sparklers on the cake, the Colonel pressing up against him, weeping and laughing so pathetically.

"Happy Birthday, Calvin," Mack said to him, so close their lips almost touched.

"Once again! I am victorious over everything!" the Colonel shouted at the top of his lungs.

With Mack's hand over his, the Colonel cut the cake with a decisive yet quivering gesture, like a man with an axe. The massive confection, responding to its wound, caved in, losing all its significance, surrendering to defeat. The sparklers fell with the candles into the chasm which had been made. Suddenly, a thunderous shout of joy rose from his men, and Colonel Connaught blubbered unabashedly like one gone suddenly mad.

• • • • •

CHAPTER XX

PICNIC TIME

Late Sunday morning, Ynez and Bruno drove out to Great Neck. The house was empty because, as planned, Alexander was gone, staying with Johnnie and Nolie while he manned the cover flat throughout the weekend. The day servants had been told they would not be needed since Ynez had correctly deduced that she would be elsewhere the whole time, wrapped in Bruno's arms for the duration of Mack's visit.

Having successfully seduced him into staying both Friday and Saturday nights in a quaint Greenwich Village inn, she could feel safe again in her own home. Her Mackie was returning. She could once more see her husband, whom she was missing so terribly, in spite of all the love-making she was getting. Bruno was now gloriously tightening his grip on her, yet still she loved Mack above and beyond anyone or anything else in her whole world. Maybe more than ever. And she wasn't sure why.

She turned the key to the main doors of her house, as Bruno retrieved the mail from its box. Going into the foyer, with Bruno following just behind looking over the half dozen envelopes, she turned to him, "Anything for me?"

"Invitations to style shows, I guess—oh—here's one with O'Couran's name on the return address."

Ynez took it from him. "Oh, it's from Peggy O'Couran," glancing at it only casually at first. "Must be a thank you note. Wasn't that sweet of her?"

But upon opening the envelope, Ynez had found only a small religious picture in full color, the size of a playing card, depicting the Virign Mary in beatific suffering.

"A holy card," Bruno noted with some surprise. "We used to get those in school whenever we did anything good."

"Which means *you* never got a single one!" Turning it over, she asked, "Is this the kind of thing Catholics send in place of bread and butter notes?" The only religion Ynez ever knew had come to her through the movies. "Oh, here's a little verse on the back—"

Bruno looked over her shoulder." That's no verse, it's a prayer, you dumb-bell!"

Ynez read aloud: "'Hail holy queen, Mother of Mercy, Our life, our sweetness, our hope, to thee we cry poor banished children of Eve, To thee send up our sighs, mourning and weeping in this valley of tears—'"

Looking up, she saw Bruno was reciting the prayer word-for-word from memory. "Don't laugh! Our mom swears by that prayer!"

"Look how she underlined these words in pencil…and so firmly, it almost went right through the card. '*Mourning and weeping in this valley of tears…*' And she didn't even sign her name. Bruno—" Ynez had turned to him. He had not even had time to remove his hat, standing in the doorway, holding the rest of the mail.

"—I think I know what she means by this. She was prevented from writing anything down…maybe she *did* phone me, but nobody was here. She's gone, Bruno! They've taken her away just as she said they would…to the Slaves of Mary."

• • •

Around noon on Sunday, Mack pulled into a roadside rest. Here, with the weather perfect, Baby set forth a snack on a picinic table not far from the park. They had been the first to take their leave and Connaught, although dismayed, was too hung-over from the night before to care.

Gathering around the table as Baby poured out hot, steaming coffee, Mack was the first to speak, looking down into his cup.

"I think we'd better all compare notes. I could start by apologizing to everybody, but it won't do any good. Each of us has become involved in this thing at various points in time. Some to a lesser degree than others, thank God."

Elliot asked simply, "Am I involved? And Wriggs? And Nolie and Johnnie?"

"I'm afraid so, kid. But…well…let's start at the beginning of it all, can we?"

"Yuh mean," Joe said, "when I wuz sent tuh shake yuz down, Mack?"

"Oh, no, Joe. Long, long before that…as long ago as before the War, when a little baby was taken from an orphan asylum in London by the Colonel's then-wife, Isolde Connaught, in order to fill the void which had been left in their marriage because Calvin was a profligate pederast."

Joe only shook his head. "And I t'ought we wuz gonna speak Englsih tudday!"

Wriggs spoke up. "This is going to be just fascinating, Mack. I'll explain everything to you, Joe, as we go along here."

"The child was raised by the Colonel's wife as her very own, and named Violet. Both mother and child were virtually neglected by him, and more or less out of contact. As Violet grew up, she was apparently seen as being not-quite-right. However, in those high circles of the military nobility, nothing was said or done."

"She was at your wedding, Mack," Elliot provided. "I took one look at her and knew she was off-base somehow."

Mack winked, then went on, "That was the last time the Colonel and Violet got along. There had been a reconciliation after the War ended. She came here, to the States to see him…but it didn't work. By that time, Isolde Connaught had been exiled. She was found to be a spy for the Germans, and a disgrace to her country as well to the Colonel—and probably to Violet as well, who had no one in the world. That's when all of this really began."

Baby asked, "Did the Colonel ever tell you what was really wrong with his daughter, Mack?"

He hesitated before answering. "Yes. He did, in his letters—but not specifically. He only said that her female organs were out of the oridnary. He made me swear that I would tell no one. And I never did."

"Not even me?" Joe queried.

"Not even you, Joe. It wasn't the easiest thing to explain, anyway."

Deucie had emptied his cup and, as Baby poured him another, said, "We never would've guessed it, and we even saw her just yesterday. Now, livin' like a man."

Mack added, nodding, "Over at the old monastery."

Deucie continued, "Yessir. It only came clear when Huck spilled the beans. And he was quite plain on it, too. Apparently Violet was prancin' about in the altogether, blamin' her problem on the Colonel! That's part of what the Babe and me have been itching to tell you!"

"You mean, of course, that Huck knows Violet Connaught is a hermaphrodite," Mack concluded.

"A *what*?" Joe frowned deeply.

"Tell you later, Joey," Mack said. "Well, go on. What else did you find out?"

"Only that the old monastery has been turned into a private sanitorium," Baby said. "By the name of The Slaves of Mary. Which brings us right back, I believe, to Brian O'Couran."

Wriggs asked, "He's the fellow who's the Director of Prohibition now, isn't he?"

"Yes," Mack answered. "And he's also the fellow who's trying to ruin me, and doing a very good job of it, too. You see, the only sure thing we might have on him is that he runs a racket which preys on unfortunate people, those with very serious physical probelms which also affect them mentally."

Deucie piped up, "So his dirty work must go way back to that devilish business down on Coney, Mackie—right after we came Home!"

"And the murder of The Whistler," Elliot said, "He was killed by O'Couran because he was going to tell you everything, isn't that right, Mack?"

Baby held up her hand. "Only in part, if I might put forth my own theory here. We went down to that place where they found Blackie's body. There was blood all over the loading dock and clear down into the driveway. Deucie and me thinkthat he was undergoing one of those crazy surgeries, having someone else's legs grafted to his! He got scared. He knew it was all a fake and that he'd die right there on the table anyway, and so he tried to get out. He crawled out to the loading dock, toppled over the side, and was crushed to death by a truck."

Mack shook his head. "But I identified his body myself. There were no legs with it—grafted on, sewn on, or otherwise. There was no indication that any operation of that kind had taken place from what I could gather."

Baby demanded, "You never told us what was left of the Whistler, Mackie. You've got to try and describe it now."

"This is the part when I go pee," Joe hoisted himself around the bench of the picinic table and headed for the trees.

"Well, the truck hit him from the area of the abdomen all the way up to the neck. His body was intact otherwise."

"You're sure about that?" Baby asked.

"Yes. There he was on the slab. It was too clear. So ghastly and sad, Baby!"

"If he were cut in a place you couldn't see, by looking at his body there in the morgue…well, you might've missed something." Baby pressed on, in a thoroughly medical manner.

"Yes, that's true."

Baby continued. "Let's just say, for conjecture now, that the Whistler was made to feel he couldn't possibly offer them enough information to pay for the grafting of someone else's legs onto his body. So they made him a deal. They told him they needed his male hormonal glands and that he would undergo a simple painless operation. These would be used to turn Violet Connaught into a true man."

"But," Elliot interrupted, "if Violet is what you say she is, isn't she both already?"

"Hermaprodites often don't possess tesitcles," Baby stated in her most clinical manner. "Many times, they are born with a penis which does not function at all and a vagina beneath it. This is what Huck described to us."

Wriggs elbowed Elliot, who was turning green. "Got that now?"

Baby conjectured, "Possibly, they doped him up and entered his body behind the testicles, and he bled to death."

"Well! This is hardly table talk," Elliot said, gulping. "Maybe I'll just go and join Joe. "

But Baby, munching away on the other half of her corned beef sandwich, enjoying every bite, was ready to add still more theories. "Now I've thought a lot about what Huck described as far as Violet's malformation. All last night in fact, when that birthday cake gave me gas and I couldn't sleep, I fell to musing—what would anybody like that want more than anything else in the world? Caught betwixt and between a girl and a boy. With a Father as a War hero. Well, Deucie and I talked it over."

"'Cause I couldn't sleep either," Deucie went on. "Well, it figures that—oh, you go ahead, tell 'em, Babe. This ain't stuff for the layman, unless you know your oats like she does."

"Well, the answer is *balls*. She had everything else but." Baby's conclusion was firm.

Joe had just returned. "Boy, I musta missed an awful lot! Now all of a sudden we're talkin' dirty!"

"Sit down, Joe," Mack pulled on his tie. "This is very interesting. The sickening stuff is over—I think."

About a hundred feet away, a young and merry family was just unpacking for their noon-time picnic. "Gee," Elliot said. "I wonder if we should invite them over! Maybe they'll have some bright ideas, too!"

Joe got up once again. "I'll go see!"

"Joe! He's just kidding!" Mack motioned him back. "Can you imagine," he now leaned in, whispering, "what anyone would think hearing us all talk this way!"

Climbing over the bench, Joe sat back down next to Mack. "All I need tuh know is how dis funny stuff is gonna bring you down!"

"Well," Mack replied. "First of all, that sanitorium called The Slaves of Mary is on my property. I bought it for the Colonel. I'm sure if they ever get found out about that, the whole thing will come back to me."

"And what about dis Doctor Sloane—or whatever his name is?" Joe wanted to know. "Remember dat stick pin we found?"

"Hold on, I've got it right here in my lapel pocket." Mack pulled out the small piece of jewelry wrapped in his handkerchief.

"We've got something to show you, too." And at that Baby reached into her purse, bringing forth the small note which they'd wrenched from the mailbox during their investigation. "See. Somebody with the inital of 'B' was kept waiting and didn't like it."

Side by side, on the wooden picinic table, the note and the stick-pin seemed to possess an eerie parallel.

"Hold on a minute!" Elliot pointed to the letter "B" at the bottom of the note. "That's the number thirteen, if you look at it carefully. Thirteen! Just like on the stick-pin!"

Wriggs patted him on the back. "Right you are, Elliot! You see how all those arrangements you do in sharps and flats come in handy! Now just tell us how this all ties in."

Elliot took a moment. "Well, it's a nickname, just like yours, that's what it is. It implies something someone does—or is…"

Joe snapped his fingers. "Yeah! Like when yuh get sent up! The number on yer uny-form!"

Elliot shook his head. "Although you're both right, this particular number would have to be something someone would be proud of. The pin is gold, after all. And the signing of the number at the bottom of the note indicates to me a code name of some kind."

"Come to think of it," Mack replied, "there might be something in one of the Colonel's letters about a code name. I believe that Isolde Connaught's code name was Operative 13, in fact. Yes, it was, come to think of it!"

Deucie insisted. "She's long been court-martialed as a spy. Now how could that be, Mack?"

Mack nodded with certainty. "Sure. In Luxemburg, right on the heels of the Armistice. Calvin even sent me the newspaper clippings."

Joe couldn't take any more. "Jeez. Ghosts!" Jumping over the bench, he ran for the bushes.

"The t.p. is in my knitting bag!" Baby called after him, adding, "Musta bin the corned beef."

"Honey," Deucie marveled. "You got a theory for everything."

• • • • •

CHAPTER XXI

REVEILLE FOR A LOYAL SON

At Miss Harrison's townhouse, Alexander lay dying. Johnnie, in the next room, was barely conscious. Overnight,with the help of her friend Dr. Elizabeth Sutton, Annabelle Harrison had turned the second floor of her home into an instant hosptial ward, enlisting the services of the best private nurses she could find, and a leading surgeon as well.

Keys had spotted the getaway car carrying his sister away from the cover flat and, by a harrowing and bizarre chase, saved her life. But for Alexander, there was little hope.

There at his bedside was Ynez. Annabelle had telephoned her out in Great Neck to give her the awful news. She then telephoned Nolie, who arrived almost immediately, hastily writing a note which she left at the lobby desk: "Johnnie badly beaten, Alexander dying. Miss Harrison taking care of things at 37th Street. Go there now. N."

The errant party-goers arrived back in the City early Sunday evening, dropping Elliot and Wriggs off first. Leaving their bags in the lobby of the building, they ran back out with the note and sped with the rest to Murray Hill. Once there, they were taken at once to the second floor, meeting with four women in white, silently, efficiently going back and forth. No one knew what to say, and nobody recognizable was about.

Baby stopped a nurse on the way down the stairs. "We're friends of the Parkers and of Miss Harrison. This is Mr. Daly, Mr. Armstrong, and we are Mr. and Mrs. deVol—"

"This way, please." The nurse, handing her trays to another, led them through the upstairs hall and into a bedroom. Before them, Alexander lay barely visible within an oxygen tent, bandaged except for his eyes. Sitting beside him was Ynez, her hand clutching his beneath the tent.

Only a sigh from Mack's lips caused her to turn. "Oh, Mack! Look what they've done to him!"

A nurse, trying to quiet her as she attempted to stand, held a wavering Ynez. Finally falling into her husband's arms, she wept. Another nurse entered with Alexander's Mother, Keys standing beside her. This tall and dignified black woman showed no signs of emotion, but emanated a courage and a strength which now filled the room. Just behind them was Dr. Sutton.

"Mr. and Mrs. Daly, I am Doctor Sutton, and this is Alexander's Mother, as well as the Mother of Johnnie and, of course, Keys." Mack, unable to speak, saw her nod and, reaching out to touch her hand, found himself embracing her instead.

Then, she went at once to her son. "He's going to die, isn't he?" she asked, looking up at all of those gathered about.

Doctor Sutton gestured to a man standing just outside, introducing him as the surgeon, saying, "We're going to do everything we can to save his life, and must at once operate. This room must be prepared for surgery."

"May I stay here with him, please, for just a moment more?" Mrs. Parker asked.

Dr. Sutton nodded but led Ynez and Mack from the room. There, they met Joe, Elliot, Wriggs and the deVols.

"Mr. Armstrong, your wife is just there, to the right, with Johnnie." At first Elliot could imagine what she meant. He had not done well with anything this real and this horrible since the War. Then he got it: she was talking about his sister, Nolie.

"We want to know how all of this happened!" Elliot said, with tears of rage in his eyes.

Ynez tried to speak but then, with a gesture of her head toward the stairway, indicated Bruno's presence there. Coming forward, he began speaking at once, softly but firmly, taking them aside.

"They got into the cover flat at the Club deVol and worked your right hand man over to such a degree that his lungs are shot. His clavicle was completely crushed and his neck possibly broken. You just heard. He probably won't make it."

Baby asked, "But Johnnie? Where's Johnnie? What happ—"

"Same thing. She went across the street to save him. They threw her in their car and Keys hopped a taxi, forced the cabbie into chasing them, apparently took over driving it, smashed the cab into their car and pulled Johnnie out. This was down by the fish market wharf about three this morning. The crumbs got cindered. Their car blew up."

Wriggs stopped him. "What! Johnnie—did she—?"

"No. He got her out just before..." (Mack kept shaking his head, trying to speak.) Bruno pressed on, "No hospital down here would take these two, of course. So Keys Parker and Miss Harrison figured this arrangment out here. She called Ynez up at Great Neck at about 3:20. I was out with her because we found that someobody had broken in...Mack! Listen to me—are you o.k.?"

Mack leaned against the balustrade. "This is all my fault. What have I done—"

Baby held on to him. "Stop it, Mack. We just have to make sure these two kids are going to be all right."

"Mrs. deVol!" Dr. Sutton leaned out into the hallway. "Would you please lend us your expertise at once?" Baby left them.

"Listen, all you," Bruno was definite. "Elliot, you go in and see to your sister and Johnnie—but first of all, hear me out. No matter whose fault this was, it's affecting us all." His voice was lowered to a whisper. "I had my boys down at the wharf where the car caught fire just after 3:30. The cops hadn't even gotten there yet, so I had 'em roll both the car and the taxi into the river. That way we'll stall for time."

Ynez said, "We'll go in and see Johnnie now…Nolie has been in there the whole while."

As Baby was preparing to assist, she also put on her mask of courage. Worn so very often throughout her life, she had never allowed another soul—not even Deucie—to see what lay behind it—the acknowledgment that death is ever waiting.

Looking over at Mrs. Parker, who sat with her hands folded in prayer, the two exchanged a look, and as Alexander's bandages were being cut away, Mrs. Parker threw her head back and closed her eyes. What they had done to her son was not human.

Dr. Sutton touched Mrs. Parker lightly. "Will you step out, now, please?" Resigned, she turned and went.

Baby looked down at what was left of Alexander Parker, his young body now exposed. What would cause one mortal to do this to another? she asked herself.

Johnnie was propped up and fully conscious, with Nolie sitting on the edge of the bed, holding her right hand, which was only partially bandaged.

"Don't try to speak—" Nolie whispered to her as Mack and Joe joined Elliot and Wriggs around her. Keys was called to be with his Mother at this moment, and silently left the room.

But Johnnie insisted. "I'm…just…all banged up—that's all," she uttered hoarsely.

"—but my brother—"

Nolie looked up at Elliot, shaking her head. He said simply, "It's o.k., honey. He's going to be o.k." Johnnie seemed reassured and closed her eyes.

A nurse standing opposite Nolie made a gesture. She must sleep now and should, for a time, be left alone.

In the hall with the others, Nolie's voice trembled. "I'm going to kill whoever did this," she announced with tremendous ire. "And don't think I won't."

Her expression changed then because, looking past the men who were gathered around her, she saw Mrs. Parker, standing with Ynez and Keys. Walking toward her, she held out her hands.

Mrs. Parker, raising her head, said to Mack, "He's loved you and your wife more than anyone else he ever knew." She paused, holding back a sob. "...and I know you how much you loved him."

"So much. So very much," Ynez whispered, as Mack put his arms around them both, embracing them in all his bigness. No one spoke for a minute or two until, coming up the stairs, they saw Annabelle Harrison. In her artist's smock, with her hair coiled in braids, she was possessed of that eternal compassion only a woman has.

Elliot met her there. "God, Miss Harrison, we can never thank you."

"We're all here together," she answered. "And that is what counts most."

She then turned to Mrs. Parker. "My room adjoins Alexander's. We can wait in there."

Threading past them, she took her down the corridor and was joined by Keys.

Mack stood apart from the rest and slowly walked, alone, toward a window at the end of the hall. There he stood, engulfed in the darkness, looking out at the night. Joe went to him.

"I did this this to them," Mack wept, "—to all of them."

• • •

One hour later, at April's end in that Year of our Lord, 1928, Alexander Parker died. He was only 22.

His funeral was held in Harlem, with Elliot's orchestra accompanying the choir. Far from reporters, police, unknown enemies, and all of those who would not understand—all of those he held most dear came to bid Alexander adieu.

Down on Fulton Street, Bruno went about the kind of work he knew so well with quiet and solitary swiftness—making sure anybody who was around the night his boys dumped the taxi, the getaway car and two charred bodies into the river were given hush money. In the midst of all this, he was told that Blanche King had completely vanished.

A police report described a large black man spotted overtaking a taxicab driver near Fifth Avenue and Forty-Sixth Street. The driver never came forward to admit or deny it. Between Annabelle's millions and Mack's unlimited coffers, he was more than well paid off, purchasing a new hack, and sworn by Bruno to secrecy. It was lucky that Keys was not still in his major domo's uniform when he saw his sister being thrown into the car or the matter would've been traced to the Club deVol.

As it was, Deucie and Baby closed the club down for a week and all was quiet. Annabelle Harrison postponed her gallery opening and, at the Daly house in Great Neck, everything was changed. It would never be the same again without Alexander's presence. The house's sanctity had been violated by the break-in—naturally, not reported because of the dangerous situations which now defined Mack and Ynez's very life.

Strangely, nothing had been taken, with the exception of the bundle of letters from the Colonel, once encased in the ivory box. Mack decided to call in an expert on the matter, and that expert was Joe.

On the day he and Bruno returned to the Great Neck house, Ynez was in her bedroom with the door closed. There she had remained, alone for that entire week following Alexander's funeral, looking over his school books, putting in perfect order his notebooks and tests which he had so proudly brought home to her.

It fell to Mack to rally the day servants into working even harder in an attempt to replace the gap made by Alexander. Mack felt utterly desolate. There would never be another who could so easily and so lovingly take care of all Mack's secret business dealings, keep Ynez in tow, and make them both laugh the way that Alexander did. Mack now continually damned himself for Alexander Parker's death and Johnnie's beating. Repeated telephone calls during which Elliot, Baby, Deucie, and even Bruno attempted to pull him out of it did no good.

In his own bedroom on that sultry May afternoon two weeks after the funeral, Joe watched him burying his head in his pillows, not knowing what to do or say. Finally it came to him, "It comes wid duh job, Mack. We all is in on it, and dere's no turnin' back. We all coulda backed out, but we didn't, now did we?"

Mack turned over. "Sure, Joe, isn't that how it is in gangland? But I don't head up any gang and I'm not an underworld boss who expects my friends to end up in constant jeopardy!"

"You better t'ink again, kid," Joe said, putting his thumb under Mack's chin and lifting his face so he could look into his eyes. "Even if youse and me hadn't hit it off, you still woulda been taken down by O'Couran an' his mob, and you still woulda bin in the middle ah danger, an' criminal stuff, an' possible vi-lence an' murder." (Joe saw tears in his eyes.) "Now I ain't stoppin' dere nei'der. What you did wid your booze, whether you wuz forced to do it or not, still ain't legal, and nor is runnin' a speak, for dat matter, see? All of us is in on dis 'cause it fits us like a glove, and dat's it. Nobody would be woykin' for yuz if dey wasn't duh type to wanna do it."

"But I don't want to live this way, Joe! Do you?"

Joe sat down on the bed. "Hey! Me? I'm a lower East Side Wop who wuz born into it. I'm queer and I'm happy. All cuzza youse. Duh rest of it—well, I jus' figger it's part of duh game, see? For me, Mack, I wouldn't have it no udder way but you an' me!" And Joe smiled.

"Yes, but, Joe, Alexander was beaten to death! And Johnnie just barely survived! And up North, the Colonel is getting his end of it, too. It's so terrible."

"You gotta fight back. Please. Dat's why you got me, pal!"

Mack sat up and then went to the window. A thunder storm was gathering power over the Sound. In the garden, he saw Ynez, who had at last left her room, a basket at her side, holding a bouquet for Alexander's grave which she'd just picked. She'd put on a black organdy picture hat, and was trailing yards of black chiffon behind her—a solitary figure there, beautiful and lonely on that cloudy day.

Earlier that she told him that she was going with Mrs. Parker, Johnnie and Nolie to visit Alexander's grave at the cemetary in Harlem...then something about having to keep an appointment with the columnist from the *Graphic* who'd written about her.

"You'll never guess who telephoned me today, Mack," she had said to him just earlier.

"I can't stand any more surprises, Ynez," he'd muttered.

"That gossip monger, Walter Winchell."

"For what reason?"

Ynez had sighed. "God only knows. He wants to meet me at the Broadway Child's."

"What a spot!" Mack replied with irony. "—well, suit yourself."

She had gone ahead, toward her bedroom. "It's too much for me to think about just now," he'd heard her say as she shut the door and softly left him there.

Just afterward, when Bruno stopped by, Mack seemed to rally due to Joe's heart-to-heart. He got up, fixed his tie and went down to greet him. "Did Ynez tell you that she was going to meet with that reporter from the *Graphic*?"

Bruno answered, "That's why I'm here. I'll watch her back, don't worry."

Mack drew a deep breath, standing in the foyer, both brothers watching him. "I'm going to sell this place," Mack announced abruptly. "It's just not the same anymore without Alexander. Elliot, Nolie and Johnnie have to get out of their apartment in less than thirty days now, so I've made up my mind—I'm going to buy their building. I don't care how much it costs. Ynez can have her own place enitrely. And Joe and I can be together." Bruno and Joe followed him into the living room.

"I won't say I'm all that surprised," Bruno said, making himself a drink. "It's jake by me. Ynez hates it here since she realized she was being watched.

Then the robbery, and with Alexander gone. I just don't blame you."

Joe added, "Yeah, a whole new clean slate, as dey say!" putting his arm about Mack's shoulders. "It's gonna be just slick tuh be wid youse! You mean we're gonna have our very own place, just like a coupla fairies?"

Mack managed a laugh. "Yes, Joe, and we'll get Bootsie Carstairs to help you fix it up, too! Whatever you want."

Bruno left them, two drinks in hand. "I'll go up and see how Ynez is doing while you two fairies plan your new digs."

Mack said quietly to Joe as soon as Bruno had gone, "He's not such a bad egg these days. I wonder what's gotten into him?"

"Listen, when you cut dat deal wid him so's he could make dough of the O'Couran scam, a lotta his troubles was over. Pop left our rackets in a kinda mess, and he really needed some big new job to pull us outta it. See, he's jus' grad'ally takin' over. Pop ain't got long."

"—but he seems to be getting a little soft, Joe! Is he falling for Ynez?"

"He tol' me he feels like he's gotta take charge ah her. See, he's goin' up tuh tell her duh news right now. Gotta be foyst, yuh know. You didn't tell her yet, did juh—about giving up dis dump?" Mack shook his head. "See? What'd I tell yuh?" Then Joe thought a little, adding, "'Course he also sez she's a great lay. My brudder used'ta go for very common blisters, yuh know, Mack. She's bin good for him!"

"Speaking of common blisters, what about Blanche King? Has she turned up yet?" Mack continued as he went around opening the draperies which Ynez still insisted on keeping closed.

"We got duh boys tuh comb duh boroughs lookin' for her. No sign ah her, high or low. She never did dat title search on duh 68th Street buildin', an' she wasn't keepin' up wid collectin' Bruno's protection payments neither. All she really done was to put tugedder dat business plan for O'Couran an' his control over duh Moran's Elixir racket."

"She probably went over to his gang, don't you think? That's common in the underworld, I hear."

"Dat's a common occurrence in whut we calls life." Joe's eyes rolled up at the ceiling. Would he never get it?

Upstairs, Ynez was heard talking to Bruno. From the tone of her voice, he apparently had told her of the move. She sounded cheered.

Bruno came down the stairs with Ynez. "I'll drive her up to Harlem, then cover her while she meets with this Winchell character, then meet up with you both. O.k.?"

"We'll be at the rehearsal hall right nearby with Elliot and Nolie. I want to break the news to them person," Mack answered as Ynez entered the drawing room in a black suit. "Ynez? I take it you've heard?"

Holding out her hands toward Mack, she nodded. "Yes, Bruno just told me. But I don't want you to do this just because of me, Mack."

"It's best for us all, I think." He took her hands in his. "This house wasn't ever much of a home, was it?"

"You tried. And I did what I could, too. I think it's a good idea." Turning, she quickly left, taking Bruno's arm rather suddenly.

Mack waited until the front doors shut. "She does blame me for this whole thing, Joe." He gestured, taking in the whole house itself. "Not just Alexander's death, or Johnnie—but everything. She just never had things the way her dreams demanded. It makes me wonder if she'll want a divorce soon."

"Nuttin' dat dame does or is would surprise me, Mack." Joe paused. "She's my compy-tition! But I do know she loves yuh just as much as I do, pal."

They headed for the library. "Joey, what in this world would I do without you? Couldn't she be talked into a divorce by Bruno—now that he's had this change of heart, do you suppose?"

"Yuh mean so he could grab her alimony?" Joe again paused. "Well, he may be pretty low, but I don't t'ink he's dat low. What's in here?—udder dan books?"

"Just books Joe.That's what it's here for. This is why I asked you to come out. Now look, I kept the Colonel's letters here, in this box. "

Mack showed Joe the large, exquisite antique ivory casque on the big library table at the center of the room. He then pointed out its lid, which was overturned on the floor nearby. "I haven't touched a thing since the break-in. Only his letters were taken. Nothing else was moved or even touched. They got in by those French doors over there."

Walking to the doors, pulling back the drapery, he noticed that one of the small, leaded panes had been neatly cracked then removed. In this manner, the thief merely reached in and unlatched the door.

"Somebody had tuh have cased duh jernt foyst. How would dey know duh letters was in dat box dere in duh foyst place?"

"I can't imagine! Calvin gave it to Ynez and me as a wedding gift. I think it was a casket of some kind. Perhaps for a baby. Some dead little princess. Anyway, it seemed a fitting place in which to keep them."

"Jeez. Dat guy's got screwy taste! But in dese letters did he spill duh beans, so tuh speak?" Joe asked, trying to reach his hand through the lead frame which had held the broken pane of glass.

"Oh, sure. He poured his heart out to me. Always one thing or another…in anguish about his wife being condemned and executed as a spy for Germany…So," Mack looked wearily at him, "what's your take on this…crime scene?"

"I sure as Hell can't get *my* mitts t'rough here. Hafta be a small kinda guy—or a goyl. I myself wuz never in dis room before, as yuz knows. You ackchullee *read* all dese books!" Joe looked all around the room, then at Mack in astonishment.

"Well, sure, when I had time. Now, Joe, come on, keep thinking!"

"Okee-dough-kee! Now let's go back to when we stayed overnight at dih Tumble On Inn. Dat night, when we wuz goin' over duh room where duh quack doctor slep' and I found dat l'il pin, we did note dat Bootsie Carstairs' stoodeo wuz turned over, too. I'm puttin 'em bot' tuggedder. Just' watch me now!" Joe, smiling from ear to ear, then commenced to humming, his hands shoved in his pockets.

"Say, don't hold out on me! What's your theory, Sherlock?"

"Well, you saw how he draws up every single room foyst before he goes an' decorates 'em, right? Didn't you say he did up dis whole jernt here?"

Mack looked with admiration and amazement at his boyfriend. "—you think the doctor lifted the designs for this place when he stayed up at Bootsie's!"

Joe nodded eagerly. "He mustah. Orchid said he was gonna check duh designs against duh inventory—and we ain't spoken to him since."

"That just might be it, Joey! By God! I'll bet you're right. Good man! Come on, we've got to go see Elliot and Nolie."

Joe took a good long look at him. Somewhere behind that sad smile of his, there seemed to be a glimmer of hope.

At the rehearsal hall on Eighth Avenue, Mack and Joe were treated to some new songs and dances while waiting for the Armstrongs to take their break. The place was filled with chorus boys and girls, rehearsing some sort of routine with Elliot scowling in the middle of it all, simply going through the motions. It appeared that this new diversion, set to open in Atlantic City the first week of June, was more than a revue—it was a full-fledged musical comedy, produced by the impresario "King" Tuthill.

It was Tut who had formerly owned the Daly house at Great Neck. As he had acquired even greater fame and fortune, "King Tut" had looked to even more palatial surroundings, moving his fragile, phobic wife and their two kids to a modernistic pile farther out on the Island.

Sitting importantly before a table littered with sheet music, scrawling away at various scripts with vehemence and puffing away at a cigar, Tut (known as the Broadway Time-Bomb) seemed ready to explode at any minute. As Elliot wearily waved to Mack and Joe, wiping his brow with his neck scarf, shaking his head in despair, Nolie sent unseen daggers in the direction of Tuthill.

At last the break came. It had grown so humid, due to the pending cloudburst, that the cast headed at once for the stairs and for some fresh air. Nolie rolled her eyes as King Tuthill motioned them toward him.

"It's mahvelous, kiddies!" he was saying as they approached. "This new gimmick will make it a sure hit!" He then addressed Nolie, "Wanna have lunch with me, dollink?"

She shook her head. "We've got some friends here, thanks anyway, Tut."

"Ah! Mack Daly!" Tut shook Mack's hand as if he were cranking up a car. "Love your new speak! And your wife, too! She should really be in the follies—so beauty-full!"

"Thanks," Mack replied. "I appreciated your coming to the opening of the deVol. Too bad your wife was ill."

"Always ill!" He shook his head. "I wish to Hell she'd snap out of it sooner or later 'cause it just means more worry for me." He shrugged and went on his way, with something of a leer directed at his leading lady.

As Nolie and Elliot gathered up their belongings, she wise-cracked, "Is he kidding? He keeps her perpetually drunk so that he can screw every chorus girl from here to Jersey City!"

"Nolie!" Elliot laughed. "You be nice now."

"If you can't guess what's in the back of that nasty man's head by now, I'm here to tell you that it is none other than my ass!" she fumed, tugging at her cloche.

As they walked toward the stairs, she related to Mack and Joe how the Broadway Time-Bomb's two children, Junior and Peaches, both in their early 'teens, were doing anything but behaving. Utterly neglected by both parents! And Gladys Tuthill, a one-time great beauty herself, was rumoured to be bed-ridden.

"Well, I hope it's not in *his* bed!" Elliot added, always siding with fellow drunks. "He's nastiness personified. Got one thing alone on his mind. And now he's changed the name of the show to 'Hotcha Honeymoon' and had the whole thing rewritten to dirty it up!"

"That's his angle on bringing in the crowds," Nolie interrupted.

"As if we need 'em! He's got my sister here and I in bed together through a lot of it now." Elliot, looking around the rehearsal to make sure they were alone, saw that the pianist was just leaving, waving moodily to them.

Nolie took over. "It's about us getting married, and what happens *right afterward*!" She breathed deeply. "It's just plain dirty. And I don't like it one bit." Tut was famous for his naughty shows. "Originally, it was a cute little thing called 'Powder My Back'—about our start in show business. Nice! Well, then he decided that I possessed that mysterious quality called It, and if we detailed the more nasty events of the honeymoon which my brother and I, of course, never partook in, it would be the sex-hit of the season." She rattled on a mile a minute. "I now go through half the show in my undies getting mauled by Elliot the moment the curtian goes up. So all at once the magazines want sex stuff about us too, naturally."

"This, on top of getting kicked out of our dump!" Elliot concluded.

"Well, I think I can solve that problem—" and with that Mack told them of his plan to buy their building. Nolie, burying her head in his arms, sobbed away and Elliot rose, walked around in circles, speechless, then wiped a couple of tears from his cheek and started giggling.

"Don't you just love him, Joe!" he whimpered.

"I shoor do," Joe answered. "You gotta love a guy like dat!"

Mack looked at their faces. If only he could see this kind of happiness surrounding everybody he loved all the time. If only he could stop that machine that churned out evil day and night. If only he knew where it was hiding.

• • • • •

CHAPTER XXII

THE DOCTOR IS IN

Walter Winchell was seated at the Broadway Child's, a meeting place for queer theatrical types, armed with notepad, coffee and cigarettes, when Ynez entered. Bruno waited outside for three full minutes then took a place at the counter near enough to overhear what was about to be said.

"Mrs. Daly, I thank you for coming," he said. "Won't you have something?" Ynez ordered iced tea. "Now, I'm not going to beat around the bush with you, Mrs. Daly.There's a whispering campaign going on about you and your crowd. It wasn't started by anyone in particular, it just got going around town and before you knew it, everybody was talking…"

"About what?" Ynez flatly asked.

"—about your relationship to some shady stuff, I'm afraid, Mrs. Daly. Like the death of that Negro boy, for instance. He worked for you, didn't he?"

"Yes." (Same tone of voice.)

"He was murdered, wasn't he?"

"No." (Same tone of voice.)

"Wasn't there some dirty business across the street from your club on 46th Street? Didn't another Negro overtake a cabbie and make him follow a car down to Fulton Street which held another Negro—a young girl?"

"What does this have to do with anything at all, Mr. Winchell?" Her iced tea arrived in a frosty glass, matching her tone.

"Well, if you must know, Mrs. Daly, people around town are saying things. This other Negro—the big one—does he work for Miss Annabelle Harrison, the Society blueblood?"

"Why don't you ask her?" Ynez daintily sipped her tea through a pair of straws.

"She's a bit out of my league, I'm afraid," Winchell snickered, waving to a passerby.

"And I'm not?" Ynez lifted one brow, looking straight through him.

"Well, let's put it this way, Mrs. Daly, if you help me out with this thing, I could be very good for you."

"In what way, Mr. Winchell?"

"Well, I could put you on the map! Make a real item out of you! Every day you could be in print, in fact—if you like."

"That piece you wrote about me a while back wasn't at all nice, Mr. Winchell. I don't think I need any more of that kind of publicity."

His voice rose, and he gave her a narrow look. "Well! Then why'd you come here today?"

"—just to see what you were after." She paused.

"I'm after some answers, Mrs. Daly. In exchange for launching you."

"Go on."

"Well, it so happens that there are those people involved in your crowd who just might be getting very hurt. Not by me, or by anybody in particular—but only by their actions. Their behavior, don't you get it? It'll ruin them—the way they're acting."

Ynez decided to take a chance. Slowly she said, "Describe this behavior, Mr. Winchell."

"Well, for one thing, running all about with Negroes! And for another, and here's one for you, Mrs. Daly, getting in with pansies—and gangsters. Not knowing where to draw the line, you see."

Ynez wondered if Winchell and the detective sent up to the Armstrongs' had exchanged notes. "Pasnsies and gangsters, my, my. People just eat that stuff up, don't they, Mr. Winchell? That's what keeps your electricity on!"

Winchell threw his head back and laughed. "You got me there, sister! The reason I asked you here today is only because if anybody knows about the real dirt, it's gotta be you! That bunch you run with is all sewn up tight as a drum, though. I can't get a thing on 'em. But, oh, boy! If I could! If I could!"

"If you could, what then! Of whom are you speaking?"

Still laughing, he replied eagerly, "O.k.! here it is; what's the story behind Elliot and Nolie Armstrong?"

Ynez proffered her cigarette to be lit, mentally congratulating herself on her instincts. "Well, let's see. Elliot shaves only every other day and Nolie is wearing handkerchief hems this season."

Winchell's eyes became mere slits. "Cute. So you won't talk, huh?" (Ynez smiled, cat-like.) "Well, whadda you know about the Tuthill bunch—Gladys, King Tut and his two brats?"

Ynez was taken aback. That was the set that Mrs. Mack Daly had made every effort to avoid by aligning herself with Annabelle Harrison! "Oh, that Broadway crowd—well, only that she's an invalid, I guess."

"Oh, come now, Mrs. Daly. I got it from one of her maids that she's under this doctor's care who's cast a kind of spell on her."

"What?" Ynez sat up. "Do you know this doctor's name?"

"Say! I'm the one asking the questions here. It doesn't matter—gee, are you pale all of a sudden! Something wrong?" Winchell, leaning forward, patted her gloved hand, which she at once withdrew.

"It's possible that this doctor is a very, very dangerous man," Ynez murmured.

"How do you know that?" Winchell demanded.

Ynez felt she had to say something, to do something about this awful fiend Mack had told her about. "If you want to print anything at all, Mr. Winchell, write that anyone who is falling prey to a certain quack doctor in this town must at once report him to the authorities!" Ynez confided, leaning over the table.

"All right! Now we're getting someplace. You're not telling me something, Mrs. Daly! This is real dirt here."

"I've only heard that Gladys Tuthill drinks very heavily due to her husband's endless cheating—everyone knows that by now! " She stopped, feeling Walter Winchell's eyes burrowing through her. "I'm not lying. I had no idea she was in the clutches of this certain doctor. I am horribly shocked."

"Didn't you know that Tut married her for her money?" Winchell pursued. "—so he could produce those shows of his?"

Ynez nodded. "Of course. When they moved from Great Neck, it was because *she* built that new house for him. All in the way of ostentation, I would imagine."

"Did you imagine that whatever money he made on those shows went to paying for operations on the gals he got–well—You Know What?" Winchell was by now leaning so far over the table toward Ynez, his chin was almost touching the coffee cup.

"Of course. That's no news." (But it was.)

"But what would you say if I told you that Gladys Tuthill was flat on her ass broke, Mrs. Daly? What would you say about *that*?"

"I'd say both that doctor and King Tut bled her for every penny!" she found herself suddenly saying.

Winchell now pointed at her with ferocity. "But how, Mrs. Daly—how do you know that?"

"Mr. Winchell, I find that certain people who go in for such things always get taken for a ride." Ynez covered her surprise with the veil of sophistication.

Winchell was shaking his head now, lighting a fresh cigarette from the one he was just putting out, thoroughly agitated and excited. His eyes gleamed.

"Uh-uh. No soap, sweetheart! You come clean with me, Mrs. Daly, and I'll give you a story that'll blow this town wide open."

"We shall be in touch, Mr. Winchell!" Ynez purred, rising unexpectedly.

"Promise?" Winchell was insistent, also getting up, bowing.

"I never promise, but only *tempt*!" and with those words, she managed to get out of there, but fast.

Ynez waited for Bruno across the street, shadowed by the confines of a theatre marquee, watching Walter Winchell leaving Child's with a satisfied look about his mouth.

"Well, toots, all I can say is you've got that thing!" Bruno looked at her, marveling. "He sure has a hard-on for you."

"Yeah, and he can stroke it himself, too," Ynez answered. "Can you imagine that poor Gladys Tuthill and the shape she must be in!"

Bruno's eyes narrowed. "No, but you can."

"Come on, it's starting to rain. We're supposed to be meeting Mack at the rehearsal hall."

By the time they got there, the Heavens had opened up over New York. Thunder and lightning turned Broadway into a chaotic jumble of people under sagging, soaked newspapers dashing into traffic, umbrellas sheltering those lucky few who'd remembered them.

Bruno and Ynez arrived only slightly damp, finding Joe sitting on the steps just inside the rehearsal hall offices, while Mack plugged nickels into the nearby pay telephone. Just above them, dozens of tapping feet were causing the floor to shake.

"—been on the blower for a half hour now," Joe told them. "Talkin' to his lawyer. Decided he'd better put in to buy the apartment buildin' pronto."

Just then, Mack emerged from the phone booth. "Wait'll you all hear this! H'lo Ynez, Bruno…oh! Just let me sit down! Talk about dollars and sense! Nonsense it seems!" He sat on the steps beside Joe and lit up a cigarette.

"Are you in some sort of financial trouble, Mack?" Ynez almost meekly asked, standing over him.

"Not financial trouble, thank God—real estate trouble—and not from having enough of it, but too much! It seems that Colonel Connaught somehow put himself in charge of some of my affairs when we were vacationing in Europe right after our marriage, Ynez. I don't know if you recall, but he and I had a joint bank account then, in order to initially help him out of going under—due to his purchase of the land which The Slaves of Mary now occupy."

"I do, yes. But wasn't it closed?" Ynez asked.

"Not at all. Even though I bought the land and manse outright for him. Anyway, he used the account and my name to buy that place on 68th Street, known as *La Maison*!"

Joe was confused—Ynez and Bruno clearly surprised.

Bruno asked Mack, "You mean to say he owned that joint and ran that racket out of it?"

"No. No. He bought the place on 68th Street in my name! I own it. My attorney just told me he has all the papers on it, with my name on them, and Connaught's underneath as Power of Attorney. When Ynez and I were abroad, you see, he arranged this all through some lawyer who has since been disbarred and has suitably vanished. He never told me anything about it. I'm completely shocked."

Joe spoke up. "Yuh mean he rigged it when you wuz away, so that you would buy dat buildin' where all dat shit went on? Where Ynez here woyked and where Lady Lee got her feet separated from her?"

"Yes, Joe. And all this time, I've owned it without knowing it. I still own it! See? That's what I've only just found out about!"

"But, Mack," Ynez said. "There couldn't have been enough money left in that account to buy the 68th Street place."

Bruno waved his hand in the air. "No. No. Betcha anything money was pumped into that account in order make the sale happen. They just needed Mack's name and his credit, was all. It's an old game."

"Yeah," Joe said. "I gets it. You wuz a shill, used as a front." (Mack just shook his head in disbelief.) "You t'ink mebbee duh Coynull's daughter put him up to dis?"

"Possibly. Anyway, my lawyer said the building was, and is, mine, but blessedly, that business called *La Maison* had nothing to do with my name. When it got closed down, they never could trace any of those people. Apparently, it's been empty all this time. Two years."

Bruno thought otherwise, "What makes you think it's empty, Mack?"

• • •

Now and then, the rain would cease. Before them, the house on 68th Street still looked much as it had whenYnez did her dirty shimmy there two years before. Heavy black velvet draperies still covered every single window, now coated with a fine layer of the city's dust and grime. Beneath the front steps, the little book shoppe' s sign still swung eerily in the wind. It seemed uninhabited, except by evil.

Ynez, looking out from inside Bruno's touring car, said it gave her an awful case of the willies. This former repository of depravity-for-profit and even murder was more foreboding than ever on that stormy late afternoon in May.

Joe was the first to get out, dashing up to the front entryway, attained by six steps, and encircled by a glass and wrought iron bay. It was littered with newspapers and trash. The door was locked, Joe turned to say, but just then he noticed something within the enclosure, amid the dead leaves. Peanut shells. Lots of them. He motioned to Bruno.

"Looks like we found Blanche!" Joe called, going up the steps as Bruno followed. "Should we break in?"

"Too difficult and too obvious," Bruno whispered. "Let's go around back."

"Shouldn't *we* be doing something, Mack? It's stopped raining." Ynez, there on the sidewalk now, tugged at Mack's collar, seeing the brothers going around the mews to the back of the house.

"Do you really want to go back in there, Ynez? After all that's happened?"

"Well, I know the whole house better than any of you. I'm game!"

Following close behind Bruno and Joe, they proceeded gingerly down the mews which was flanked by the carriage house to their left. Upon reaching it, Ynez rubbed some of the grime away from the panes of glass above the doors.

"Mack! Look! It's the brown sedan that's been following me!"

"You're certain?"

"Of course! I memorized the license plate!"

Just across the cobbled drive, they saw Bruno and Joe, hard at work on the door to the kitchens with Joe's lock set. It was easily opened, but as he pushed the door forward they discovered some furniture had been shoved in front of it. "Sure sign somebody's in dere!" Joe commented.

"Wait. Look here, boys—" Ynez indicated a stairway to the left of the kitchen door, dropping down past the street level, revealing yet another entrance to the house. A pile of dead leaves and branches had accumulated over the past two years. Suddenly it was growing dark again, and rain threatened again.

Joe went down the steps on tip-toes, as Bruno, Mack and Ynez stood above them. As he descended and lit a match, there was a slight crunching noise. "Shit!" Joe whispered. "What was dat? It ain't me!"

Mack bent over. "I stepped on something. Hold on."

Feeling about the cobbled drive, he picked up a handful of debris. "I've got about a dozen peanut shells here!"

"Blanche is in there, you can bet on it. Either dead or alive," Bruno hissed. "And if she's not dead yet, she will be soon."

"I got it open!" Joe called out softly, pulling a small flashlight from his back trouser pocket. "Now take it easy and follow me."

Inside with Joe leading, they were treated to a somewhat dusty medieval torture chamber which no one had enjoyed in quite some time. There was no sign of life.

"This is where they birched the clients," Ynez explained. "Come on, this way." Continuing stealthily on, now through an ornate arch, she led them into Lady Lee's Oriental theatre of sin.

"This is where she did her stuff with those feet of hers," Ynez whispered.

"Jeez," Joe breathed. "I just got duh creeps real bad. And I still don't undertstan' what she did wid her—"

"SSshhh! Listen!" Bruno waved his hand, as they proceeded out into a narrow corridor. "What was that?" Just above them…voices…as if inside a cave.

Opening the door a crack, the voices now became completely audible.

Ynez motioned to them. "There's a laundry chute over here. You can hear everything going on upstairs." Guiding Joe's flashlight, she opened its small door just a bit.

They heard:

"I believe in him! He is my master!"

"But just how much more pain can you endure?"

"—but you see how close I am, don't you? I believe I look quite like the male member of the species now! You see how my breasts are just as good as gone! It is only a matter of time until my manhood rears its head! Then, very soon, my beloved, all our efforts will prove themselves and the world will genuflect! Genuflect, I say!"

A strong upper-class British accent was evident, but the voice itself was strained and tremulous.

"Not until we get *him* out of the way. And it's got to be soon, too. We can make it look like a typical underworld murder."

("That's Blanche's voice, all right—" Bruno whispered.)

"Cut that stuff! My Master will have ingenious ideas for his disposal!" said the other, with sarcasm in her voice, her accent clipped, a guttural laugh following. "Everything would've been so easy had he not come in on it! How I hate him, Blanche! Still, I don't want anything traced to us. You and your gangland techniques! Oh! Leave it all behind, will you? We're past that! Ours is a messianic manifest destiny!" Again that laugh.

Joe whispered, "What's all dat crap mean?"

"Ssshh. The other one—it's Violet Connaught," Mack said.

"Tonight, if he doesn't come up with the money he's taken…" Blanche's voice this time. "—then that will be the end of him!" A horn was heard suddenly honking outside.

"There's our darling Trevor! Hurry, Blanche! Get dressed!"

"Jeez! Dey was havin' *nookie*?" Joe whispered.

In a short time, the pair could be heard going toward the kitchen by the clatter of their heels. Through the floorboards, the mixed aromas of heady perfume and ether leaked. A kerosense light came on from what seemed to be the larder off the kitchen—then, the creaking of hinges, a door opening, then slamming shut.

"Trap door…" Ynez whispered. "—goes underneath and into the carriage house."

Bruno was out of there at once, ahead of Joe and Mack. "I'm gonna follow them. You three meet me later at the Armstrongs'."

Waiting until the car had picked them up, he proceeded down the mews and out into the street, with the others following. Bruno then ran ahead, jumping in his own car and slowly pulling out after the sedan.

Mack reasoned that the driver of the brown sedan had walked into the mews from the street, unlocked the carriage house, backed the car out, then sounded the horn.

"I wonder if there's anybody else in here?" Ynez whispered, as Joe pulled forth his gun.

"My guess is dere ain't—unless it's a corpse or two! Come on, let's look aroun'."

Because the electricity had been shut off, the place was dotted with old-fashioned kerosense lamps. It still looked much the same as Ynez had remembered it, with nothing touched. Even the office, once occupied by Baby, was the same. Mack picked up the phone. Out of service.

"Well, at least there's one bill I'm not still paying!" he quipped. They proceeded up the grand stairway, Mack now with the flashlight, Ynez holding onto them both, urging them on, familiar with the building's design.

It was there they found evidence of the place being presently occupied. In one room, far at the back and out of sight from the street, a supply of tinned food, a burner for cooking, and some china was placed here and there. Another room revealed sleeping quarters, with medicine bottles and hypodermic needles everywhere. Neatly laid out on a chair was an army uniform, just the right size for Violet.

Mack commented, "The Colonel must've given her this. Sad, isn't it?"

"Oh, I'm weepin'," Joe replied.

Going toward the back of the house, Ynez showed them what was once the master bedroom, now turned into a kind of meeting room. Someone had dragged a refactory table there, with chairs around it. Stacks of notebooks, journals, calendars all sat in a row. The bundle of letters stolen from Mack and a very well accomplished watercolor sketch of the Daly library lay at the center of the table.

"Joe! You were right. Look at this design, and right there–look—Bootsie has drawn the ivory box!" Mack proudly smiled at Joe, for a moment forgetting his dilemma.

"See? I ain't no master-minded crimmy-null, but I do know my stuff! Dem small hands which got into yer place belonged to Violet Connaught. But what in Hell kinda gag is dis anyways?"

He sifted through the piles of papers with the end of a pencil. "Must be a big-time black-mail racket or sump'in."

"Look here," Ynez pointed to a large scroll on the table, "a diagram showing the cycles of the moon. and some charts, used by astrologists."

Meanwhile, Mack was pushing aside a heap of papers, revealing a photograph of a man holding an orb and sceptre, dressed in long white robes and wearing a a crown. He looked like a middle-aged college professor, except for his eyes, which were those of a madman.

"Get a gander at dat guy!" Joe focused the flashlight on the picture.

Mack looked closely. "It looks like a fellow either dressed up for Hallowe'en, or some kind of secret society rally. But I'll wager it's none other than Doctor Soames!" Folding the picture, he slipped it into his jacket pocket.

"You know, boys," Ynez whispered. "I've seen a lot of things in my day which were Goddammed peculiar, but this really takes the cake!"

A thunderclap and a flash of lightning, accompanied by shrill cries of fear, caused them all to jump. Startled, staring wide-eyed at one another, Ynez and Joe clung to Mack. Barely breathing, they heard the cries again.

Joe whispered, "Anny-mulls. Somewheres in here! I've hoyd dem kinda noises before…at duh zoo!"

Joe led the way to the back, where they found themselves in a conservatory. Flashing his light on a large cage which occupied the entire length of the room, they saw looking back at them, blinking and whining in fear, two very large apes.

"Monkey gland suppliers," Mack commented, as Joe fed one a handy banana.

Ynez was transfixed by the pair, who now calmed down and seemed to feel the same way about her. "Oh, Mack! The poor things! Look how sweet their eyes are!"

"They've no doubt been worked on. How cruel!" Mack added.

"Looks like Blanche graduated from squirrels to gorillas!" Joe commented, approaching the cage.

"Joe! Joe! What are you doing?"

"I'm pickin' dere lock so dey get all go home to duh jungle!"

"Are you crazy? They're ferocious, Joey! Look at those teeth!"

Ynez held Joe back, now approaching the cage herself. "I'm not a bit afraid of them! They hold some kind of awful secret, Mack! Look how gentle they are now! Joe, that one looks just like you!" she giggled, holding a perfumed handkerchief up before her nose.

"Jeez, t'anks." Abashed, he finished off the end of the bannana himself.

Mack turned away. "Look over here, you two. The rest of this room was his laboratory!"

Joe flashed the light all around. "Dat crazy doctor's? Talk about unsannytary! Smells like poop in here!"

"Hand me your flashlight, Joe. It surprises me that he has so much conviction about what he does," Mack said, drawing their attention to a small, functioning ice box containing phials all labled SEMEN. "He must really use the semen from those apes on his patients!"

"Jeez, now he's got duh Navy involved!" Joe shook his head.

"What? No, not seamen, Joey, semen," Ynez provided. "—you know...goo-goo."

By now, she had wandered to the far end of the chamber and pointed to a door. "Whatever do you think he's done with that room?"

"What was it used for when this place was up and running?" Mack asked.

"It was a Roman bath. You can guess the rest."

Mack pulled it open, focusing the flashlight within. "What the devil?" Then: "Oh, my God!" Mack gasped, quickly closing the door.

"What is it!" Ynez asked, frightened.

"Well," Mack answered shakily. "It's not what I'd expect to see in a Roman bath, that's for sure."

• • •

Bruno drove on until he reached Forest Hills, where the Packard sedan made a turn into a Tudor Revival neighborhood of upper middle class homes. The storm had ceased, leaving the kempt lawns strewn with fallen boughs, as gutters ran in torrents and puddles reflected the rising moon.

He parked his car out of sight at the corner, got out and, pulling his hat down far over his eyes, walked quickly toward the dimly lit house before which the sedan had just parked.

Hiding behind a tree growing on the lot next door, he saw a thin man of average height and effeminate appearance emerge from the sedan. Apparently, this was "Trevor," who had been driving. Then, a small man of corpulent appearance (Violet herself, no doubt) and lastly, Blanche King.

"That lousy two-faced bitch! What a bunch!" Bruno muttered. "And Squirrely, right in the thick with 'em!" Just seeing her mincing toward the house, made him wrap his big hand about his gun.

Violet, sporting gentleman's attire, tapped with her stick loudly on the front door. A portly fellow in his shirtsleeves, whom Bruno recognized at once as being Brian O'Couran, opened it. With little formality, and not at all pleased to see them, he nervously permitted them entrance. Racing across the lawn to the side of the house, Bruno saw open windows at the sun porch. Hiding behind a boxwood hedge, he was able to clearly hear their conversation now in progress.

O'Couran, apparently a little drunk: "Don't tell me about it! I'm handin' you over the coin as fast as I can!" In the parlor of the house, one table lamp burned. Bruno saw their shadows etched upon the walls.

Violet: "You're not playing fair and square with us, O'Couran! We've given you tremendous advantages, and you've done nothing but play us for fools! Well—you'll live to regret it!"

Blanche: "The fact is, we're not seeing revenue as we should, Brian. You know very well that I've watched every single penny that you've made out of that Moran's Elixir partnership. Don't lie to us, Brian!"

O'Couran (attempting to soothe them): "But I got my own expenses to cover, you've got to understand!"

Violet: "Of course you do! But you do your business on a cash basis, and we've come to the conclusion you're stashing it away. We need money now, Brian. Please hand it over before there's trouble."

O'Couran (stammering): "But I don't keep no cash in the house!"

Blanche: "You're a filthy liar, Brian." (Her shadow crossed the room. She had apparently pulled out her little .32.)

O'Couran (shouting): "You'll not go so far! You've done your very worst with me and I'll not have it anymore! I'll report you, I will!"

Violet: "You look rather under the weather, Brian. Not feeling well, what? Shall we call a doctor for you?"

A gesture, angry and swift, was made. The shadow of the fellow called Trevor crossed the room, apparently going to the telephone stand. As O'Couran protested, sounding like a man about to go mad, the call was being placed. Bruno could not make out either the exchange or the number itself.

Then, without so much as a prompting, the shadow of Violet loomed over O'Couran's. Cursing under her breath, she slapped O'Couran twice across the face. It proved effective.

Almost six feet in height and wide as he was tall, Brian O'Couran began crying like a child. Bruno lifted himself up to look in the window, seeing the fellow called Trevor now finshing his call, Blanche standing by with a strangely ghoulish smile on her face, and Violet castigating O'Couran.

"You're a two-faced shanty Irish ignoramus, Brian O'Couran! And you've consistently cheated us out of a good deal of money! Now where is it!"

O'Couran, dropping to his knees, pleaded, "No! No! please! Ain't I loyal and in good standing with the Order and our all-powerful Master?"

"Oh, shut up. You've got cash hidden around here somewhere, Brian," Blanche was saying, turning around, beginning to tear the place apart.

Now Bruno saw the fellow called Trevor bring a a large hypodermic needle from within his jacket as Blanche went into a fit of rage tossing sofa cushions everywhere.

Violet and Trevor held O'Couran down, like a squealing pig. "I ain't lying, for God's sake! I'm poor! I'm poor I tell you!"

Whatever his three aggressors were saying back to him, Bruno could not make out, but they wanted him rendered defenseless—that much was clear. Violet took great glee in slapping him over and over. As O' Couran buckled, the fellow with the needle jabbed it into the side of his thick neck. Bruno saw him collapse backwards, landing with a thud. All three of his guests laughed in a manner which reminded Bruno of certain types he'd seen in the stir watching rats writhe and squirm as they were slowly squeezed to death in the bare fists of his fellow inmates.

Bruno figured the time was right. He pulled out his gun and aimed it at the lone table lamp in the parlor. A shot rang out and the house was plunged in darkness. Silence.

Bruno, now going to the front door—left unlocked—slowly and without a sound, turned the knob, then dropped down to the floor of the entryway—flat out, on the ground. Feeling about, he discovered an umbrella and, using it as a spear, threw it inside across the room.

Blanche fired in that direction. The little .32 had come in handy. His birthday present to her, with her name engraved on it.

"Whoever you are," Violet growled, "don't think we frighten easily! Now come out and fight like a gentleman and tell us what it is you want!"

This little speech was accompanied by a slight stirring from within. Etched by the moon through the living room windows, he saw her strange little profile and fired. A sharp cry followed. Another shadow fell away. He had hit the man named Trevor instead.

Porch lights were going on all around him now. Bruno saw both Violet and Blanche supporting Trevor, hurrying him to the back toward the rear entrance. Skirting the side of the house just in time to see them getting into a big, official-looking car which Bruno knew to be Brian's own, he saw Blanche frantically attempting to place the wounded fellow called Trevor upright in the driver's seat. Amazed, Bruno remained in the shadows.

"I can't…I can't do it," he sobbed in a light, thin voice—blood coming from a shoulder wound, gleaming in the moonlight.

"But you've got to! Neither one of us can drive!" Blanche shrieked.

Violet screamed, "What good are you then?" grabbing Blanche's gun away from her, pummeling him with it. Blanche tried wresting it from Violet, all three of them screaming, weeping, cursing.

"Don't!" Bruno heard her suddenly scream. "Blanche! No!"

Three shots rang out, aimed at the wounded fellow's head, blowing his brains out, sending the whole side of his head in smithereens everywhere, all over Blanche. All over Violet as well.

"You've done it again! Lost your mind again!" Blanche screamed half—mad, sobbing.

Just then, Bruno turned and saw the most peculiar sight: A small delivery van pulling into the driveway at great speed; with the motor still running, two men hopped out, advancing toward O'Couran's car.

"She's killed him, that's what she's done!" Blanche shouted toward them, her voice shaking.

Violet, however, was remarkably sane, covered as she was with blood and brain matter, issuing orders, "Never mind that, lads! Had to be done! O'Couran is in there! Here! Put this body in the back of our van and mind the head!" She stepped out of the car, and went toward the van. "Wrap it up in something. Might come in handy!"

As Violet was about to open the side doors, a pale, gaunt man with a pince-nez reflecting the moon flung open the door with his walking stick.

"Stop! Leave that body just where is is. This is simply unacceptable!" His voice was deep, sepulchural. "Demanding I leave my patients for such nonsense!" He had on a surgeon's coat, which he now removed and threw at one of his men. "Clean up that mess at once!"

Far in the distance, sirens could be heard approaching. "Get in!" he commanded. Both Blanche and Violet obeyed at once, disappearing into the van. He continued his orders, speaking rapidly, with Shakespearan intonation, "Ian, take Brian's auto out of here—leave poor Trevor as he is. I shall have to speak with Brian." He now turned to the other thug. "And you, Reggie! Take the youngsters back in this thing." He sighed in a matter-of-fact way. "I suppose I must drive the Packard back myself. Ah, well!"

Now proceeding toward the back door of the house, Bruno saw clearly him—a man of distinguished appearance, his aquiline features stamped with a look of perpetual ennui. Bruno hopped over the porch,watching him sweep by as the sirens grew louder. Two patrol cars—he estimated, less than four blocks away.

Peeking through the window in the kitchen door, he saw the gaunt man neatly and methodically putting everything back in place, muttering to himself about how everyone was so incompetent.

Then, kicking Brian in his side, he demanded, "Get up! You prehistoric, bog-trotting warthog, you! Get up I say!"

Bruno heard the van backing swiftly out of the drive, followed by Brian's automobile.The sirens, now so very near, were beginning to make Bruno wonder how this weird- looking guy could cover all of this up with about five minutes left before the cops stopped in front of the house!

But he was manging to get O'Couran seated in his armchiar and, with the aid of another injection—this time in his arm—revive him within mere seconds.

"Here, take a bit of this," he said, offering O'Couran his own flask. "You'll be better in the wink of an eye, you old souse!" The sirens were heard just rounding the block.

Bruno couldn't see Brian O'Couran's bloated face, but he pictured his flickering, bloodshot eyes lifting groggily, as he moaned, "Master? Is it you? Have you come for me?"

"Oh, shut up, you ignorant Mick. Here's our boys in blue! I'll do the talking! Just tell me where the money is."

"—oh…sure. I'm sittin' on it!" O'Couran slobbered, giggling.

The man known as "master" shoved Brian's fat behind out of the way and reached down between the cushions. Out came a grocery bag full of cash. The police were now at the door. Composing himself, and even smiling, he elegantly opened it.

"Sorry to disturb you," one cop said. "But we got a complaint from the neighbors. Thought some bootleggers might be rilin' Commissioner O'Couran!"

"Oh, officers, do come in. I am Dr. Soames, Commissioner O'Couran's physician." He proferred a business card. "Ever since his wife was taken away for treatment due to her nervous condition, Brian has been terribly depressed. Haven't you, Brian?"

"Hmm? Oh.Yeah." O'Couran looked up at the policemen, smiling foolishly. "Evenin', Donnelly, evenin', Donahue."

One cop said, in an aside to the doctor, "Drinkin' again, is he?"

"Oh, my, yes. D.T.s setting in, I fear. I've given him something to calm him down. No doubt the poor neighbors were startled to hear gunshots?" the doctor purred.

"That's right, doctor," one replied.

Bruno saw Doctor Soames bend and pick up what proved to be Blanche's .32 calibre pistol, skewering it with his fountain pen. "Here is the reason, gentlemen. Commissioner O'Couran was taking pot-shots at pink elephants. You see the mess he's made!" Then bending close to them, the doctor whispered, "I'm trying to get him off the stuff, officers, but I may have to send him away for the cure!"

O'Couran heard it. He reared up, tears sprouting in eyes. "No! No! You'll not do that to me! Anything but that!"

One policeman replied, shaking his head sadly, "I heard before he took this job, he never so much as touched a drop of liquour to his lips! You see what Prohibition does to people!"

"Indeed, indeed, gentlemen." The Doctor smiled wanly and, dipping into the pocket of his striped trousers, pulled out a wad of bills. "Here, divide this up amongst you both! Keep mum about our dear cohort! Say nothing! Godspeed! Good night!" And with that he had them out of there, closing the door firmly but gently.

Now, turning to O'Couran, gazing down on him, he proclaimed, "You know what? I think I'm going to have you removed from office, Brian, dear."

"*Good*! Do it! Do it tomorrow! You put me in there, and you can get me out! Only please don't send me to that Gehenna up North!"

"*A bientot*!" The Doctor looked, with a smug but imperious grin, at the spectacle lumped in the armchair before him then, placing the bagful of cash under his arm, simply walked out.

Bruno dashed around the house to see him getting in the brown sedan. As soon as the Doctor had pulled out, he ran to his own car, jumped in, and began to follow him.

• • • • •

CHAPTER XXIII

THE DOCTOR IS OUT

Just after ten o' clock, at the corner of 67th Street and Third Avenue, Mack, Joe and Ynez were strolling downtown toward the Armstrongs' building, all deep in thought. They were unaware of Bruno's touring car speeding in from Queens, with a certain brown sedan right in front of it. Just a few blocks north, both automobiles were turning right back into the very street which they had just left.

It appeared that the mad doctor was going back to 68th Street and Bruno was determined to get him. But the doctor was a skillful driver and knew, perhaps, that he was being followed. Sneaking through a stoplight just changing to red, he darted ahead.

"You won't get away from me, Goddammit!" Bruno shouted from behind the wheel of his own car.

Only a couple of moments later, back in front of the 68th Street place, Bruno brought his automobile to a screeching halt, leapt out and ran down the mews. Where had the doctor gone? Then, he peered through the windows of the carriage house doors. There, nicely parked, was the brown sedan, giving off enough heat to be felt through the locked doors. Turning toward the rear of the main house, out of breath, he hollered, "I'm coming in there, you Goddamed freak, and beat the fuck out of you!"

Taking off his hat, he threw it on the ground, swearing, then headed for the kitchen door, where he simply kicked it in and threw aside the furniture that had been piled there. Climbing over it, throwing it everwhere, he shouted into the darkness,"Hey, you crazy asshole! I saw everything! Hey, in there!" Pulling out his gun, he advanced into the cavernous mouth of the place.

• • •

Not quite two hours later, Bruno showed up at the Armstrong penthouse, covered in dust and grime. Johnnie stood in the foyer, gaping at him.

"You need a good dry cleaners!" she observed.

Ynez, Mack and Joe, who had been there only a while, got up and went to meet him.

"What in Hell happened to you! We were so desperately worried, Bruno!" Ynez chided, pulling him into the living room.

"Please," Bruno replied in a hoarse whisper. "Those pricks downstairs almost didn't let me up and I was about to kill 'em."

Nolie motioned to him. "You look like you just crawled out of the grave!"

Bruno's hand shook as he lit up a cigarette, going into the living room and parking his dust-laden self on the quilt under which Johnnie had just been cuddling. "I don't want to dirty anything in here." He leaned back and shut his eyes. "Chaaarrriiist! What a night. That goddammed Blanche King!"

"You catch a beatin', brudder?" Joe asked, as Mack proffered sandwiches and a lemonade.

"No. I'll tell you everything from start to finish, just don't anybody speak until I'm done, 'cause I've some new theories as a result of what's just happened to me."

He began talking and held them transfixed for a half an hour. At the conclusion, he looked around. "Anyway, I checked the whole goddammed house and the crazy bastard was nowhere to be found. So I figured he must live right nearby—someplace! So what about all of you, huh? What'd you come up with?"

Mack let go a deep, deep sigh. "Tomorrow I'll have some of my men from work hose that place out and board it up. Then we can go around checking the other houses that are near it to see if we can locate this guy."

Bruno, gulping down the aspirin Nolie had brought him, nodded.

Mack went on, "We haven't filled the girls in on anything much yet. So here's what we found after you left." He related what they had discovered—the little army uniform, the apes—and a brief summary of what was stored in the Roman Bath. "And that's all. So far," Mack concluded grimly.

Johnnie said, "Well, if it isn't, I can't even imagine what'll come next! It looks like O'Couran and this doctor are partners, and they've got more than a few irons in the fire."

"But somehow," Nolie added, "it all seems to pivot around you, Mack, and your relationship to the Colonel and his daughter, Violet."

Bruno, eyes still closed, his head on a pillow, raised a hand. He was more than emphatic. "There's something going on here that's way beyond me, pal. This just isn't like anything I've ever come up against." Then he paused. "It seems like what we thought all along is really the other way around. Like O'Couran is working for the doctor, feeding him money through bootlegging, and using you, Mack, as his prime source. Easiest touch around since you work for O'Couran himself! From what I heard, this doctor genuinely believes in his own crazy-ass vision. Like it's some kind of mission. And so does O'Couran and so does Blanche and that Violet whatever his-or-her last name is!" He shook his head and shrugged. "It's like some kind of nutty religion. They call him Master and treat him like he's a god!"

Ynez shuddered. "Well, all I know is it ought to be the scenario for the next Lon Chaney picture!"

"That Roman bath in the 68th Street house," Mack reluctantly explained, "was filled up with containers of body parts. Maybe as many as one hundred different varieties."

"Didja see Lady Lee's feet in dere?" Joe asked.

"Joe, to be honest with you, I really didn't pause to look for 'em," Mack answered, patting him gently. "But I'm sure they're in there somewhere!"

Nolie became suddenly very emotional. "How can we get these monsters off our backs!" She looked as if she might even start to cry. "Look at what they've done to us all! What in Hell is next?!"

Ynez said, "Well, we certainly can't go to the police, my darling! Not just because we're in with the mob here, but because the cops are all paid off anyway, it appears."

Bruno gave her a look. "Oh, Ynez, do you even think the police would believe you if we told 'em all this stuff?" He laughed mirthlessly. "I don't know how big this combined operation is, but I'll find out! And if I have to call in some of the other families to wipe 'em out, then I'll do it."

Joe waved his hands in the air, a half-sandwich in each. "But what's in it for dee udder famb'lees, B.! Dey don't want nuttin' tuh do wid body parts and spook doctors!" Joe reasoned.

Johnnie, curled up like a cat and sipping her lemonade, offered, "They're both after you, Mack—these two maniacs. They want you brought to your knees. O'Couran wants all of your sideline business, and he's under this doctor's thumb. He takes some off the top for himself which angers the doctor, apparently because it takes a lot of jack to run his cult! And somehow, the Colonel's daughter Violet is precisely in the middle of this whole awful thing."

Mack agreed to a point. "But the Colonel himself is absolutely not in on this. He's innocent. We know that. He's being shaken down by her to keep this secret society running." Mack stopped speaking, as Ynez suddenly grabbed his arm tightly.

She looked around at everyone. "These people go through dough like termites go through front porches. I told you what Winchell said about poor Gladys Tuthill! How does it all get spent?"

Bruno had the answer. "Mostly enforcement, I'd guess. They hire thugs to protect 'em, they have a secret network that pushes this doctor's miracle cures and, finally, they must be paying off the people who run that asylum up north."

Nolie went back into the kitchen, raiding the refrigerator then returning with a bottle of pickled pigs' feet. "Oh, God, why did I bring these in here when we're having this conversation?"

It was now far past midnight, into the wee hours of the morning. Elliot, coming in with Wriggs after playing at the club, found them all sittting there. Nolie, as was her custom, went to make a midnight snack for them both, tossing the pigs' feet in the trash.

"Morning, everybody." Wriggs managed a smile. Neither were very happy.

Elliot, looking around at the weary faces of his friends gathered, asked, "Now what?"

"Elliot," Mack smiled. "Give us some good news. We could all use it."

"Well, we've got a roof over our heads, and that's good news! The rest of it is all bad, I'm afraid." He went to change out of his white suit of tails, while Wriggs joined Nolie in the kitchen, helping her out, also avoiding any response.

Mack whispered in Johnnie's direction, "John, is something wrong?"

She patted his hand, winked, and gave him a vague nod.

"How *did* it go tonight?" Ynez asked, feeling the sudden freeze.

Elliot, emerging in one of his modernistic dressing gowns, threw himself down on a chair. "Well, Nolie is greatly missed, I can tell you that. Now I sing my duets to myself. Attendance at the Club deVol has, as they say, fallen off drastically."

"But I told you all over and over," Johnnie said. "I'm fine here by myself. Keys and Mama come by, Nolie! You don't need to hang around here night after night."

Coming out of the kitchen followed by Wriggs with trays piled high with eggs, sausages and muffins, Nolie blandly replied, "Honey, I intend to hang around here not only night after night but day after day as well."

Elliot shot her a withering look. "How about our rehearsals for 'Hotcha Honeymoon' day after day, huh, Winola?"

"All I'm asking is that both of us go in there tomorrow and speak to Tuthill about making some modifications…It's just not—" Nolie began.

Elliot interrupted. "He might agree to make some changes, but he's in it for the dough, Nolie. This show is going to really put us on the map!"

His sister answered, "Well, he's grabbing more than sheckels, like my ass for instance! Black and blue from his pinches!" Nolie sashayed back into the kitchen. "And then goes bragging about his family to everyone like he's a model husband and father! Those horribly spoiled kids of his! If I ever saw two brats who need a sober Mother, it's Junior and Peaches Tuthill."

Ynez said, "I feel so sorry for her. Drowning her sorrows in booze. By the by—" She looked about, "Can't a gal get a drink around here anymore?"

Bruno pulled out his flask. "If King Tut is counting on profits from this new show because his wife gave up her fortune to a miracle racket that didn't pan out, he's not gonna change a thing to suit you, Nolie." Rising, he went to the empty bar and scoured for glasses.

Elliot, by now devouring his eggs, announced sullenly, "Just go out and drink that stuff on the terrace, please." Now addressing Nolie, "And if he won't agree to cut the sex stuff, does this mean you'll refuse to sing at his kids' dance this Saturday night?"

Nolie brought in coffee with Wriggs in tow carrying the cups. "Elliot, I know how much it means to you to please Tut. But you let him talk you into hiring our band for far less which means *we'll* have to make it up to them!"

"It's for his kids, Nolie!"

"Oh, all *right*! Let's just drop it! We've got other, more serious things to worry about," she huffed and puffed a little. "—and I'm sure if I sit on his lap and call him poopsie-woopsie, he *will* modify that second act!"

Mack attempted to lighten the pervasive mood. "Well, anyway! This building will be all ours soon enough! Think about it! Our citadel!"

Bruno, still with eyes closed, head on the pillow, muttered, "Yeah, and we're all gonna need a citadel, from what I can see."

But Johnnie, putting her head on Mack's shoulder, said sweetly, "Honestly! After all you've got to deal with, you can still find the silver linin' behind every cloud." But Mack wasn't listening. He was explaining to Joe what a citadel was.

• • •

Saturday night found Nolie reluctantly climbing into the offical orchestra bus with the rest of the band headed out to the Tuthill estate in Manhasset. King Tut had, after all, agreed to 'change a few things, here and there, in act two,' and so Mrs. Armstrong was appeased, yet thoroughly expecting him to maul her as soon as they were alone.

With them came Johnnie, out and about for the first time in weeks, dressed once again as Nolie's maid. "Don't be surprised," Johnnie told her, raising a recently unbandaged fist, "if I slug him."

"Be my guest!" Nolie laughed.

Junior and Peaches Tuthill were thrilled to see the Army of Charm alighting in front of their modern mansion, proceeding to show Nolie and Elliot around, acting very sophisticated, dolled up just like flappers and sheiks.

"Kind of reminds me of us when we were that age," Elliot told his sister as they were setting up in the ballroom.

"Well, I hope they don't follow in *our* footsteps!" Nolie replied. "She's got enough paint on that little face of hers to cover a three-bedroom house. Both of them smoking—and they aren't over fifteen if they're a day!"

"I smelled liquor on Junior's breath!" Wriggs put in, opening Elliot's fiddle case.

Elliot smirked, folding his hands like a parson in prayer. "Tsk. Tsk Tsk. What a couple of bluenoses you both are. They're just a product of our modern age, that's all. Going to the bow-wow's!"

Johnnie, passing by with an armful of Nolie's costumes, took this all in. "Oh, come now, Elliot. He ain't even old enough to shave, and she's just out of grade school!"

Elliot looked narrowly at her. "Kids with that much money don't *go* to grade school, Johnnie. They go to boarding school."

"That's not the point. Just look around. There's not a child here who's yet reached sixteen," Johnnie replied. "Where do you want these, honey?" Johnnie asked Nolie.

"Well, I'm supposed to change in some room just off Tuthill's office, or so I was told. Uh-oh. Here he comes now."

"Hello, kidlets!" King Tut greeted them jovially. "Ain't this going to be the catapillar's trousers, though? Nolie, dollink, come with me, I'll show you where you'll dress." He gave Johnnie a look which was a strong suggestion that she remain behind, but it did no good.

"This is my private bathroom, Nolie—now don't you worry about me. I've got some telephoning to do!" He left, going into his office just beyond, leaving the door which connected both rooms wide open.

It was a swanky mahogany and nickel-fitted affair, with a large mirror set into the door. "*Two-way glass*," Johnnie whispered.

Tut looked up from his desk twelve feet away, positioned to give him a clear view.

"Say, Johnnie," he sang out sweetly, now rising and standing at the threshold of the bathroom. "Would you mind running out to my car? I left a little present for your boss-lady there!"

Nolie and Johnnie exchanged looks. *Go ahead, but hurry back.*

With Johnnie just gone, Tut smiled at the boss-lady, about to close the door. "Why don't you start changing, sweetie? I seem to hear the band tuning up!"

Nolie shut it firmly, locked it, then counted to five and opened it fast, banging King Tut almost up against the wall.

"Say, what's the deal here, anyway? Can you *see* through this mirror?"

"My dear, I was just curling my eyebrow hairs," smoothing one brow over with his pinky finger.

Suddenly, a buzzer on his desk sounded. "'Xcuse me, sweetie pie. House phone. Yes?—oh, all right!" He told her that some big shot had just walked in with his daughter all in tears. "I'll be right back, Nolie, pet. Meanwhile, you go on ahead and step out of your step-in's!" And off he went.

"Like Hell I will!" she thought and, gathering up her costumes, bustled out, meeting Johnnie coming toward her, breathless.

"I ran back! You o.k.?"(Nolie nodded like a prize fighter.) She produced an elegant little box. "Look—must be an anklet. Cartier, no less!"

"Well, you know what he can wrap *that* around! I'm not changing in there." She headed for the stairway. "Come on!"

Running after her, Johnnie cautioned, "But we were told not to go upstairs!"

Nolie abruptly opened the first door she encountered. There, across a salmon-colored expanse of what was obviously a female's lair, a woman in a swan bed stared out at nothing. "Oh! Mrs. Tuthill! I'm so sorry…" Both turned to leave.

"What's *wrong* with her?" Johnnie whispered, transfixed by her appearance. Creeping closer, they both paused.

Mrs. Tuthill was very obviously not a well woman. Her eyes, glassy, surrounded by deep circles, were absent of all reason. Her mouth sagged into an expression of stupor. These features were set into a wizened face, the color of ashes, all wrapped up in a tulle scarf. They did note, however, that she was breathing and seemed, somehow, to be aware of their presence.

"My fix, honey…my fix…" came from her lips in a scratchy, barely audible tone of desperation.

"She thinks I'm her maid!" Johnnie whispered, aghast. "What'll we do?"

But behind them, Mrs. Tuthill's official maid was heard clearing her throat. "I'll take care of her, thanks. Do you want to change in Mrs. Tuthill's powder room, Mrs. Armstrong?" This efficient servant indicated a door to their left, then went over and propped up her employer's sagging self.

When they went out to play the opening number, Elliot whispered to Nolie, "Gee, I feel like I'm teaching a music class to third graders!" Then he noticed how upset she appeared. "Did he try and put his mitts all over you, Noles?"

"No. But John and I just happened to run into his wife," Nolie replied, looking toward the back of the ballroom where the mothers and fathers had gathered around mah-jongg tables. A small bar had been set up for the parents, which was being patronized very heavily. Yet, a battallion of servants made sure it was well-patrolled, keeping the kids away. At the opposite end, an ice cream parlor from one of Tut's shows had been installed. Somehow, right after the fourth dance and their duet, Elliot, Nolie—everyone in the band—began to notice that some of the kids seemed a little tipsy.

In between their second and third sets, Wriggs took it upon himself to do some patrolling of his own. Going out on the terrace, he took in the kids at close range. Here, he saw the girls in low-cut frocks with short hems and rolled hose—the boys, cigarette smoking, swearing and acting smooth.

"Trying to be something out of all the movies they've seen!" he thought to himself. "Rich, spoiled and pretty darned pathetic if you ask me!" He approached a crowd of boys and girls, all whispering to one another.

"Say, mister," one peach-fuzzed boy drawled, "we'll slip you twenty clams if you ankle it into town and buy us a pack of Murads."

Jack Wrigley was genuinely shocked. "Say! You shouldn't be smoking at your ages!" he told them all.

"Aw, go to Hell!" a be-rouged pre-flapper snarled and thumbed her nose at him. The kids all laughed. Another, coughing away, told him, "Mind your own beeswax, why don't you! We'll do anything we damned well please, see?"

Wriggs continued on, nonplussed, into the formal gardens. Hung with Chinese lanterns, the effect was charming, but what he was hearing from behind the topiary was not:

"Come on! Give me another swig! I can take it!"

"Ooo! That burns all the way down!"

"Golly, I feel like I'm gonna be sick…"

Out from the hedges, a young kewpie doll staggered, falling into his arms. "Hello, big boy!" she whined cutely. "You're just my type! How about a l'il kiss?"

"Say, watch that stuff—" Then he was overpowered by the scent of alcohol. The poor little girl reeked of it. "You're drunk! You're disgustingly, low-down drunk, missy!"

"Don't 'missy' me, hot stuff! Do you know who I am? Well, I'll tell you…" Wriggs had to steady her, almost holding her up. "I'm Peaches Tuthill, the hostess of this riot here, and you've got some cheek, Buster!" But suddenly she clutched his arms, her eyes becoming a burning red and filling with tears. "I can't see! I can't see! Help me! I'm going blind!"

Screaming hysterically, she writhed in a sudden spasm. Wriggs held onto her, not knowing at first what had happened.

Within seconds, there were terrible cries of agony from everywhere within the gardens. Around him, boys and girls began vomiting blood, writhing in seizures—then, more than a few passed out cold. Shouting and screaming for their mothers and fathers, careening into one another, almost a dozen of them acted in a way that was frightening to the rest; shaking violently, clawing at their throats and their eyes as if on fire.

Wriggs, holding onto Peaches, yelled out, "Somebody help out here! Help us!" Servants and band members were now all running from the ballroom, picking up the young people, holding them tightly in their arms as they went into uncontrollable fits.Their parents, responding to what now was complete pandemonium, broke through the crush.

"Get a doctor!" Wriggs ordered. "These kids have been poisoned!"

"Peaches!" Tuthill cradled his daughter in her arms, holding her tightly to prevent her from shaking. "What is this? What have you done!"

Tuthill's son, crying like a baby, coughing up blood, reeled right toward Jack Wrigley. "My eyes! My eyes! Help me!" From his trousers fell a pint flask of Moran's Elixir.

"Who gave my children this rotgut!" Tuthill shouted, looking at the band members.

A dignified gentleman broke through. "I've called the police and the Manhasset Hospital. These children have alcohol poisoning. Get them inside, into the kitchens at once."

But three of the kids had already fallen unconscious and were hyperventilating.

Elliot and Nolie pushed through followed by Johnnie. Some of the young people, unaffected by drinking the volatile liqour, had become so frightened they were running back toward the house, crying out for their parents, who took them up in their arms.

Embracing one girl, already in convulsions, Nolie managed to get her to the kitchen, forcing water down her throat. Johnnie followed with a boy who had scratched at his eyes until they bled. Everyone tried to help, but four of the children who were poisoned appeared to be, by that time, in nearly critical condition—choking to death on their own blood.

Down in the garden, just past the terrace, one mother yelled out, "Look here! Bottles of hooch! How did they get hold of this!" Littered about, barely hidden under the shrubbery, were dozens of pint bottles, most of which had been emptied.

Another answered, sobbing over her little girl, "That orchestra brought them in!"

Elliot stood in disbelief, dumbfounded, looking around, seeing these mere children so very near death.

Johnnie and some of the servants were now back on the terrace with a tea cart holding pitchers of water. "Get over here and drink this!" she called out to one boy. "Drink all you can!"

"My throat is burning up!" he yelled. "My eyes are are blurry! I can't see anything now!"

At the Manhasset Hospital, Tuthill received the shocking news that his son had died in the ambulance of alcohol poisoning within less than an hour after drinking the rotgut. His daughter, Peaches, had survived but, he was told, would be partially blind for the rest of her life.

The police came to the hospital after searching through the Tuthill mansion for any more of the bad liquor. None was found. But all the bottles of the rotgut hooch, which littered the garden, whether emptied or left half-full, were taken in as evidence.

In the vestibule outside of his daughter's room, Tuthill confronted Elliot. "I hold you and your band members responsible for all of this," he was beyond crying. "I know what kind of people you are. I know you brought that stuff into my house. You killed my son and made my daughter blind."

Elliot and Nolie were taken into custody, with Johnnie and Wriggs wondering what they should do next.

• • • • •

CHAPTER XXIV

BLANCHE BAILS

As a direct result of the terrible events at Tuthill's party, a special investigation committee was formed, headed by Mayor Walker himself. Behind it was an angry and outraged public, who believed that Prohibition had done more harm than good, serving as a foundation for corruption, producing more drunks, more crime and more deaths than America had ever seen in its history.

In the midst of this, the Commissioner of Prohibition, Mr. Brian O'Couran, announced suddenly that he would be voluntarily stepping down. His eyes had been opened to the shameful state of his administration almost as soon as he'd walked into that job. He wanted no part of it.

Commissioner O'Couran was reviled. A clean-living, moral and upright gentleman, whose wife had become so terribly melancholy since departing the Old Sod, he had decided to leave it all behind, take care of her, and get back to his church work. Not only would he fully co-operate with the committee to make a clean sweep of the corruption within the Prohibition Bureau, but would "personally see to it that those who had covertly and arrogantly broken the law were brought, at once, to justice."

That very same week, shock waves continually numbed all New York. A chemical analysis done on the hooch found at the Tuthill party revealed that it had been cut with radiator fluid and formaldehyde. Now the question on everyone's lips was: Where did those kids ever get this poison? Whoever purveyed the stuff was going to the chair, and there was no doubt about that! The very heart of the City was wracked by sorrow and sympathy for the Tuthills.

Mack Daly, looking down from the terrace of the Armstrong penthouse atop the 55th Street building—now his very own—faintly heard the newsboys yelling. There, high above Manhattan, he and Joe also had just come to dwell, occupying the apartment next to Elliot's. Ynez was ensconced in the two others, now joined together as one vast, luxurious home for herself and Bruno—when, and if, he was available to Live In Sin with her.

Mack could not help but feel that all of them were simply hiding out up there…or perhaps, trapped—high above the conventions and moral platitudes of the city that he loved.

The investigation committee had not yet subpoenaed Mr. Daly. But, on that sultry morning in early June, 1928, hearing the latest develpoments in that day's news being hawked far below, he was certain that his time would soon draw near.

The committee had begun by immediately arresting small-time bootleggers around town, and raiding the less posh nite spots. Photographs of the raids were everywhere, showing respectable people manhandled and humiliated by the police—nite spots and supper clubs axed to pieces. Many officials could now bathe themselves in a roseate light, with the elections just around the corner. But they were just as guilty as those who made the stuff, cut it with poisons and sold it to the unsuspecting. Many editorials and radio reports courageously were saying as much!

But the big shots retaliated. Some of them shouted for Repeal of the 18th Amendment, because Prohibition was killing more people than the electric chair and the noose combined; others held out for National Temperance. Whatever road they chose, each faction was perversely safe as long as they made a big noise in defense of their position. As long as they kept raking in the bucks.

The biggest racketeers were still held as sacred because so much political funding was shoveled their way, with many leading American families behind them. Indeed, many leading American families were them.

Mack Daly wanted to get out of it all together. Go back to Europe, taking Joe with him—or, as Bruno was proposing, virtually vanish into the Underworld. Couldn't Bruno set him up in Chicago, where he had powerful relatives who knew gangland Jews who would welcome him into that kind of life? Either way, he only wanted one thing: to have Joe with him.

Turning around, he saw Elliot sitting on a hassock, looking over yet another tabloid.

"Well, I guess we had to expect as much," he commented looking up at Mack, sliding the paper over a gin bottle, lying there, half empty. Rather than embarrass Elliot, Mack left it there. Anyway, the headline was so big you could read it from across the street:

KING TUT'S CURSE!
GLADYS TUTHILL DIES AFTER LONG ILLNESS
HUBBY MOURNS: "FIRST MY KIDS THEN MY WIFE!"

"Winchell's interview is in there," Elliot said. "The things Tut's saying about us are just awful."

Mack sat down opposite him. "Couldn't be worse things than yesterday's, and the day before that, I hope to God."

"No. Nothing could be worse than that. But it hurts Nolie so to know that he's such a goddammed liar. He *wanted* his wife dead, Mack! He was slowly murdering her! She and Johnnie witnessed it. And now they'll never be able to make the truth known."

Sighing deeply, he rose, grabbing the newspaper and his bottle underneath it. "I'll just file this one with the rest." Just then, the gin fell to the floor with a rattle. "Just gargling, Mack, as usual." Then he added, "But do you blame me?" With a defiant thrust he tossed the tabloid in the corner with the rest.

A whole pile of both morning and evening editions had acummulated there. Theatrical papers, respectable papers and every tabloid available on the newsstands formed a kind of tower of Babel, which now, like Elliot's bottle, also toppled. Elliot shut his eyes, because every headline of the past two weeks suddenly revealed themselves, reviving in him all the feelings he had been trying to drown in drink.

Sarcastic, nasty headlines:

OOPS! THEY'RE NOT MARRIED!
BUT ARE THEY EVER LIARS!
INCESTUOUS JAZZ COUPLE FAKE
"MISTER AND MISSUS" ANGLE!
ARMSTRONGS KAPUT IN SHOW BIZ
DUE TO TUT SCANDAL

...and on and on.

Right after the incident, Elliot and Nolie had been brought in for questioning, then released pending an inquest. They both sensed this ensuing hearing would mean the end of their careers, and the end of the Army of Charm Orchestra itself. Everybody out of work. A dozen or more lives ruined by smear campaigns which now dirtied the reputations of everyone even remotely connected with their music. All recording and radio contracts were getting cancelled left and right. All future concerts, all public appearances—suddenly gone.

In the end, it had nothing to do with the entirely false accusation that they had brought the rotgut to the party themselves. A thorough search found not even so much as a hip flask on any orchestra member.

But Ynez knew better. A lot of good it did. She had telephoned Gladys Tuthill the night before her kids' fatal party. Gladys, Ynez reported later, told her she was being helped "beyond her wildest imaginings" by a certain Doctor. Soames.

He was giving her injections to not only bring back her beauty, but to stop her from drinking as well, and had replaced her cocktails with some panacea called "Moran's Elixir." He was, she said, her single consolation. A real savior—

with Tut gone night after night out chasing show girls—and all that booze lying around everywhere. Ynez heard her crying over the wire. Pretty soon, Gladys was certain her vision would be restored and she would even be able to walk again. Coughing horribly, left alone to slowly die while the servants hung the lanterns and crepe paper for the party downstairs, she whispered in a sepulchural voice that Soames was encouraging her to divorce King Tuthill.

Ynez told Annabelle at once. "Straight from the horse's mouth. She was getting it from both ends! Soames and her husband both wanted her dead so they could get her money!"

Annabelle mused, "I wonder if she's left a will. It wouldn't surprise me at all if she had left something rather sizeable hidden away somewhere from Tuthill…intending it for that monstrous doctor."

But all of this was soon forgotten—overhshadowed by Eliot and Nolie's court date. The judge put one simple and shattering question to them both on the very first day of the hearing. Before they had even had a chance to testify, their fate had been decided.

An open courtroom had been decided upon for the sake of the parents of the young people involved. Reporters, photographers, fans of the Armstrongs, and a sea of morbidly curious rabble elbowed their way in, breathlessly waiting for the lions to enter the arena. But it was all so simple and over within only a couple of minutes.

"Mr. and Mrs. Elliot Armstrong?" (the judge asked this, by way of mere identification, as they both stepped forward to the bench.)

"Professionally, yes, your Honor," Elliot had answered truthfully.

"And privately—?"

"No, your Honor."

"*No*? Are you both single? If so, give your legal names, please."

Elliot (clearing his throat): "Your Honor, those are our legal names. Except for the Missus part. We're…not married…you see…but we are both named Armstrong."

A murmur of shock passed like a wave over the crowded courtroom. There were many standing outside the court house, being lifted up to the windows, thirsty for any drop of scandal. A warm day, windows open. And for those out of earshot, notes were scribbled rapidly, then passed from hand to hand until these reached the windowsills where eager hands grabbed at them. Within those few seconds which passed, audible shocked whispers were heard over the buzz of the electric fans. They were both not married? All this time had they been living in sin? *And* they had the same last name—?

The judge called for order, then looked down at his papers. "How is it you can legally use the same last name then? What are you? Distant cousins, perhaps?" he was reported to have continued reasonably.

"No…we are both…both…brother and sister."

"The handsome crooner's head was bent low. He dared not look up." So the papers said.

"Speak *up*! What was that?"

Nolie (clearly): "Brother and sister. We're both brother and sister, your Honor." (Blurting out): "But it's not what you think—it's not what you think!"

The whispering turning into a roar, a stampede of reporters running out of the court room for the nearest pay telephones. What a story. Incest of all things!

"Order! Order in the court! Or you shall all be dismissed!" the judge scowled down at the packed court room. "This matter is not relevant to the business of the day!"

And even though Elliot and Nolie had been cleared of all charges, their careers and their lives were forever ruined within those few seconds.

KOLLEGE KAPERS, a monthly rag for the jazz-mad younger set, printed an open letter to:

"Mister and Missus Phony-Baloney Armstrong:

YOU LIED TO US AND LET US KOLLEGE KIDS DOWN!

LIARS! PHONIES! FAKES!

Sure, brother and sister acts are numerous—that's all right! But why masquerade as man and wife? Fooling everybody, letting everybody down, making everybody hate you both—when we all loved you so much! We wanted to be just like you! Married and cute and full of pep with so much love for each other! Well, what kind of love was it anyway? And why did you both have to deceive everybody? Why did you touch each other that way and hug and kiss like that? You have hurt us and shocked us and we can't forgive you. What are you both hiding? <u>And why</u>?"

Tuthill, meanwhile, was refusing all interviews. But then, Walter Winchell penned one truly horribe story stating the fact that all his money had been dumped into "Hotcha Honeymoon" and now he was broke on top of everything else!

He wanted nothing more to do with those Armstrong perverts. If his son and daughter hadn't so blatantly imitated both of them, none of this would've happened, Tut had told Winchell.

And Winchell wouldn't let go of it. In Tut's own words: "When I saw my poor Junior in the arms of that fellow Elliot Armstrong's got glued to him, I just finally saw the light, and let me tell you it made me sick to my stomach!"

(Wriggs couldn't believe it when he'd read the article. "*But I was trying to save his life! That's all!"* Meanwhile, his parents disowned him.)

The interview went on: "What exactly do you mean by that,Tut? That you finally 'just saw the light?'"

"I mean that they're connected with this present lavender feeling in New

York, dammit! I've been in the show business for far too long not to know how certain types of people like that work hard at covering up their sick, filthy lives. I tell you both Elliot and Nolie Armstrong are hiding something." Then, adding: "Anyway, they're blacklisted from here on in. They'll never work again. Not in this town, or on the road, or even in Burley-q. You'll see, Walter. You'll see. And I'll make sure of it, too."

"Those are serious words, Tut, and I need proof of such accusations," Winchell had replied within the article.

Then, the very next day…

WINCHELL WRITES: "*Could it be that this brother and sister team have been fooling around with The Love That Dare Not Speak its Name? And that's why they've been fooling us? I'm only guessing, folks, but as I continue to poke under the rocks paving Your Broadway and Mine, I'll let you know!*"

On the heels of this, Winchell himself had boldly telephoned the pair that was suddenly making New York's stomach turn.

"Elliot Armstrong?" (Elliot, on the other end, muttering in the affirmative.) "Now that Tuthill has told his story—and made some infererences which just might make perfect sense—why don't you and your sister there tell *yours*! And this time, why not make it the *truth*!?"

To which Elliot had answered: "What's the use? What good would that do except to make you look like some kind of crusader!"

"Crusader, you say? Hey, I like that word! Can I use it?" (A smile, lookng more like a leer from Winchell.)

And so it was that Mack, watching Elliot fumbling with that tall pile of newspapers, trying to put his gin bottle in his pocket and looking as if he'd aged ten years, began to realize that very, very soon their whole world would end and everyone in it—buried alive.

And then the doorbell rang. Mack himself went and opened it.

"Where is Mr. Benjamin Leventhal? His name isn't listed downstairs."

"That would be me…I've only just moved here, " Mack answered and was handed a summons to appear in court that very next week.

"Now who was that?" Elliot asked wearily.

"Oh, nobody in particular," Mack answered, shoving the official letter in his breast pocket. "Just a guy selling tickets to a circus."

• • •

"You know," Nolie was saying to Johnnie at that very moment, "I should be ecstatic that Mack went and bought this whole dump and saved our asses…but I'm not!" Both of them were hiding out in their bedroom, Johnnie curled up beside her.

"You're worried about leaving Elliot, and I can see why! But what's left for you here in America, honey?"

"Not a Godammed thing. Still, going to Paris would mean starting all over. I'm not worried about all this stuff following me. I can sing and play the piano. I can speak pretty good French and, best of all, I've got you!"

"Yes, and my friends who are over there are makin' lots more money than they ever could here, don't forget," Johnnie added.

"Sure they are—but they're black. I'm nothing more than a novelty singer with a white gal's baby face and blonde locks. Without Elliot, I'm like a million others." Nolie stifled a yawn. She just couldn't sleep a wink these days.

"You take a nap, honey, and I'll go for a stroll." Johnnie kissed her gently and tip-toed out.

Finally she was going to get some sleep! Maybe the notion about moving to France had given her girlfriend some a ray of hope in all of this. Princess Johnnie Parker was that particular type of human being who looked for a blessing within every single shadow.

Leaving the 55th Street building, she felt quite like herself. For the first time in ages!

"At least I don't have to wear that damned maid's uniform anymore!" she was thinking. It seemed like a good idea to stop by the florists just beneath the Elevated and buy Nolie a bouquet of posies.

"I hope," she uttered a little prayer up to Heaven, "if you're lookin' down on me, dear brother Alexander, you aren't objectin' to me wearing this light blue frock instead of a black one!" Looking at her relfection in the store windows, she decided that all her bruises were entirely repaired, and that Alexander was smiling down on her, proud of his sister.

Turning the corner of 55th Street, she walked across to Third Avenue, toward the Elevated.The afternoon was warm and sunny, and it was beginning to feel like summer. There, at the 59th Street stop, a mingling of all classes confronted her. So many sad souls in the world, thought the princess, noticing a desperate and haggard-looking woman being jostled along as she went toward the stairs.

Now, of all things, the woman turned, stopped, and stared at Johnnie. Was she one of the building's cleaning staff so used to seeing her dressed in uniform—not sure if was she was a maid anymore?

Johnnie went along, crossing the street in the direction of the flower shoppe, the shadow of the El overhead blotting out the sun. Still the woman stared on, and walked right toward her.

Reaching the opposite corner, the woman called out to her over the clattering train. "Hello! Hello!"

Johnnie turned and was confronted by the face of a spinster, pinched, superior, alone—obviously well-educated. Yet, her eyes were those of one deep in throes of an opium or morphine addiction.

"You don't know me, but I believe that you are the sister of that poor boy who was so horribly killed recently," the woman began. Johnnie noddded slightly. "Well, I just want to say how sorry I am about your brother's death. Please accept my most profound condolences," she stated simply.

"Thank you so much. How kind of you…do you work in our buildin'?" asked Johnnie, as the train overhead wheezed off.

The woman looked off to the side, her mouth suddenly wrenched with emotion. "Nnno—I—I—*say*, would you very much mind if I spoke to you in confidence for just a moment? I won't take up much of your time."

Johnnie felt instantly sorry for her. She certainly wasn't poor. Plainly dressed in a severe tailor model, she carried no purse, but evidently had filled the pockets of her jacket, Johnnie now noted, with bags of what appeared to be peanuts.

Just before the El stop, Johnnie indicated a bench in front of a delicatessen but a few feet away. The woman, sitting down in a stiff, pathetic way, mechanically began tossing the peanuts at a squirrel. *(She's just plain crazy, poor thing,* Johnnie thought.)

"I am a lover of life, you know," the woman began with a poetic ring to her voice. "But I am a staunch opponent of impurity! That is why, for a few years, I had to do what I did." (Johnnie thought she'd better just hear a little bit of this, then be on her way.) "Your brother was *not* killed by *my* people, you know. He was killed by Brian O'Couran's gang."

"Yes, that's what we've thought," Johnnie answered simply, looking around for any possible excuse to leave this woman by herself.

"Did you! Did you really?" Now turning to Johnnie, her eyes bulging, encircled by deep shadows: "Well, that puts my mind at ease a little. You see, they are trying to prove that Mack Daly is a homosexual. They want to find that out in order to see that he is fully brought to his knees and, in so doing, shatter the very soul of my darling Violet."

"What?" Johnnie's heart began to beat rapidly. "What do you mean?"

"I mean that O'Couran and his gang are relentless in pursuing those awful rumours about Mack Daly being a pederast! Oh, we ourselves have trailed him and that wife of his and have found absolutely *no proof*!" (This, accompanied by a gesture of finality from a hand covered in a crocheted glove.)

She continued rattling on, indignantly: "We have found out that Ynez Daly, his wife, is, of course, a whore. Displaying herself in the nude…dancing vulgarly as she did! Then—consorting with Mr. Bruno Imperio, my former employer!" It almost seemed as if she were talking to herself now.

Johnnie knew little of Bruno Imperio's syndicate, but she had heard of a woman who suddenly left her job as his right hand. She had also heard Ynez,

Mack, Joe and Bruno talking about this woman. What was her name? Then Johnnie recalled it: Blanche. Blanche King. Was this poor thing sitting before her the very same? A gun moll? It seemed highly unlikely yet, Johnnie realized, whoever she might be, this woman was revealing some horrible and very important facts which had to do with her friends.

"You were employed by Mr. Bruno Imperio?" asked Johnnie softly.

"Yes. I had to worm my way in to find out all I could, you see." Another couple of peanuts were tossed to the squirre with a gesture like a wind-up toy.

Johnnie was by now having recurring goosebumps. "How clever of you," she murmured. "And what exactly did you find out?"

"Well," Blanche King began matter-of-factly, "ony that Mack Daly isn't a pansy at all. He and Joseph are only just friends, you see."

"Isn't that something now," Johnnie heard herself saying.

"Oh, and I am so glad you realize it. You know, you should really join our society. You could be turned white."

"Wha—what did you just say?" Johnnie felt her hand fly upward, pressing againist her heart.

"Oh, yes. My Master can do anything. Someday, all of the black, brown and yellow races will be white. You'll see. Oh!" She paused, smiling vaguely. "But I forgot to tell you. If you don't want to be turned white, we must kill you." Then she looked Johnnie over. "Anybody imperfect—goes! You ought to try it. Soon."

Not knowing what to say, and becoming frightened by her words, her whole demeanor, Johnnie humored her. "All right, I'll be sure to look into it. Let's get back to Mr. Daly, can we?"

But before Johnnie could continue, Blanche reached inside her jacket and pulled out a small book, upon which was printed "MY TRAVEL DIARY." Opening it to the inside cover, she showed Johnnie a photograph which had been pasted there. She lifted it to her lips and kissed it.

"It's my Master! See?" She then closed the little book, put it back inside the bag of peanuts and announced, "I'm going to kill myself now." (Johnnie—her blood freezing—just looked at her.) "I can no longer hold all of this inside, don't you see! If O'Couran's gang should find me and torture me, perhaps I'd even…no! No! Never that! For I would never ever betray our cause and my Master!" Now, with a peculiar stare punctuated by rapid blinking, she asked Johnnie, "I hope that *you* don't know anything about it!"

Her mouth dry, Johnnie mouthed the words, "About…*what*…?"

"Well, *about what*! What indeed! About Mr. Daly and Colonel Connaught, of course! What else, at this point, matters?"

Johnnie had to think fast and she knew it. "No. No, I don't, but I…I…agree with…with…your notions…yes! I really do! Precisely!"

"Ah, hah!" The woman clapped her hands together, uplifted in a suddenly ghastly way. "You see? I have my supporters! You *do* agree then, of course?"

"Completely. Didn't I just say so?" Johnnie answered, hardly able to swallow and having no idea to what she was agreeing.

"Mr. Daly is not homosexual at all! He is merely in partnership with the two Imperio boys to expand his bootlegging business." She smiled broadly. "And he permits his wife's behavior because she is letting him know if the Imperios are doing anything behind his back!"

Quickly, Johnnie asked, "But they wouldn't do a thing like that, would they?"

She let go a hollow, insane little laugh. "Pop Imperio will die any day now, then Bruno will officially be in power—oh! You just wait! You just wait!"

Johnnie saw her rise and, still smiling, the woman pulled open the tattered top of the paper bag and shoved it under Johnnie's nose. Amid the peanuts and the diary were four or five large hypodermic needles.

"Eenie, meenie, minie, moe," she sang to herself, then picked one out and incredibly jabbed it into the side of her neck as Johnnie sat watching. She then turned slowly away and began to walk.

"But wait! Who *is* your master!" Johnnie called after her.

"Good-bye…!" the woman gave a tiny wave, a sad smile, and vanished into the throng.

"Wait! Please! Wait!" Johnnie called out, seeing her advancing quickly toward the elevated train stop and mounting the stairs.

A simple fact now burned itself into Johnnie's mind, knowing at once what she was going to do. Pushing through the crowd, racing for the stairs, running up them—she arrived on the platform just as Blanche was passing through the turnstile.

Walking toward the opening of the tunnel just as a train was approaching, she stepped out in front of it. A Hellish screaming of brakes, of humanity, of Johnnie's own voice emerging from her, followed. Johnnie, not even realizing what she had seen or heard, screamed out the name of Blanche King.

As people ran toward the suicide and others panicked and headed from the station and down the stairs, Princess Johnnie Parker stood there—paralyzed by what had just occurred. Feeling something clutched tightly in her hand, unconscious of holding it, she looked down. Blanche had forgotten her bag of peanuts, all of those needles—and…her diary.

• • • • •

CHAPTER XXV

THE DIARY

Joe and Bruno were just then on their way into the building. There they saw Johnnie, just a few steps ahead of them, in an apparent rush.

"Where's duh fire?" Joe called out to her.

Clutching her purse as if someone might snatch it away at any second, she turned to them, forcing a nervous grin. As they got closer, it was clear to them that she was shaking all over.

Stepping into the elevator ahead of them, she murmured, "I guess I'm getting one of those awful Summer colds, that's all."

The elevator boy asked, "What's all that mess up on Third Ave?"

"Must be a derailment," Bruno said. "We just came through there and it's all blocked off at the station." He turned to Johnnie. "You'd better get right into bed, kid. Nothing to fool with."

"Good idea!" Johnnie replied, her voice shaking. "Going to see Mack, huh?"

"Yuppers," Joe answered. "We'll stop by later an' look in on yuz if yuh need anyt'ing."

Johnnie got out, waved goodbye and dug in her purse for the latch key. The bag of peanuts, with its half dozen needles, was in the way, which she now pulled out. Opposite was the incinerator door. With shaking hands, she dumped the whole bag down the chute, saving only the diary, then let herself in.

A note on the hall table told her that Nolie, Elliot and Wriggs had also gone to see Mack. She was alone.

In the bedroom she occupied with Nolie, Johnnie shut the door, tore off her hat, sat on the bed and pulled out Blanche's travel diary. Amazing. All in this tiny, lucid writing. Going into their bathroom, she searched for the aspirin bottle, beginning to read it immediately. It occurred to her that if she locked the bathroom door, took her apsirin and sat down on the toilet, she could not possibly be disturbed. Her fingers flew over the pages.

Short entries. About one hundred pages or so. It might take her an hour or two. She could even lie and say she didn't want to be disturbed if someone came to the door. Summer cold. Good excuse.

Two hours later, Johnnie Parker emerged from the bathroom to Nolie's calling her name.

"Honey, are you sick? Bruno and Joe said—"

"Nolie, we've got to go someplace where we can be alone. I've got to talk to you. Come in here. Look at this."

"Travel diary? Whose is it?"

"Nolie, I just read this whole thing. It's incredible. Like pages out of a nightmare. Only it's all real and it's all happening right now! I want to see that those monsters who killed Alexander and beat me up are punished. I want to see that Mack and Elliot and you and me are free of this evil. Nolie, everything is in here."

"Honey! You're sweating and chilled to the bone! Sit down here—"

"No. Please. Come on, let's go up on the roof. Just you and me. We can climb up and nobody will know it. It's a nice day. Come on. Right now, Noles." Before Nolie knew it, she was following Johnnie out into the hallway, then up the ladder and onto the roof.

"At least take my jacket, " Nolie suggested, looking around for a place to sit, utterly mystified.

"Thanks. Here, right here." Johnnie, sitting on a tool box the maintenance man had left behind, slid over for Nolie. She drew a breath. "This was Blanche King's secret diary, Winola. She just jumped to her death up there—at the El. Look at the police cars and that ambulance up on Third. I was with her. I saw the whole thing." Nolie held onto Johnnie, putting her arms around her.

"I'm going to be all right. It's just that—oh, Nolie—listen. Blanche King was a devotee of this Doctor Soames guy, who heads a group of suckers who he bleeds for money to keep his racket going. They have this perfectly insane cult, which is based on this crazy idea that people must be made perfect or die. Die, Nolie. Through all these operations and drugs and different kinds of treatments with electricity, they think they can make them perfect. If not, they just carve 'em up!"

"This stuff is all in here?" Nolie pointed to the book.

"Well, she also mentions a kind of bible that they go by, where it's put down in detail. But let me go on, and begin at the beginning. Back, before the War, Colonel Connaught had a male lover who lived with him disguised as a woman, assuming the role of his wife, and was never found out about. They went about in society and were accepted even by royalty, so Blanche says in here. They had to cover up the fact that were both queer to such a degree that this man dressed like a lady all the time, see. This man was of German blood—called himself Isolde. Well, after a year or so everybody in high society began to get suspicious because the Colonel and this Isolde drag hadn't produced a kid. Sound familiar?"

"I'm with you all the way, honey! Proceed!"

"So the Colonel's lover-man, now entirely fooling everybody into believing He's a She, went to an orphanage and found this little baby who was born a herm-aph-ro-dite. Now that's a new word for me."

"Who turns out to be Violet."

"Right. And, who, as she grew up, developed breasts and a full-fledged pussy, but who also had a You-Know-What as well, but was missing a pair of You Know-What elses!"

"Commonly referred to as testicles, I believe," Nolie interjected.

Johnnie drew a breath. "Right again. So really, was not all-man. Now you might wonder why Isolde picked such a poor unfortunate baby like that. Well, he—Isolde—was a medical student back in old Heidleberg, and got booted out for fooling around with other boys, ending up in England. He met, and fell madly in love with, the Colonel, and never forgot his dream of becoming a doctor. He believed in—oh, it's right here—making people perfect. Something called…hold on—how do you say that word?" She pointed to it in the diary.

"*Eugenics*. It means just that. Perfecting humanity."

"Yes! Anyway, Isolde really wanted to help this poor orphan kid! He wanted to make her into either one or the other. He was all conflicted within himself, see, about being a pansy. Well, the war came and, of course, the Colonel was called to serve. And now it gets really juicy. Isolde began his activity as a spy for Germany, and was really a hit at it, because he could be the wife of the Colonel and learn all the military secrets of the allies, then run over to Germany, turn into the man that he was, and sell out Merry Old England, see?"

"So the Colonel was married, all right, but not to a woman, to a man, who was a rotten dirty spy that could change his spots at will, so to speak. Yes. And, oh, boy, did this man love the Colonel! It was something intense, from what it says in here. So, as we know, Colonel Connaught met Mack Daly and fell fatally in love with him during the War. And, oh, my, was Isolde ever jealous. In fact, it drove him nuts. At least, that's what anybody reading this little book would conclude. Isolde convinced himself that that the Colonel and Mack were NOT lovers, not at all! And that Mack Daly was not even queer."

"*What*? How on earth did he—or she—ever sell herself that bill of goods?"

"Well, figure it out. It was a well-kept secret, as we know from Elliot, except among those within the old regiment. And the Colonel was a British hero, remember that, Nolie. So there was the Colonel off fighting the War, and Isolde trying to care for little Violet in England, teachin' her pro-German sentiments, actin' like a real mother! Then gettin' back into her masculine attire, goin' over the front lines and handin' the enemy everything! She—or rather HE—knew the Kaiser! She had two full-time jobs! As a Geman spy and a mom! And, as he went crazier, Isolde became obsessed with the fact that the Colonel had ever and only loved HIM, and his daughter Violet. Almost as if they were a happy, perfect and normal family, in fact. Throughout the War, continuing to study Eugenics on the side, Isolde was given the opportunity to experiment on captured prisoners in Germany. It was his goal to operate on Violet and turn her into a regular male...And the Colonel, being a military man, would've much preferred a son to a...a...whatever that was you just said."

"I said *hermaphrodite*! Ghastly!" Nolie cried out, her hand to her lips.

"Isolde ended up back in London, thirsting for the Colonel's love—still playing the part of the returning hero's wife, mind you—was captured and got deported. Presumably, executed as a spy in Luxemburg. But he esacaped because he shed his drag and got out of Europe dressed as a man. He ended up *here*, in the USA, as Dr. Tristan Soames, following the Colonel secretly to our shores! Unfortunately, Colonel Connaught was left in charge of their adopted daughter, Violet."

"The Colonel came here to America just to be close to Mackie, right?"

"Precisely. Well, Doctor. Soames managed to get Violet away from the Colonel one day, and Violet says to Isolde—something like, 'Well, just who in Hell are *you*, anyway!' And Isolde says: 'I'm your mother...Isolde!' And so Violet says: 'How can you be my mother if you're a man?' So he tells her that he operated on himself, turning himself *into a man* because he was German and believed so much in the German cause and became a spy for them, and that was his only cover."

"WHEW!"

"You see, he *did* sell her a bill of goods! She actually believes that this pansy was once a woman and surgically turned himself into a man! Off came the boobies, the ding dong and the balls!"

Nolie took a very deep breath.

"But there's *more*. So Violet says to him, 'Oh! I recognize you now! Have you come to help me?' And he says, 'You shall be my masterpiece!' Then asks her, 'Do you love men or women, my child?' And she says, of course, 'Well, um, come to think of it, I love women.' And so Tristan Soames, alias Isolde, says: 'Well, *of course* you do, for you must be a man, and I will complete what God left unfinished.' *Then* he starts up this secret cult, getting money any way he could. He starts operating on her over time, but meanwhile goes into practice hooking in innocent folks...monkey gland serums, grafting body parts, abortions...anything, really! But he had this weird power over these suckers and they stuck to him like flies to fly paper! A lot of them came from that joint *La Maison*. It was just a recruiting center for nut jobs. He went through thousands and thousands of dollars he took from his followers over these last two years, Nolie! If they didn't *have* it, he insisted they *get* it!"

"—and that's where O'Couran comes in?"

"Yes, and Blanche King, too. Doctor. Soames' goal is to make everybody into absolutely perfect normal men and women in every way, so that they will give birth to absolutely perfect and normal kids. Nobody could be a pansy or a dike. Nobody could be anything else but—well—boring, I guess!"

"And when it didn't work on these poor slobs, he shipped them up to The Slaves of Mary?!"

"Sure did, honey, sure did."

"But how did Mack end up the fall guy in all of this?"

"Well, Mack just happened to have the one source of big money which could be secretly diverted into this weird dream, thanks to the advent of Prohibition. O'Couran met Doctor. Soames years ago and they became partners down on Coney by supplying him with alcohol used to preserve the body parts he was collecting. At that time, O'Couran worked within the Prohibiton Bureau as a phony dry agent, cutting secret deals. Soames asked him who his associates were, and when the name of Mack Daly came up, Soames wouldn't let O'Couran go no-how. "

"And so, when Mack married Ynez, Soames' theories got closer to the truth," Nolie surmised. "It just served to underscore what he'd been trying to talk himself into all those years!"

"—because it confirmed what he'd been hoping all along. That Mack *wasn't* queer, and that the Colonel was the perfect heroic man...the prototype of all men for the future."

"But all along, hasn't this Doctor. Soames—formerly Isolde Connaught—been trying to prove that Mack *is* queer?"

"No. Not at all. O'Couran has been behind that side of it! Because O'Couran is under Soames' thumb, handing him over all his profits, Nolie! Like everyone else in that ring—he's deathly afraid of Soames."

"Oh, my God. So who's winning?"

"O'Couran is nothing more than Soames' stool pigeon. However, his relationship to Mr. Daly is somethin' else again. It was O'Couran who placed that gigolo who Ynez tricked with in front of Violet to confess all he saw! So she didn't want to hear it, and just shot him, point-blank. Violet did that! And O'Couran also sent those thugs up to get me and Alexander. He killed my brother. He's looking for facts dealing with Mr. Daly's bein' queer, so he can expose him, take Mack down, grab his liquor and his money, and an eventual seat in the Senate, which Soames believes he can wrangle when his followers take over our country!" Johnnie drew a deep breath. "See, that's one reason O'Couran stuck with Soames. O'Couran wanted to go places in government and told Soames that he could push his crazy vision toward national attention. Soames loved the idea, and said he'd back O'Couran all the way."

"This is so frightening. O'Couran has separate issues from Soames about Mack, you might say," Nolie mused. "He despises Jews and faires, that's easy enough—and he resents Mack's class and his fortune!"

"Blanche's final entries were all about O'Couran. After that night when Bruno followed Blanche and Violet to O'Couran's place, Dr. Soames was not happy about the way things were turning out because of the way O'Couran had messed everything up."

Johnnie turned to the final entries. How the hand-writing had changed, appearing child-like, the pages ink-smeared!

"Now that Soames has gotten him to step out of his present office and go into politics," she continued, "O'Couran can whitewash his efforts as Commissioner of Prohibition and call for a full investigation of Mr. Daly. Then get him tried and convicted on everything from bootlegging to sodomy and give O'Couran a clear road to Washington! You've got to see Blanche King's final words. Look here—" Johnnie opened the book to the pages which had most recently been written in.

Nolie began to read. "Look, it's dated as of only yesterday! Let's see what it says: '*Talked at length to my Master about the future of our organization and the difficulties we have undergone due to Brian's stupidity. Master says that Brian never should have let his personal feelings interfere with our great mission. I felt that Master was going to put him in the S. of M. and just leave him to rot! But instead he wants to perfect him then send him on an upward political course into federal government! Oh, the glorious and merciful heart of my Master! He says that O'Couran will be most useful to us in this way and, of course, Master is, as always, infallible.*'"

Nolie looked up. "I just can't believe that Soames would have this much money and power behind him, do you?"

"Sure. He's got lots of people suckered in who are in very high places."

"I think Mack ought to read this through right away, don't you?" Nolie asked. (Johnnie nodded, resolutely.) "And you should say nothing to anybody else about what happened to you today, you poor darling!"

"But what about Mrs. Daly? Shouldn't she be told as well?" Johnnie asked.

"Well, her life *was* being threatened, and still could be. Is it O'Couran who wants her out of the way?"

"No. They truly meant her no actual harm. It was Violet herself, working with one of Soames' followers—to make sure Mrs. Daly wasn't a lezzie and a real girl. And she was! And is! Soames and Violet both broke into the Great Neck house to get those letters from the Colonel to Mack, hoping-against-hope that they would not reveal the fact that their hero, husband and Father was having a full-fledged queer affair with Mack Daly."

"And did they reveal as much?"

"No. The Colonel never hinted at such a thing, for fear someone else would read them. Blanche states plainly that the letters proved only that Connaught loved Mr. D. like a gentleman would love any good soldier. Violet and Doctor. Soames are more certain than ever that Mack is *not* queer and that he and Joey are only friends! Through all of this, that single delusion has kept 'em going."

Nolie looked off, her eyes widening. "O'Couran will prove otherwise, though. Don't you remember the boys telling us that someone was taking photographs from an airplane on that orgiastic weekend they spent up there? It had to be O'Couran's gang. When he presents all his evidence in court it will be the end of Mack and Soames, too! Oh, it's so all so horrifying, Johnnie!" Nolie was overcome with a chill, as warm as it was up on that roof.

"I don't know what to *do* with all of this information!" Johnnie shut the little diary firmly. "I just wish it wasn't me that had to meet up with her, that's all."

Nolie rose, tapping her index finger against her cheek, looking down at Johnnie. "You've got to let Mack in on this. Let him read every word of that thing."

A somber pause arose between both women.

"I will," Johnnie nodded, whispering, "I only hope he can use it all to defend himself against O'Couran."

• • • • •

CHAPTER XXVI

LIEBESTODT

Violet Connaught casually picked up the late edition of the *SUN* while passing her downstairs neighbor's door. She unfolded it and read the headlines:

MOB GIRL LEAPS TO DEATH!
GANGLAND MOLL BLANCHE KING
HURLS SELF IN FRONT OF ELEVATED

A piercing scream echoed throughout the corridors of the 67th Street rooming house where she and the doctor were living. Tenants, rushing out from their little efficiencies, saw a small mustachioed man lying unconscious on the third floor landing, with the tabloid at his side. Having heard what they thought was a woman's cry, some ran about searching for a female in distress, while others knelt to pick her up—one pulling forth a handy flask of gin.

Revived but dazed, the undersized fellow scrambled to his feet, paper in hand, and went for the next flight of stairs, breathing hard, choking back heart-wrenching sobs. They let him go. Apparently something in that evening's spread had 'gotten to the little shrimp' one said, while another bent to scrutinize what at first looked like a centipede, dead, there on the floor.

"What the dickens is that?" the tenant wondered then, looking closer, picked it up. An artificial mustache all caked up with glue. Of all things.

"Blanche is *gone*, Tristan! Gone!" Violet rushed into their cavernous garrett rooms, shouting out the words.

Here, within the gabled and towered attic of a once-grand mansion of the Victorian era, now reduced to a refuge for chapfallen boarders, Soames and Violet hid out. Littered with a vast arsenal of surplus war paraphernalia—guns, buzz bombs, flame throwers, potato mashers, useless artillery shells and surgical equipment—they'd made their home.

One area was reserved for the doctor's experiments. He had salvaged from the garbage all he could from the 68th Street property which Mack Daly had cleaned out from top to bottom. Here, an old kitchen table served as the Master's desk, upon which was dumped wads of cash and mountains of coins.

A scowl met her, as the gaunt man known as Doctor Soames lifted a silk kerchief from his piercing eyes. Seated in an armchair turned away from the door, his head jerked quickly about, revealing a face frozen with a look of awful fate.

"I know! I have just awakened from a trance wherein I saw the whole thing!" He rose and caught her up in his arms. "Oh, my darling, my darling, my darling! Don't you see, it was fore-ordained? She was no longer of any use to us or our Cause!"

"But I *loved* her! And she loved *me*, Tristan! We were so *blissful* together! Why would she go and *do* such a thing?!"

Pushing Violet away from him and holding her at arm's length, he said, "I was only just given a message as to her reason, my son! It was not suicide, but rather sacrifice! Our dear friend Blanche offered herself to the jaws of Death so that others might live."

Violet lifted her odd little face to Tristan Connaught's. "But why, oh, why, oh, why?" she sobbed on. "*Who* must live that she would kill herself?"

"Why—*you*—of course, my child. She died for *you*."

"I?" Violet looked into his piercing madman's eyes, searching therein for an answer.

"Don't you see, my darling child—come, here, rest now, I'll give you another injection. "

Leading Violet into a bedroom which they both shared, he forced her back, caressing her head as it descended upon the pillows. "Blanche was never certain of her own sexual habit. She began by falling in love with you as a woman, and ended by requiring herself to love you as a man."

"But I'm not yet *there*, Tristan! Blanche understood!" Now she turned her head aside and wept bitterly again.

"Now, now, be a man about it! Buck up! Where's my little soldier?" He had brought the needle to the bedside and raised her up, removing her snappy little hat, her suit jacket, then her cuff link, rolling up her sleeve.

"There. There. Blanche could not have continued to love you as you will soon be! She would not love my child, my son…as a MAN. The time had come! That is why she went away. Soon enough, you will wed a *normal* woman who will bear your children!"

"Do you mean that…I'm *really* ready…at last?"

Soames now put the needle back in its case and lay down beside her. "My guides have told me that we must leave on the morrow," he whispered in her ear, caressing her. "Then I will make you look just like me in every way!"

"Where will we go? Our facilites have all been taken from us." Violet whimpered, snuggling up to him, unbuttoning his fly.

"North, to the Slaves of Mary, my son!" Through the darkened room, his eyes glowed up at the ceiling, like two cinders from Hell. "Ah! How good it feels to have your touch upon my manhood."

"Oh, Tristan, you did such a wonderful job on yourself! I can't wait!"

"I didn't do such a bad job on *you* either, my son. It only remains for me to attatch the nuts!"

Violet let go a short, anguished sob. "Please don't ever say 'nuts' again, Tristan. They make me think of Blanche."

• • •

The news of Blanche King's suicide reached Brian O'Couran by way of a phone call to his City Hall office made by one of his mugs barely two hours after her fatal plunge. The gang was on alert to see what Brian would do next. They had ceased to trust him. The most important members were directly involved in the Moran's Elixir mess, now waiting for the Commissioner to expose them in order to save his own skin.

And that was just what the Commissioner was intending on doing. O'Couran slammed down the phone. Had she been killed by one of Soames insane devotees? Would he be next?

Reaching across the desk for his telephone, fumbling to punch his fat fingers into the dial, he began making frantic calls, trying to ascertain whether or not she had truly jumped to her death or was pushed. Nobody knew either way, and it was not until the evening editions hit the stands that it was declared an obvious suicide.

Now, he only had to worry about the reason behind that leap. Why?

Sloppy drunk and still in his office long after everyone had gone home, he rifled the papers for the whole story. There was little to tell, except that some low-lifes around town had recognized her as a known moll.

All the papers still carried stuff about the Moran's Elixir scandal, though. The ownership of this questionable enterprise was sure to be traced to him soon enough. Looking over the notes that his secretary had left him, he skimmed his recent legal advice:

1) Admit having owned the company only briefly, believing it to be an honest operation—a harmless patent medicine manufactory, makers of a fair and square product, easily purchased over the counter, intended to help thousands. OR:

2) Tell them that the infusion of deadly chemicals into the product, and the purveying of it, had nothing to do with you! OR:

3) Tell them that *the same men* continued to run it when you took the

company over, and rather than terminate these dishonest employees—big-hearted fellow that you are—you allowed them all to stay on. OR:

4) Tell them that these fellows were taking money off the top, leaving you with nothing. *They* were the culprits—*they* deliberately added the poisons to stretch the product, (not you!) making it go further, until the end result was rotgut hooch. OR:

5) That they swindled you by profiting off the stuff; you ended up taking all the blame and will now suffer a terrific loss of both money and reputation.

("It'll be some task to convince my boys of this," O'Couran muttered to himself. *"But maybe I can get away with it."*) He read on:

NOTE: True, you should've now and then checked up on the operation! But you were too *busy*—because this sort of thing is happening all over! Companies being turned into illegal businesses by disreputable employees behind the backs of their owners everywhere. It has gotten to be a national pasttime. SO YOU MIGHT CONSIDER:

6) Accusing the plant supervisor, the chemist, the accountant—all of the heads of the Moran's Elixir company. Have them sent up, and let that be the end of it.

7) Using all of this to your own advantage. Publicly state that since you went into office you've become nothing but a scapegoat! *A perfect excuse for stepping down!*

Well, it sounded pretty damned good to O'Couran. Anything to save his arse. Brian didn't trust Soames, even though he called him Master, and now Soames was his only recourse.

What if the Master couldn't pull off his grand vision of a better America by bringing forth a perfect generation from the present one and catapult him into a Senate seat?The millions required would first of all mean that his experiments would have to be astounding successes, and thus far not even the monkey gland serum showed much improvement on anyone. And look what happened to the wife of that whoremaster, King Tut!

Fingering his own boys who had taken over the running of the plant would be touchy. Oh, he could bribe the D.A. and the judges and the jury, too, and get 'em off on something or other, but that would take more money than he had! Mostly because the Master kept on demanding it—kept on making Brian all those promises. First, however, didn't he have to get his boys who worked in the Moran's plant to take the rap for him? That was what he had to do. Bribe 'em.

But how—and with what? He had surrendered most of his cash profits from the Moran's Elixir racket to Soames, after paying off the fellows who trailed Ynez and took those goddammed out-of-focus photographs from that aeroplane. He only had a bit left…hidden here and there, to keep him going once his salary stopped.

How was he to continue his booze racket if he no longer had his wonderful position? He could certainly bring Daly to his knees! But—without endangering his own reputation and angering Soames to such a degree that his Master would kill him?

If the evidence that he had gathered against Daly was presented in court, it might just reflect their joint affiliation with the Imperio gang! That would do the Jew in for sure, but would also mean his own ruin as well. At least he could close down the Club deVol!

There had to be plenty of stuff hidden there which he could commandeer, then trace the bottles directly to Daly, and use the haul to finesse his boys into taking the rap for him. Let 'em cut it and re-cut it! Such pure hooch would bring 'em in thousands once diluted with several hundred gallons of turpentine!

He at once pulled forth that most dreaded and official-looking form which would send his agents down to the Club deVol. Filling it out in a matter-of-fact way, he dropped it into his outgoing inter-office mail tray. That was that.

"Hullo, Morrisey—is that you?" Brian was on the phone again, this time to a key mug who had managed the Moran's plant for him. "We're goin' to raid the Club deVol down on 46th Street in the next couple of days. I want you to be first in on the take, you old s.o.b. you! It's gonna be some haul." (O'Couran let go a chuckle, but the man on the other end did not respond in kind.) "—now the nerve of you, Morrisey! Don't we go way, way back? Ain't we made from the same cloth? I would never turn on ye! Me? Brian Patrick O'Couran?"

But Morrisey wasn't buying the Commissioner's blarney this time around. He was sputtering threats. Death threats. The whole gang was ready to draw and quarter Old Man O'Couran, who was nothing but crazy for going in with that quack doctor as he did! His boys put it all together; they knew what he was going to pull next!

O'Couran, cursing at him, slammed down the telephone and, feeling himself sliding off his chair, grabbed for anything to pull him back up. Yanking his blotter forward, the photograph of Margaret, his wife, was revealed under it. Until recently, the picture had always been before him on his desk.

"Oh, what have I done to you, Peg, my Peg! It was not my doin' but his!" he blubbered, pointing across the desk at a frame which had formerly held his wife's picture, and now displayed that of his Master, Doctor Soames.

• • •

Another member of the medical profession, one greatly respected and esteemed, kept a telephone at her bedside table, instructing her servants to allow it to ring through no matter what the hour. Having been On Call for two full days and nights, she was exhausted. Luckily, no one had phoned.

As a result of helping her friend Annabelle Harrison prepare for the long-awaited opening of her gallery, Doctor. Sutton felt she could at last look forward to a good night's sleep.

However, at six-thirty a.m., she heard an operator's voice distantly crackling over the wire: "Will you accept a collect call from Mrs. Margaret O'Couran?"

Doctorr. Sutton said of course she would, then heard hysterical weeping coming from the other end.

"Mrs. O'Couran! Is that you? What is wrong! Please, please compose yourself!"

"Oh. I…I can't. Sweet Jesus, help me! It's all burnin' down! The whole mountain is on fire! The loonies are loose runnin' everywhere! The big lodge next to it will be goin' up like a tinder box soon! I don't know where Mr. and Mrs. Daly went!"

"But they've moved into the City—where are you!" Behind the voice, sirens and shouting were heard.

"Tell Mr. and Mrs. Daly! Everyone is burning to death! God help me!"

"Mrs. O'Couran—are you injured?"

"No, no, I managed to get out and walked all the way here, into town. I had your business card in my little prayer book and so I didn't know who else to telephone. Thank God I was spared! I've got to hide before they come and get me! They'll kill me once they know I've told you!"

The call was suddenly cut off.

"Hello! Hello! Operator! Can you please trace that call? It was collect!"

"Hold please—" (Doctor. Sutton waited breathlesly.) "Sorry, Madame, we cannot trace it."

Poor Margaret O'Couran, thinking of course she could reach the Dalys! They were not yet listed! What was on fire! Mrs. O'Couran sounded sane, but horribly alarmed, overwrought, terrified for her life! What lodge was on fire? Loonies, escaped? All these thoughts flew through Doctor. Sutton's mind as she placed a call to Annabelle Harrison's studio out in Great Neck.

When the operator rang back, she heard Keys' voice, answering sleepily.

"Perhaps Belle can help me, Mr. Parker. Margaret O'Couran, the Commissioner of Prohibition's wife, is in terrible trouble and I don't know the Dalys' new number! " Keys had, by now, handed the phone to Annabelle.

"Elizabeth! Yes, yes, of course I have their numbers," she told Dr. Sutton. "And I think I know what has happened, too. Mack's got to go up there! There is no time to waste. I'll telephone Mack. Ynez needn't know. I don't think she could take it."

"Is it very far? Shall I go with them?"

Annabelle paused, then said, "It's in the Adirondacks. Don't be silly. They'll have to fly up—and–oh! I know how I can get them there! I shall ring you back—"

Peggy O'Couran had, by then, replaced the ear-piece on the telephone at the post office, and wandered dazed back out into the streets. The entire sky blackened with smoke, townsfolk running from their homes, as all the Volunteer Fire Companies from the neighboring villages roared and clanged through the main street, heading for the mountains which now were engulfed in leaping flames.

A few of the more fortunate inmates of the santorium had, like Peggy, made it into town; wretched characters, further terrifying the already frightened natives. Walking about, filthy, dressed in tattered nightgowns, they screamed and moaned.

An elderly man cried out, "I am Avery Hopwood, the stock broker! Please won't someone try and reach my family! I was imprisoned up there and tortured!"

But no one came to the aid of these poor souls because it was apparent that the fire was already spreading to the edge of town. Peggy sat on the stoop of the general store and began to cry, already adding more tears to those caused by the overwhelming smoke. "Why, oh, why did I ever come here and leave the old Sod!" she wailed, burying her head in her arms.

Up on the mountain, the Slaves of Mary had been claimed by the great blaze the night prior, and now seemed like a white hot entrance to Hell itself. That was where it had all started. The strong winds played havoc with the fire, sending it first down the mountain, and finally past the little valley at its West side, where that great war hero, Colonel Calvin Connaught, had created his great lodge.

As dawn broke, the house and grounds were surrounded by columns of flames devouring the tall trees, dropping great boughs alive with fire everywhere. Huck had risen to see the sky a horrible red and black, the land all about the house no longer distinguishable from the sky. Waves of heat distorted anything he could make out at even a short distance. The Colonel was gone. The horses could be heard shrieking, the dogs frantically barking. His first thought was to find his man, then round the animals up, cover their heads with rags soaked in water, and get them down to the lake with Calvin and himself. As he passed along the balcony, he could see trees engulfed in flames, careening down over the veranda.

He shouted out Calvin's name, pulling on his jacket, running down the stairs. Somewhere, amid the crackling and tumbling boughs, he thought he heard an anguished voice.

Looking out from the front door, he saw the strangest thing.

A woman was attempting to carry a little man toward the house by way of the path leading to the lake and then toward the old monastery. It appeared that the man had on a hospital gown and was bleeding. Bearing her burden, the woman would put him down, adjust her picture hat, then struggle upward again, coughing, reassuring the wounded soul that they had not far to go, continuing onward.

Huck went back inside, looking all about for Connaught. Hearing yet another strange sound, the playing of the tune "Over There" on the gramophone, he located the Colonel sipping tea at the dining room table, dressed in full uniform.

"They've taken Paris, lad! I knew it would come to this! Goddammed heinies! But, I've got everything under control, we shall attack within the hour!"

"We gotta take care of the horses and our dogs, Calvin! Come on! Gotta get the truck!" Huck went to him, taking his arm.

The Colonel, rising majestically, peered out at the fire engulfing the lodge and smiled. "This is the moment I've been wating for, my boy! War! War is upon us! And we shall have victory!"

Looking at his man now, Huck saw that, at last, it had happened. He had completely lost his mind. Startled from this realization by the bell clanging outside the front door, he realized the lady and her wounded burden had arrived. He ran to the entryway.

There, the woman stood, imperious, holding the sagging body of a small man in her arms. "I am Mrs. Isolde Connaught," she said. "Will you please announce me and tell the Colonel that his wife has returned, and has brought with her…our son."

• • •

In the hydroplane that Annabelle Harrison had secured, Joe, Bruno and Ynez sat on the edge of their seats, peering down at the miles and miles of billowing smoke. Mack, up front with the pilot, flying courageously with little visibility, was attempting to guide him toward the lodge and Caisson Lake.

"We'll probably be able to take her down right on the lake, sir," the pilot said, intent on his mission, his eyes never leaving the strange sky. "Do you see any sign of the place you're looking for?"

Mack peered through binoculars. "It's impossible. I can't make a thing out. There's the little town nearby but—wait! Look! There it is! The lake! Right on his property!"

"That must be the lodge," Bruno said. "It's still in one piece. So far."

"Not for long. Look how close the fire is," Ynez added grimly.

"Dat must be duh ol' monastery," Joe called out. "See it?"

As the smoke cleared briefly, they looked down upon the building.

The pilot shook his head. "Whatever it was, it's gone now...just like a giant piece of red hot coal."

Mack pointed down. "The far end of the lake looks untouched."

The pilot began his descent. "I'll bring her up clear to the opposite edge, and wait for you."

Now the lodge came clearly into view. The fire had already taken the northern side of the veranda, spreading its sinister fingers toward the tower where the American flag flapped eerily in the breeze, still untouched.

The airplane's pontoons touched the surface of the lake.

"Steady now, everybody!" the pilot called out as the craft was engulfed in billowing smoke. They had landed, but could not see a thing in any direction.

"There's the shore! See it? I can taxi in!" The pilot called out, cutting the engines, skimming his craft into the shallow waters of the shore. "Now you'll have to jump out, run like the bejesus and get your pals and be back here lickety-split!" He then turned to Ynez. "And you'll be waiting in here with me, ma'm."

"The Hell I will! I didn't come all this way to sit and twiddle my thumbs!"

Bruno and Joe leapt from the plane, ending up almost knee deep in lake water—so hot it nearly scalded. Mack hopped out then lifted Ynez from the plane.

"Why did you insist on coming, Ynez?" he shouted to her over the roar of the fire.

"I couldn't leave you boys! When I was a kid we had lots of big fires in the coal mines! It was exciting!" Wrapping her scarf about her face, she headed with Mack toward the path's edge where Bruno and Joe waited.

They set out upward, toward the lodge—Joe, close to Mack, then Ynez, and finally Bruno. On either side, and even ahead of them, the fire had come within less than thirty feet.

"If dis operation takes more dan ten minutes," Joe yelled, "we are all fried eggs. Let's make it snappy!"

On they went, with the great blaze encroaching now, inches away from the brush along the path. As the heat became more and more intense, the smoke unbearable, Bruno spotted the lodge, entirely surrounded by collapsed trees all on fire. "It's over there to your left, Mack! Can we even get to it?"

"There's a side porch, at the west side of the place! Come on!" Mack yelled.

He led them toward the stairs where Huck, Wriggs and Joe had earlier piled up logs. Here, the fire was but a foot from that portion of the house, but had not yet touched it.

"I'm going in!" Mack hollered. "It's only a matter of minutes before the whole thing comes crashing down—"

Joe, without hesitation, ran after him, turning around and shouting, "Don't worry! We can do it! We'll get 'em bot' outa dere!"

Bruno shook his head. "You're both crazy!" he hollered.

Ynez (screaming, "Mack! Mack! Don't!") was not even heard as Joe and Mack proceeded into the lodge, like some great funeral pyre.

Suddenly, shots rang out. Through the mist of the smoke, they saw Huck, doubled over, clutching his left shoulder. In his blood-soaked hospital gown, the little man could also now be seen through the clearing smoke on the floor before them. It was this figure who held the gun and had shot at Huck.

A thin, high voice emerging from this man shouted: "Go away! We don't need anybody! We're back together now as we should be! A family once again!"

Mack recognized her at once: Violet Connaught. Attempting to pull herself up, still managing to hold the gun in one hand, she frantically began undressing herself with the other. Looming over her, Mack and Joe now saw the Colonel, head held high, standing at attention—his eyes, that of a trapped beast.

Joe started to run toward Huck, as Mack, baffled by what he was seeing, called out: "Calvin, it's me, MacDaily!"

The Colonel turned slowly toward his beloved. "MacDaily! Get away from here! Look what's come for me! My wife! My wife and my son! They mustn't know about us! The Germans have taken Paris! We've lost, Mack! We've lost the whole goddammed war!"

From nearby, a hollow, insane laugh rivaled the crackling, tumbling timbers. Mack now saw what appeared to be a haggard woman in a picture hat perched on top of a red wig—a man's body protruding from a long Edwardian dress, hairy chest and Adam's apple encumbered by pearls and diamond necklaces. His face, with a two-day growth of beard, was painted like a clown's, smiling ghoulishly.

"Now I seen everyt'ing!" Joe muttered, doing a double take and pulling out his gun.

Doctor. Soames, having again assumed the role of the Colonel's wife, hissed at Mack, "You lied to the world! You seduced my husband and turned him queer and made him into your lover! But *I've* got him back now, and we have won over those sick fiends who took him—and our perfect vision—away from us. We have at last triumphed!"

Joe hollered, "Shut the fuck up or I'll kill yuz both!"

"Joe," Mack whispered under his breath, "Violet has a gun…be careful."

"That little guy dere is Violet?!"

Outside, the pilot had left his aircraft to warn Bruno and Ynez that they must all leave at once—or surely die. Ynez told Bruno she was going inside and, fighting him off, ran toward the building shouting Mack's name.

Bruno, turning to the pilot, ordered him to start the propellors. "I'm sure as Hell not leavin' my brother in there! Turn your hydroplane about and prepare for a take-off!"

Running to Ynez, he shielded her with his coat as torrents of hot ash carried by the wind rained down on them. "Ynez! For Chrissakes, GO BACK!"

"I'm *not* leaving my Mack!"

They arrived in the Great Room of the lodge to witness Mack attempting to reason with Colonel Connaught. "Tell Isolde that you and your son will die in a matter of seconds if you all don't get out of here."

Looking quickly at Ynez and Bruno,who had just arrived, he cautioned them with a look and subtle gesture to remain absolutely still and quiet and then resumed talking to the Colonel in measured tones, "We have been sent by the high officials of the Kaiser to render you and your family to safety." He paused. "Even though we did lose the war, Calvin, you are still a hero and will be celebrated."

As he was speaking, Joe inched closer to Huck who, still conscious, was slumped over an armchair. Above them, a tall pine engulfed in flames toppled right outside the dining room windows, hitting the veranda roof, causing it to suddenly collapse. Flames and glass crackled about the place where the Colonel stood directly under the valulting of the tower, which now began to sag.

"Mack! Be careful!" Ynez shouted out.

Soames, only just at that moment aware of their presence, whirled about, regarding her archly. "*You*! Here, in my encampment! Whore! Filthy, dirty bitch!"

Advancing toward Ynez, he lifted his hands, covered with blood, making them into claws.

Bruno was slowly drawing forth his gun. "You keep away from her, you goddammed freak," he yelled.

But Soames kept approaching, now but two feet from Ynez, as the roof of the tower above them was collpasing. Then, but inches away, he suddenly spit directly in her face.

Before anyone there realized what she was doing, Ynez grabbed Bruno's gun and began shooting straight at Soames.

Six full shots rang out. Ynez' face was impassive as Soames' reacted with a horrible spasm, crumbled to the ground, blood gushing from his mouth, the hat and wig falling away. The figure, dying there before them, was that of a man.

He had opened an old wound which Ynez had buried, unhealed, going back to her childhood, on that day when a stranger had spat upon poor dear Al.

Violet screaming out, rising, staggered to him. "Tristan! Where is my Mother? What have you done with her!" She had removed the hospital gown and stood nude before the corpse of Soames, weeping.

To everyone's shock, the result of her last surgery showed itself. Below her flaccid penis, the doctor had stitched a pair of fleshy sacks holding the male glands of the Whistler. These receptacles were the precious and tiny feet once belonging to Lady Lee, completing, at last, what Nature had omitted. Dangling there, they did perhaps resemble testicles, had it not been for the delicate little toenails which Chollie Fong had painted the shade of "Was My Face Red."

Transfixed, the four visitors to the Colonel's lodge did not at first notice the whole roof of the tower over them groaning under the flames.

"Quick!" Joe shouted, grabbing Huck, as Mack ran forward to get Colonel Connaught. But as he was assisting him toward the door, the Colonel's gaze fell upon Violet.

"What have I done? What have I done to my child!"

He seemed then to come to his senses and, standing bolt upright, looked squarely at Mack. "I must remain here in my castle and die with those who loved me. Go now! I order you!"

Joe hollered, "Leave him, Mack! Come on!" holding Huck in his arms.

The tower roof fell inward. Mack, blinded by the vast white hot explosion, felt the Colonel's hand force him back and away. And as he was pulled from the place by Joe and Bruno, he saw Connaught saluting him, then fall over the bodies of Violet Connaught and his lover, Tristan Soames.

"Calvin! No! Calvin!" Huck sobbed, barely conscious.

The fire had now taken over the stables. With the horses and dogs running down the path to the lake, wild and terrified, dust, flames, hot cinders all conspired to make them lose their way. "We'll be trampled to death!" Ynez screamed. As they ran from the lodge the entire structure collapsed toward them.

Turning, Mack watched the great lodge being swallowed up in flames, surrendering in blinding defeat. The lodge had become one with the greater fire which had overtaken the mountain that it had crowned.

Joe, holding onto Huck, yelled for Mack to follow them to the lake. Mack looked up and stumbled toward him. He was the last one in the aircraft, looking behind in disbelief.

"Did you really love him that much, Mack?" Ynez asked him, breathless.

"Never. I was haunted by him. Always under his power—but now that feeling is over, at last," Mack whispered hoarsely.

He shook his head, bending it low. Joe put his arm around him, after maneuvering Huck into a reclining position.

Bruno opened Huck's jacket and shirt, looking at his shoulder wounds.

"That little freak of nature was a lousy shot, kid. Lucky for you."

Huck buried his head in Bruno's chest and wept. "My man's gone…" was all he said.

The hydroplane gained both height and speed within less than an hour. A sinister, distant, blackened sun, surveying the earth like the eye of a devouring monster, protruded angrily just up over the top of the smoke-blackened heavens.

• • • • •

CHAPTER XXVII

THAT FINISHES THAT

Baby was telling Bruno, "We had two bluenoses in the club posing as butter and egg men just now." Then, the operator at the front desk telephoned.

Joe answered. "Fat Tony's downstairs, Bruno. Must be Pop died. Finally."

And he had. "Only back for a day, too," Joe muttered sadly. "And now dis." It was just past four.

That whole day, Mack had been at the hearing, grilled by the investigation committee. He had still not arrived back at the apartment when this sad news came in.

Deucie and Baby were worried about what must've been Prohibition agents. With no one else to tell this news to except Bruno, they were left with no answers as to what to do. As he was rushing out the door of Ynez's place (who had sequestered herself in her bedroom since returning from the Adirondacks), his only order was: "Have Mack call me down at the restaurant as soon as he gets here."

He and Joe left the 55th Street apartment at once. Joe cried a little, Bruno not at all. Both were concerned about how their Mother would take it.

"Yer it, now, B. Yer duh man," was all Joe said.

Ynez rose as soon as they'd left, rallied by the door slamming, wandering through her cavernous and sleekly modern new digs in search of a cigarette and a drink, pulling on a chiffon peignoir. Somewhere between the double living room and a space which still had no function or name, she found the deVols standing there, staring at each other.

She murmured, "I couldn't sleep and I think I heard Bruno leave—" Then added, "*Now* what?"

Baby told her.

"God! I can't believe it's taken the old geezer took so long to croak! Well, there'll be celebrating, I can tell you that much—now that Bruno's in charge of everything!"

"Not at the Club deVol, there won't be," Baby would've expressed condolences except that she was so concerned about what had just happened. "We just had two dry agents in there. Wait and see, with Mack on the pan, we're gonna get raided."

Ynez told them to sit down for God's sake, and so they did, just opposite her, as she fairly collapsed on a white sharkskin sofa. "So you closed up and came here?" she asked wearily.

Deucie nodded. "They were in there with maybe only seven or eight reg'lars. I served 'em and they paid and walked out. They didn't swallow the stuff."

This meant that they carried the liquor from the club in their mouths and spit it into a phial once outside, proving the establishment was, without a doubt, a speak. It was now only a matter of paperwork, a paddy wagon and a yellow padlock.

"Well, you did the right thing," Ynez said. "Now don't go back—it could mean the raid'll be on for tonight. Even if you're the only two folks in there—you know you'll both go to jail!"

No one spoke. Then Ynez sat up, rubbing her forehead. "Christ, somebody's got to get the booze out of there *now*, or it'll be traced to Mack!"

"That's why we're here, Ynez," Baby said curtly. "With Bruno's father On The Other Side, we're as good as cooked! And just when you need 'em most, too!"

"What a time for this to happen!" Ynez leapt up, heading for the telephone. "I'm going to call up the plant. There's this guy named Abie there who could bring the trucks around and get the stuff out of there before the cops hit it!"

Baby saw her racing back and forth between the maze of rooms. She said, "Maybe we'd better let Mack handle it, Ynez—"

But Ynez was already calling Brooklyn.

All the boys were at the restaurant when Bruno and Joe arrived. They had gone upstairs to console Mama, who was surrounded by her sisters and friends. Dry-eyed, holding a rosary, sitting in the middle of everyone, she was the picture of composure.

Looking up at Bruno, she said in Sicilian: "*Ora si tu figghio mio qu aue ha portari sangu e lacrime e tutto u resto di noiauci amo ha fari chiddu che ni dicinu iettari sangu e cianceri*!"

Bruno left Joe with their Mother, and went back downstairs to join the men. It had begun.

For a whole hour, Joe sat with his arms around her, then also left to return to the restaurant. He was just going through the kitchen toward the dining room when Fat Tony came in, but it wasn't to pay his condolences. Joe stopped there to listen.

He had been at court all day taking in what was happening to Mack. Then, he'd gotten a tip-off about O'Couran obtaining a court order to get all of the booze out of the club. It was going to be used as direct evidence against Daly.

Joe heard his brother asking, "How bad is it for Daly?" and Fat Tony replying, "It's over." Then there was a pause. Joe could only hear, over the respectful silence, the heavy breathing of the dozen guys coming from out there. They were waiting for Burno to make his first big decision. Joe hung back in the shadows, his heart pounding faster than it ever had before.

"We'll need Mack's trucks. That's all." Then he outlined a plan. They would go to the plant, steal them, and proceed at once to the club. No one would ever suspect that a quartet of bakery trucks with the name "Leventhal" on them were hauling the biggest cache of liquor in Manhattan.

"We'll bring the stuff right over here—store it underneath my offices."

"What's gonna happen when Daly finds out?" someone asked.

Joe heard Bruno answer, "Well, he's fucked anyway, isn't he, so what difference does it make?"

Joe was stunned. He didn't move a muscle. Where was Mack? Why hadn't he called? Racing back up the stairs, through his own bedroom, he pulled open his bureau drawer and got his gun…then out of the window and across the rooftop…down the fire escape…

He had the grace of some wild animal, driven to save what it loved more than anything else in the whole world. And as he ran, he was filled with anger.

It was well past six in the evening when Mack returned to his new home. Nobody was about, except Elliot, who, by this time, was a little tipsy. Wriggs, it seemed, had been spending a lot of time with Huck since Elliot had started drinking again.

"Well?" Elliot said as Mack entered.

"Well—" Mack gave it right back to him, with a little laugh, taking a soft drink and lighted cigarette from him, then slowly lowering himself on a big satin ottoman. "Well, indeed…I told them the truth, Elliot."

"—about—?" Elliot just barely asked.

"Oh, not about my marriage, or about me being queer, or anybody else really. Just about how I got into this in the first place. You know, the big boys demanding I supply them in secret—back when I delivered the stuff to them for free."

"That musta gone over just grand," Elliot quipped bitterly. "Were some of 'em sitting right in front of you?"

"Sure," Mack answered. "And just behind them, the feds—in from Washington for all this next week. And maybe the week after that, too." He let go a deep sigh. "But I couldn't do it any other way. I had to start…at the beginning, you see. So I did." He made a helpless gesture, his hands rising slightly from his knees. "And these are just the preliminaries. O'Couran goes up tomorrow. Last. Out of deferance, I guess, since he used to be the commissioner."

"Then what?" Elliot asked.

"Then?" Mack stopped. "Then…well, then, I'll have to have my lawyer come in on it. I'm going to be indicted."

Elliot was suddenly very lucid. "How do you know that!"

"Oh, word's gotten around. I should've stepped down as O'Couran did, but I didn't even think it would come to this—"

"Come to what? What does this all mean Mack—" (His best friend trying to hide his concern, but doing a bad job of it.)

"Just that the big boys are going to use O'Couran to finish me, so I don't let much more out and into the open. Nobody else really knows how corrupt this prohibition mess has become, you see." Again he laughed. "And I certainly ought to know more than anybody because I got myself in *deeper* than anybody else has!"

He drew forth a small ring of keys from his trouser pocket and tossed them in the air, catching them in his hand. "I'm in charge of the whole East Coast bonded alcohol racket, by way of a gift from Uncle Sam. I was reminded of that over and over again today. A very big responsibility. For somebody who wasn't born here. Who also happens to be a kike."

"Aw, Hell, Mack. How long were up there…in front of them?"

"Well, 'til just now. About an hour ago."

"From when?"

"All day. All day long, kid! From eight in the morning until six at night."

That single sentence told everything.

Elliot cleared his throat. "What about your marriage to Ynez? Have they gotten into your—private life yet?"

"Somewhat."

"Oh, Mack! That's terrible! It's none of their business!" Elliot realized something was happening to him—sitting crunched up before Mack, shaking his head. Just shaking his head. Coming apart. Feeling like he couldn't stop himself from crying.

"They can *make* it their business. If they're out to get you—or rather me." Mack looked down at Elliot, almost void of all emotion, his voice hoarse and strained.

Taking another swig of his soft drink, smashing out the cigarette he had not even smoked, he slowly said in a whisper, "And they *are* out to get me, Elliot. You know that as well as I do. And they will, too." He rose and went alone out to the terrace.

It was then that they heard the doorbell. Elliot went to answer it. There was Joe, sweating and all out of breath.

"Gotta see Mack. Right now. Alone."

Elliot pointed to the terrace, then left them alone.

Joe put his arms about Mack. "Listen to me." It all came out in a confused horrible way. Somewhere in there, he mentioned that Pop Imperio had just died. Then Joe said, "No matter what happens, you and I are always gonna be tuggether, see?"

"You mean they're going to the plant and hi-jacking my trucks!" Joe had to admit it. His brother was, after all, a real son of a bitch.

Mack held him, staring into his eyes. "There's something they discussed today which I want you to understand, Joe. Something that might finish me. See, I'm a naturalized citizen. What I've done—what I've been doing—well…they've put it in so many words. It just isn't *American*. A real American would never have done what I did. They're all up against me just to save their skins." (Joe sputtered, fighting mad.) "But, Joey, they've got tremendous power. *Tremendous*. Joe—now listen to me: they're talking about deporting me. Taking away my citizenship. Sending me back to Austria."

"Can I come wid yuz?" Joe asked instantly.

Mack sighed, looking at him with tears in his eyes. "Oh, God, Joe." He really didn't understand. "Would you want to? Now that your father is gone, aren't you Bruno's right-hand man?"

"Well sure—but, you don't hafta go! We could hide yuh out. Take yuh to Chicago!"

"No, no, Joe, I'm up against the federal government here. They'd find me. It's better that I just turn myself in."

Joe was fiercely enraged now, he wasn't sure at just what…not at Mack, but at life…at God, probably. But he felt like doing something to save Mack, thinking with his heart, the way a gangster would when he could no longer think any other way.

"WHAT? Give up! Give up to duh goddammed law! What'd dey ever do for you! Goddammed feds! Naw, naw, Mack. Not you. I won't let yuz. I won't let yuz, dat's all!" He turned away to wipe his eyes. "I won't let 'em take yuz away from me. I'll kill 'em, Mack! I'll kill every single Goddammed one of 'em!"

He twirled about and Mack saw in Joe's eyes something that was never there before. Joe was a killer. He hadn't been until then. But he had always had it in him. For love only, of course. He could kill for love. And he would—and he was going to. Because Joe Imperio loved Mack more than anything else in the whole world.

"I'm gettin' your booze away from Bruno!—t'inks he can get one over on me! I'll show that bastard! I'll kill him, Mack! I'll kill him for what he's doin' to you!"

Mack called after him, loudly, throwing open the doors. But Joe had gone.

• • •

Joe had stolen Mack's car and sped crosstown, then downtown, not going through any lights, but swerving in and out of the traffic, pounding his fist on the horn, blinded by his anger, wiping tears from his eyes.

Ynez had not been able to reach anyone at the plant. There was no answer, which was odd. Most odd. And so, in her typically dramatic way, grabbing Deucie and Baby, she hurried out of her new home, located a taxi driver who would take them all that way into Brooklyn, and arrived there to find that the gates had been chained and padlocked.

A notice placed prominently at the guard house read:

**CLOSED BY ORDER OF THE FEDERAL GOVERNMENT
IN COMPLIANCE
WITH THE NATIONAL PROHIBITION ACT.**

For a long time, as twilight descended over the canal, the three stood staring at it. Finally Deucie sat down on the curb because his good leg was aching so badly. Ynez went up to the gates, rattling them, yelling out, "Hello! Anyone in there?" It was like some awful desert out there. Not a soul around.

"How we gonna find Mack?" Baby asked. "How we gonna get back? What'll we do?"

No answer came.

• • •

With no trouble at all, Joe broke into the Club deVol by the back service door in mere seconds, then sat in the darkness of the place, on the floor, his back up against the stage, sobbing his heart out, twirling mechanically the barrel of his .32.

Bruno arrived soon after. But he had no trouble getting in by the front door. He had stolen a key and had it copied. He heard his brother—sniffling, swearing out loud at no one, at everyone.

Silently, he went in and sat beside him. For a long time neither brother spoke.

Bruno finally said, "You heard what I said back at Mom's, didn't you?"

"You coulda tol' Mack, yuh know, you lousy piece of shit! Everybody fucks Mack over, Bruno! You ain't no help!" He was crying, but mastering his sorrow; replacing it with terrible vengence, he continued: "Now jus' becuz Pop's gone you t'ink you can fuck everybody over, cuz yer duh Man. Well,

I'm here to tell yuh dat I got some say in what's comin' down, see!" He paused to wipe his nose, then put his gun under his brother's chin. "Mackie is gonna need dough to break town. So's we're gonna hide him out an' use duh dough from his booze to set us up in Chicago! You and me and Mack and Mrs. Daly—we're gonna get the fuck outa dis Hell-hole an' go to Chicago. Yer gonna see dat Mack gets his booze back and we're gonna start all over and never, ever, ever play by nobody's Goddammed rules again."

"Joey—Joey, listen to me…" Bruno had something between a smile and smirk on his face. He yelled at him, suddenly: "Come on, Joe! Get some sense, will you!" He shoved the gun away. Then he shrugged. Disgusted. "Oh, you can't. You never could. You're just a dumb ass."

Joe shouted back: "You gonna leave my Mack open tuh gettin' deported?" Shaking his head violently—"No, no, you ain't, my brudder. You an' me, we bot' of us saw him comin! Like a fuckin' sittin' duck, Bruno—an' went after him! You know we did, Bruno! You set *me* up and him, too!"

Joe stood up, facing his brother, gun clenched in his hand. "You made out just swell, too, you got duh wifey, you got duh rackets, you got his dough and you get off widout so much as a fuckin' SCRATCH. And whut's he get! SHIT, brudder, SHIT! An' I ain't goin' tuh stan' by an' see it happen!"

Bruno stood as well. "You're crazy, Joey—this is our business, Joe. You got yourself in too deep, that's all!" He laughed. "I never meant you to fall for Daly! You've got to think this out. You're fucking nuts, Joe! You're a crazy fairy, that's all!"

Both brothers stared at one another.

Joe asked, "But what're you gonna DO! You gotta help Mack, Bruno! You gotta!"

Just as Bruno was gently taking the gun from Joe, a vehicle was heard coming up the alley.

• • •

Baby helped Deucie to his feet. A big black Phaeton was rolling into veiw.

"It's Bruno's goons," Ynez said.

Fat Tony squeezed himself from behind the wheel, while four other guys peered out. He read the notice without even aknowledging the three people standing there.

"Now what?" he asked no one in particular.

"You tell us," Baby replied.

"We're s'posed ta get duh trucks," he said. "Gotta break in."

"For what?" Ynez asked.

"—get duh booze outa duh club usin' bakery trucks. Ain't you all hooked up wid Mack Daly somehow?"

"Only directly," Deucie answered. "And you're talkin' about *our* club. Which," he added, "sounds like a good idea, except that I don't think Mack would jeopardize the Leventhal bunch by commandeering their trucks if anything...well...if you fellows should get caught."

Tony was slow. He had to think about it. "Well, dat is troo. Only we're under orders." Baby asked, "Whose orders?" Tony said: "Bruno Imperio's."

Baby, Deucie and Ynez exchanged looks, then Ynez whispered (also, to no one in particular), "Oh, he wouldn't really do *that*, would he?"

But Deucie jangled the big yellow padlocks and smiled. "Well, you men had better get to it! Be dark before too long!"

"How in Hell we gonna cut t'roo dem!" Tony had turned to his boys.

They had no answer.

• • •

The engine had been cut. Breathing hard, Bruno and Joe stared at each other. Bruno whispered, "That's not Tony and the boys. It's too soon. "

Then, a voice from outside said: "There's been a break-in here."

"You think they took the stuff out?" another asked.

"Not Daly. He's got keys. Somebody else has been in here."

"—there's gotta be a secret vault somewhere—" Two more men were entering the place.

It was the voice of O'Couran. Moments passed and a terrible silence fell over the Club deVol. Then: "Here t'is, boys. Back of this broom closet."

Bruno whispered, "He's not gonna get that stuff. That suff is mine."

Joe still couldn't believe it. Stringing them along. Just like always. He wasn't any pal to Mack. He didn't care about Mrs. Daly. He was a rat. Now, he was turning from his own brother.

Bruno eyed Joe and hissed, "Don't look at me like that. Forget it. Forget everything. We gotta save our asses here."

Joe took back his gun with no trouble, shoving it into his brother's back. "Get outa duh way, Bruno. I'm handlin' dis job."

There were sounds of the police and O'Couran rattling down the cellar stairs. He had three men with him.

"You crazy, Joe? Hear me out. I've got a plan! I wouldn't screw you over—listen to me!"

"Let's hear it. Only don't try an' stop me."

"We'll get 'em on the way up the stairs. You hide on the right, I'll be on the left, see?" Bruno was calm, but Joe was ready for blood. He wanted blood. He wanted to kill O'Couran then maybe kill his own brother. If he was lying to him. Again. Like always. But maybe this time he wasn't. And maybe he was.

"O. k. but let's do it now," Joe replied.

Bruno pulled his gun from his shoulder holster, with Joe firmly gripping the pair he had carried into the club. Into the darkness of the back club the brothers went. The cellar light was on, shedding a faint glow through the broom closet, revealing that two dry agents, fully armed with rifles, were down there along with O'Couran.

Someone whistled low. "What a haul this is!" And O'Couran said, "Just as I thought! We'll keep it all for ourselves, my lads, except two or three pints for evidence That'll be plenty enough to convict Daly with."

That was enough for Joe. Running to the door of the vault and leaping down the stairs, he opened fire with both guns. But the dry agents aimed upward, completely surprised, shooting Joe through and through, over and over, at first not even knowing who he was.

Joe just kept shooting, crying out, rifled with bullets, falling down the stairs. Two men fell by way of Joe's bullets, O'Couran shouting, "It's the Imperio fellow! Get him! Don't stop! Kill him! Kill him!"

The agents opened a second round. Joe fell forward finally, at the foot of the steps, pitching down to the cellar floor in a pool of blood which mingled with the liquor there, like a lake of death. Joe was dead, but the agents kept firing and firing.

Up above, Bruno hid behind the vault door, his brain reeling. His brother was down there, shot over and over, killed by those bastard pricks—those pricks who were taking all of his hooch. It was then that Bruno felt he also had to kill.

But he was no fool. He turned away, leaving his dead brother there below; leaving the two dry agents murdered by Joe. Leaving the two who had survived standing—one cop and O'Couran himself, both panting like animals.

Going toward the service door that Joe had busted open, he saw, in the driveway, the federal agents' cars—those big bullet-proofed closed touring cars. He had to think fast. The sidewalk was filled with people hurrying past—having heard the gun fire.

It was a sultry dusk for that time of year. More folks out on the street because of the weather. Someone surely alerting every cop that could be found. And Joe—down there, too—dead. Shot by them.

Where was Tony with the trucks? What would Ma do when she found out about Joe? Joe. Her beloved Joe. Her favorite. First Pop…now Joey. Always her favorite.

Bruno felt himself grow cold. He had to think fast, but now, when he needed his mind to do all the tricks he'd always counted on, it spun.

There before him was Brian O'Couran, the other cop at his side. Both covered in blood. O'Couran wheezing away after his climb up the steps, his pockets bulging with booze bottles.

"You as well!" O'Couran growled. "I might've known!"

Bruno raised his gun. But just then, shots rang out from behind him.

Another agent had been posted at the front of the club and, coming around to the back, saw what was happening. With a single bullet from his rifle, he hit Bruno at the back of his head.

O'Couran, standing aside, put four more bullets into him. But still, Bruno remained standing. Then, he dropped his own gun and suddenly lunged toward O'Couran, his arms out, his hands ready to choke him. The other agent pulled back as well. Bruno staggered back into the club.

Breathing his brother's name, he fell forward down the stairs on top of Joe's body.

"Well," said O'Couran wearily, "that finishes that—just shove 'em both aside, boys, and bring the stuff up!"

• • • • •

CHAPTER XXVIII

ONE WAY PASSAGE

With Joe gone, Mack Daly had also ceased to live. Now, only referred to in the hearings and the newspapers as Benjamin Leventhal, he had lost the defining radiance of that once-proud sun which shone above him. He no longer knew who he was, but became, almost overnight, aware of who—and what—he had been.

The former Mack Daly remained silent now, and when he would speak, murmured that there was nothing left of him.

He would, of course, comply fully with his prosecutors. There was some reason for a defense. It seemed fatuous. Whether guilty or innocent, he only felt certain of one thing: that he had most certainly been in the right place at the right time…however briefly.

Ending finally in January, 1929, the hearings resulted in a judgment which found him guilty of many things. The reasons, enumerated before him as he stood sentence, amounted to Conspiracy with Organized Crime, Collusion within his official position under the Prohibition Bureau to remove, transport and sell government bonded alcohol, Grand Larceny—he had amassed a fortune from these practices.

As to his character, it was not, at first, revealed. But during the summer and autumn of 1928, as the hearings dragged on and on, the manner in which he, his wife and friends had lived gradually came out into the open.

What hurt him most was a newspaper article which, after listing his crimes, also suggested that he be charged for High Treason, because of what he had done—and *what he was*. All of it was Un-American, to put it simply. He had betrayed the nation which made him.

And there, alone in his apartment which he'd intended on sharing with Joe, Mack Daly sat, night after night, through it all. He would not see anyone or answer his telephone. He was a man preparing to die.

Baby and Deucie moved into the building and cared for him. After the killings of the Imperio brothers, and the closing down of the Club deVol, they could not return there. And Mack had automatically spared them from court action by taking all the blame for the speak-easy operation himself.

Johnnie took Nolie away with her to Paris and Wriggs abandoned Elliot, due to his drinking, for Huck. Elliot drank harder than ever, and in a relatively short period of time he became very, very ill.

The Countess, Mack's very old and dear friend, let him be. Ynez telephoned her early on, sobbing, demanding to know what would happen to him now that he had to go away.

"My Benjamin has very bad luck when it comes to governments," she said. "It was always so, since his childhood—and it always shall be so. This present regime, here in America, has damned him. But it will come to an end very soon, anyway—with dire consesquences for everyone living under it. And, as for the one one under which he will live, there, in Austria...it also will pass away very soon. Then, Ynez, something terrible will happen over there. Worse than before. Not to be imagined."

Ynez whispered, "Will he never be spared?"

The Countess paused. "Pray that he will be—" she answered. Then in her voice, Ynez heard a hollow and faint sigh.

Soon afterward, Walter Winchell cabled Mrs. Mack Daly. She had taken none of his calls. King Tuthill wanted her to know that he had purchased Annabelle Harrison's statue of her, and wondered if she'd consider starring in a vaudeville tour entitled "I Married a Fairy."

Ynez tore the wire up and went back—somewhere into the confines of her vast apartment, to cry her eyes out as she had done for weeks on end.

As Mack merely waited on and on, Ynez was unable to face him, sensing more than ever his crushing loss bleeding through her walls, feeling his war which had never really ended. Realizing that she loved him so...and that she *always* would...Mrs. Mack Daly accepted something which was living within her heart. This love she had for him...it was going to lay waste to her every day, every month and every year of all her tomorrows. And even in every moment that her heart went on beating, it would also go on aching...for him...for *them*. For what never was—and never could have been.

People now passed by the 55th Street apartment house gazing up at it as a Tower of Depravity where all those perverts lived...and where they now merely existed, self-exiled, damned by all their sins.

That man who thought he was such a big shot was going to be deported—stripped of his citizenship—sent him back to Austria. He could never return to America again. And nobody ever guessed all this time that he was a Kraut...as well as a Jew and a fairy. What that s.o.b. got away with! Well, see? It served him right.

• • •

On a cold February morning in 1929, Mack Daly walked alone toward the ship that would take him away forever. This was his explicit wish. That all his friends remain behind. That no one see him off. That he would make this final departure alone, leaving everything, everyone that had ever been so clearly a part of his spirit and heart.

As he mounted the gang plank, he turned to look at the fog shrouding the City which had claimed him, created him and celebrated what he was, and what he had stood for.

Then, reaching the ship itself, Mack saw standing, high up on the bridge, a young sailor wrapped in a long dark coat, looking down at him.

No one else on deck, and no one embarking...for Mack was very early on that day and ready to meet his Fate.

How very much he looked like Joe, Mack thought—that man up there on the bridge! Yet, now and then the fog would nearly cover him and Mack could not see him at all. Sometimes, it was as if he wasn't there.

"Good morning, sir—" a voice called down from up there on the bridge. Mack saw nothing. The fog cleared again. It wasn't Joe's voice but whoever it was, he did look so much like Joey. Mack stared up at him.

"Hello!" he called back, going forward, still looking up, the mist clinging to his face—his overcoat—chilling him to the bone.

"It looks as if we are both the first ones onboard today! We will be sharing this final passage together, it appears. Are you all ready, sir?"

Mack stared on. He said nothing.

Then the sailor asked him, smiling down through the fog, "Do I look familiar to you, sir?"

Mack at last found the words to answer. "You remind me of someone, that's all."

Mack saw him smile exactly the way Joe would've smiled.

But he had stared on for far too long, and that was impolite. Mack wanted so to say something else, but his eyes were so full of tears and his heart beating so very loudly that he could not bring himself to speak.

Wiping his eyes with the tip of his glove, he looked up again; the fog—so dense. No longer could he see him now...the wonderful guy who had so looked so very much like his Joe.

Then, just where the young man had been standing, a ray of sunlight, piercing the grim dawn, found him still there, coat flapping in the wind, etched against the sky.

"Come up here with me and look!" he called to Mack, extending his hand outward. "The sun is breaking through the fog over the City!"

With the light still dancing there, on the bridge, Mack Daly mounted the steps, placing himself in the very center of its piercing brilliance.

Caressed by it all around him now, he felt Joe right there at his side. And in his empty hand, Mack Daly knew another's, grasping it with every ounce of strength, firmly holding his own. Joe was there with him and would be, throughout eternity.

The foghorn sounded and the clouds came again, embracing this man standing alone, there, on the bridge, made so suddenly golden by that light, his head lifted high, smiling up at the newborn sun.

FINIS